'The best fictional account I've read of the way the internet has shaped our inner lives. A literary thriller that confirms the arrival of a major new talent'

Alex Preston, *Observer* Fiction to Look out for in 2017

'This impressive novel is alive with clever ideas'   *The Times*

'Inventive and highly charged... good at evoking the tensions in a world where we can't switch off... a compelling mystery'

Daily Telegraph

'A shrewd examination of how love stories are transformed by the distorting filter of the internet... super-smart... intriguing'

Daily Mail

'[An] exceptional debut'   *Literary Review*

'Shot through with dark humour and prose that burns like a laptop overheating on your thighs... captures the exquisite agony of life online'   *AnOther Magazine*

'If last summer's must-read debut was Emma Cline's *The Girls*, this year it's undoubtedly Olivia Sudjic's remarkable *Sympathy*'

Vogue UK

'A brilliantly claustrophobic read'   *Psychologies*

'*Sympathy* will double-click your heart'   *Vanity Fair*

'A powerful and original novel'   Diana Athill

'A memorable debut, Sudjic's acute observation and sharp wit engage readers from the off, but the real revelation here is how *Sympathy* deepens and darkens as it goes into something altogether rawer, wiser and more challenging'

Peter Ho Davies, author of *The Fortunes*

OLIVIA SUDJIC

SYMPATHY

Leabharlanna Poiblí Chathair Baile Átha Cliath
Dublin City Public Libraries

AN IMPRINT OF PUSHKIN PRESS

ONE,
an imprint of Pushkin Press
71–75 Shelton Street
London WC2H 9JQ

First published in Great Britain by ONE in 2017
This edition first published in 2018

1 3 5 7 9 8 6 4 2

Paperback ISBN 13: 978-0-99350-626-0
Hardback ISBN 13: 978-0-99291-829-3

Grateful acknowledgment is made for permission to reprint lines from
"Amenimo makezu" (Not Losing to the Rain) by Kenji Miyazawa, submitted
by TRANSCEND member Satoshi Ashikaya. This version of the poem
originally appeared on Transcend Media Service (TMS) on 4 August 2014.
https://www.transcend.org/tms/2014/08/
not-losing-to-the-rain-amenimo-makezu/

Book design by Victoria Hartman
Offset by Tetragon, London

Printed and bound by CPI Group (UK) Ltd, Croydon CR0 4YY

www.pushkinpress.com

For Pat

Because the mountain grass
Cannot but keep the form
Where the mountain hare has lain

     —*W. B. Yeats*

I wouldn't mind being a pawn, if only I might join.

     —*Alice*

1

I wasn't with her when the fever started. I didn't even know she was sick. I'd known nearly everything about her until then, and could have recalled the smallest detail of any given day, whether she'd spent it with me or not. For months her presence, and telepresence, had given shape to my new life in New York. Now, with the stroke of a finger, it had gone.

Unfollow. Intended as a symbolic gesture only, a symbolic *fuck you*, assuming that I'd still have a level of public access. I'd observed her this way long before we met, but it appeared that her privacy had been altered since then. Very recently, I guessed. I was alarmed by her inhibition or what it meant she had to hide. Before, anyone could find her. Just by typing her name they would get an instant synopsis of her life: the neat grid of her pictures, captioned with her thoughts and feelings, tagged with a location and timestamped. Anyone could track her progress through the city, or slip backwards into her past, to her vacations and graduations. I can't have been the only one who'd done it so successfully. But now I was locked out. A white wall had descended, blank except for a padlock symbol.

More than her physical absence, it was this whiteout that was disorienting. There was little to suggest that time was passing. No news of her mornings or meals, no filtered sunsets or stars. As darkness fell in my world, the light from hers tormented me, remaining the same bright hospital white. I butted my index finger repeatedly against the wall, but her defiant little mouth, just visible in the porthole containing her profile picture, turned my symbolic gesture back towards me: *Fuck you*. It was all symbolic. I touched the mouth; it was hard and would admit nothing. Her face was hard too. It denied, or felt nothing. No amount of pressure made any difference. There was nothing I could depress except *Follow* or *Back*. I couldn't decide which, so I waited, hoping that the unhappy choice would be taken away. Sometimes I would cover the glare with the palm of my hand, cancelling her light completely by squeezing my knuckles together. I'd count out sixty Mississippis and then flare them open again, hoping with this expansive motion to have magically sprung the lock, or to discover that the wall was only a temporary measure and she'd now restored her previous settings. When she did not, I tried more inventive routes. Rather than typing in *her* name, like any fool, I interrogated other names I knew—the names of her friends—pressing on every back door I could think of for a glimpse of where she was and who she was with, hoping to find her sheltering in one of their pictures. Not one of them had seen her, or if they had, they were hiding the fact. Or she was hiding somewhere in that labyrinth of other people's lives, but behind the lens itself.

It didn't take long for my resolve to weaken; then, after I'd admitted defeat, tapping *Follow* again, the time spent waiting for her to approve my request passed impossibly slowly. For whole minutes I convinced myself that it was the best thing to have happened, that this was in fact the only way out: to know nothing more about her from now on. It was useless, however. I knew too much already, and for long hours in between those minutes I tortured myself with grim fantasies—what was happening behind the wall as I waited for reentry.

Follow, once white, was now an arresting grey, the word replaced by *Requested.* I felt this new word did not convey proper urgency. For a start, I did not like the past tense. I glared at the word as I lay in bed, certain that my envoy was not requesting hard enough. I wondered how I might take back control of the situation. When we had spent rare nights apart before, I'd kept our message thread open, in order to watch her name waxing on- and offline in the grey bar at the top of the screen, pressing it every so often to keep it lit. By doing this I'd felt as though I had her next to me, as if she lay beside me breathing, but trying that trick then felt more like lying beside a corpse for comfort.

When I wasn't watching the white wall, I watched the grey bar. At least there time moved on. It didn't tell the *actual* time, but how long had passed since she'd gone off-grid. I wanted to breathe in the same atmosphere as her. I opened the windows as many inches as I could, felt the currents of air that moved between the tall buildings, and imagined liquefying them, creating a hydraulic system between us, so that I could position and push her finger down just by levering mine above the button. Once, I felt sure I'd seen her status morph from *last seen* to *online* and from *online* to the pendulous *typing:* a sign of life, like steam on a mirror. Then I had blinked hard, and again the grey bar, the headstone above the message thread, confirmed that she was not.

I waited for her to appear for so long that occasionally I had to turn over, onto my front, and lower my device-holding hand to the floor to steer the blood into my fingers. If I managed to fall asleep, my mind pinballed through possible encounters, following her to every intersection of the Upper West Side. Depending on the intensity of my despair, the streets either connected or separated us, and though I barely moved, each time I woke I was exhausted, fingers pruned with sweat as if I'd spent the night stalking the fifty blocks between us.

This limbo period taught me everything there is to know about the terrain between longing and revulsion. Where they met, I felt sickly warmth seep up from the mattress. Whenever I found it, I had the sensation, like a neck twist, a violent muscle spasm, of having briefly possessed her. Just there our bodies snapped into alignment, and it was, for an instant, *me* doing whatever she was doing while ignoring my *Follow* request.

From the limited amount I do know about her activity then, the sickly heat makes sense. My intelligence came later, from the doorman in the building where she lived on West 113th. He reported that by the time she'd arrived at the hospital, two blocks away, as a walk-in with a high fever, a parasite had bored into her brain. He explained that it had all begun, like most things covertly bent on death, with "flulike symptoms," and the first doctor had dismissed her on that basis. Sent her off to buy a stronger version of Theraflu. When she made her second trip, it was by ambulance. The doorman had called 911 himself. Ambulances, he informed me gravely, are usually reserved in America for the very unconscious or the very rich, but he had reasoned that she was both.

"It probably began its life's journey at the bottom of the ocean, in a crustacean. Found its way into something like a frog, and from there into something like a snake, and then a bird—"

"Or," I interrupted, with a croak, "some other creature."

He studied me for a moment. I had barely spoken to anyone in days, and it had become a strain to keep my theories to myself.

"Right," he continued, "before being eaten or petted by her. She loved cute stuff, right?"

"Right."

"The demon." He rolled his eyes and I nodded. Her cat was a menace, it was true.

After her operation, she was moved into a room in the ICU, with a prime view of the Hudson. It would have been the first day of October. I remember the air outside was still warm, hot in the sun. The summer, the summer of *us*, lingered in the soft light and the thick end-of-day heat, but she retained little memory of any of it. The latter half of July, all of August and September had been disemboweled with the removal of the parasite. She first met me in August, and she later assured me that my part in it all had either been eaten up by the parasite or burnt away in the operating theatre.

In a story she wrote after it happened, some time after I left New York, she says she remembers nothing but waking: a "burning sensation," the "wet bloom" of her own eyelids, gluey from surgical tape, seen from inside as she "swam into consciousness" in a bright room. The memory, suspiciously literary, excludes her mother, who had travelled there from Tokyo to keep a vigil. Either the wet bloom is made up and she remembers nothing about waking in that room, or she has purposefully edited her mother from the scene. The mother was definitely there. She even took a picture of her daughter coming round and beamed it back a generation to her own mother, at that moment still sleeping in the curve of their ancestral archipelago. The picture was accompanied with the word *Waking!* in Japanese.

Kakusei!

Back in the lobby of her daughter's apartment, as she returned the spare key, the mother showed the picture to the doorman, plus an x-ray which revealed the strange looping path of the parasite. She thanked him for all his help. He'd saved her daughter's life, no doubt. She would be discharged soon. It was only two blocks for her to walk back, or she could take a cab. She might need help, more than usual, in the coming weeks.

You will have seen the *Kakusei* picture. It ended up in the news. It isn't flattering. Her determined face is flushed, the jaw juts out, though I suppose her beauty is a fact so absolute that vanity is beneath it. The picture is now the first to come up when you search for her. Mizuko Himura. I have set a million traps for that name. Whenever she does or says anything, or anyone else does or says anything in connection with her, across whichever ocean, the name reaches me in a Google alert. Each time I reel in the net, experience rapture for about one second, and am then overcome by acute nausea. I will read without breathing, scanning to see if any of her words are about me, or secretly addressed to me, and feel a creeping mortification when nothing stands out and she slips back into the water. Though I am still hoping for a message, even now that more than a year has passed, I have to assume that the omission is the message, and that her long silence contains all the answers I need.

Looking at the pictures of her taken since, I can tell something has shifted. The charm has become strange—stronger, if that's possible—though that might be the effect of distance, or professionally applied makeup, or my reading into her face what I know to have happened, or all of the above. Her features appear somewhat dismantled, less symmetrical, as if you are looking at the remnants of something perfect but you can't properly remember it whole.

I still don't know how she really felt about me. I've gone through all the things I kept; they're inconclusive, flotsam and jetsam that could mean anything or nothing. I am sure there is something very deep, lying far beneath the surface, which, if disturbed, maybe even provoked, might finally come up for air. I used to be able to summon things that way, pulling things towards me on invisible strings, making the sky dense, a febrile blue screen shivering with all that I wanted to keep close. In fact, right before I left for America, my mother had passed the power on to me. A singular inheritance. She'd poked her head into my bedroom, where I'd been holed up, packing relentlessly for weeks. I'd grown used to stepping over and around two halves of a suitcase in the middle of my floor and had forgotten that at some point I'd have to a) close and b) transport it without assistance. After a period of silent observation, me furiously folding things without looking up, she advised that I try to "live lightly" in New York. Back then, knowing nothing of what awaited me, I'd assumed this wisdom was aimed at my suitcase, split open on its back, leaking onto the carpet my too-difficult books (Baudrillard, Deleuze) and too careful ensembles. Then she'd pinned me to her chest, the first hug from her I could remember as an adult, and I felt her press the power into me. It slid like mercury, tingling in my fingers and toes, giving me a new sensation of their weight. She'd never lived lightly herself, of course. She suffered from incurable apophenia. "In Manhattan," she said, "either you need to be light, so light you float above the city as a solitary spore, or"—and this was the sudden flipside to her warning, the part that lodged in my mind "you have to be really, really heavy, pulling everything there is towards you."

2

When I look at the *Kakusei* picture of her in the hospital, I remember waiting for her to wake up the first time I slept in her bed. It was August. I lay there for hours, until the morning sun that streamed through the window became painful, my body on fire but unable to move. Very, very slowly, I turned my head so that I could see the back of her neck. The clasp of her necklace had left its imprint like two tiny teeth marks.

I tried to remember all the things, each little link in the chain, that had brought us to this point, this place, my eyes boring into her back, her outline so much sharper than in pictures. It felt strange that I couldn't stretch out my hand through her body, push it out the other side, or turn her over in my palm. Until then, having spent hours on end, day after day, sliding my finger through her pictures, I had thought of her more like a liquid or a gas, but in fact she was a solid. It was strange too to see her from new angles. In short, to be so close. I don't mean in the way it is to go from strangers to lovers. I mean the exact opposite, in fact. It was more like I'd gone from lover (intimate, easy in her company, despite her never knowing I was there) to stranger. She didn't know me at all, and that felt unreasonable and surprising. I also found it hard to accept that the Mizuko I'd known in multiple miniatures was one physical person. I suppose it would feel the same waking up in bed with Jesus or Father Christmas, or any long-dead figurehead of an ancient cult. You know every word of every doctrine off by heart and then you see their toenails, gums, and vertebrae, not in pieces but all held together, and it's hard not to lose your shit.

I'd trawled through all the comments under her pictures, mainly from girls she didn't know but who, like me, had noted how imperceptible her pores were and praised her skin for being like a baby's. I'd also read the ugly phrases like "assimilated Manhattanite" and "*enfant terrible* of a Japanese banking dynasty" in various short profiles of her in trendy literary magazines. There seemed to be more of this type of thing online than her own writing. It's true she didn't work that hard, or produce much writing in the time I knew her. Back then she spent most of her sweet time not go-getting but posting pictures of the things she wanted and liking the pictures strangers posted. She rarely said no to people, but not because she was actually nice; she just knew a way to make everything work to her advantage, shaping it into something she could use, usually in the brushwork of a story. There is probably a precise Japanese term for that kind of person. I should have asked.

There was a time I could just turn around and ask her a stupid question like that because she was literally right *there*. I can hardly imagine it now. Very occasionally I feel like she is standing behind me, watching me struggle for the words, or daring me to use them, and sometimes as I type I get that feeling that comes at night when windows become mirrors and you begin to sense that you are being watched. That your bright interior world is being inspected by eyes you cannot meet. Whenever it comes over me, I stare aggressively at my reflection so that whoever is out there will think I've spotted them. At the moment I live alone in a studio flat in Wood Green, England, an eerily lit subterranean bowl that can be peered into from street level. In case someone is there, hidden by my reflection in the dark glass, I raise and lower the blind with mysterious purpose and stare angrily at myself in the window, but really through me and at my imagined stalker.

But how *did* I get there, in bed beside her for the first time? That morning, August 11, I felt no different, morally, from the way I had as I'd walked to her apartment from the sushi restaurant the night before, August 10. Just following, not really knowing where I was going; one of the few things I had not known about her already was her exact address. I had obediently trotted from one thing to the next without feeling like I was moving much. It felt that way for all the time that I knew her really, until I got to the end and looked back. When I look back, of course, it goes way, way back.

Mizuko was thirty-two when I discovered her that summer at twenty-three. I have the email that dates the discovery as July 23. She looked like a child, and certainly younger than me. We met a couple of weeks later at the Hungarian Pastry Shop opposite Saint John the Divine. In June, I had moved from where I'd been staying on the Upper East Side into her neighbourhood, Morningside Heights, up by Columbia University. I already knew the majority of what I still know about her before we met. She was born and grew up in Japan. Her grandfather founded Himura Securities. Her mother had her own company back in Tokyo. She had lived in New York since turning eighteen. She had always been sure of what she wanted to do in life, and now she was a writer with representation, teaching a number of classes in the creative writing MFA programme at Columbia which she had taken herself a few years previously. Her most successful short story so far had been "Kizuna," or "The Ties That Bind." It was the one I liked best. Back then she was working on a novel, tentatively titled *Kegare,* which she translated for me as "Impurity," though I was never allowed to read it.

"Origin stories make us feel secure; untangling them can undo us."

That is the first line of "Kizuna." It was also the first of her stories I read.

Sure, I thought. Yup. I started to imagine that those words were even written by me. Reading about her life felt like pressing my two hands together. She seemed a perfect match. I made her into my origin story—a way to explain myself to myself, as if she alone would give me a reason for being in the universe.

New York is my birthplace; that's why I went back, which is how I met her. I went there hoping I'd fall into place. It was spring 2014. The Malaysian Airlines flight had recently gone missing, and on the flight over I was terrified I'd disappear into grey ocean and be lost forever. As a result, I did some of my best existential thinking on that plane. Suspended, disconnected, stationary, yet hurtling through the sky at hundreds of miles per hour, unable to effect any change at all.

I remembered when I had first heard the words *what goes up must come down.* My mother discussing some kind of comeuppance. Now I think of my flight to JFK and the trajectory I have been on since: the apartments on floors that got lower and lower to the ground, until I moved into a basement. *What goes up must come down* was a maxim I'd heard my whole life, so often and in so many different mouths, like glass made fuller but dull by the sea. On the plane I understood it in a new way, a way that blew my mind with the simple, universal truth of the words. When the captain announced that we were at last making our descent, I reacted to the inevitable news as if I'd been called on to land the plane myself. Although my view was thick white cloud, I had to screw my eyes shut. When the seatbelt signs went off and each row broke into a frenzy of personal electronic noises, I was the only person who remained in my seat. I stayed until the last passenger had passed me, and read my landing form over multiple times, digesting all the forbidden articles. Fruits, vegetables, insects, cell cultures, disease agents, snails, soil. With great care, I copied out Silvia's address from one of her envelopes, even though I knew it by heart. I checked the form again. Gambling? Yes. Violent pornography? Yes. Moral turpitude? Not quite yet.

In the end I outstayed my tourist visa by some months (four), accruing what is called "unlawful presence," meaning I am barred from reentering the United States for three years. Though the customs hall was heavily air-conditioned, I was sweating, and on being asked the purpose of my visit, I blanked. Being born in New York, I had once possessed a U.S. passport, but my mother had claimed that for tax reasons I should give up my American nationality and get a British passport to match hers. The man at the desk took my picture, then feigned interest in the gap-year stamps I had collected, I suppose to signal that he was more human than his outsize shoulders suggested.

"Cambodia? They eat a lot of crazy things out there. Seems like they eat whatever runs past them."

"Yes," I said with a big smile, even though I do not hold that view myself.

I was ready to mimic, to learn customs, to please.

Reacquainted with my suitcase, I decided not to try the subway just yet. In the back of a cab, a ribbon of text slid from right and vanished left at the bottom of a screen set into the partition, bringing breaking news of an escaped elephant, followed by a drive-by shooting in Queens. Because the language was the same, I was not prepared for just how foreign-feeling everything was. I had to tell myself that this was a place once populated by Native Americans, where there were *arrowheads in the ground*. I reminded myself of it often during my time there. Every time something happened to make me feel like an alien, I thought about the Native American arrowheads. A certain sensibility in the soil which slipped into the water that came out of the taps, tasting so different.

We rode most of the way to Manhattan alongside a law enforcement vehicle, a van that said CORRECTIONS in blue along its body. It was the kind you expect to see John Malkovich jumping out of and then fleeing into the graveyard that bordered the road. I was immediately transfixed. Everywhere I looked I saw movies. There were backyards, garages, solid-looking porches, clapboard houses. The words *downtown, crosstown, uptown*, also solid as tree trunks. I had brought a little brown journal with me. Silvia, who was in her eighties and would be my host, had recommended the idea, suggesting that, like saving money, it might aid my recovery. I turned to the first page and, interested primarily in lighting effects, wrote: *beautiful light on Van Wyck Xpwy, oily afternoon sun, anointing my forehead.* Mizuko later mocked me when I showed her, but that was exactly how it felt: an ancient sunburst that had anointed so many before me, bestowing on them a second, or third, beginning.

Outside Silvia's building, the air was damp and delicious, with a diffuse smell like a mysterious cinema snack—a prickly, popcorny breeze that made me feel light-headed. I forgot to tip. I realised as I shut the boot, exhaust hot through my jeans, that I was ready either to cartwheel for miles or to collapse where I stood. Her building was on East 72nd, constructed from glass and mirrors, and looked after by three identical men—all, I think, called Tony—who supposedly took turns but were always huddled together behind a desk in the lobby.

"Go right up," they chorused. "Twenty-three, apartment A."

It was an efficient lift. My stomach lurched and I put my arms out behind me. I wanted to stop off at another floor so I'd have more time. I hadn't thought of what I might say as I crossed the threshold. I had all the big conversations rehearsed but not the start or the build-up to them. At her door I knocked a few times, but there was no answer. I considered returning to the lobby but then tried the door, and it opened.

"*Hello?*" I called, gripping my case. "It's Alice."

I waited to be acknowledged. An intense heat emanated from within. Slowly I made out that the hall was lined with mirrors, glinting darkly, with Persian rugs along the bottom. I took cautious steps, calling Silvia's name. It occurred to me that it might be a hoax. There was a chance I'd been writing back and forth with a very wise and supportive Nigerian scammer who had for two years been effecting the typewritten script of a grandmother with cancer. It was plausible. My mother had once received a beautifully descriptive email explaining that a Nigerian astronaut had been left on the moon since the seventies, was in good spirits, but was ready to come home if she could help. Surely, I told myself, even such creative people did not deal in typewritten *letters*.

The first door I came to was slightly ajar. There appeared to be a figure beneath a sheet laid out on the sofa. I'd been taught not to disturb sleeping figures and so retreated. After some minutes I decided I should make a noise and located a bathroom. It was covered floor to ceiling in framed photographs of Silvia and her late husband. The area around the sink was littered with Spry cinnamon mints, and there were a few different iterations of a plastic device, like a larger-than-normal turkey baster, perched around the bath. I flushed the toilet, but the flush was too gentle, barely a whisper. When I emerged, the body was still sleeping.

I tiptoed through the rest of the apartment. It felt like I had intruded onto the set of an American sitcom, and I was surprised to see that each room actually led somewhere, with enormous windows so that you could see across the city for miles. There were three bedrooms, two with en suite bathrooms. One had clearly been a man's and was now annexed as a study. One was filled with boxes. The other was Silvia's, though she never slept there and later told me I should sleep in it myself because the bed had the best mattress and she always slept on her sofa anyway. There was a living room that was also a dining room. It had saloon doors into a kitchen, the guest WC that I had used, and then the den that Silvia was currently sleeping in, with a television playing TCM on mute. Back in the living room, I picked up a pair of binoculars from a coffee table. The city was still there. After twenty minutes, I sat down on the living room sofa and immediately fell asleep.

When I woke again, the sky was dark, but the orange glow of the streetlamps radiated upwards. Silvia was standing in front of me.

"Who's that?" she said, peering.

"Alice," I said through other words in my dream.

"Who?"

"Alice. Hare," I qualified. "I'm here."

"You're not supposed to be here until tomorrow."

"Oh," I said, starting to right myself.

"I didn't want you before tomorrow. I've had an operation."

"Sorry," I began, trying to stand up.

"Okay," she said, and shuffled back into her den.

I listened and waited, blinking in the up-lit dark and feeling that everything was upside down. After a few minutes, in which I could hear her fall asleep again by the resumption of shallow breathing, I lay back and tried to breathe deeply, because I could feel that I was about to get locked into the anxiety attack that had threatened at various points on the journey every time I thought about the plane that had disappeared into thin air. I felt unreal, like a phantom in her apartment that she'd walked right through. My breaths were getting shorter and faster, as if I were sucking on a straw with no opening, until I felt my lungs expand much too much, so that when I tried to exhale it felt as if they had stuck together and were tearing from the effort of pulling apart again. Then I was crying, gulping and crying, also then roaring. Then, when no one came, the tears stopped and I was very still and totally quiet, like an infant silenced by the profound shock of something shiny reflecting on the ceiling. Except all that had happened was that the sound of the roads far below had made a pin drop, locating me, reminding me where in the world I was, that I was really there, and it had stunned me.

I settled back onto the pillow and recalled the start of my correspondence with Silvia, or the scammer pretending to be her, nearly two years before. July 2012. The summer before my final year of university. I was ploughing through a reading list outside on a khaki canvas camp bed from the army surplus store. Most of the furniture we owned was portable in some way. I came inside when I heard shouting. My mother was standing in front of the television set. We watched a room full of physicists officially declare the discovery of the Higgs boson. Peter Higgs, a kindly-looking, beaky-nosed man, shed a single tear. My mother cried too, much more than Higgs. "Okay," I said, patting her. "But it really doesn't have anything to do with us."

A week later I got the letter from New York, with a postmark dated the day of the discovery.

Dear Alice,

So it turns out we are immersed in an ocean. No doubt you will have read about the discovery of the Higgs particle. It makes my brain ache to think of the largest machine—they keep saying it's the size of Chartres Cathedral—finding the smallest particle in existence. Do they talk about it at your school? Forgive me, you are over that by now. Are you still studying? I wonder what sort of girl you have turned out to be. I last saw you when you were very small, and I assume now you are much bigger. I suppose you will wonder why I am contacting you again after so long. Well, I don't feel like going into it much unless you want to know. If you do, write back.

Yours truly,
Silvia Weiss

3

I had little trouble appropriating parts of Mizuko's origin story because in practice my own origin story didn't belong to me, and it was always evolving. If I challenged anything—dates, names, places—my mother would respond not with an answer but with a question, like why didn't I go and find my *real* parents and leave her in peace? She meant my birth parents, and each of us knew that was impossible. One was dead; the other had been in prison but was maybe dead by then too. I knew almost nothing else about them.

Memory is our first tool. We learn the face of whoever feeds us, and other things—less corporeal. We remember feelings, or persistent doubt. Then it starts to trip us up, starts to manipulate and mess with us. I suppose you could say I went to New York that spring because I wanted to escape, in England, what Mizuko's therapist had named *a toxic cycle of self-doubt*. I wanted a single, coherent narrative to explain who I was and what it was I was supposed to be doing.

In fact both my mothers were possessive of facts. With my second one, every detail, if you record and compare, is contradictory. The main focus is always her absent husband, my second absent father, Mark. Sometimes he is a deserter, his memory despised and insulted; other times he gets to be a kind of destiny that is worshipped and wept over. How I fit into the picture has continually shifted. I have been a marriage-saver and a marriage-ruiner. The one line she's held on to throughout is that I will mess everything up if I try to lay my hands on any part of it. I've told her practically nothing about last year.

When Mizuko asked me to sum up my childhood in a word, I said *claustrophobic*. Susy would never ever, she assured me, let me go. But I should have said *contradictory*, since at other times it was the opposite. I would wander around our cottage on my own or settle secretly in the attic, where she kept countless fragments of fact in unpacked boxes. The sheer volume of information was overwhelming, rendering it close to useless, and I think she intended it to be, to put me off searching through it. It would have taken a million robots a million years to reassemble what had really happened to us from looking in our attic.

In her letters, Silvia gave me her version of events.

> I'll start with when you were born. Manhattan in 1991. I called you Rabbit. That was what I called Mark when he was a little boy too.

Rabbit's stuck, at least for me, in my head. I often say it aloud to myself, or aloud but in my head. *Rabbit*. I prefer it to Alice Hare, and I was in heaven when Mizuko started calling me Rabbit too.

> You might have had another name before Alice, but your real mother fled with that detail (among others) from the maternity ward of Lenox Hill Hospital in her green gown

—I imagine her balloon-belly leading, bottom winking—

> to surprise a red Moishe's moving van on its way down-
> town. She was smashed like a watermelon before anyone
> could ask what, if anything, she might have had in mind
> for you. Neither, having a flair for surprises, had she told
> your father you even existed. Himself, disdaining both
> women and authority, would most likely not have followed
> orders anyway. He was incarcerated in Baybram Correc-
> tional Facility for crimes that require, for their successful
> undertaking, something as poetic as an "abandoned and
> malignant heart." It became clear that your real mother,
> who could not have afforded even your delivery, had no
> plan for you that the state could execute, though the au-
> thorities raked through her few personal effects for a clue.

I know, from what Silvia told me, that inside the steaming belly I had so recently exited they found only collard greens, string beans, whiting, and schnapps, and that those who saw the accident reported that my mother's last words were barely intelligible, seemingly addressed to herself: "Nigger, leave me alone, let me be. My son will blow your brains out."

All the best stories begin like that, Mizuko said when I told her. Lucky *you*.

> You were put up for adoption. My son, Mark Hare, and
> his wife, Susy, took you in. They had a name ready: Alice.
> I was there when you were handed over, a tensile ball of
> fists and fuzz, a lifetime of fairy knots. They were older
> than normal parents. Mark was a physics professor, Susy
> was an illustrator, at least on the adoption forms, and

they lived near where he worked at Columbia University
in Morningside Heights.

This is the bit I had heard over and over from Susy. I knew
they met there as undergraduates, during the student protests in
1968. I've been told the story *so many times*. I think everybody
who has ever had even the briefest encounter with my mother
knows it.

Their first conversation was broadcast on the student
radio station, WKCR. Susy, then Susannah and eighteen,
an earnest freshman from England, interviewed Mark.

"Very tall, strong arms, one raised in a fist like a divining
rod" (the divining rod, a staple, is one of Susy's few landmarks in
the story). It pleased me that when I fact-checked Silvia's letters,
all their details appeared online, rooting it in the real, repeated
almost word for word. It made Silvia feel comforting, as if with
her I finally stood on solid ground. Back then I had no reason
to mistrust the medium; it seemed reassuring, impersonal, objective, with no particular bias or axe to grind. Google was the
arbiter of truth.

Susy wanted student voices for her "Columbia in Crisis"
segment. Most of the Class of '68 used their graduation
as a platform for another protest. The ceremony was
conducted at Saint John's that year, and many students
hid radios under their academic gowns, silent until they
burst into Bob Dylan, when WKCR played "The Times
They Are A'Changin'" and the students marched out into
the sunshine.

They got married in 1976. Your mother looked like a dessert. Mark began working toward becoming a professor at Columbia. I guess he felt claustrophobic, having been born, raised, and then worked his way up in academia within the same two-square-mile pocket of Manhattan.

Susy always says she knew he was the man she would marry right after she first slept with him. She had gotten up, dressed with her back to him where he lay in bed, then sat on his one armchair in his poky student room. As she sat there, watching and waiting for him to wake, she got that intuition that her period was about to arrive, slightly ahead of schedule. She leapt up at once, but it was too late. Mark refused her offers to recover his chair, saying, perhaps still high or half asleep, that it was a marker. *A stain that made her part of the furniture.* I have never heard her tell that story and not found it slightly creepy, but she always uses this anecdote as if it were a litmus test of good masculine character. *He sounds nice,* she will say about some man, but you can see she's thinking he wouldn't pass the period-stain challenge like Mark.

After he finished his PhD, Mark accepted a position as a theoretical physicist at Columbia. A theory emerged to explain the elementary architecture of the universe. He began focusing on superstring theory, and gradually M-theory. *M* stands for mother of all theories, magic, mystery, or matrix. It is an adaptation of superstring, a simple equation by the standards of particle physics, that, if proved, will "reconcile what we think of as incompatible things, explain the nature and behavior of all matter and energy." And he became, shall we say, preoccupied. Susy (Mark was the one who contracted her from Susannah to Susy, the abbreviation of *superstring theory*) was in awe but could not work him out. I guess women love mystery. Trust me, you want to go for a nice, safe one like my late husband, Rex. I made that mistake with Mark's father. Your mother doesn't like there to be things —any things—that exclude her. Physics was like a secret language between Mark and his friends. She used to make jokes, funny for no one at all. Things like, "As a physicist, he should be taking *more interest in the physical,* or in patterns which repeat, and small things, like babies." She raised it around so many mortified acquaintances and waitresses that, because Mark would do anything to avoid a scene, they began trying for a baby even though it wasn't the right time with his research. They tried for four years without success.

I knew a lot about their sex life already, because, in that area, at least, my mother has no filter.

I remember the year it became an issue, when I sent Susy to a doctor, because it was when the Chinese loaned two pandas, Ling Ling and Yun Yun, to the Bronx Zoo. I had decided I wanted a grandchild by this point. I guess now that it seemed possible I might not get one. I did a lot of reading about the mating process the zookeepers were trying to facilitate. I think pandas lose their libido if a human walks through their enclosure, much as a human would if a panda crashed through the bedroom.

Susy mentioned the pandas too. Mark was a kind of Ling Ling, the male panda. To get him interested in mating, Susy would create a set of imperceptible conditions—the right temperature, the right light, the right meal—and to boost the chances of this rare, involuntary urge—the Great Hump Day—occurring at a moment when she could make use of it, she barely left his side.

> Though she went with him pretty much everywhere, even to work, where she would seat herself in a library near his office, she was oblivious to *him*. She had wished so hard, for so long, for a particular future to manifest itself in a blue cross that the blue cross overlaid Mark's face.

I know the feeling.

> Mark said to me that whenever he woke up, Susy was lying beside him, already waiting, with her eyes wide open. She kept talking about how they would soon be the Three Hares. That's the famous symbol of the three hares chasing each other, something Mark had explained to her once, early on, before he knew how she would turn it against him, as a classic example of rotational symmetry. My only input was names. I always said it would need to work in a crisis, over a loudspeaker, and in a foreign accent.

When I stayed with her, Silvia could always be counted on to summarize the nature of something about to happen so that then there was little need to actually *do* it. Susy still wanted to do it, and had dutifully chosen a name with an eye on death, destruction, and crisis management.

> I made a list of all the possible things *Alice* might rhyme with if yelled down a busy street, and it didn't appear

there would be many emergencies where you would mistake *Alice* for *palace, malice,* or *chalice.* Susy stopped going to all the expensive doctors I'd sent her to. She believed by going to fertility doctors she was pulling infertility toward her. Instead she read horoscopes and did Tarot cards. The paved footpaths in Riverside Park were riddled with cracks. It was all code. I remember she even bought that candy that comes with messages inside and left the pertinent ones on Mark's side of the bed, which went undiscovered and were slept on, leaving troubling brown stains on the sheets. My cleaner then was Mark's too, and she used to complain about it all the time. But the big sign came when she was standing by the Alice statue in Central Park. She got talking to a young woman who swiftly became her friend, confidante, and then, despite Mark's and my attempts at intervention, surrogate. Susy could befriend women at the speed of light. I always say that those friendships are more like falling in love and always finish as quickly. And of course the surrogate ended up miscarrying the first Alice. So Susy was forty-one by the time she finally brought you, Alice II, home in a Moses basket.

This is my favourite part of this particular letter . . .

By then they lived on Claremont Avenue in professorial housing. It was covered in snow when we carried you up the steps of the building. It was January 19, 1991. I have a Polaroid I'll show you when you get here. In the hour between leaving and returning, there had been a power cut and water had flooded everywhere. The long, dark hall was knee-deep, the elevators were out of service. Mail had floated out of an open mailbox on the bottom row, spooling all manner of personal information around the faux plaster columns. I hated that apartment. I remember Mark looking so depressed, and I made, in retrospect, an ill-judged joke like "Don't throw the baby out with the bathwater."

I had to admit that it seemed a lot of what Susy had told me about that particular moment appeared to be true. Once I had even found the note that my mother had said was pinned to the noticeboard in the entrance when they got home to the flood:

> *Dear tenants, someone has a faulty flusher in their toilet.*
> *If you notice your toilet is not flushing properly, or if you*
> *hear noise when you flush, please notify the super.*
> *Thank you, Ramon*

Susy told me that Mark smiled, took the note off the board, folded it neatly, and put it in his pocket. This was normally the thing she would have done—something that seemed out of the ordinary and was perhaps a sign—but she was carrying me in the Moses basket and had no free hands.

"What are you going to do with that?" she asked him.

"Mark this day."

Then he had apparently started humming "The Power of Love" in the flooded hallway, lined with broken columns just like in the music video for that song where Luther Vandross is up to his shins in water and the screen crackles with electricity bolts, suggesting an invisible field of love permeating a Roman-bath-themed nightclub.

At first, when I was a child and my mother used to recount

the homecoming, bringing it into sharper relief each time until you'd think it had happened the morning of her telling it to you, I thought it was a story about how happy Mark must have been to finally be a father. That's the way she tells it. Even before Silvia got in touch, as I grew up I realised that by that point he was a forty-four-year-old particle physicist, and so gradually I saw that singing Luther Vandross was another kind of sign. My arrival meant he could finally leave the city, where he was cracking up under the conviction that he was wasting his one chance to be great. For him to take the note meant that, like Susy, when he wanted something badly, any rough-edged, fragmentary thing became as smooth and unequivocal as an arrow.

> Mark was by then part of a team setting up the SSC
> (Superconducting Super Collider) in Waxahachie, Texas.
> It was, if you know nothing about physics, supposed to
> have been what the Large Hadron Collider in Geneva
> later became, except the American version, of course, was
> going to be ten times more powerful and hunt the Higgs
> boson "ten times faster."

In 1988, the year of that first, miscarried Alice, the area around Waxahachie was chosen, by a committee that included Mark, as the site for the collider. He was then enlisted to convince coastal academics to move there. Young physicists had followed, not yet in his footsteps, but his directions. Settlers in big white sneakers, mavericks in Hawaiian shirts. Though he still lived in New York, he had been spending more and more time in Dallas (Susy, for national security reasons, was forbidden from accompanying him) and less and less at Columbia or the Morningside Heights apartment, where Susy occupied herself by drawing. Her condition for relocating to Dallas had been that they would first adopt and that she and Mark would write and illustrate a children's book together, *Alice in Dallas,* which would make particle physics accessible to three- to six-year-olds.

> Seventeen shafts were sunk and fourteen miles of the tunnel bored out of Austin chalk before the site was abandoned. Congress pulled support, canceling funding, citing fears about committing to its projected cost. Many physicists went to Wall Street; a few who remained got involved in ranching.

That's from an article Silvia showed me. Susy sometimes says that too, wistfully, as if cattle might have been the answer. Other times, depending on her mood, she speaks self-importantly about her sacrifice—as if the fate of American science, the discovery of the origins of the universe, rested solely on Mark's permanent physical presence there.

When it was cancelled, Mark felt betrayed, *not,* I now know, by Congress, and *not* by the physics community, and *not,* Silvia assured me, by me, but by Susy. If she hadn't made him wait in New York until they found me, if he had been there, in the field, sooner, he was sure the project would have succeeded. I'm sure he felt guilty. Not for us, but for all the other families and lives he had uprooted, abandoned in the middle of the desert, and exposed to early failure.

> In 1993 he and Susy came ingloriously back to New York, with you in tow of course. You had just started talking. You came right back to the same bit of Morningside Heights, but his Columbia accommodation had

been reallocated in your absence. For a year you all
stayed in an apartment owned by one of Mark's friends
—another professor, who at that time rarely used it—in
the area. Someone had used pieces of boat interior to
establish a new life within the building at some point,
so the apartment looked like a 1930s art deco ocean
liner inside.

I imagine this to be the kind of unique interior that can
only have come into being when one of the residents came into
the possession of an ocean liner and didn't know what to do
with it.

It was possible it was supposed to thematically connect
the building with the Hudson, but it bothered Mark that
there seemed to be no explanation for your new surroundings. I remember when I first visited you there, he
was sitting in the middle of the apartment, sleepless and
malevolent-looking. He didn't look like himself at all. All
of the rooms intercommunicated, so you could see from
the hall to the living room and from there to the dining
room. He had the central vantage point on the couch,
and he kind of glowered at me and didn't say anything.
It did not, I told him, as usual trying to make light of the
situation, match the buoyancy of the building. He ignored
me. I could see it was this deliberate sabotage. He was in
opposition to everything around him. None of it made
sense anymore. He had gotten used to seeing his equations
overlay every surface, and the blank white walls held no
meaning for him. He moved with his eyes only, conversing
with every object, sometimes as if he were trying to sink

it, sometimes as if he were just trying to restore it to its original course, somewhere out to sea, by force of will.

When its rightful occupant needed the apartment back and we had to disembark from the ocean liner, we moved in with Silvia.

Just when I got you settled in, Mark revealed that he was accepting a job at a bank in Tokyo. Trading desks, he told us, wanted quiet, clever men who could bring scientific theories to chaos. He had, apparently overnight, made up his mind to quit both physics and America.

Susy tried to ship Mark's armchair—the dark period stain had been hidden under new upholstery—but Mark was no longer available for compromise. He had already embraced Japanese minimalism, and the chair could not be part of our ascetic life there.

The bare minimum was shipped ahead, and you three followed a week later. I came in the taxi to the airport. I remember I hummed a kind of hymn to Saint John the Divine, an unfinished monument that to me embodies all the qualities I so admire in physicists who wait a lifetime for a theory to be proved. We sat in silence and stop-started, making incremental thrusts along 125th Street, just as schools were being dismissed. As we passed the Apollo Theater, Susy turned to you—you were sitting in between us, Mark was sitting in the front. She looked at you with big, meaningful eyes, of course addressing me and Mark, and said something like "Feels like moving to the *moon*, right, Alice?" And I remember you began to cry. Such a heartbreaking sound that I could have cried too, but I couldn't because I was so angry. I already blamed her. If I'd known it was the last time I was going to see him, I wonder how I might have tried to stop him, what I would have said. I go over emotionally manipulative maternal speeches in my dreams. Do you know Volumnia, Coriolanus's mother? I remember the last "conversation" Mark and I had pretty well, because we barely spoke and your mother did most of the talking with the taxi driver while we listened and I tried to tell him by looking into the curve of his right ear that I was forbidding him to leave even though I was coming to say goodbye. The driver had polite questions, phrased as if all four of us were going on a happy vacation, and Mark left Susy to field them from behind. We were given a brief history of the driver's wife and son.

"Are you going to have another one?"

"Wife?"

"No, son."

"Yes, I hope so."

"Do you have a name yet?"

"Not yet."

When we drifted into silence, the driver said brightly, "My name is *very* short."

"That's important," I said. "Names have to work in a crisis. What is it?"

"Haseeb."

"Spelled H-a-s-i-b?"

"No, H-a-s-e-e-b."

"So not that short, then."

At which my beautiful son finally turned, shooting me a look that meant STOP.

4

In the time which passed between the discovery of the Higgs in July 2012 and my arrival in New York in April 2014, I came to know Silvia through her letters, which she always typed on a typewriter. Through whatever she chose to tell me, piece by piece. There could be no rushing ahead, and sometimes I grew impatient waiting for a response to arrive, but there was never a time when I asked her a question and she didn't give a direct answer.

I had considered trying to find and contact her before she found me. There had been projects at school—some of which I knew better than to bring home, and others that I thought might be harmless enough—which required grandparents. A teacher once encouraged us to ask our grandparents for recipes to put in a class cookbook that was supposed to show how life had changed between rationing and microwaves. I suggested Silvia. It did not go down well, and Susy, in her rambling explanation for why I could not, went as far as to claim that her mother-in-law had passed away.

The discovery of the Higgs boson opened up more questions

than it answered. The implications, plus the letter from not-dead Silvia, meant I became even more concerned about my place in the universe. I'd wanted to study physics at university, but Susy had barred me from continuing past school, so I'd opted for a degree in philosophy instead. As far as the physics went, the space I inhabited was either the centre of some cosmic attention or one self-important speck in an infinite multitude, a bubble in an ocean of foam. Either there were physical laws, which governed every single thing that happened to me and thus connected me to everything else subject to those same laws, or everything I thought and did and everything that happened to me was essentially a mistake, in which case what was the point of physics? I consumed all the news reports when I was supposed to be revising for my finals. Some people claimed that the finding meant our universe could be doomed to fall apart.

Philosophy works best when you come up with a highly improbable, impossible, or imaginary scenario to test something —you work out what something is by what you can deduce that it is not. Creating little fantasy scenarios is what I liked about it.

I enjoyed Descartes's demon, Locke's soul swaps, the neo-Lockeans, and especially quantum theory, which said that an exact replica of you could suddenly appear somewhere—next door, or in another country, or even on another planet. That replica would be identical to you: same memories even, but the unity wouldn't last long. Different environments would estrange you; for example, your replica's parents might emigrate.

When I wrote back to Silvia, I kept it secret. Partly because it felt good to have a secret and partly because I tended to avoid doing or saying anything that might cause a disturbance in the house. I liked it when things were quiet.

To answer her first letter's provocation, Silvia told me that she did not have email or a cell phone. She would sooner die than possess either. She had decided to write to me when she did, yes, inspired by the discovery of the Higgs, but also because she was at that time starting to lose the use of her right arm, meaning that soon she would not be able to write on her typewriter and so she would be cut off. She said she'd become increasingly isolated, marooned in her Upper East Side apartment. It seemed from the way she wrote about it that she was unhappy about this, but when I finally pitched up at her door, I began to view her solitude more as a lifestyle choice. In any case, she had decided to write all the letters she had ever meant to write, and send them, before she could no longer do it. She had recently been widowed by her third husband, Rex, and so was writing her acerbic letters to me in between reading her condolence cards and shredding them.

I can now make educated guesses, having both been to Japan and felt depressed myself, about what Mark might have wanted from moving to Tokyo. To surround himself with people who didn't know him, couldn't disappoint him, strangers who didn't speak his language but whose ceremonial politeness reached across. Otherwise it was a bizarre plan to go to Tokyo, given that the bubble had burst and Japan, the victim of a "liquidity trap," was already in the first of its Lost Decades. I don't know if he was properly employed by the bank he claimed to be working for. Susy says he was, Silvia says he wasn't. He said he worked at Tsuki Bank, which was owned by Himura Securities, the company Mizuko's grandfather started. By the time Mark joined, it was known as a "zombie bank," just being kept afloat by the government, with no one doing any real work, though on a typical day Mark left home at 8 a.m. and returned at 2 a.m. He said he was friends with other men at the bank, with whom he went to play mahjong in the evenings and sometimes just sit with, watching NHK television until very late. Silvia thinks this was all made up and that he just sat on a bench in the park and wandered around Tokyo on his own.

Nothing about moving to Tokyo is very clear, because Silvia did not come with us. All that is certain is that three of us left New York in 1993 and only two of us left Tokyo for England in 1994.

When I was ten, wanting a conclusion for what had happened in the interim, I faked his suicide note. I tea-stained it, burnt the edges with a candle, hid it in an old shoebox, and then pretended to find it in the attic. Susy saw past my attempt and forbade me from going up there, but I still did in secret. It was sifting through those things as a teenager—the beautiful ornaments, scrolls, and prints the dusty boxes contained, as well as all the packets of real photographs of me, nearly three, in front of temples and neon crossings—that started my fixation with Japan. I wanted to restore, maybe more like *invent*, the future suggested by their contents.

Susy seemed to have decided my birth family could not be as interesting to me as hers, because she used the former as a threat. I could go back and live with them if I was so unhappy with her. It was a clever strategy, leaching the rebellion from the idea. My cursory searches of the Internet found nothing. Susy maintained she had lost the adoption papers in our many moves, but Silvia felt sure she had destroyed them to keep me from straying. Silvia also blamed Susy for her long silence, as well as for Mark's abandonment of physics and relocation to Japan. She blamed her most of all for his disappearance. They had barely spoken in the aftermath of that. In my replies I went over all the contradictions Susy had glossed over—about Silvia, the SSC, Tokyo, and Mark. Silvia pulled each one apart in her responses, not angrily but with a sense of moral duty, as if Susy's falsehoods presented a tiny fish I might choke on and which she had to debone for me until it became just a few white flakes on a spine. When she was done, the spine itself became a sharp little skeleton key to pasts which resembled mine.

In quantum mechanics, no object has a fixed position, except when colliding with something else. The rest of the time it is midflight. Silvia's letters helped me to finally get away, but they also, for a while, made me feel more rooted to where I was. Silvia hadn't got to grips with any modes of communication that did not require a person to be fixed. The most technologically advanced tool she owned apart from her shredder was a cordless landline. This meant I felt fixed when I corresponded with her. Every time I opened one of her envelopes, I had the exhilaration of arriving, after a long journey, at a familiar place.

I told her about my studies, and in return she would send reviews and clippings from *The New Yorker* and the *New York Times* about books she had found interesting. These were the first things I found in my college mailbox that weren't my own essays handed back to me or university-wide mailings. Sometimes she asked me what my plans were for after university, and I said I didn't know. I said I didn't want to think beyond my exams at that point because then I would freak myself out. She said that sounded wise, because after exams life became just a series of days and weeks and years with no markers and very few rules, and nobody told you what to do anymore. I said this freaked me out even more. She said I might want to come and visit her in New York if I didn't know what to do with myself when I was free.

After the exams, everyone else poured outdoors into the sunshine to do the things they had been waiting to finally do now that they no longer had to study. I didn't feel free at all. I felt bereft. Agoraphobic. Even though philosophy wasn't the subject I had most wanted to study, I had liked studying and running to a schedule. I had loved a particular tutor. At our last meeting, this tutor told me to "go have fun, go wild," and I'd burst out crying. Within days I had developed a debilitating fatigue. I ached, I had dry eyes. I lay in bed but could not sleep. Then a rash appeared on one side of my torso. It was dark and patchy and a doctor said it was from stress. Since I was waiting, with growing dread, for the results of my exams, stress seemed likely. But when I got my results, which were fine, and there was nothing else which tied me to any dates or places and nothing else to wait for, things started to feel really bad. No one was coming to watch me in the graduation ceremony, so I decided to skip it. Technically, I hadn't actually told Susy it was even happening, as I hadn't wanted her to make a spontaneous and unnerving decision to come.

I lay on my single bed for hours after graduation, until there was a knock at the door and an old crone put her key in the lock, hearing no answer.

"No," she said, annoyed. "You're not supposed to be here now. They've rented out these bedrooms over the summer to conference guests from Kuala Lumpur."

I went back to my mother's. I itched all over. My rash became raw. I drifted along in a kind of haze—never really awake, never really able to sleep. Then I began getting migraines and panic attacks. When I tried to speak I kept forgetting words or reversing them in my sentences, making me feel like a foreigner. I remember the first time it happened: a waitress in a café asked what I meant when I tried to ask for "a tap glass of water." It definitely wasn't as humiliating as it felt at the time, but soon I barely left the house, and then, the longer this went on, I found it less and less necessary to leave my room. My eyes felt cloudy. Each bit of my body felt strange to me, as if someone else's hands were attached to my arms, and this weird, foreign feeling crept up and up until my brain felt like it was in the wrong head. Even the skin on my face felt like someone else's, like I could have peeled it off without its hurting, the way you do candle wax that has cooled on your finger. Whatever I did, I felt like I was impersonating myself.

Susy asked me to help with one of the joyless art therapy retreats she occasionally hosted at our home for people with many feelings. If someone held a door open for me, I had to pretend to walk through. When I answered the house phone, I found myself having to think about how to make my voice sound like what I remembered it sounding like before this feeling had come over me.

Silvia was convinced it was the outcome of too much time spent online, eroding my memory and brain. She had read *many articles* about kids who had exactly the same thing, though mainly in South Korea and Taiwan, and said I should be out and about, meeting people and being active. I said I didn't have the energy, but I didn't say that I also didn't have any friends who were friends I could see in real life. Most of my friends were behind screens, dispersed in random parts of the globe thanks to my having been signed up to a school for kids whose parents were always moving. Silvia sent me all kinds of clippings to alleviate my anxiety, or at least my sense of being unique. She underlined some of her typewritten words in pen: Stress. Shrinking population. Recession. Housing market. Occasionally she suggested that I might be depressed on account of my anemic graduate ambitions. In an effort to inspire me, she sent quizzes, flowcharts, personality tests which were supposed to help you work out what you were meant to do with your numberless days.

I couldn't work the flowcharts. I couldn't get down them. I pawed and then retreated from the first question like a dog stuck at the top of a staircase. I could not think more than one hour forward in time. The only direction to move, it seemed, was back. When I considered the future, on the other hand, I felt like I was shrinking.

> Get a job,

Silvia wrote,

> any job. Just to give you some dignity. Or, better yet, come here, no dignity needed.

I couldn't go anywhere, I assured her. I might have locked-in syndrome. I might have had a stroke. I lay in bed in my old bedroom, my mother making alarming thudding noises in the attic. But the wisdom of what Silvia said did slowly dawn on me, and after some research, I found a way to make minuscule amounts of money without leaving my bed, writing marketing copy for a company that made diagnostic toys for children with autism. I used this money for buying lottery tickets and playing online poker, spending hours picking my numbers for the former until my login timed out. The gambling was perhaps the healthiest of my pursuits. One morning I opened a link contained in an email from a girl called Miki, who said in the subject box that she wanted to be my special friend. Nothing appeared particularly amiss until I clicked on the link.

Having never before watched any kind of pornography, I quickly caught up on everything I'd missed. I liked scenes with Asian girls, and one actress especially, called Maria Ozawa, who was half Japanese, half French Canadian. She made movies for a Japanese porn company called Attackers. It wasn't that I had gone specifically looking for videos which simulated rape, torture, and bondage, but those were the films which happened to have the girl I liked best acting in them.

During this pornography/gambling/autism period, a fear was planted in me that I was infertile. Though I had never contemplated the idea of having my own children before, for some reason I decided I could not, and this became a symbol of my utter uselessness and dislocation from normal society. I first remember it coming over me as I was listening, in and out of sleep, to a radio programme coming from Susy's room, during which it was announced that an osprey called Lady had broken her own record. She had laid her sixty-ninth egg at age twenty-nine, and had flown to South Africa and back to do it. Birdwatchers had noted in the middle of the night that her behavior had changed, and hundreds of people had been watching her lay the egg through a live stream broadcast all over the world. I woke up fully at this point, cold and sweating. As I lay listening to the birdwatchers praising Lady's accomplishment, I did an online self-diagnosis on my phone for slightly irregular periods and decided I had polycystic ovaries and total sterility. The family line, I told myself, wherever it had started, ended with me. They played a recording of people cheering as Lady stood up to reveal Egg. I was only twenty-two, but I felt like I'd failed already.

At this point my correspondence with Silvia lapsed. Or my replies did. As usual, her letters arrived, trying to rouse me, comparing my indulgent postgraduate malaise to Mark's after the cancellation of the SSC and offering advice on how to shake it off.

> You should be waking up every morning at the same time, eating avocados, and going to visit places of historical interest. You should be playing with animals and updating your collections—didn't you say you had some? You should be applying for real jobs and going for long walks.

You should limit the time you spend online and read or write instead. What good is your degree otherwise? You should also, sweetheart, as I have said before, COME TO NEW YORK. It is so healthy to be somewhere where the view always changes without your having to move. Just come and sniff the air.

Move was underlined in red pen.

Cancer had moved into every part of her body. She later told me that pushing the invitation was not so much for my benefit as for hers. In the end I earned a tiny portion of the money towards my flight from my online job and she made up the difference. She thought it was character-building for me to at least try to earn a portion of the fare. I remembered this later and felt guilty when I saw the inscription on the building I walked past on my way to see Silvia in the home she had been moved to on Amsterdam Avenue: THE HABIT OF SAVING MONEY WHILE IT STIFFENS THE WILL ALSO BRIGHTENS THE ENERGIES. IF YOU WOULD BE SURE THAT YOU ARE BEGINNING RIGHT, BEGIN TO SAVE.

In the end I guess it was that which hooked me—the idea of another beginning, begun right. Although Silvia had offered to help me understand at least a part of my origins (not my birth parents, written out entirely except for the lost adoption forms), I wanted to build—half reconstruction, half my own design—a version that belonged entirely to me.

When the ticket confirmation arrived in my inbox I punched the air, staggered downstairs, unsteady on my wasted legs, and told Susy I was going to New York. Her face fell. *To find my real parents,* I added. I had decided to stop caring about what was real and what was not, because it never seemed to trouble her.

In the weeks before my departure, when she saw that I wasn't going to change my plans, she started telling me instead that I should hurry up and go, as if it were she who had planned this all along. But she looked at me now and then like she was slightly afraid, even impressed. In the end she even drove me to the airport, saying the whole way that she was glad I'd finally listened to her advice and booked a flight. I sat in the passenger seat in silence, saying goodbye to it all through the car window. It felt good but strange to be outside the house. There was a heavy blue cloud with a narrow strip of white at the horizon so that the sky looked very low. Under it, Olde Worlde streaked into the past. Places I had known forever, but the landscape had already begun to feel foreign to me. It looked like memory already. Mock Tudor houses, dinky cars, a white man digging in a field next to a parked tractor and a yellow Labrador at his side, two people —a white man and woman—both in black trousers and brown jackets crossing a railway line, a flock of white-and-red turkeys running through the forecourt of a white-and-red petrol station, a dilapidated lawn, an old white man cycling through a mud-green field with a red hunting cap on, the flaps under his collar tied tightly, and a young white man wearing an FBI sweater selling grapes by the roadside. I peered at them, Little Englanders, as though they were people from another time. When the view became suggestive of the airport, for the first time I began to feel that it was all really happening. I sat up straight in my seat when I started to see the signs under the white motorway bridges, dipping like whale backs below the grey sky.

Waiting to board the plane, I counted how many hours I had before me without an Internet connection. Silvia had mailed me a short, slim book about New York, a long essay she loved, which I planned to read on the journey. The essay was from a long time ago, but the writer also said it was the duty of the reader—meaning a reader in the future, just like me—to bring the city up to date.

"When a young man in Manhattan writes a letter to his girl in Brooklyn," I read, holding the book close to my face under my lone spotlight, "the love message gets blown to her through a pneumatic tube—pfft—just like that."

5

My first morning at Silvia's, like most of the mornings before I transitioned fully to Eastern Time, was shocking pink. I woke up with the sensation of floating, levitating between the sofa and a pink triangle of light which edged down the slope of my forehead, over my eyes, and towards my chest as I lay still, thinking. Mainly I was thinking about the pinkness, the startling colour of it everywhere. I had never woken so high up, and so effortlessly early, and with nothing obscuring the dawn. It felt like a time and a colour I had been missing my whole life.

I went to get my journal—again, as on the Van Wyck Expressway, intending to note the light quality, in place of any more concrete feelings—but when I returned from the hall where I'd left my unpacked suitcase, the colour had already started to dissolve.

When Silvia finally emerged to get the papers from outside the front door, she looked more the way I'd hoped she would and less like the spectral presence that had stood over me in the night. She looked clean and beady-eyed, her hair wet, with one roller in it. She opened and quickly shut the door again, the papers rolled in the bony crook of her arm. I could hear the sound of muffled barking. I disliked dogs, and it was usually mutual. My impression of Silvia was of a bulky middle perched on tiny legs. For the rest of the time that I knew her, she almost exclusively wore the same pinkish pyjamas and a lamb's-wool throw with sheepskin slippers. She had maybe six sets of the same. The only time she modified her dress was for medical appointments, when she added coats and scarves no matter the weather outside. She had shorn white hair that I remember resting my hand on later, when we were in the hospital. When it wasn't wet and flattened against her skull, it was very soft, like an earlobe. Then eyebrows which were no longer there but delicate creases where they had been once. She said she had no need for eyebrows anymore anyway, as nothing surprised her. Beneath them, her stately liver spots, and her calm, all-knowing eyes. Even her lips were a line, smooth as an envelope, with a paler part beneath where the bottom gums pressed against the skin of the chin.

Immediately I had many burning questions for her, all of which seemed too complex to broach except one: "What's the Wi-Fi password?"

"No idea," she replied, engaged in a one-armed struggle with the rubber band around the papers. "Sorry about last night—my medication is pretty strong. You *are* supposed to be here. I thought it was tomorrow, or the day before, and I got mixed up about which day my operation was on when I booked your flight."

Her voice was frail.

I stood up. "No, not at all. *I'm* sorry if—if I arrived unannounced. I didn't have a number to call, and downstairs they said to go straight up."

"Oh yes. They do know who you are. They're very helpful boys. I'm always calling them up to do things for me."

I began to speak, but she shuffled away and the conversation was over.

Later I realised that Silvia's manner diverged, at least at first, from her letters because she found it difficult to speak and was often heavily sedated. She wished to communicate with me only when it suited her. When she was not in the middle of something else—usually reading. When she had something particular to say. When she was feeling well, and when her speaking apparatus was well lubricated. None of these conditions happened all at once for a while.

Silvia seemed to have settled in her den with the papers, so I wandered over to the window. You couldn't see the East River exactly, but there was a sense of it from the light that bounced off the water and some very narrow shining cracks visible between buildings. The sight of the city was like a machine that I could not isolate the significance of any part of. Later, when I had learnt my way around by walking, I could situate myself when I stood in that same spot looking down. I could trace an imaginary line to Mizuko's, beyond that to Columbia, and, on the far side of it, Claremont Avenue. On a diagonal line back down and east across Central Park I would soon be able to add Nat Rooiakker's place, practically across the street from the Metropolitan Museum. After that I could go further, imagining behind me, backwards and over the bridge, what I would soon know to be Dwight Nutt's place in Dumbo.

An hour or so later, Silvia shuffled in from the den again and showed me around the apartment I had already seen, with a croaky guide to garbage disposal, mail, laundry, a porcelain dish where she kept tip money for delivery boys, and the schedule for when the cleaner was due to come. She also handed me a credit card with a PIN number written on a Post-it, for "emergencies."

"You won't need your own key," she explained. "I always

leave it unlocked and I'm always here. If I'm not, you'll be with me."

I wrote down a list of various tasks as she dictated them to me. My main duties comprised receiving deliveries and paying for them, taking prescriptions to Duane Reade, winding Silvia's watch (which she found impossible because of her increasingly useless arm), crushing pills, twisting bottle caps and lids (such as that on eyedrops), and other intensely satisfying ministrations, which I accepted gladly and later tried to re-create when I took care of Mizuko.

My first official engagement was receiving a delivery of twelve bottles of vodka. The big ones, not the miniatures. I was charged with releasing each bottle from a heft of packaging, then laying six in the freezer, side by side. I did so with a jaunty swing of my arms from box to freezer drawer. I put the remaining six upright in the cupboard. Once I had completed this task, Silvia informed me that I needed to take her purse to buy a new kettle from Bed Bath and Beyond and that on the way there, or, if I preferred, on the way back, I was to introduce myself to Donna and Denise, identical twins in their late forties who took it in turns to have cigarette breaks and who worked in a grocery store across the street. They had been helping her, before I came, with supplies. She said I could take a stroll around, pick up the kettle, and say hello in any order I chose.

I am going to switch to using the word *elevator,* as it was a word I had to start using to make myself understood. The woman who joined the *elevator* on the twentieth floor had stumps for fingers, which I could not stop staring at, and then I could not stop wondering whether I should have offered to press the button for her or if that would have been worse. They went towards the gold buttons, casting a fleshy tint, and I shivered and she saw. I had to remind myself I was really *here* in this shiny, sitcom world, an audience whose reactions could be seen. I bit my lip hard as punishment. The speed of the elevator drop made me dizzy. I hadn't eaten since the previous lunchtime, when I had been too anxious to eat much, and I felt billowy, the April breeze outside moving me more than any sense of direction.

Walking the streets felt instantly different from driving through them in the cab from the airport. The mythic scale of the buildings shrank me at the same time as it made something grow in size inside me. I began to sense this feeling, the first manifestation of what became my special power, travelling towards my fingers, a gradual itch that became harder and harder to ignore, until I realised that along with the feeling there was something ulterior. I wanted to take a picture.

I stopped on a bench and contemplated the blank canvas of my Instagram account. It was six months old but with no pictures and only a handful of followers, whom I did not know and who mostly appeared to be corporate robots, perverts, or porn stars. I had so far used it only to survey the progress made since school of people I barely knew or had never known. I also followed many beautiful women on personal journeys, pursuing their dreams with a ruthless determination that left me exhausted. It had been a constant torment during my seclusion. Now it was different. I wanted the world to know I was here, not me as I had been but a self constructed from bits of New York. My vision zeroed in on a city made up of little squares. I began popping them like vitamins.

As I continued walking I began shaking out my arms, rolling my neck back and around, tugging at my hair and clothes, tracing my finger along walls. Silvia had been right: some kind of transfusion was happening as the outside came rushing in. It was good to be somewhere where all you had to do was arrive —where that was all that was expected. My first walk took me, without my having made any perceptible decisions except one left and one right, to East 65th and Park. I stopped all of a sudden at a narrow white townhouse where the sidewalk smelt of fresh laundry. It seemed that something in my feet, controlled remotely, had brought me to a halt. My brain, calmly hovering above like a drone, had not made the command and was surprised by it. *This stroll is over,* my feet said; *time to turn back.* I stood still. Not wanting to stop walking, to stop touching things and taking pictures, but I sensed that Silvia was waiting.

A small boy stood sucking his teeth at me while he waited for someone to unload something from the boot of a car. I stared back at him, repossessing my feet and then my body, drawing myself upwards and making my stomach taut. I admired his monogrammed uniform, wondering what a Preschool of the Arts might be. I realised it must be three already. Children were walking in formation along the sidewalk, all in yellow overalls and holding on to each other like a human school bus. There were also older ones—tribes of girls in partial school uniform with sprain-injury socks over their knees and elbows. Thick hair elasticked in low ponytails, flowery kit bags, after-school tangerines, pastel Converses, orthodontics. The care with which these luminous angels were marshalled along the street, the ease with which they were normal and good, lay all over them in a healthy sheen. None of them felt familiar. I stared longingly after them, wondering which of them I might have been if I'd stayed here to grow up.

Everything at this point was pretty. There was dogwood and sprays of blossom shining on black branches. This was the first picture I sent out into the world. Sometimes I return to it and note how many hundreds of weeks have passed since and how much has changed. From then on, from that blossom branch, I was addicted to walking around the city, documenting it, breaking it down so I could hold it. I explored alone, on foot, occasionally using buses or taxis when it got dark and my feet were bleeding.

My solitude, as Silvia and the slim book she had given me had promised, no longer felt like a burden but a gift. As I walked, my thoughts could leave my body. I had no more itinerary than the blossoms descending towards the gutter or alighting on the arms of benches. I floated down every morning from the Upper East Side, ending up around SoHo or City Hall. I liked gliding, like a robot on the ocean floor, from point to point on the city grid. When I came home, exhausted, I would stick my head into Silvia's den and holler triumphantly, "New York is the best place in the *world!*"

It is certainly the best place to walk that I have been to. You don't have to have any idea where you are going; you can advance without being aware of anything but vague progress into time stretching out before you. In this way I discovered moments of light-headedness, which led to a feeling that my body was somehow becoming less and less material. The exact opposite of what had happened to me at home in England, when everything had become gloopy and masklike. I felt, after a time, like I could float upwards, into the air, as well as down. At its most intense, I felt like I was only a heartbeat inside my brain.

You can also cope better with strange things when you are slightly tripping out like this. It is certainly easier to fall in love with a stranger. You can answer the question "How you doing today, señorita?" in a way you never would in England, if you were asked, which you wouldn't be. You can get talking to a woman who is wearing a smart grey suit but sitting on the sidewalk, begging. There will likely be a snappy dachshund parked beside her in a pram when you realise you have no coins in your purse, only dollar bills. This will not embarrass you; you'll just give the bills. You can wonder with detached amusement what a Philly cheese steak is and make your mistaken judgment based on the smell of spicy sausage in the air, which in fact comes from an adjacent cart you should have gone to instead. People will make comments about how slowly you count the change. Doesn't matter. It's novelty. It might as well be another language. You can pass a man holding something strange and highly personal in the street and look away because it feels like he is doing it on purpose to make people look. You can sit in a café downtown whilst a family holds hands in prayer and gives thanks because somebody graduated today, and you can watch them unselfconsciously because they are so deep into it. On the Lower East Side, you can count the ornamental cockatoos within dusty windows. In midtown you can buy something for allergy season when you see a warning about it outside a juice shop. You can do whatever you like—you can go completely mental—and no one gives a shit.

6

Japan is the opposite. As everybody knows, it is a place that cares deeply about attention to detail. This is at the root of all the other impressive national stereotypes about Japanese people—being polite and respectful to strangers and their personal space, obeying rules, keeping a shared environment pristine, co-operating. I had finally returned to Japan for a few weeks as part of my year out before university, to see for real the mini-Japan my mother kept in the attic, collecting the stamps the U.S. customs official would later admire. As I waited for my case, black wheelie bags were going round like identical sushi, all neatly wrapped and shiny in plastic, and dummy bags were going round too, with rhetorical questions on them and an imagined Person A and Person B who might go home and realise they had each other's bags. Their futures altered, their lives entwined forever. I considered taking someone else's bag just so this simulation would play out.

Outside, I felt sure that I remembered the warm rain and, encouraged by this, a woman who bowed deeply to me. She continued bowing until, as far as she knew, with her eyes to the ground, I was long past looking. It seemed rude to ask if I knew her when I felt so sure I did. An old man in a smart uniform helped with my correct case, covered in stickers I had peeled away to their white fuzz. Then he bowed too. That is the thing I liked best about Japan: all the soothing acts of ceremony and little rituals, which made me feel like no moment was too small for me to hold and keep. The maid who cleaned my room even took a polythene bag that I had intended to throw away and folded it into a neat little square.

I try to remember moving there as a child. I try to remember the ground shaking, but now I know I am thinking of news reports and clippings from the attic, or Mizuko's stories, so I allow myself only a series of neat mental pictures. In them my silhouette varies gradually, and, like a flipbook, the faster I go through them, the more I appear to be running.

Susy sometimes said the earthquake happened just after and other times just as, or just before, Mark decided to get lost. As a national natural disaster, it was a good, roomy cover for whatever really happened between them. If it hadn't occurred, no one could have tolerated for so long the victim she became. She talks about Mark constantly, unaware, or unconcerned, that she has come full circle at the end of a sentence. She does not accept whatever it was that took place and so has a compulsion to repeat her stories to me or, better, to strangers, whose polite incredulity grants her some kind of temporary relief.

Although the real split between us came when I returned to New York, my solo trip to Japan marks the fault line. There was even an earthquake just as I landed—a small one. For the most part, I feel like I have managed to separate my memories, my way of seeing things, from hers. If, very occasionally, I feel us move together or overlap again, I have to stand still, and when I do I feel like my feet are sinking, as if water is coming up through fractures in the ground. There is a sudden stomach lightness, a toe wetness, the floor beneath giving way as her vision seeps into mine. The feeling isn't exactly unpleasant. Sometimes in New York I went to places Susy had spoken of, following her footsteps like chess moves, not to know more about *her* so much but as if this would somehow grow me up too.

Though Susy didn't know about my real itinerary (if she'd found out exactly where I was going, I'm sure she would have taken my passport), my gap year involved a guided tour of Japan with a few days in Tokyo alone first. To get to my hotel, I rode in a beautiful blue taxi with a glowing orb on top, milky with navy kanji. It was clear to me I did not fit in. When the taxi stopped in traffic, an old woman in the adjacent taxi, with cavernously large ears pushed forward by her face mask, stared at me, unblinking, through the window. Outside my hotel were three men employed just to stand on the same zebra crossing, waving and halting traffic, who would drop their arms and stare whenever I passed.

Outside Tokyo, everything got smaller and I felt even bigger. Millions of fireflies and moths floated and sparkled in the half light, taunting my human bulk as I walked in silence behind the tour group. We took a bullet train to a town that was preparing to celebrate the festival of Tsukimi, the moon-viewing festival based on the Japanese folk tale "The Rabbit in the Moon." The story of the rabbit in the moon deeply affected me, even though when the tour guide pointed out the pareidolia that identifies the markings in the moon as a rabbit, I seemed to be the only one who couldn't see it.

Some people in the town did not seem to care about the festival and were watching football on TV. The players were dotted about in neon green. They looked unreal, the way they might be seen by the forgotten man in the moon and the rabbit if they were watching the floodlit pitch forlornly from above. The occasional wash of noise and the sight of the screens, their halo of green flickering when the tour guide had promised an authentic experience of moon viewing, caused one of our group to complain because it wasn't "historically accurate." The man, who seemed to think the events of the story had a basis in historical fact, demanded to be taken somewhere more historical, and so we went to a temple, where some people, copying the example of our guide, prayed to their ancestors. I hung back and watched.

The man had a family—a wife and a son a bit older than me. Something about them interested me, and I began watching them exclusively. On the last evening I saw the son alone and walked over to him.

"I'm Alice."

I realised that I was drunk as I said my name. He turned to me with a face that showed he also knew this, answering in a deadpan way, "I'm Rupert."

He didn't say anything else for a while, but as it was the last night of the trip and we were back in Tokyo at a nice hotel, I persevered, because I was lonely.

"This is the edge of town in a way."

"The edge of town?" he asked, as if pleased to be talking about something with a parameter, though Tokyo still sprawled far beyond it.

I did deep nodding and let there be a pause so that we could look at the view together and so that he might say something else.

When he finally did, it was, "It looks like a necklace," meaning the lights and the roads.

I considered and agreed that they looked like rubies or emeralds.

After a while he stopped looking and walked away without a

word. I went back to my room and spent all night contemplating whether it was possible in life not to be constantly let down. If it could ever be worth pinning your happiness to another person, when all other people ever seemed to do was disappear. Tokyo was a place you could quite happily exist alone and be self-contained. It seemed to promise that it was *better* to be by yourself.

When I got back from that trip I was insufferable. I trailed Susy around the house reading koans under my breath to annoy her, so that sometimes she would turn around and say "What?" and I would smile and say "Nothing." It pleased me greatly that I had managed to conceal the trip from her. When I began university, in the autumn of 2010, I did not make any attempt to hide or even temper my obsession. If anything, I exaggerated it, sleeping on a mattress on the floor, lining up a series of strange rocks and twigs which stood for the whole universe outside my door, drinking exclusively green tea or brown rice tea while deep in books about Japanese history and culture. I ate only Japanese food, spoke only about Japanese philosophers, and read only Japanese literature, which I bought in translation mainly but also, as souvenirs, in Japanese. I told people who asked that I had lived there for longer than I had. I made up other things too, I'm sure, which I can no longer remember. When the chain reaction of earthquake, tsunami, and nuclear disaster happened the following spring, I talked about it as if I were an authority.

It was in my second term of first year, while watching the coverage of the 2011 tsunami in our college communal room (a mysterious sign on the door said THE MEDIA ROOM, though there was only one TV), that I first saw Rupert again. Rupert who would, in the not-so-distant future, become Mizuko's boyfriend. He called me out on some of the things I was saying about Japanese culture. People looked at me and then back at him—two enemy samurai. Then, me first (and because of that him too), we recognised each other from our conversation while looking at the view in Tokyo the year before.

Rupert Hunter was a permanent student. I'm not sure how old he was then—he didn't have Facebook. I think he was doing his second master's, and I think he was supposed to be writing something on masks in Africa. Something anthropological with the word *culture* in it. His hero was Bruce Chatwin, and later Mizuko talked about him having spent time with the Baoulé people in Côte d'Ivoire. We didn't become friends. I got the sense that on top of being reclusive, he did not like me personally, and we rarely ran into each other. When we did, he would pretend he hadn't seen me. Even when we were in a narrow passageway he would pretend to be checking the time, slowly, with disbelief, and then making some mysterious calculation that required his full concentration.

The chance of both Mizuko and her boyfriend suffering from short lived comas only a few years apart certainly seems *slim*, but that is what happened. I can't imagine many things worse than waking from a coma. I feel depressed waking up and finding evidence that others have been up for a while already. Whenever I woke up to find that Mizuko had already left her side of the bed, I would lie there for a few moments feeling like the wind had been knocked out of me, before jumping up to check that she was still in the apartment somewhere. Wherever I am, I try to make sure I'm the last to fall asleep and the first to wake up. I hate anyone watching me sleep. I hate it even more after last summer.

Midway through my second year, word spread that the elusive Rupert Hunter had disappeared. It took some time for an already solitary person enrolled in an esoteric master's program where foreign field trips were common, and whose interests qualified as obscure, to be noticed by his generally self-involved peers as being consistently *not there*. I *did* notice, and asked the porters if they knew anything about it. I was informed by one of them, who was quickly reprimanded by another for sharing the information, that Rupert had claimed to be on a year abroad in Senegal but that he had, only moments after sending his parents a message about Lac Rose, the beautiful, strawberry-milkshake-coloured lake in that country, been hit by a car while on his bicycle three roads away from college. He was now in hospital, and his father—the one who wanted everything to be historically accurate—was staying in his college room. He had been investigating while his son was unconscious and had discovered that Rupert had been living inside a Winnebago the whole term, teaching himself to play the kora, a West African harp, and highlighting pink every other line in *Utz*.

7

The only reason I got to sleep with—in the same bed as—Mizuko after I first met her was thanks to Rupert Hunter.

"Are you sure you don't want to go?" I'd said to him.

Mizuko had two tickets for a talk at Columbia. One she had earmarked for Rupert, who, since the last time I'd seen him at university, before his cycling accident, appeared to have left England for real, transferred his mysterious academic studies to Columbia, and become Mizuko's all-consuming passion and central neurosis. Though he presented a definite obstacle, without him I might never have had the guts to approach her in real life.

"Sure," he said. "I have tonnes to do."

"And you don't want to give it to someone else?" I said, turning to Mizuko, trying to sound casual but also trying not to let her actually give the ticket to someone else. "Because obviously I'm dying to go. I tried to get a ticket myself," I lied, "but they're all sold out."

The talk was being hosted by the Japan Society at Columbia. I had breathed on their glass-covered noticeboard on my evening walks around the campus and noted the talks that were advertised there. There was one called something like "Sacred Cows and Kobe Beef."

"It looks so interesting," I said, trying to suppress the note of desperation in my voice. I tried to remember what the board had said, but I could only think of words to do with meat. "I boned up on it the other day." Then suddenly it came to me: "I was reading all about the 'Bovine Revolution.'"

Rupert looked at me in a weird way.

Boned up was a phrase I had never used before. From their expressions, I decided I would not do so again. I had the same feeling I'd had in college every time I'd bumped into Rupert and he'd avoided my gaze, except now worse, because she was there too.

"The *what* revolution?" Rupert asked with an incredulous look.

"Bo-vine," I repeated.

"The talk she's going to is about the Holocaust," he said, looking over his shoulder towards the door.

I froze. That was the other talk on the other board, a few paces along. I had forgotten it.

Mizuko looked pained by the silence.

"Are we talking about the same noticeboard?" I asked.

"It was on the Donald Keene board," Mizuko offered. "Not the Institute for Japanese Cultural Heritage Initiatives one. You might be mixing them up."

"Oh," I said, tensing my hands into fists under the table. "Probably."

"I also want to go to the one about Takuboku," Mizuko said warmly.

She evidently thought I was a much better acquaintance of Rupert's than I was, an impression I had tried to give as I sat down.

"You had to register, and the registration is now closed," Rupert said.

"Oh no," I said, not knowing what Takuboku was and deciding to keep quiet.

"Anyway," Mizuko said, "it starts at four in Kent Hall. That's in ten minutes. Shall we walk over?"

I felt the hot air of the café ripple through my lungs and stomach. It was the kind of nervous excitement that can sometimes cause me to pass wind, so I tightened everything and smiled at her. "Great."

I turned the beam of my smile on Rupert. A subtly altered smile, a hint more smugness, a touch less warmth, that I hoped conveyed I was out-Japanning him with his own girlfriend right in front of his fine-boned face. I had not forgotten how he had publicly embarrassed me in my first year with the tsunami coverage rolling in the background. This would be payback.

"Don't worry, Roo," Mizuko said. "There's another coming up we can go to together."

She brought up a page on her device, covered it with her hand so that the sunshine did not fade out the words on the screen, and read mechanically, "'A critical reflection on liberal humanism in Japan's transformation into a nation-state. Katsuya Hirano, associate professor, Department of History, UCLA.' Oh! Here's the one you meant"—she looked at me, realising with embarrassment that she had forgotten my name—"underneath." She looked back at the screen. "'From Sacred Cow to Kobe Beef —Japan's Bovine Revolution. Daniel Botsman, professor of East Asian studies at Yale.'"

Rupert snorted, swung a black canvas backpack onto one shoulder, and pushed his chair in. "I've got to go."

"Right," Mizuko said. "See you later, baby." And, turning to me, her new shadow, "Ready?"

On the way, Mizuko gave me a short introduction. It would be about a Japanese diplomat sent to Lithuania to serve as Japan's consul. She said his name softly, and so fast I couldn't catch it. The visas he granted had saved thousands of Jews from the Nazis, who, I interjected so I could save some face, had invaded Lithuania in June 1941. I had been looking this up on my device as we walked by, briefly turning on my data roaming and pretending to send a text.

Suddenly it was working out so much better than I had hoped for. But I felt that it was immensely disrespectful to be in such ecstasy prior to a talk given by the descendent of a Holocaust survivor. I felt sure I would be punished for it later in some way and tried to bite my cheeks whenever they threatened to break out into a lunatic grin. The more I bit, the more the grin prised my cheeks apart. Suddenly I had to laugh. It was like realising you definitely need to projectile vomit when you thought you had it under control in some imprisoning form of public space. I had to stagger off the path and grab hold of a Beaux Arts streetlamp, where I leaned over the grass and heaved and retched and laughed like a maniac.

"Are you okay?" Mizuko asked.

I made a soft moan, the serene expiation of breath after vomit when the threat of imminent projection has subsided.

"Feeling sick," I said. "Nauseous." I waved my hand at her. "Not actually going to throw up."

Mizuko waited silently. I wondered how to proceed. If I was sick she might not want me to go with her to the talk, and in any case, a sane person who felt sick would not go, they would go home. My mind moved quickly, too quickly, searching for a suitable lie. I lifted my head up and returned to the path she was still standing on.

"I'm actually *pregnant*," I said gravely.

There could be no arguing with *that*. It came out and for a second I felt better, as with vomit, but then, almost immediately, the next wave of complexity I had just created for myself made me feel sick for real.

"I'm not *keeping* it."

I knew she was pro-choice. I'd seen two or three pictures with captions that confirmed it.

"Oh man," she said, repeating her earlier question but in a softer voice: "Are you *okay?*"

Her apparent concern—dimpled chin and knitted brow —brought me dangerously close to smiling again, so I put my hands to my face as if to wipe away tears, and she put her hand gently, or cautiously, as if it might burn her to touch me, on my back. My ability to make up lies on the spot chills me as much as it saves me.

The inside of the auditorium was heavily air-conditioned. It was an egg-shaped room with shiny wooden walls, a waxed floor, and a small stage inside one of its elongated curves. I had been worrying it would be too intimidating and too grand for my purpose, which was to forge intimacy, but it was not an imposing room. It didn't look like there had to be audience participation, or like everyone there was Japanese or Jewish or a member of Columbia, which meant I would have been conspicuous. Six or seven rows of white chairs were occupied by all sorts of people of all ages. The back row consisted mainly of student types, all frenziedly stroking luminous screens held in their laps.

Mizuko and I took the first two seats in the second row. I tried to smile at her reassuringly. Maybe I would keep it, the laughter baby, and we could move back to Tokyo and raise it, dress it up in tiny kimonos. She too laid her device in her lap. It had a splintered screen despite a protective case designed like a slice of watermelon. I'd seen it in the many photos she took of herself in mirrors. She hung her head as she put in her pass code, which, I correctly guessed, was the year of her birth.

1 2
  8 9

She had long nails, filed to demonic points, with just the tips painted pink. She had to use her fingers lightly, flexed so that only the pads of them touched the screen. Still there was a slight click. I felt at ease by her side now that I was not required to speak. I could simply sit and cast sidelong glances in her direction. It was like sitting next to a film star. This person I had only ever seen in miniature so vital beside me.

A wiry man ascended the stage and put things on a small lectern, and then another man joined him and turned on a white projector screen behind them both. Mizuko glanced up briefly, noticing the change in light. The lights above the audience dimmed, and I felt bliss expanding from my chest and sliding down into the rest of my body, collecting in my shoes like warm pools of butter despite the air conditioning. *This,* I thought, is the reward for making things happen rather than just waiting for them to happen to you.

The talk itself was of course horrific. The speaker showed us pictures of Jewish women in Lithuania. He also showed pictures of women undressing in a forest before their execution. The Nazi terminology for *murdered,* he said, with a steady voice that made Mizuko shed tears and wipe them delicately away, was *liquidated.* The part at which I myself cried was when he described the Jews in long lines, allowed to carry some baggage as a sham, to create the impression amongst them that they were simply being resettled rather than shunted to their death. The speaker was the descendent of someone who had been saved by

the Japanese diplomat. Disobeying his bosses in Japan, the diplomat had issued thousands of exit visas. Over July and August,
he and his wife had stayed up all night, writing visas. The Japanese government closed the consulate, but even as the diplomat's
train was about to leave the city, he kept writing visas from his
open window. When the train began moving, he flung his visa
stamp out the window so the crowds could continue to stamp
visas for themselves. The speaker's father had eventually settled
in America, where he met his wife, who was in the audience.

Mizuko leaned over to me when he pointed her out, sitting
in the front row just to the right of us. "She has such a beautiful
profile," Mizuko whispered, her breath warm milk.

I nodded and then kept my head very still so that she might
admire *my* head in profile too.

Because the diplomat had issued the unauthorised visas, he
was dismissed, but quietly, without reason. He worked odd jobs
after returning to Japan and later moved away for a time. He
fell into obscurity and never spoke of his actions, but in 1968 a
survivor who had become an Israeli diplomat tracked him down.
His name was Sugihara. Mizuko, I knew, loved all stories about
people who tracked other people down.

The talk, we were reminded, was being recorded. When it
was time for questions from the floor, I put up my hand first,
wanting to show Mizuko how I had as much interest in this subject as in beef, only to lower it when the hammering in my chest
meant that I didn't think I would be able to keep the tremor from
my voice. Mizuko, however, perfectly composed, asked a question of her own. I often listen to the talk online, and I have come
to love the diplomat and the memory of Mizuko and me being
there together, because this was when anything felt possible and
barely any lies had been told.

When I listen, the question right before Mizuko's is from a

law student who says his name into the microphone. His surname I can't catch, but his first name I took as a sign. It is Mark.
Mark, with a voice that slides, eliding words, asks the speaker
what he thinks Sugihara's legacy is. By this point I was used to
how unapologetically earnest Americans are. After a pause, the
speaker says that Sugihara has taught him the power of an individual. "Most people," he says, "think that they don't have an
impact on anyone else, but you're having a huge impact, or you
can have a huge impact, without even realising it, even on the
course of just one other person's life." When I listened to this at
the time my eyes blazed; I was hoping Mizuko was receiving it
with the same fervour I was by directly applying every word the
speaker was saying to my own situation and, more specifically,
to the possibility of a relationship between *us*.

Then there is a lull as the person with the microphone brings
it round to our side of the seats. In comes Mizuko's voice, followed by a little bump of her breath into the head of the microphone, like a train rolling into the air cushion at the end of the
track.

"Hello. I'm Mizuko Himura." Her voice is smooth and
self-assured.

Something inside me clenches. A phantom breath on the back
of my neck.

"I teach creative writing here." The present tense makes me
wince. "Thank you so much for giving such a moving account of
your family and of Sugihara."

She pronounces his name with a Japanese accent. The lightness of the word, thrown up into the air like a child, makes her
subsequent American English sound plodding.

"I was wondering if you could shed light on how he came to
carry out such an extraordinary act of disobedience, given that
in Japanese culture respect for your elders is inviolable."

Her question floored me, still floors me.

Every time I hear it I repeat the word *inviolable* over and over in my mouth, as if rolling a grape and trying not to break the skin.

This, she later explained, was a question she had prepared and already had her own answer to, but she was interested in hearing the speaker's point of view and, more importantly, in alerting the non-Japanese in the audience to just how exceptional Sugihara's actions had been. His father had pushed him to become a doctor, but he, more interested in foreign cultures, wanted to study English. His father forced Sugihara to take the entrance exam for medical school, but Sugihara wrote only his name on the test. His father was furious when he found out and disowned him. She also, I knew, liked stories about this kind of rebellion. I could see why this talk was exactly her sort of thing.

After everyone clapped and the men descended from the stage, we went out into the warmth of the early evening. The sun was low in the sky, its light arrowing straight across from one side of the island to the other, west to east, blinding us. We looked down at our feet as we walked. The spokes of light picked out each herringbone brick and made it redder. Our shadows cast us as a ludicrous double act. We walked around a corner of a building so that Mizuko could have a cigarette out of the glare. We came out onto a platform above Broadway. I have been told that when I concentrate intently, as while watching something and forgetting myself, I am a heavy breather. It is something I am always at pains to correct. There were red and off-white squares underfoot, and she stood on red and I stood on white. I peered out over the dark red exterior of Teachers College and then across to the cream church spires as Mizuko tried to light her rolled cigarette. It was a wind-spot, and the cigarette wouldn't light. The way she was holding it in her mouth and her pointy little nails fiddling with the lighter for so long made me want to take it from her mouth and lean in to kiss her. I wondered, from the way my feet felt as if they might be standing on a waterbed rather than on solid ground, if we might have been standing on the site of Mark and Susy's first kiss. I hoped not.

"What are you up to now?" she said finally, giving up.

"I think I need to decompress," I said, pleased with this word, and then, inspired by the talk to take the initiative more often, "Shall we get a drink?"

"*So* yes," was her reply. SO YES, I thought to myself, writing it in loop-the-loop letters across the sky.

As we walked down Broadway to a bar Mizuko had thought of, we passed a bookshop. As with all her favourite things, I already knew what and where they were, so I mentioned it before she did. "This is my favourite bookshop," I said.

Outside the bookshop we heard a fragment of conversation between an older woman and a younger woman, an assistant, who was wresting a book out of a red bookshelf standing outside the shop door. "I know someone who'd love it, but they've gone and *died*," the old woman said to the younger woman, who looked embarrassed. We seized on it with our eyes and turned to each other, panting with stifled laughter. It wasn't necessarily as funny as our laughing suggested. Perhaps the laughter was prompted by having just left the Holocaust behind. But I believe it communicated to Mizuko that we had the same sense of humour, as well as the same taste in bookshops, the same ear for what was funny and how. And we were fixing on things, or at least I was. I wanted to make it natural, the encounter and our subsequent fast friendship, as if it had all happened by chance.

My boyfriend at that time had told me that very week that love is really the feeling of atoms from exploded stars reunited after billions of years.

"Who said that?" I had asked immediately, knowing that he would not have come up with this himself.

"A physicist," he replied after a hurt pause.

He'd read the most recent *New Yorker* cover to cover, as he liked to be able to pass things off as his own. I found myself thinking of it again as I and Mizuko walked, and now I knew that it was true.

After examining something on her phone, Mizuko changed her mind about which bar she wanted us to walk to. She was also suddenly desperate to pee, so we stopped at a café called Nussbaum & Wu. I waited outside while she asked to use the bathroom. I remember I felt unsure, now that the side-by-sideness had been broken, whether I should stay. It seemed easy to roll from the Hungarian to the Holocaust to here, but now she was gone, and I was creeping about on the sidewalk and it broke up the flow. What was a perfectly acceptable thing to do online seemed wrong in this context. I imagined that she was standing in the bathroom waiting, hoping I would go away. Maybe she was texting Rupert right now along these lines: *Your friend STILL here. Help.* And then I imagined his reply, with wording I was more sure of: *NOT my friend. You were one who invited her along. Why are you always so nice to people you don't even know?*

I had been staying in New York for some months by this point, but I had not yet fully acclimated. Or at least, saying I hadn't yet *acclimated* was still my default with people who asked how it was going. Like professing to be tired or stressed or suffering from a minor ailment is the default when you're not in a new city. As I waited for her to return, I determined not to make this the default, but by the time she came out again I had gotten so nervous I couldn't say anything except "Ha."

"Hi," she said, unfazed.

She was all grace, continually saving me like this, and yet it also made me sense that the moral distance, the distance of civilised adult years, between us was widening all the time. It made me doubt my actions, the wisdom of what I was doing. Before I could answer, her phone rang. Out came the smashed watermelon. Rupert, I thought, pushing my tongue into the back of my top row of teeth.

But after the way she greeted the caller, it became clear that it was not Rupert. In fact, it became clear quite quickly that it was a call *about* Rupert. A call that began in great audible detail very abruptly, no doubt precipitated by a messaging exchange, which had presumably been going on in the bathroom while I was on the sidewalk, buffering, wondering if it was okay to follow people in real life. I dithered in a circle around a scaffold pole as I waited. When the conversation showed no signs of ending, I began to swing around the pole. With each swing towards where she stood, rooted to the spot, I could hear the words Mizuko was saying, and then, on the other side of the pole as I swung away from her, I could hear only the traffic on 113th Street.

"He sleeps much better with me. But I sleep so much worse because I'm so stressed that he's not getting enough sleep."

"Hey hey, he could have taken a teaching post at Saskatoon. He stayed here for me."

"Bad."

"Bad since he stopped drinking."

"I'm not *allowed* to be quiet, but he's *always* quiet."

"Here's the line—"

"Here's the line and if you cross it . . ."

I did a few more turns around the pole before sensing that this might possibly be very annoying. It was Mizuko's turn to be silent as she listened to the person on the other end. I knew this was the kind of call I should probably not be present for, but wasn't it also rude just to walk off and leave her without explaining or saying goodbye? I supposed I could retreat to the stoop of one of the buildings around the corner, but without my presence there as a reminder, the call might last even longer. But was it rude to make her sense my physical presence? What was the Japanese etiquette on this point? I wondered.

"The good times are really good."

"No, I can't take it."

"He always insists on coming, like he doesn't want me to be around anyone else, and then always bails."

"He was shaking at the table."

"Two days in a row he leaves in a bad mood, but I barely have any real friends left."

"Apart from you, yes."

"I gave the ticket away."

I realised that Mizuko was indirectly including me in this conversation, even though she wasn't explicitly describing my presence or mentioning me by name. It was a significant moment for me, being tacitly relayed as part of her call to a friend. I was now a real person with real effects on her life.

"Everything's about *him,* but he can't commit to anything. He can't even commit to a musical instrument. I can't take it."

I tried not to look like I was taking any of this in, which was impossible because it was so encouraging.

"Yeah, I think it's because of his family."

"They're British."

"Mm-hmm, really uptight."

"Yes, I think he even has a title. He's like son and heir."

I turned her words over in my mind as I pretended to play with my phone.

Sun and hair
Son and heir
Sun and air

"It's not always like this—he just blames everything on me. He blames all tension on me. It's so unfair, *so* unfair." It was the same *so*, I realised possessively, as *So yes*.

"It can't *all* be me. I'm so fed up of being blamed for everything, June, I can't take it anymore."

I made a mental note of June's name to search for later.

"I'm not always easy, but no one is. I don't want to break up with him, but he can't say all the problems are down to me and me just swallow it."

"I don't want to walk. A lot of the time I'm very happy."

It was June's turn to speak, but only briefly.

"He just walked off."

"I'd just love there to be a third person with us, because I feel like I'm going crazy."

An impatient silence while she waited for June to finish.

"You've been in lots of relationships—you know that's not true."

I began listening very intently now and not hiding it. What was it that June could know?

I had no idea where this conversation was leading me, but it seemed to be a secret tunnel straight into Mizuko's head.

"It's *not* cheating."

"She told me to *embrace* it."

"She told me I'm not mentally ill, it takes two."

"She would fucking tell me that because that's what therapists do."

"Exactly, it's immaterial."

"But he was having a panic attack—an anxiety attack. He

did it in Paris twice. One at the airport. I need to be better at dealing with it."

"He can blame the relationship all he wants, but he has his own issues."

She vacillated between defending herself and defending Rupert, which reminded me of my mother.

"He *is* working on them."

"Neuroptical therapy kind of working on them."

At least it sounded to me at the time, standing in the street with the noise of the wind and the cars and the passersby, that she said *neuroptical,* but when I tried to search for it after, the only likely-looking result was "NeurOptimal neuro feedback," described as "an amazing therapy with benefits for autistic-spectrum disorders, ADHD, Lyme disease, depression, anxiety, and eating disorders, to name just a few." It seemed to involve lying in a comfortable chair with sensors placed on your head and ears, listening to music while "neurofeedback" provided the central nervous system with moment-by-moment feedback on its current activity and then the brain used this information to improve itself.

"I just get fed up with its all being about him and his feelings."

"It's just the way he *says* things. If I mention meeting anyone that's *my* friend, he immediately tenses up and says, Well, I don't want any pressure this weekend."

"I suppose I feel like I owe him chances."

"Oh fuck, he's trying to get through now. Shall I answer?"

Mizuko looked down briefly at the object in her hand as it morphed from June to Rupert.

"Hi, baby, are you okay?"

"No, that deli place on Broadway."

"Are you all right, baby?"

"Speaking to June."

"I'm worried about you. I do feel like you're suffering from anxiety and I want to help you."

A long pause.

I decided to signal walking. I split my middle and index fingers into two legs and alternated them forward and back in the direction of the subway. Her eyes flashed and she held up her palm to convey a stop sign.

"It *can't* be all me—it's not humanly possible."

Or was it a goodbye/okay, you go sign?

"I understand, baby, but I feel like we need to be able to talk as adults and you shut me out."

"What am I doing that's so shit?"

"What do you want me to do?"

"You didn't say it like that, baby."

"Why can't you meet me halfway?"

I searched her face for a sense of whether this was a metaphorical meeting or whether, having spent an hour and a half hearing about genocide, waiting for her to pee, and then listening with saintly patience to her two consecutive phone calls for about fifteen minutes now, she was going to leave me here to meet him.

"It often feels like we're not even a couple."

"But you never reply to them. It's like I'm having a relationship with myself."

And once again I was content to let the conversation take its course.

"Couples *do* things for each other without it seeming like a chore. With Andy and Sophie, Andy . . ."

Rupert did not care what Andy and Sophie did, but I resolved to find them later too.

"You're the only one."

"You . . ."

Stop, I willed her. *S-T-O-P.*

A divine, unseen force heard my thoughts and translated them into sound, triggering a car alarm. Its piercing, insistent noise ended the call.

8

Sometime before we met, a friend at Columbia gave Mizuko a book that was always next to her bed. She liked to pick it up and read parts of it to me. It essentially said that my generation used the Internet too much. Hers was fine. It also pointed out that the carbon that fuels our electronic life is melting the icecaps. The melting ice is relieving gravitational pressure, and this, the book said, meant that the Japanese earthquake in 2011 was "no coincidence." There was a picture in it of a lonely Japanese house adrift in the Pacific, which Mizuko would shove at me occasionally as if I were personally responsible for the devastation.

When we met, we were both online constantly. In fact, I would say I was only online constantly because she was, and I was monitoring her usage. For her, the Internet was primarily a tool of self-promotion and reinforcement for her multiple selves while for me it became a tool designed for the sole purpose of observing her. It was the only way I could have been brave enough to approach her in real life, having dissected the pictorial equivalent of her DNA in advance.

I still have a Google map with pins in it that she made. She sent it to all newcomers or people visiting New York who asked her for recommendations, because she didn't have time to do a new list for everyone. Some of the pins have gone grey so you can't click on them anymore, but you can still read her sweetly enthusiastic, dairy-free annotations:

> *almond milk lattes are the best!*
> *best vegan ice cream ever!*
> *get the scallion pancake!*
> *compost and blueberry cookies!*

We once went to a place from the list together, and she ordered an "S&M" salad and a raw juice called "Spanking." I kept the receipt because it felt like something particularly significant was happening in the development of our friendship that she would make that selection. Other things I saved indiscriminately, simply because I was less clear what, if anything, they meant. Remnants of all the chunks of time and money we spent together, like receipts and ticket stubs, I kept as if I knew that one day I would have to account for what really happened.

Mizuko said that she and I were "born either side of a divide." I felt that she was trying to create one when she said things like this. And yet she didn't want to push me *too* far. She wanted to keep me, I think, on the other side of this invisible line, for me to watch her, which was good for her self-esteem after Rupert appeared to lose interest, or, I hoped, so she could watch me watching her. I was an object of curiosity. She used to ask me questions like "Do you really not remember *chain letters*? Did you even have those growing up? I guess you didn't grow up IRL," and I wouldn't even need to reply; she'd have made her mind up. She seemed obsessed with my *generation*. She had led a class about how my *generation* couldn't physically cope with books anymore; they had been rewired and could now learn only through "gamification." These little morons, she explained, had to be able to interact and adapt and insert themselves somehow into everything; otherwise it wasn't worth knowing. "I'm a Digital Immigrant," she said primly. "You're a Digital *Native.*" That name drove me nuts. Digital *Native? Not me,* I said. Only I didn't say it, I thought it and then nodded, because I would take any name she gave me and be anything she asked me to be, even though it pained me to be made into anything but her image. Apart from everything else that was wrong with it, back then I was, if anything, a digital *novice.* I had no idea.

Now I make sure everything I do is encrypted. I have tried to educate my mother too. She is always making up dumb security questions and passwords using maiden names or using public Wi-Fi in coffee shops or falling for phishing scams. I have told her she should think of encryption like a letter in a sealed, addressed envelope rather than a postcard. To imagine whenever she is using her web browser that she is walking down an ordinary street. She can be seen by anyone. Susy needs real-world metaphors like this to understand. I have taken more advanced measures to keep my private business private. The main thing I rely on is an operating system called Tails. It provides me with total security, anonymity, and amnesia.

At the time, despite Mizuko's insistence on this digital divide, I was sure her mind worked like mine. Her thoughts were nonlinear, more like a lattice, and this predisposed her to getting distracted. She would get lost in Wikipedia wormholes, so lost that she would sometimes have to disconnect the Wi-Fi or give her doorman her electronic devices. I said I wanted to help. After she was discharged from the hospital, I said that I saw my role as midwife to the birth of her still unfinished book, *Kegare,* helping out with memories she had lost over the summer, cleaning up, doing chores, playing house whilst she wrote the Great Japanese American Novel. Apparently that level of concern and care was in itself distracting.

"I know you—you're standing there looking for things you can move around," she said, sensing me behind her. "You're like a beaver."

It gave me the sensation of being loved that she knew me as well as this, and then it made me think of my home and my mother, whom I had not thought of in months.

I got so caught up with Mizuko, my beautiful, quantum self, that I neglected many of the reasons Silvia gave for why I should come to New York in the first place. Next to me are three frosted plastic crates that slot one on top of the other so they become a cabinet. The contents, mainly clippings and letters, belonged to Silvia. Under my desk is another plastic storage box, which has things in it that I collected myself from my time in New York. I have lived with this mini-museum for a long time, and I'm sure the right thing to do is to convert it into something else, something lighter. I want it to become so light it could float away. The heaviest thing is a copy of Henry James's *The Golden Bowl*. This belonged to Mizuko and was the one she used to write her thesis as an undergraduate at Yale. In her more fatalistic moods, Mizuko often said that novels were dead because we have the Internet everywhere we go now and we can find out anything we want to know straightaway, which tends to kill a plot. That was why she wrote just about real life. It feels true in some ways. In other ways, I reassured her, stories must be more like chess, a game of perfect information in which all the moves that can be made are right there in front of you, but the problem is knowing what your opponent knows and what she plans to do.

The Golden Bowl has her notes, which continue to make me happy and sad at the same time. Seeing her mind at work, knowing that she had thought of other things and been charmed by other subjects before me. The cover has a woman with a loose bun, a romantic but off-limits green dress, and elbow-length gloves. Beside her are three yellow books and a green hat, and she is sitting on a bench staring at the viewer with disdain. Between pages 60 and 61 there is still a scrap of lined A5 notepaper with square holes in the margin where it has been ripped out of a ring binder. On it is a list, broken down into four subdivisions: TO BUY, TO GET, TO DO, TO PAY. From looking at the back, where she has turned the page on its side and drawn a calendar which begins on Tuesday and runs until Sunday, I can tell that the list concerns her twenty-first birthday. On Wednesday there are three bullet points, spaced down the column according to the segment of the day. At the top it says "back to NY," in the middle it says "5:15 wax." At the bottom is a boy's name I don't recognise. The next day there is a name I do recognise, because I met its owner. She was a friend of Mizuko's from Yale. On Friday it says "4 p.m. nails" and, at the same level as the two names written in for the previous two evening slots, another boy's name I don't recognise but which is not the same as the first boy's name.

On Saturday there is a flurry of aphoristic activity at 1:30, 3:30, 5 p.m. (the mysterious initials MD), 6 p.m., and 7 p.m. At 9 p.m. are the names of two more men (not the same as either of the first two), who I assume must have been in charge of music at the birthday party from that point, since succeeding them at 10 p.m. are the names of two other men, one of whom I recognise—a DJ who was still friends with her by the time I knew her. I never met him, I just know his name from following her. On Sunday it says "Yale" at about the middle of the day. One thing from the list gets me every time. "TO BUY: camera film." *Every time.*

Mizuko was born in 1982, which means she turned twenty-one in 2003—when I was twelve—and that she used a real camera to take photos at her birthday party. I respected her; she was an authority figure, a guide . . . but sometimes I wondered if my young blood was the draw for her, and I would be relieved that whatever else might change, the years between us could not close.

Also to buy are tinfoil, matchboxes, labels, stickers, mini-sparklers, pink roses, Satellite Wafers, pens, and something shoes (a brand of shoe, I think), which is crossed out. On the TO DO division of the to-do list is an Emerson essay, which makes me reevaluate certain assumptions. When I knew her, it felt like she just knew everything and could quote everything, and not like she had ever had to absorb it by effort. I looked up Satellite Wafers because I didn't know what they were. Turns out they are the American name for Flying Saucers. Looking at her handwriting makes me feel like she is lightly touching me by mistake, on the arm or the back. Some of the notes in the margins of the book itself are in Japanese, and these make me jealous, like I am looking at her but not touching, or watching her touch someone else. I try to imagine her writing the list and the calendar on the paper, not yet even twenty-one, younger than me, with adolescent concerns, recently arrived from Japan, but it seems impossible that she could ever have been younger than me.

Before I met her, I saw pictures she had posted of the original printed photographs of her twenty-first birthday party, which she must have taken with the film on the TO BUY list. She looked exactly the same. Her hair was still long and dark and sat flatly either side of a central parting. Her eyebrows in the photographs are the only thing that make her seem younger. They have been overplucked and are not as long as her eyes are wide, but still, like everything else about her, they are perfectly symmetrical. In the photo she is pressing her finger just above her top lip towards a deep philtrum—a word that I felt came up too often in her stories—which I know that Rupert liked to put the tip of his finger into also. His academic ability to provide the correct words for things extended to body parts and their absences, such as the philtrum, and was held in high esteem by Mizuko. I told her that *philtrum,* unless spoken by a medical professional, was the kind of phony word that appears in ads using love stories to sell mobile phone plans. My then boyfriend had made one of those ads, which I showed her as proof.

When I try to remember how she looked without using pictures to aid me, I think of her outline first. Sometimes she wound her dark hair up into two plaited doughnuts on either side of her head. Whenever she worked on her novel, she would begin by sitting down but would soon be crouching on the seat of the chair. She said she preferred to crouch on things rather than to sit on them. Somehow it made her look even more beautiful, crouching, even smaller and more impossible as a creature. At other times she wore one bun, right on the top of her head. Always one bun in the bath. Her hair had blunt, thick ends as if it had recently been cut. I knew it had been, and I'd run my fingers over the picture taken in the hairdresser's many times.

From there, I move inward. I think of her beautiful clothes and jewellery. She had very simple gold jewellery, but it was unlike anything I ever found in shops. When I asked her about it she said it was *inherited,* as if it were a special type of milk or meat, and I felt annoyed that Susy had never given me any jewellery like that. She always wore a gold chain with rings on. When she was close by, it jangled like a cat coming towards you, so that when I hear a cat following me behind a hedge or down the street I still feel cold joy in my stomach. The ring on the chain with the most sentimental value to her was a wedding ring that had belonged to her grandmother.

For our first meeting, she wore a white blouse and black cu-
lottes, what some people call a skort, or her skirt was so short on
her thighs that I assumed it had shorts hidden underneath it, but
then, she was comfortable showing her body in a way I was not.
She would never pull her skirt down in a breeze, she would just
let it billow about her as if it didn't even register. She had short,
shapely legs. She was, that first day, wearing little white leather
clogs like hoofs that made her legs look more elegant because the
clogs were so ugly. She had a long, lightweight coat made out of
beige silk hanging on the back of her chair, and a black leather
bag swung to one side over the coat. I located her from behind.
The coat was rolled up at the sleeves. This accentuated her thin
wrists and long fingers when she put it back on. Under the table
she had slipped one foot out of her clog, and the other was half
in, half out, so I could see that she had crazy small feet in real
life. They didn't seem like the kind of feet that could support a
body. And I had never seen her walk. To date I had only known
her through her mainly static online presence, or videos in which
she captured one small movement, which was then repeated on
a loop. When she did walk, to the bathroom between the chairs
and the customers leaning back in them, oblivious to her ma-
noeuvres, the sight felt strangely moving and profound, like a
baby, or a veteran getting out of a wheelchair, or a deer in snow.
That is perhaps overdoing it. Maybe I didn't quite know that at
the time, but it was striking. If you have not seen a deer in snow,
I mean: moving with precision, but as if she might leap away in
a completely different direction at any moment.

The second story by her I read—also about origins—was
written just after her twenty-first birthday. This fell on the day a
space shuttle disintegrated during reentry over Texas and Loui-
siana, killing all the astronauts on board. She said the party had
been ruined but at least she had managed to make something

good out of it afterwards. A piece of insulation had broken off and hit the wing during the launch, so there was a hole. When the shuttle reentered the earth's atmosphere, it slowly broke apart. Notable places that had debris included a university and several casinos. Searchers also found "human body parts, including arms, feet, a torso, a skull, and a heart." Some worms living in Petri dishes enclosed in an aluminium canister "survived impact with the ground and were recovered weeks after." I verified this on Wikipedia. The worms were on the spacecraft for research into the effect of weightlessness on bodies. Apart from the worms, people also found data from a disk drive—results from an experiment on the properties of certain kinds of liquids. There is a special property in things like lava, ketchup, whipped cream, blood, paint, and nail polish. They flow in a certain way. In this story, first published in a Yale student magazine, Mizuko wrote about how on that birthday more than any other, because it was her twenty-first, she was expecting to hear from her father, and so she and her mother had a big row on the phone from Japan to America, and how then the space shuttle crashed and only some worms in a Petri dish survived. Mizuko told me about all this and then said we had to listen to Kate Bush, as if this were the obvious next step in female friendship.

It was especially unfortunate that the shuttle had disintegrated on her twenty-first birthday because the party had been space-themed. That is why she had the Flying Saucers/Satellite Wafers on the TO BUY section. My nearest newsagent in Wood Green does not sell Flying Saucers, but a kind of old-timey food shop has just opened on the high street that sells vintage sweets and I bought a little plastic bucket full of them. My current ritual is to open my mouth and place the pale pink disc lightly on my tongue. At first there is no taste, as if it is a communion wafer. Then, as it settles, I feel it start to stick. I leave it, not biting, waiting for the spit that gathers in my mouth to dissolve the rice paper. Everything is suddenly wet. It breaks apart and then there is the powder texture of the sherbet, the taste sweet at first but then sour. When I swallow I think of her smooth, easy handwriting and her Biro moving on the paper of the Henry James novel.

As in the book, Mizuko herself was given a golden bowl. But rather than being covered in gold to hide a crack, hers is an example of the Japanese art of fixing broken pottery by filling the cracks with gold. The bowl belonged to Mizuko's family. It had been an ordinary ceramic bowl in the family *butsudan*—the special miniature cupboard or portable shrine Japanese people have —for a long time, in one piece, but it broke during the earthquake that Mark disappeared just before, in, or after. Mizuko's grandmother had it repaired using the technique.

Mizuko explained it to me like this: "Instead of the breaking diminishing the bowl, its resilience made it even more valuable and filled it with new meaning. It became a living object when it broke."

I said that that was *beautiful,* and she said, *Of course.*

To sum up: my attachment to her was cultivated through her pictures and photographs and quotes and all the things she put online, not just because of what they were and how they related to me, but because of the attitude, the way of seeing the world they suggested. The way she saw and spoke about things was the exact way I wished I could see and speak about things. I began to try to look at plain, ordinary-seeming things the way I thought she might look at them and so try to remake them like she did. And yes, primarily it was the pictures of her that did it for me, but also the pictures of things. She transfigured ordinary pavement markings into arresting images, for example. She could do the same to slants of light, shadows on brick, foam, feet. I told her once, very earnestly, drunk, that I was a plain thing she managed to transfigure into something more interesting by looking at me. In that sense it can sometimes be good to be plain-looking, because it is a temptation to those who pride themselves on having a good eye.

That much I know to be true. I have yet to decide why she chose me. My plainness, my youth, and my interest in Japan all help to explain what first drew Mizuko to me and across the age gap, but she didn't say these things explicitly. The one thing she did say suggested it. I remember showing her this trick I learned about how to work out what your special purpose was in life —a kind of diagram.

"So this is the part where you write down what's special about you, in this intersection of the circles, there."

"About me?"

"Well, we've done yours, so what's special about me?"

"You?"

She thought for a long time and I started to feel uncomfortable. Finally she looked like an idea had come to her. "You have the zeitgeist."

That is still all I have written down, just "the zeitgeist."

I remember when she finally also noted that I dressed like a figure in a Dutch painting, too late to add to the diagram, which she had not noticed when she was introduced to me.

All Mizuko's outfits were puritanical. Monochromatic. This was why I dressed like a figure in a Dutch painting, that first day and every day after, because I studied her pictures (some of which were of the paintings themselves) and their captions: *This is everything*.

I've pretty much given up trying to pin down what she saw in me, and instead I've tried to come up with an answer for what happened to me as a result of her minor interest. Even before she knew I existed, I saw myself in her, and whenever I did anything, I was watching her in my rearview mirror. I was like a rubbernecker who causes another crash by mistake. Things often happen that way, crashing into something when you have your eye on something else. Kathleen Drew, the scientist researching seaweed whose work unintentionally saved the starving population of Japan. The idea of an invisible something permeating space, interacting with particles to provide their mass, was first deemed "of no obvious relevance to physics." This irrelevance, of course, was later discovered as the Higgs field. You don't always know what it is that you've found.

It was like I'd aborted one search and started a new quest but the World Wide Web had not forgotten the first. Some sinister controller behind it all still remembered I was in the market for a father figure. Finding the Internet incomprehensible, suspecting it to be by nature immoral, my host provided me with alternative research tools. On my third day, Silvia, who had still not felt the inclination or the necessity to probe me much beyond greetings and goodnights, told me to go into the bedroom full of boxes and locate the three crates that are now under my feet. They then contained Mark's things, mainly childhood remainders and funny school memorabilia, and items from Silvia's own life in scrapbooks and folded letters. Books, including *Quantum Field Theory, Special Relativity, Perfect Symmetry, The Primeval Universe, The Popper-Carnap Controversy*. She said I could look through these if I wanted, and I supposed it was her way of breaking the ice—letting me know things, as promised, without saying them herself. But it was noticeable how much ice there was to break, and how much less close to her I felt now that I was actually there.

As I began to sift through them, I was not prepared for how

excruciatingly personal a lot of it was. I wondered if Silvia had intended this or hadn't looked through them herself recently. I was trying to work out why she wanted me to have them, especially when at least half of their contents turned out to be unrelated to Mark. I wondered whether it wasn't a test, like refusing the last thing in the dish when your host offers it to you.

I could hear wheezing in the next room as she did the exercises demanded of her by her physical therapist, whom until recently she had approved of but who had that day scandalised her by confessing to having met her husband online. She was on to number six, the buttock squeeze—saying "tight, tighter, tightest," lifting her tailbone slightly off the sofa, holding, relaxing, repeating.

What I did read then, mainly the angry exchanges (faxed) between Silvia and Susy, and even ones in which Silvia had implored her to let me visit, did not make me feel any closer to Silvia, nor to Susy or Mark. The intimacy and admissions the crates contained, raw and unvarnished, faintly repulsed me. I shut the lid on them as if they were embarrassing odours or bodily secretions.

Most of the time Silvia and I kept to our separate spaces. There were days in which all she could do was sleep sitting up or lie awake horizontal. She hadn't slept in her own bed since Rex died. Sleeping on the sofa in the den had started when he was very sick and nurses had moved into the apartment. To move back again would mean that a new normal had been accepted. Sometimes she would come into one room from another and sense something, or its displacement. A life stirring somewhere. And then she would realise it was me and she would look down and ask why I was inside wilting on such a nice day. So there was no explicit bonding. Certainly not the kind you might be expecting if you like films like *The Parent Trap* as much as Mizuko and I did. We watched it together once, and I dared to say that we were like two little Lindsay Lohans in the isolation cabin, to which she made a kind of grunt.

When Silvia did speak, her voice would often dry out mid-sentence, and at these moments I would seize the opportunity to suggest turning the heating down. She would always refuse. She was very thin and very still, so she was always cold. Because of the cancer in her throat, Silvia claimed she found not just speaking but eating and drinking (nonalcoholic beverages) very difficult, so there was no structure of mealtimes or getting to know one another that way. The first portion of my trip was therefore largely mute. Nil by mouth. And it followed me, the muteness, whether I was in or out of her building. Nor did I eat much of anything. Inside, I never felt hungry. The central heating, despite the rising temperatures outside, was always up to maximum, and so the air moved in shimmering waves. My stomach shrank. The heat dried up your words even if you didn't have cancer in your throat. But in the silence an unspoken understanding was growing between us. Although we weren't related by blood, I think we could relate to each other as solitary beings.

I was still expecting Silvia to talk to me directly about Mark at some point, but it seemed she felt either that she had said everything she needed to in her letters or she couldn't do it in person. It was so different from life with Susy that at first I couldn't understand it. How could someone be sad, deeply, permanently sad, as she had attested in her letters, and not need, as Susy evidently did, to draw everyone else into her misery?

"Do you not miss him?" I asked finally, broaching the subject a few days after she had given me the crates.

"Rex?"

"Mark."

"Of course."

"So then . . ."

"You just start to accept that you can't do anything to change the facts. You can't control what happens to you in life, so you learn to let go."

The facts, according to Silvia, were that Susy had pinned Mark down when he hadn't wanted to be pinned. I noticed she would deflect any conversation about Mark to talking about Susy.

"She made him retreat as far from any emotional warmth as possible—deep into equations and the desert—and when that got pulled out from under him, he had nowhere left to go."

"So you think he killed himself?"

"Yes." She blinked. "I know he did. I knew my son, and he was so different that last time I saw him, before you all left. He looked like he'd just completely checked out already. After he disappeared, when no body was found, my friends tried to persuade me to get therapy. I went once and the therapist told me I didn't need to come back as there was nothing wrong with me —it's everyone else that's the problem."

"A therapist said that?"

"In so many words, yes."

He had loved me, Silvia said, but in an abstract, detached kind of way. As a little goofball that belonged to someone else. He would have made a good uncle.

"Susy had this whole different idea of who he was," she said, rousing herself and pointing a finger at me. I felt the anger in her voice. "She thought he could handle the blood and guts, the innards of life, but he wasn't *ever* that kind of boy." She gasped as if in physical pain. "He even found it difficult to say he loved me when he was little. It made him kind of freeze up when we said goodnight, so we just used a special hand squeeze instead. He was very good at empathising with people at a distance. If he saw a homeless person or there was a sad story in a movie he'd cry, he'd be more upset than perhaps was normal, but Susy made it her mission to get emotion out of him at close range and he just turned to stone."

I considered this. A perverse part of me found myself wanting to defend Susy. I tried to imagine her, fresh off the boat, arriving at Columbia. Finding someone who made her feel like she had a place in this strange new world. It was easier to feel pity for her from far away. Now that Silvia had given me the crates, I guessed I was free to draw my own conclusions, and that was the main difference between the two women.

Following that awkward and unusual conversation, Silvia suggested I go up to look at the Columbia campus. It was the day before Memorial Day; she explained that everyone in the city would therefore be wearing white. She suggested that I wear white too, but I said I didn't really have anything but a white T-shirt and she said that was no good. She offered to lend me a white linen suit she had in her closet with a pair of white leather brogues. I was too polite to refuse, since she seemed unusually animated by the idea of dressing me up, and I was fascinated by her closet, full of smart city clothes I could not imagine her wearing when I looked at her pink pyjamas.

The minute I got outside, it occurred to me that it was possible Silvia had not been outside on Memorial Day for a very long time. No one else seemed to be wearing white, except very occasionally a troupe of handsome sailors. I walked the whole way there, a relic in white linen and shoulder pads, the white shoes (a size too small) cutting painfully into my heels. First across the park and then up further until every other car had a fish bumper sticker and every other shop front was Redeem and More Church of God or the Church of God in Christ, Inc.

I felt the stares and became grudgingly angry at Silvia for put-

ting me through this well-meant torture. The discomfort reverberated in my belly. I had mainly been subsisting on iced coffee
and green juice, consumed in transit. I'd lost weight, which I'd
noticed only because my clothes were looser, and I'd begun to
think I could live on air. I found that it helped with my walking
meditations in order to achieve my trancelike state. On the way
up to Columbia I spotted a place called Miss Mamie's Spoon-
bread Too. This promised "down-home Southern dishes and
sides served up in a country-style kitchen with a red checkered
floor." I thought it would also make a good tile for my Instagram.

At my table, I began writing in my journal.

> *Saw the outside of Natural History Museum. Tired so went*
> *to sit on a bench. Sat next to two cool Asian kids who*
> *were squeezed together at the end of one. A wide stone*
> *bench. They were both looking down at their devices. The*
> *bench was set down beneath an engraved slab which read*
> *NATURALIST. I looked at the other benches—different*
> *professions were inscribed above them.*

As I wrote I was unsure why this memory, alongside equally
dull observations about light quality, was taking precedence over
any ruminations about weightier matters. So far I had not written anything in my journal about anything that I imagined Silvia
would deem useful. I wondered if in choosing the bench I had
had a subconscious motive. Was this to be my profession? A nat-
uralist.

I carried on up toward Columbia. The sidewalk was smooth
and wide, the buildings punctuated with unbroken views through
to the river. I watched a suited man holding a shiny gift bag stride
ahead while a small woman in a pink kimono, white socks, and
wooden clogs moved carefully and slowly behind him. I felt my-

self resisting Silvia's suggestion of going all the way up to the Columbia campus. I hovered, feeling that not to go would disappoint her and appear somehow ungrateful and unorthodox, while sensing that to go would put me in a bad mood or in some way compromise the persona I was beginning to fashion. The longer I hesitated, the more anxious and conflicted I felt. Going seemed like the right thing to do—like eating vegetables, or getting sleep—and I usually felt better obeying instructions than not. It is probably more like the storyline you were expecting. Don't all adopted kids, or abandoned kids, neglected or dislocated kids, feel a certain way? I had thought I would feel excited by it, or compelled simply because I knew Susy would have tried to stop me. And it seemed that Silvia expected me to want it, and so I wanted to want it to please her, but now that I was here, I found that I didn't. I wanted to forget it all. For the first time in my life, I felt like I could.

Half an hour or so went by, cars passing on either side of me as I sat on a bench in the middle of the two lanes, from which vantage point I studied the furry green exterior of a Barnard building. It was overwhelmed by an ivy brighter and greener than any I'd ever seen. There was no brick, or stone, or whatever the material was, visible. The façade was wholly organic, with only hints of the architecture underneath, and recesses that marked windows. It was thrilling in contrast to the surrounding metal, stone, and glass, but the longer I looked, the more it began to take on a dystopian air, like a scene from a lost city. This, I supposed, was what it might look like were academia abandoned as the SCC had been. Was this what the city would look like when knowledge was no longer enough? When the desire to turn inward, surrendering entirely to one's own private world of nonresistance, overwhelmed, like creeping ivy, our desire to know worlds beyond it?

The building's aspect became so profoundly depressing that I felt desperate to leave but suddenly unable to do so. My limbs became lead. I wanted to weep for future generations. I blamed myself. *This is the reason you must respect your elders*—I sensed that the strange, disembodied controller had come back, the disapproving drone operator or whoever it was, pulling me upright. *Not so fast!* it said. *It would be wrong, in fact it would be rude, not to preserve something of the past.* I felt a prod, though no one was behind me. *Go up there!* The voice had a Dickensian, moralising quality. It was certainly conservative. *It's your duty to the ancestors. Doesn't matter whether they're directly yours or not. It's the principle of the thing. You can't just stop halfway. You're supposed to be following in their footsteps.* I stumbled to my feet as if the bench had tipped me forwards.

In my mind, this quest, resistant as I now felt towards it, was steeped in the self-help language that was all over Instagram, which chronicled so many million journeys of self-discovery. I don't know what those people felt they didn't know about themselves, but I think it's fair to say I had some legitimate concerns. Have you ever truly, keenly felt like you don't know who you are? Do you ever do something and think, Who is at the controls? Like some mad pilot has locked you out of the cockpit? I definitely do. I feel a kind of vertigo that makes me shake afterwards. I guess we all feel it when making a difficult-seeming choice, and sometimes you seriously don't know what you want because you don't know who you're supposed to be, or who you want to be. Physics, my first and second families, my philosophy degree, had all failed to help me answer that question. The former has led me to wonder whether I am one of an infinite number of Alices in multiple universes. A quantum fuck-up, which is someone who fucks up in every one of those universes but in different ways. My first family took no care at my making, and my second family got me, essentially by mistake, out of a million possible babies going spare. It was Silvia's offer to come to New York, an offer which had a simple yes/no answer, that finally pulled me out of that. I could make the choice because I knew I wanted to be the type of person who said yes. When I did, it was as if all the lethargy, all the time spent motionless in my bedroom, had been to allow for the winding of something tighter and tighter, so that now I had to get physically as far away from Susy as possible or implode.

As I moved through the part familiar, part unfamiliar topography of Columbia, I tried to imagine being Susy, looking out for Mark always. Stalking him, essentially. I imagined I was stalking the ghost of her stalking the ghost of him. There was potentially something comforting about this, to see a pattern emerging. I tried to enter the building Susy had often mentioned as being where Mark had spent most of his time working, but having located it with the Columbia map, I came up against twin revolving doors, which both had signs that read, PLEASE USE OTHER DOOR.

Walking around the campus did not have the emotional intensity I had once hoped for, now feared. I guessed there had been a lot of modernisation. It savoured less of sixties activism than I had imagined it would based on Silvia's accounts. I did see that the sign on a bathroom in one of the campus buildings had been changed from WOMEN'S ROOM to WOMEN'S WOOMB. Other than that, little political ferment was obvious. The one place that did give me the feeling—similar to the moments in Tokyo when I had been sure a memory was coming back—was Sakura Park. This is the small park right by where I had lived, beside the school of music on Claremont Avenue. It was green and canopied with linden trees. Somehow it was quiet and I stopped hearing the big red New York Sightseeing buses rumble past. When I lay in the grass by the pagoda, I had a fleeting recollection of being tiny. Of looking at blades of grass as objects of fascination, broad as my fingernails. The swings too did something. Their chains tinkled, and that sound did something too, it was hard to say what. Whether it was memory or clairvoyance. As I walked around, I noticed more things which struck the same chord. A tōrō, a heavy stone lantern, at the northern end of the park. This had been installed when New York became Tokyo's sister city. I feel sure now that it was a kind of second sight, but I did also know such details from Silvia's letters. Parts of which I could recall word for word, having read them so many times before my arrival.

> The bronze statue of General Butterfield, in the southeast
> corner of the park, became my son's mute sympathizer.
> The general's likeness was cast by the sculptor better
> known for his presidents on Mount Rushmore, who'd
> had a studio at Saint John the Divine. In life, Butterfield
> (an avid composer of bleak bugle calls) had been beset by
> an English wife of his own, who, much like your mother,
> I'm afraid, continued to dictate his whereabouts even in
> death. The general's wife directed the executors of her
> will to erect an enormous statue of her husband, stipulat-
> ing where and in exactly what pose. In accordance, the
> sculptor depicted the general at a heroic size, in full dress
> uniform, head held high, arms folded in defiance, and
> on a rock intended to simulate the faraway terrain of his
> proudest achievements.

Much of this is borne out, almost word for word, by the signs in Sakura Park. Every time Silvia was proved correct this way, I felt stronger, surer of myself. By six, gold light began radiating from the West Side, and I found myself drawn towards the river. More from Silvia's letters came to life as I stood there.

You had just started speaking, but he seemed to have forgotten how. Whole days went by without his saying a single word. When he did communicate, your mother said he gave "only the merest of hints" that he was suicidal, a distortion I never forgave her for. She wanted me to think everything was fine. She always thought she could manage people, as if we were all little children like you. I later found out from him that he had spent most of his new-found unemployment, if not on the couch, then staring at the Hudson. A few people drown in the waters around New York City each year. The Hudson moves swiftly, pushing bodies out to sea. The water can travel at the speed of four knots, and it is the same for the East River, which races on the other side. He would walk the approach of London plane trees to and from Grant's Tomb, sometimes with you tottering at his side, and then back toward the apartment you were staying in via Sakura Park.

I stood looking down at the Hudson for a long time, until the empty feeling, the dizzy feeling behind my eyes, reverberated so much that I shook. I thought it might be best to try and eat. All I'd ordered in Miss Mamie's was iced coffee. I wandered back towards the university, through the emptying main thoroughfare, into a deli which had a bad smell. Walked out again and headed across the street to a sandwich store, Subs Conscious. But the sight of all the spills and flaps of meat, gelatinous, oozing sauces, made me sick. I looked for something plain, like a yoghurt, but could only find yellow, crayon-smelling pots called banana pudding.

In person, New York was not exactly like I'd hoped. The initiation seemed indefinite. I was Zeno. I was walking and walking, I couldn't stop, but I never got there; if anything, I felt further away.

Apart from walking, the other compulsion of the two I had developed since arriving was the posting of pictures. At first this helped to counter the strange sensation that in pressing ahead, I was in fact being pushed back. What I haven't properly conveyed is that it wasn't actually a *social* activity at this point, as I had no friends, and second, it wasn't even instant, as I couldn't actually post pictures unless I was somewhere with a Wi-Fi connection, because I was trying to avoid expensive roaming charges. This meant that I couldn't get online for large portions of the day, which helped fuel the other addiction—the trancelike walking —and that when I arrived at somewhere, rarely by design, I saw only what was immediately apparent, not what Wikipedia said about it. The observations I wrote down in the journal I kept are therefore often grand and also naive, as if I am the first to discover something, or totally missing the point of it.

As I didn't have any followers at this point, taking pictures was really only for my benefit. But I noticed that there was a difference between just taking them and posting them so that they were public. The first made me feel okay. The second made me feel good. Like bursting a bubble in bubble wrap, or plucking a hair from the root, but after a while, when more random fitness gurus and a few strange men with pictures of their cars and weird personal mottos started following me, I felt like I had joined up with something bigger than myself. I sensed that whatever I was doing was in some way happening on a grander scale.

I still didn't really know what it was, though, that I was doing. I guess I was following instructions — *come and sniff the air.* Well, I was sniffing. I was scratching and sniffing. Occasionally Silvia had enquired after the state of my career aspirations. She seemed to think I would make a good journalist. Maybe it was the way I looked like a kind of Wall Street Grace Jones in the white linen suit. I must have reminded her of her heyday. Silvia had once been a journalist.

She'd suggested it first that morning: "Why don't you just be a journalist?" I found myself having to explain that it was trickier now to just *be* anything, except an entrepreneur, and particularly with newspapers and periodicals like the kind she'd worked on, which had a kind of moribund vibe, and the people who had made it had only the very tip of the sinking ship and weren't keen to share it.

"Did you see *Titanic*?" I'd asked.

"Yes. But in my day —"

"Well, now it's like the bit at the end."

"So what do you *like* doing?" she had said, with a hint of exasperation. "Isn't there anything you've seen in the city that caught your attention?"

I hesitated. "So far?"

She nodded.

"Walking," I said helplessly. "And taking pictures."

She shifted more upright on the sofa. "Really? I didn't know you'd brought a camera with you."

"Oh, I haven't."

"So then how —"

"On my phone. That's how everyone takes pictures now, I guess."

Silvia looked revolted, and I felt worse than I had done at the start of the conversation.

But it was true. I did enjoy taking pictures, even if the medium constituted a small betrayal. I wasn't sure it was the same level of joy that qualified pursuing it professionally, so that a name like *photographer* could be mine, but it made me feel like I was participating in the city. Each picture implied a kind of fantasy life beyond it, like a window, and every time I posted one, I felt that it added a new room around the window and each room housed another self. It made the whole city more manageable, was a way to take apart the pieces of the machine.

I tried to explain this to Silvia.

"So it's like a scrapbook," she said finally.

"No," I replied, faltering. I wasn't sure why it wasn't.

"What's different?"

"The grid format of the app means you play with juxtapositions."

"So?"

"Um. It's public, I guess. And if you put one of these—" I pushed my device towards her and she jerked backwards.

"Number sign," she said warily. "Yes, I know what that is."

"Hashtag," I corrected, detecting impatience, even arrogance in my tone.

"Well, what happens if you use that?"

"Then it links you up with all these other people who have used it for something they've posted, and people can look through—they're called threads."

"What people, strangers?"

"Yes, I guess."

After this conversation, which had a distancing effect, I stopped talking to Silvia about that part of my trip too. Talking about it with her made me feel like a stranger in her eyes. The way she had cut it down to size had also made it feel less like I was part of something bigger, more like I was spreading out my experiences too thin, so that nothing would grow out of them. It didn't feel like an initiation quite so much anymore; it was more juvenile than that. I knew Silvia was disappointed in my new pastime. And this meant that when I got back from Columbia, her white linen suit all creased and damp with sweat, I avoided walking past the chink of light coming from the door into her den. I didn't want to tell her about my day, because I felt guilty that instead of going up there and writing relevant observations in my journal—which is what she had recommended I do, as a *journalist* might—I had gone round taking pictures and putting them all up online. Given that it was a pilgrimage she said she found too hard to make, I knew it would upset her to know this.

I had come back tired, and feeling on the whole less heady from my return walk than usual. I'd finally discovered that though walking alone in New York can be healthy and encourage mindfulness, it can also make you feel like shit. Halfway there, halfway there again, destined never to make it. Though it seems like everything is in motion and you are changing and growing as a person with every step, your belief in yourself and your progress all at once turns out to be mistaken. An illusion, like legs that have spent too long at sea. You laugh at yourself like you laugh at someone alone in a gym at night, pounding at a treadmill. The kind of laugh that echoes and makes you feel empty. I'd finally let myself notice the rats scurrying in and out of garbage, the cockroaches crawling amongst the rotting fruit, the overripe smell outside the 7-Elevens, and the currents of warm urine from mystery recesses that seemed to follow me wherever I went. It was the first time that random strangers calling after me on the street upset me, an irony I am now aware of, given my willingness to interact with strangers online. But it's exactly this kind of interaction that makes a stranger acknowledging you on a public street seem like an impertinence, possibly a sign of psychosis. The city is tricky. The highs are so much higher, but in the lows you drop straight down again to bedrock. It helps that streets are snapped to a grid. There are also psychic boutiques and sidewalk prophets, but until you contrive your own love story set in that city, even one as warped as mine, you remain outside it, looking for signals in the white smoke that rises from under, in the sudden hot laundry smells and the LED typos of street vendors — *donut* easily becomes *dount,* ominously like *don't,* to my mind. There was a DOUNT sign on Second Avenue which more than once redirected my superstitious footsteps.

Back in my bedroom, I saw that Silvia had left a Post-it on my pillow in her shaky red pen:

Nat coming tomorrow, 11 a.m. Red alert.

I went to bed in all my clothes, wanting to be ready for whatever was coming.

9

After such an extended period of silence between Silvia and me, Nat's arrival the next morning was a shock. I opened the door and she practically fell on me. She was tall and muscular and wore ruby-red lipstick.

"*Hap-pee Memorial Day!*" she bellowed.

I hadn't known if it was appropriate to wish someone a happy Memorial Day.

"Hello, hello, hello!" she continued, stepping around me into the hall. "How are we, how are we *all*? You must be Alice. I never forget names."

This turned out to be a kind of threat.

"I remember you when you were tiny and now you're e-normous."

She was carrying a box. "Pastries," she said emphatically, shoving them at me, and then, baby-voiced, "Do you want to put them nicely on a plate?"

I nodded as if I couldn't wait.

"Where is Her Majesty?"

I indicated the den. My voice had dried up from lack of use.

"Don't get up, Silvia. Coming to *you,* sweetie!" She swung the door open violently. "Good Lord, it's hot in here, Silvie. Hi, hi, no need to get up."

Silvia hadn't gotten up but was smiling at Nat from a supine position on the couch. She was holding a magnifying glass she used to read the small print of her financial portfolio. They blew kisses at each other across the coffee table that Silvia kept books and papers on. Silvia looked even smaller and frailer now Nat was here.

"I won't stay too long," Nat continued. "I'm going across to Roosevelt Island to meet Ingrid and see her new project at two."

I looked at Silvia and felt newly protective of her. Two was a long way away, and I imagined she would not be able to talk for that long.

"How are you, sweetie? I feel like I haven't seen you for ages. Not since this one arrived."

Nat waved away my offer of the sofa adjacent to Silvia's. "I do yoga, so I prefer the floor," she said, squatting gingerly and then losing control. There was a loud crunch as she sat on her glasses. She retrieved them from the pocket of her flat, square rear and inspected the damage. "Well, these are *fuck,*" she declared, leaving the obscenity dangling uncertainly.

I went to fetch two vodkas and arrange the pastries on a plate. When I came back, Nat was looking for something on her device to read to Silvia.

"Here it is!" she crowed. "'Greeting I am Mrs. Olive Jana Lofer the daughter to the cancer woman copyright sign.' 'The cancer woman' is copyrighted," Nat explained, looking over the top of her cracked glasses, held to her face. She read in a stilted voice, uncertain how to punctuate the text. "'My precious mom may her soul rest in perfect peace contacted you some time ago in respect to the funds transfer of her late husband Lofer Jana, to help take care of me Olive Jana Lofer, before my mother passed away, she issued a cashier check to you for your help initially although you—'"

"Spam," I said, hearing my voice burbling up from some deep reserve and rising to meet the volume of Nat's. I felt instantly self-conscious.

"That's what my daughter told me too," Nat said. "She asks for a thousand dollars, which I was just about to send before Ingrid stopped me. I was just reading it to your grandmother. Silvia's godmother to my daughter, you know."

"Email is the scourge of our age," said Silvia. "Email and cancer."

"Agreed. I filled out a questionnaire for something yesterday and I had the great pleasure of being asked if I had any of the following—Facebook, Skype, thingummy, and the rest—and I ticked the box marked 'none of the above.' How d'you like *that*? I thought."

Nat stretched out where she was on the floor. She seemed much younger than Silvia, who was eighty-one. I later learnt she was only sixty-four. I guess age gaps between friends when you're that old are less noticeable, or you have less choice in the matter.

I cleared some space on the coffee table for the pastries.

"I know you won't have any, sweetie," Nat said to Silvia. And then, to me, "She doesn't eat, you know."

I grimaced, annoyed that Nat would assume I didn't know something so basic about Silvia, after two years' correspondence and so long living under her roof.

"But I thought you might." Then, to Silvia, "She's such an enormous thing now!" indicating me. "Hello, Lurch!"

I must have looked dense.

"He's the butler from *The Addams Family*," Silvia croaked.

Nat turned back to the pastries. "They're pretty, aren't they? I get them from a little French place by me, luh pan koh-ti-dyan," she pronounced.

Silvia and I dutifully agreed.

"But the trouble with buying pastries," Nat said with a sigh, "is that then you have to eat them. It's the same with honey. I always buy it but forget to eat it. Here," she said to me, thrusting one, "you have that one. I hate raisins, I always say it's like eating blisters."

I took the pain aux raisin from her even though I also hate raisins. "How do you two know each other?" I asked between mouthfuls.

"I was Silvia's assistant at *MEA*," Nat said with pride. "Has she told you much about me already? We had the best time."

When I heard the two of them pronouncing the journal's title, I thought it was a magazine title in a foreign language that meant something like *she, me,* or *mine.* As a result, I assumed *MEA* was a kind of naff women's magazine full of arcane advice and advertorials for control pants. I didn't realise it was an acronym, or that it had been a very well-respected, though short-lived, contribution to literary criticism, championing feminist critics in particular. But I had by this point discovered how to access the Wi-Fi in the apartment by rooting around in Rex's bedroom, now the study. The password was Silvia's name. Something about that made me want to cry, even though I had never met the man. What does it say about me that I find that romantic? Knowing the password had become key to occasionally impressing Silvia, who did not fully grasp the ease with which any and every piece of obscure information could be instantly retrieved online. I had got her to think I was much smarter than I was by retreating to my magic thinking room whenever she wondered out loud about crossword clues or what films a certain actor had been in and then returning with a flourish, astonishing her with the full list from IMDb.

When there was an opportunity, I went into Rex's study to enter the search terms "MEA," "Silvia Weiss," "Nat Rooiakker." The Wikipedia page told me that the final issue had been printed in November 1968. It also explained the acronym. It was a French phrase meaning, in its literal sense, "placed into an abyss." Mizuko did her own version of this on her Instagram, taking a picture of herself and then another picture of herself holding the picture of herself, and again and again as the picture got smaller and smaller. She'd had a lecture at Columbia on the subject, which inspired her. When it occurs within a text, it gets to the point where everything becomes unstable, a loop that takes you back to where you started.

As I came back in, Nat was sitting upright on the floor, balancing a book on her head to improve her posture. All the pastries were gone.

"We travelled to Paris together without our husbands. We were very naughty—we booked a single room and that was that," Nat said, bringing me up to speed.

"Do you remember that boy?" Silvia asked.

"Did you keep in touch?"

"No, he just gave me the book."

"What was his name?"

I watched silently as the two of them rolled their eyes back into their heads like prophets, trying to remember. Nat, I noticed then, had white eyelashes over one eye, which explained the uneasy feeling I had had so far that she had not really blinked since arriving.

"Don't remember his name," Silvia said at last, defeated.

"Who's this?" I asked.

"A boy who fell in love with your grandmother even though she was married."

"He was *French*," Silvia said, as if this explained everything. "Obviously he thought I was a stupid American girl. He gave me a book called *The Intelligent Woman's Guide to Socialism, Capitalism, Sovietism and Fascism*—Bernard Shaw—probably one of the few he had in English. He thought I should be educated."

"He was no doubt right," Nat said.

"Where's it gone? I wonder. Have a look on the shelves, Alice."

Silvia had said more in the last ten minutes than she had since I had arrived. I stood up, the back of my neck prickling with something like jealousy, and began to systematically scan the floor-to-ceiling shelves around the den, which were heaving with books. I listened to the conversation continuing without me, which became increasingly politically incorrect, so that at last, out of embarrassment more than anything else, I felt I had to intervene.

"I can't see it," I said loudly. "I'll look in Rex's study."

Silvia shook her head and tapped her glass. "Don't bother. We've moved on."

I went to refresh their drinks and left the door open because I was holding the glasses. I wasn't supposed to do this because Silvia liked to keep the room hot, but it meant I could still make out their voices in the kitchen.

". . . two CT scans and a brain MRI. I can't pick up stuff with my hands much. Nothing anybody can do about it. I put away my typewriter the other day as my fingers are useless."

"If you've given up the typewriter, you really must be giving up," I heard Nat say.

"Well, you know what I say. Where there's a will, someone's died."

I heard Nat's booming laugh and felt angry.

"I fully intended to leave the house on time this morning," she was saying as I returned with more drinks on a silver tray, "but I ended up doing some research and getting more stuff down from the cupboards in the kids' old rooms. Whenever Ingrid comes round she gives me a hard time about my little project, says it looks like someone broke in."

Nat was addicted to those TV shows where celebrities find out "who they really are" by tracing their family tree. She was currently watching one—a PBS show called *Finding Your Roots*—which boasted Carole King, her favourite singer, as a participant. Later that afternoon, helping Nat with this project, I set up an account for her on an ancestry website where you could create your own tree, which then tied in to other people's trees. You paid money and that got you "coins" that work only on the website, and I could see how you could get addicted to scrolling down, down, down, falling deeper and deeper until you couldn't climb out.

I'm sure it is even more addictive if it is your own family. If the names mean something to you. And I'm sure Nat thought, when she asked for my help, that she was doing me a favour, keeping me busy, but Silvia felt it was a bizarre thing to ask an adopted kid to do. I never liked people to see that I had taken offence. That, incidentally, is why Mizuko first started calling me Rabbit. It is not on account of either a leporine appearance or something euphemistic, or even, actually, on account of my last name. It was to do with the glazed look that always comes over me when faced with somebody who has offended or hurt me and yet whose approval I want. The timidity with which I accepted each and every one of Mizuko's mood swings, or when I sensed the approach of conflict with Susy, the arguments I tried to defuse just by nodding and staring blandly, inoffensively, into her face, the twitch of my nose and mouth that suggested to Mizuko I might cry: Mizuko later told me this was how she decided on the name.

"And you, Alice," Nat said, turning to me as I handed her a heavy-bottomed glass, "what are you going to do with yourself now you're here? How *old* are you, for a start?"

"Twenty-three. I just turned twenty-three in January."

"Well, it's the end of May now, so you mean you're nearly twenty-three and a half."

"I guess."

"And when did you graduate?"

"June."

"You mean last June, as opposed to next month?"

"Yup." I recalled Silvia's note. *Red alert*. She was a bloodhound.

"Well, maybe you'd like to help me this afternoon. First, I'd like you to set up an account for me on this." She passed me an ad she had ripped out from a magazine which had the details of the genealogy website. "I really want to get some more Dutch ancestors. I want to prove the Rooiakkers go back to the first Dutch settlers. Silvia tells me you did history, so—"

"Philosophy."

"Oh, okay, well, same sort of thing—you'll still be better at this site than me, I'm sure. My kids refuse to help me. The second thing is maybe you'd like to come with me, once you've set me up a thing, to Roosevelt Island, given that it's right there. I checked with my daughter, she says you're more than welcome. I told her you're at a loose end."

I turned the words *loose end* over in my mind, cringing. I couldn't think of a reply except *No*, so I said, "Sure."

Silvia said it was shameful that all the residents of the hospital had to leave in order to make way for what they (Nat's daughter, her goddaughter) were doing. Roosevelt Island still had hospitals then—Bird S. Coler to the north, Goldwater Memorial to the south—but these were already emptied out and about to be torn down. Silvia said she sometimes looked at them through the binoculars, the patients sitting in their wheelchairs or on the benches, staring back at Manhattan.

"Wasn't it supposed to be a kind of utopia?" she'd asked Nat. "I remember they were going to have buses that ran on batteries, pneumatic garbage disposal, and stuff like that."

"That was in the sixties, though," Nat replied. "Everything was going to be a utopia. Ingrid says it's going to be an *incubator* now."

Silvia blinked and looked at me. I looked blank.

"It's where they hatch things," Nat said.

"What things?"

"Businessmen. Anyway, that's not the point, the point is"— Nat gestured towards me and looked flustered, as if she were trying to pick tactful words—"that she should be meeting *people* in New York."

"But I told her that would happen if she just walks around the city," Silvia protested.

"Then she's not walking into the right places," Nat said, narrowing her eyes. "I'm going to set you up with some *young* people. It's not good to spend all your time with the dying."

I snapped my head up from the ground as if she'd yanked me by the hair.

"Ingrid is an architect. My son-in-law is too. He's completely British, so you might appreciate his sense of humour better than me. They have a practice together, RQ + Partners, building the new thing over there." She indicated behind her, through the wall, and then through the bedroom window, which looked out onto Roosevelt Island. "I'm joining a tour of the site. You must come. You'll like Ingrid. She's . . ." Nat paused, working out how old her daughter was now. "Closer in age to you than we are."

After I'd set her up with an account on the genealogy website, we said goodbye to Silvia and went down in the elevator together. One of the Tonys on duty in the lobby told us to *have a nice day, ladies,* and I grinned through clenched teeth. We had to walk to get to the funicular that took us over the East River. We pushed through the turnstiles and stood waiting for the next of them to arrive. Nat corrected my thoughts, as if she could read them, by telling me that it was technically called an *aerial tramway.* I nodded and resolved to use the proper name aloud but continued to think of it as a funicular, because to me *a tram* sounds underwhelming, as if it just runs along rails on the ground, whereas this thing went up two hundred and fifty feet above the river.

The island, she explained, had been home to a penitentiary and a penitentiary hospital, a lunatic asylum, a smallpox hospital, and various structures that were built by convict labour. It had been renamed numerous times as well. Nat had been only once before, despite having always lived in Manhattan. It was in the eighties, when a cooperative had been established and a man she knew had persuaded her to visit.

I felt exhausted by her company already. At the same time, I felt a strange vibration, the source of it not immediately obvious, like a subway deep underground, and I knew that if I peeled away from her too soon, the mysterious feeling would disappear before I could locate it.

The funicular was crowded and we were too near the middle to see the view. I was standing too close to Nat for comfort, but there was nothing that could be done about it. Her breath tickled my ear every time she spoke. I can get quite aggravated by things like that. She was also an incurable name-dropper, and each time she asked if I knew a name, she jabbed a long red talon at me. I distracted myself from her inane conversation by wondering what sort of people went to the island now that it was no longer populated by the criminal and the insane. I studied the bodies immediately around us. Man with goatee. Man who looked like a Beatle. All the Beatles at once. Woman wearing newspaper hat. I'd grown used to how weird New Yorkers were, and I could now fit them into types. As I observed them, I noticed how strange it felt to be beside someone who knew my name, knew exactly who I was, and could have picked me out of a lineup. Up until then, the city had shown little sign of knowing me at all.

Nat gave me a taxonomy of New York society—each named individual was either *terrible* or *terribly brilliant*—and then a rundown of her own family. Her daughter's husband, she said with pride, had taken their name when they married eight years ago (at which point Ingrid was already pregnant with twins), so he was now Robin *Rooiakker* rather than Robin *Quinn*. Robin had originally been his wife's tutor at Cooper Union, nearly ten years ago.

"He's rather older than she is, actually—he's fifty-six I think he condescends to me because I didn't go to college. He can be very pompous, in fact. Ingrid says it is irony, but I don't think that's an excuse. He also," she informed me conspiratorially, "has strange compulsions about washing his hands, and he wears a mask if he has to take the subway."

I nodded, instinctively taking his side against her.

"He thinks of himself as the intellectual heavyweight of the family, but Ingrid was the one to secure the Cornell Tech project. Ingrid met the client, Walter Ruse, while doing jury duty some years ago, and they became *great* friends."

Walter Ruse was *brilliant*. But this was all the evidence you needed, Nat added in the same conspiratorial tone, to see they did jury duty by *zip code*.

"I much prefer Walter to Robin, to be frank, and I can see my daughter does too, but it was always a rebellion. Wanted to upset her father and me by picking her tutor. She also knows I disapprove of divorce, but she doesn't seem to be about to rebel against that anytime soon. Ingrid is very stubborn. She's not a quitter. Always a perfectionist, even in kindergarten, just like me."

Her candour meant that I felt I had to reciprocate with some kind of intimacy of my own so as not to be rude, but I didn't trust her. I couldn't decide what kind of person she was, whether she was one of those insects that look exactly like wasps but aren't. This wasn't because, like Nat, I was obsessed with classification, or working out how important people were and where they belonged through which names they knew and which family they belonged to. I just wanted to know if she would sting. The way I had gotten to know Silvia had been so slow, and yet I now knew nearly as much about Nat and her family, and New York society, as I had gleaned from Silvia since her first letter. There was something about this speed I mistrusted. Though I wasn't giving her nearly as much information in return, she continued to accelerate.

"You should ask Ingrid where she likes to go out in the city," Nat advised loudly as the rest of the cable car eavesdropped. "I've heard that the place people go to now is Third Square. Everyone wants to get into the Third Square," she said, mimicking the voice of someone telling her this. I nodded.

"Where do you go in England?" she persisted. "Do you like the Wallace Collection? I loved it when I went there."

It was impossible to avert my eyes from her bright and sticky makeup. Under the hot glass enclosing us it had begun globbing in her pores. Nat fanned herself, and me, due to my being pushed up against her angular shoulders, with a dark red Spanish fan. When she had finished with New York, she started on lineages of British families she knew. I said *yes, no, yes, yes, know the name, don't think so,* nodded, or repeated the name back at her.

"Robin's parents live on . . . something-mont Square, do you know it? In London. I guess not if you spent most of your time in the countryside. We've never met them—apparently they and Robin don't get on. But he says they're very grand people, British aristocrats essentially. There are lots of Americans living around that square now—I have some friends who moved in, I think. Sylvia Plath used to live there. I don't know if that's where she killed herself. Might be."

She waited as if it would be natural to ask her a question. Several moments passed. Finally I had one. "Are the twins identical?"

"No. Boy and girl."

"And do they have your surname as well, instead of his?"

"Of course. Thom and Rosa Rooiakker. I was pleased, as Ingrid doesn't have any brothers. She's twenty years younger than Robin, you know?"

I nodded.

There was a loud bang above us, like the snapping of an enormous rubber band. The funicular halted. I looked at everyone looking at each other, trying to tell whether this was normal. We hung there for a few seconds above the river.

"Don't worry," said a drawl somewhere to my left, and the whole car waited to hear why not, but that was all the relaxed voice said. Then, after a few seconds, the car started moving again and everyone acted like nothing had happened. The problem for me was that I did not feel that the real disaster had been averted. In fact, the disaster of falling down into the river, water frothing upwards and rippling out and simultaneously sucking us under, would almost have been the preferred option. Now that we continued to glide upwards, a gilded bubble riding on the air with me safely inside it, my life might just turn out to be a nothing, a name that wasn't even my own that nobody would remember. I began daring a disaster to happen, so that I might be called upon to act and so that something like animal instinct might surface. The real me, or the dead me who would be remembered for something significant, even if it was only a horrific accident.

We were descending. Gradually the chances dwindled.

"I don't suppose you want to find out your real name," Nat asked pretend-casually as everybody pushed towards the doors. "And if you did, would you switch?" I later recognised the theatrical line of questioning from PBS.

"I know what my biological father's last name is already, if that's what you mean. And no, I wouldn't." I might have added, "He's in prison," but the funicular landed and Nat strode out ahead of me.

I caught up with her greeting a blond woman in the centre of a group of about ten people. I guessed the woman was Ingrid. I didn't know which of the condescending-looking middle-aged men assembled around her was Robin, so I considered them all as if they might be.

"Hi." The blond woman waved at me. "Welcome. I'm Ingrid. I'm pretty sure my mother has told you everything about me."

She was white-blond, like an ice pop that had had all its colour sucked out. Everything about her looked bitten or swept by an arctic wind. Hard, attractive. Extremely threatening.

"Where's Robin?" Nat asked.

"He's late. I thought he might be on your tram. We'll have to start without him, I guess."

Ingrid turned to the others assembled and spoke in a much louder, more genial tone. "We're ready to begin if you are. Those of you I haven't met, I'm Ingrid Rooiakker. My partner, Robin, will join us shortly. This is Walter Ruse, whom I'm sure you know."

She gestured to a man beside her with a geometrically striking, light-cancelling beard that dipped on either side of his mouth like tusks. He wore navy-rimmed round glasses and an all-navy outfit, with an unseasonal turtleneck sweater that looked itchy and hot. He put his hand in the air at hearing Ingrid name him, closing his eyes with a deeply irritating smile. A tall, much younger man began handing round booklets with an RQ + Partners logo on the front in hot-pink foil, and I felt his eyes survey me intently as he gave me mine.

Walter and Ingrid led the group towards the water, where we turned left and began to walk along the western edge of the island. Our group was composed of two young architects, three more-senior-looking people (who, like Walter, seemed to wear outfits in only one colour), then five or six entrepreneurs and investors. Nat and I were the only women apart from Ingrid. Nat pointed out the "important" ones to me. "He is currently managing partner of a seed-stage capital firm . . . He has invested in companies like . . . He is the cofounder of . . . He does a mobile e-commerce app called . . . They do mentoring for startups . . . That one was a former chairman of something, but I'm not sure why he's here."

I started flicking through the booklet to understand how these people were, as its cover proclaimed, *creating an incubator space for digital nomads*. I hadn't ever heard of a digital nomad. I hadn't yet been called a Digital Native. I had no idea what any of it meant. I felt my feet drag slower and slower. I wanted to be alone again.

We started breaking apart into leaders and stragglers. I let myself drift to the very back, tipping my head to the sky. I listened to the seagulls crying, the low, manly sound of the tugboats, and the helicopters overhead, the wind shaking the last of the heavy blossom from the branches. I wasn't trying to catch what Ingrid or Walter was saying over it all. I was thinking I should drop back far enough to get the funicular back to Silvia's. I didn't belong here.

This is the point at which I first met him. Dwight. I felt a hand on my back and jerked my head around.

His name didn't scan well. I repeated it back to him. *Dwight Nutt*. Like it was inedible. He called himself *Walter's protégé*. He had business cards. Fistfuls.

Innovation Consultant, App Developer, Apiarist

Broken down like that.

"Let me know if you want me to show you around the city," Dwight said proprietorially, though he was in fact from Utah. That was the only way I knew he was into me, since he also gave his card to people not even on our tour.

10

When I got back, I showed Silvia the card.

"He keeps bees?"

"Yeah, I guess."

"In New York?"

"Is that bad?"

"Pretty dumb."

As we were talking, a sound issued from the next room. A beautiful, winnowing, airy sound.

"What's that?" Silvia said, alarmed.

I stared in the direction of my bedroom in disbelief. "I've got a message."

Silvia watched me as I left the room, and I felt my face get hot.

It was Dwight. He had sent me a private message via Instagram and requested to follow me, even though my account was public. Which meant, I realised with horror, he must have already seen the picture I had posted of him standing next to Walter Ruse on the site tour, which I had purposefully captioned to make it look like I knew them. Would it be worse to delete it now? I accepted the request. Immediately Dwight liked the picture of himself.

Our first date nearly didn't happen because he didn't know that he did not know the meaning of *rain check*. When I thought he was cancelling, he meant we could go *indoors or outdoors,* depending on the weather. In the end it was hot, and we met outside.

He found me at Columbus Circle and escorted me into Central Park. It was uncomfortable to have to fall into step, to keep my swinging arm from brushing his, and to listen to him instead of falling into my usual trance. My surroundings became a distraction. A threatening periphery. Something that would make me forget a word midsentence or lose my way as I spoke. Dwight asked me if I knew what the name of a certain tree was, because he had an app which told you, and I put my hand on the tree because I *did* know the name, we had them near the house in England, but even though I had my hand on it I could not think what to call it.

I guess because of the pedantic way I had explained *rain check* to him, he said he was very taken by my *Britishness.* He had deduced also that I was quirky and promised me that he was too. The not-quite compliment hovered awkwardly among the horse smells and the sour smell of garbage in the heat, the sight of drunks wearing winter fleeces in the long damp grass. He hadn't picked the right spot for a full compliment, let alone this hybrid version, and I couldn't stop thinking about how uncomfortable they must be, the drunks, and it frustrated me that they did not take their fleeces off; it was like the way you watch someone sleep upright and keep jerking awake but insist on not going to bed. As much as I tried to concentrate on him, my people-watching-while-walking ritual was too ingrained. The whole way to the meadow we walked either just behind or just in front

of a painfully anorexic woman in her fifties with a Walkman that
jutted out from her pelvis, and when I wasn't thinking about
how strange it was to be walking with Dwight, I was thinking
about who this woman was and whether she was following us.

"That's my mother," Dwight said casually when I pointed her
out. "Just in case I'm on a date with a total psycho."

"Oh!" I was startled and began to apologise. "Well, I'm actually—"

"I'm joking! My mother's in Utah."

"Oh. Okay."

"And she wouldn't let me go on dates."

When he wasn't making *quirky* jokes about his mother like
this—it happened more than once—he mainly spoke *at* me,
about his job and about his band, Jettisoned Airplane, an electronic music duo, which had been formed in March, inspired
by the plane that had gone missing and not yet been found.
Dwight was outraged that modern technology couldn't find it.
So outraged that when I admired the name Jettisoned Airplane,
he pulled a face. His collaborator, Emile, had preferred it to
Dwight's favourite, Black Box. The concept for the band had
been *born out of* a night spent with Emile discussing various
theories and experimenting with various sounds to accompany
them. The music, however, did not seem to have brought him
any resolution, and Dwight was eager to go over all his theories
with me.

"But in this day and age, how can a plane just disappear?
When I wake up, it's all about the missing plane."

Instead of this shared interest endearing him to me, or pro-
viding a platform for further intimacy, I found that I felt possessive. I therefore declined to admit to my own compulsive interest
in the case.

"The sea is pretty deep," I said.

"If it crashed into the sea," he said irritably, as if he were tired of explaining this, as if he had been personally dragged from press conference to press conference with the world's media, "then debris should be floating, as should the flight recorders."

I must have looked offended.

"Sorry," he continued, more gently. "It's just that the flight recorders, the black boxes, only emitted a signal for, like, thirty days. It's keeping me awake at night, the fact that those beeps got fainter and fainter. I'm double-dosing Ambien right now."

I was mainly interested in him because he had been brought up and lived, until only a few years before, as a Mormon. At first I didn't know this and found him strange. Then, when I did know, I couldn't tell what was weird about him because he was American, what was weird about him because he used to be a Mormon, and what it was about him that was just weird because he was a deeply abnormal human being pretending to be the type of person that Silvia felt was taking over the world. His lifelong ambition was to work for Apple so that he might play bocce on the landscaped lawns around 1 Infinite Loop. He said this had been the plan since he had arrived in the city and attached himself to Walter.

Dwight had discovered sex, drugs, EDM, and smartphones when he went to college. He had embraced them with the same enthusiasm with which he'd mostly abandoned Mormonism, though some ideas were deeply entrenched, like playing bocce. He behaved the way I imagined certain young, naive men had approached the American West at one time: as a vast wilderness for the taking. I suppose he was also, at least at first, good to me and good at showing me a stratum of the city that I had so far had no contact with. He liked the notion of taking care of me, even if he didn't have the faintest idea what it was that might be wrong. He was solutions-oriented. He believed absolutely that technology was a force for good. I think he thought of me as he had once been—a native Utahan discovering the city—which I suppose was fair enough, because when we met I was hanging out with two senior citizens.

We walked to the viewing platform of the miniature Belvedere Castle and looked at the brown turtles swimming in the green lake below. From above you could see their flippers paddling under their shells. Then we went and found a spot on the grass to spread out a picnic blanket. He told me things about himself that should have made him sound urbane but did the opposite. He told me, for example, that he liked *Steve Reich's music, modern-art museums,* and *Beat poetry.* These words flew out of his mouth and went boomeranging back as if they knew they weren't meant to take the conversation anywhere but back to him. He also explained that he *really liked interacting with different kinds of people.* When I didn't immediately respond to this, he repeated it, and so I assured him I believed it.

He didn't seem to feel that I believed him enough. A lululemon yoga rep was going round to each little settlement of picnickers and sunbathers and promoting something. I could feel Dwight twitching.

"Let me show you what I mean," he said, leaping up.

"It's okay," I said. "I think I get it."

Interacting with people, I thought to myself, remembering one of Silvia's criticisms of Susy, means finding ways to make them do what you want. I watched him sprint towards the lululemon man, turned to my phone, and scrolled through Dwight's Instagram pictures, which, if one started from the beginning, described a stark transformation from Mormon Boy to Tech Man.

After ten minutes he came scurrying back with flushed cheeks and a manic shine in his eyes. "We're going to collaborate on something. Boom. A workshop, with some other brands."

I nodded as if this were wonderful news. "Good job," I said. It was what Silvia said to me when I managed to do a task for her particularly efficiently.

"See what I mean? It just comes naturally."

"Yup. You're obviously a natural."

I realised that it was primarily this itch for interaction with strangers, rather than romance or the weather, that was his reason for taking me to the park. Buoyed by his earlier demo, he fist-bumped all seven of a group of boys in basketball uniforms and long white socks with backpacks, who were going around among the sunbathers and picnickers asking for donations. Then he followed the sound of a trumpet playing on the wind and insisted we move to a spot next to the player. He told me he was very sensitive to sound—could be hypnotised and tormented by it in equal measure. We folded the blanket in half and carried most of the things inside it, a manoeuvre that made me feel as if we were a couple making a bed together, though I had never been in such a relationship. Then we sat down again next to the trumpet player and I laid my face on the ground, just off the blanket so that the grass could cool my cheek and I could, at close quarters, watch the bees going up and down at work on the grass, soothing me with their slow, undulating movement.

Dwight brought out his business cards. I studied their heraldic symbols. *Innovation Consultant, App Developer, Apiarist.* The back had a wood-panel effect like the station wagon Lux Lisbon commits suicide in. When I noted this, he replied only, "Skeuomorphism," and winked as if we were two Freemasons greeting each other.

I liked it that he thought, at least initially, I was in on whatever it was he was in on. I guess he thought I was because I'd posted a picture of the incubator site, and I'd been there on the site tour. He liked to categorise people quickly, but in a different way from Nat. He thought about people from the perspective of what he'd learned in his business studies and digital marketing course. People were early or late adopters. I asked whether there was an adopt*ed* category, a special one for me, because I had already mentioned, when he asked about my relation to Nat, that I was adopted. I could see he didn't get my joke.

"Yeah, I guess," he said, musing as though I had said something quite profound, "in the sense that some people are so resistant to change at first, or so passive, but then it finally happens to them whether they like it or not, because they can't even pay a parking ticket without a smartphone."

He had names for every demographic. If he were telling this story, he'd say that three generations—Silent, X, and Y—all collided when I arrived in New York, no longer in its Age of Innocence, but in an age of *connectivity.*

It was the day that Maya Angelou died. When we finished the picnic, we walked from Central Park up to a restaurant in Harlem that Dwight said a former president had been photographed dining at, and on the way we saw the news on a sign outside the Apollo. Dwight thought she was a singer, and when I corrected him, he said quickly, "Novels were never really my thang."

I had to pause to ascertain whether he had definitely said *thang* or it was just his Utah accent, but he definitely said *thang.*

"Really, what I want to do now is, I want to do another degree, in *thought.*"

He would segue like this, away from whatever it was he didn't know about and into territory he felt surer of. He warned me that he liked to champion *new thinking.* For example, he liked Korean beer and some things that had a carbon fibre base. I could not stop thinking how Silvia, a bastion of his so-called Silent Generation, the one before the baby boomers, would have been dismayed. I told him his was a *new* New York for me and he seemed pleased, and then we kissed for the first time. This, I remember thinking, feels like a mushy apple.

Next we went to a bar with jazz musicians. I tried to sit down at the end of a table but the people at the other end said there was no room. "No room!" they cried when they saw me coming, even though there was. The tables were covered in paper table-cloths, with men in baseball caps and flat caps sitting at them on plastic folding chairs. We drank from miniature bottles of alcohol originating, I assumed, from a hotel minibar or a plane. I thought this would mark the end of the date, but then we went to a club after the bar. Some of Dwight's friends were there, and he seemed more anxious to show me off than to talk to me. I heard him informing one of them that though I was not his usual type, as ever he wanted to try something *new.* I couldn't tell if their presence there had been planned or not. I didn't yet know how easy it is to bump into people in New York, because I hadn't had anyone to bump into except ghosts.

Emile with the potato head, Dwight's *musical collaborator,* came over and was slimy. "I like to be a provocateur," he said. "I might just say a thing like *men are less intelligent than women,* or *blacks are more intelligent than whites,* just to get a debate started. Do you see?"

Did I? I could not stop thinking of his comment when I lost my virginity that night. At least until about three quarters of the way through, when Dwight said, "If it's your first time, you might wanna just be quiet so you can hear my dick." After which I could only think about that.

I had not been making a sound anyway, and there had already been a spongy silence all around us as I tried to ensure that the pitch of my breathing was not too loud, but from then on it was completely silent in the room, except for the strange sucky noises I obediently listened for as he made exaggerated L-shaped movements.

I can't remember how it ended. It feels like one second he was on top of me and then the next he was passing me his device as he lay next to me and telling me to look at something on it about Edward Snowdon or Israel or whatever the fuck it was, and I pretended to see but didn't. He gave me a shirt to wear in bed that said, WHEN LIFE GIVES YOU LEMONS, SAY WHAT THE FUCK AM I SUPPOSED TO DO WITH ALL THESE LEMONS?

In the morning I noticed how he laughed too easily. He laughed when I said things like *This coffee is really hot*. He would laugh carelessly on the phone when someone said *How are you?* Later on it bugged me even more, because it was usually impossible to make Mizuko laugh. On the rare occasions I managed it, it was often by accident, and for reasons which mystified me. When she asked me how I met Dwight, for example, I said I'd met him on Roosevelt Island on a site tour of the new Cornell Tech campus and we'd been on a date to a place called Red Rooster, the American Legion bar, and then to a club called Shrine. And this was somehow hilarious. So much so that I tried to laugh too: *He he he*. Lusty and low. This made her laugh harder and higher. And then I began laughing for real too, pleased and yet anxious at the same time.

I didn't mind sleeping with him. The whole time I hadn't slept with anyone at university had made it harder and harder to finally do it. Like spending too long on a very high diving board, until finally you have to exit ignominiously, the same way you climbed up.

On our second date, he explained to me a *very cool* dating app for threesomes he had just done a piece of brand strategy for, mainly around naming and positioning. It was called TriMe. It had the suggestive pun—did I see?—the connotation of three, and the evocation of a salubrious TriBeCa penthouse. I said I saw. He wanted me to go to the launch party with him that evening, but I said I had to get back because Silvia had an appointment. He assured me that everybody in New York was going to be there, and that then everybody was going to be using the app. Eighty thousand people had signed up before it had even launched. It was going to do for threesomes, he promised, what Uber had done for cabs.

"How does it work?"

"It connects to your Facebook friends and their friends, like most of the other dating apps, but you can use a made-up name, you don't have to use your real one, and there is a mode which hides you from friends and family who are using it."

"But I mean, how does it *work?* What do you do?"

"Haven't you . . ." His mouth hung open—food mulch visible—in amazement. "Tinder?"

"No." I waved my hand vaguely. "I've heard of it, obviously."

"It's pretty much Tinder. You swipe yes or no on singles or couples, depending on what you're after." He said this as if he were explaining email to an old person. "So you can connect with people who share the same fantasy as you."

"How do you know what their fantasy is?"

"It *says,*" he said impatiently. "Up front on their profile. You find out more when you get messaging. You'll see the ads for it now I've told you. They're all over the subway—*going down* and *getting crowded.*"

I shook my head. I still walked everywhere if I could. The subway map terrified me compared to the grid.

"We want people to be sitting on the subway looking at all the faces thinking who they might match with and who they want to hook up and form a trio with."

"And it's about making a threesome like getting a taxi?"

He breathed hard through his nose as though I were being particularly dense, entirely missing the nuances of the proposition.

"Have you ever tried to organise a threesome in real life?"

I shook my head. I'd only encountered them in porn, but it seemed to happen without much admin, the same way all porn skipped out the granular details of sex, like condoms and kissing, that were supposed to happen in real life.

"What are you supposed to do, just walk over to some couple in a bar and *ask* them to their *face*? *Oh hey, you don't know me, do you want to have a threesome?*"

One of his easy laughs.

A waiter came to take our order. I noticed how Dwight said, "Can I do the . . ." instead of "Can I have the . . . ," and every time he said it my buttocks clenched together.

"Can I do the Be Balanced Bowl? Thank you. I mean"— turning back to me—"do you have any idea how fucking *weird* that would be?" He began to crack himself up.

Overall, things improved for a while after I met Dwight. It felt like progress of some kind, like I was getting closer to something. He provided a lot of material and a lot of likes for Instagram. He liked everything I did, and prompted me when I neglected to do the same for him. Sometimes, when he was at work, I even made little collages of what we had been up to and posted them as I had seen strangers do, and then all his friends liked them, so that our relationship was formally approved by committee. The collages were the modern equivalent of lovesick needlepoint, perhaps.

I thought about this strange new pastime when we went to an exhibition about quilts. It was held at the New-York Historical Society. We went to lots of exhibitions together. Dwight felt they were crucial to his personal development, and in the time we dated we went to an exhibition about the Harlem Renaissance, a pearl exhibition, a shunga exhibition at the Met, and to see the quilts. He was always full of plans and day trips and itineraries, booking tickets to everything with an app that suggested stuff you might like based on stuff you *already* liked, which, I suggested, despite his unwavering commitment to novelty, didn't really count as *new.*

I took about three thousand pictures and posted about five a day. Each time I took out my phone it was like playing a slot machine. In my journal I compiled lists of those we met up with or shared cabs with or went for drinks with and made diagrams of where they sat and what I ate in restaurants. None of that seems at all relevant now, but at the time I thought I'd cracked New York. I forgot all about the contents of Silvia's three crates, which I now used as a stand for a bedside lamp. I started following people we met—Dwight's friends, Emile, two girls he used to message constantly, blond identical twins called Hatta and Hae —and even the ones who routinely liked Dwight's pictures of me on Instagram despite never having met me. Some of them started following me back so that suddenly my audience expanded significantly. I was afloat. Swallowing and spitting, spluttering and retching sometimes, but still being borne along.

"Alice Hare," I imagined people I no longer knew saying to each other, "is living in New York, is definitely *not* a virgin, has a boyfriend in tech, and hangs out with tattooed young people who drink black drinks that have charcoal as an active ingredient."

We ate only in new bars and new restaurants, due to Dwight's insatiable appetite for new experiences. He was always talking about these from the perspective of the *user,* and the main criterion of a good or bad user experience appeared to be his sensitivity to noise. At some restaurants he had to specify that he did *not* want his food brought to him on a slate. Once he found a squeaky door so unbearable in a lunch spot that he took the olive oil off the table and oiled it himself. Even outside of Jettisoned Airplane, as an innovation consultant he was constantly being asked to do naming work for brands because of his sensitive ear, and he was especially skilled at portmanteaus.

"The word *portmanteau* comes from Lewis Carroll's *Through the Looking-Glass,*" he explained, "when Alice discusses language with Humpty Dumpty. Originally it described a suitcase in two halves."

I thought of mine overflowing on its back in my old bedroom. Pushed the reminder of Susy to one side.

"Now it means the way that words can be blended, as opposed to compounded—even words that are total opposites—into one new word."

I nodded.

To him, everything in the world could be portmanteaued—people, places, time, and space. He liked separate things to converge like that—to be seamless.

I thought of him today when a barnacled chunk of the missing plane, a flaperon (portmanteau), was found washed up on Réunion Island. Then, of course, I thought of her.

Dwight never officially said I was his girlfriend. He claimed that he did not like defining such things, which was clearly an absurd thing for him, of all people, to say. Only a few hours before he told me this, I had asked him to repeat something he had said, a word he had used to describe something, and he had informed me that AOAC stood for "always on, always connected," shorthand for a marketing demographic who expected seamless communication between work and home. He had a name for everything.

As much as being with Mizuko made me look back on this period with loathing, at the time I did think it was kind of cool. It can be hot when someone is downloading things for you all the time. Taking care of you. Splitting the bill for you using an app called Spleat (*split* + *eat* = *spleat*), so you don't have to even think about spleating for yourself, and then ordering a car and then finding a bar (*cabbar*), and you can just glide through to the next thing and the next.

But I wanted whatever was happening between us to have a proper name, in order to mark the transition from who I had been before to who I was now, and I didn't want it to be a portmanteau of the two. I tried to explain this to him when we went to see the shunga exhibition. Without directly commenting on what I had just said, Dwight told me that now that he was no longer a Mormon, he liked to be very *free*. He said it like a foreign, maybe Italian word I might not know the meaning of. He said he liked going to *Burning Man, did I see?* and a night called Kinky Salon when he was in the Valley. In general, he said, he was a fan of radical free expression and did not want to be tied to anything or anyone. He said confidently that he could pick up the same vibe from me.

Even though I was the Japan fan, it had been he who'd suggested going to the shunga exhibition. His device was constantly sending him those alerts whenever something was happening in the city that was his *thang,* and we'd been to a lot of Japanese fusion restaurants recently. Shunga are very explicit erotic images; that much I knew already. We hovered by the introductory explanation on the wall. The scenes we were about to see depicted sly-faced women engaged in all sorts of "duplicity," cuckolds, "nubile ingenues," fantastical contortions as if the figures were invertebrates, "virgins in the snow," spurned wives armed with snowballs ready to pelt them, a cunnilingual octopus, a salesman having sex with six women, bald nuns in suitcases, "torrid nights under mosquito nets," visible, sometimes shocking age gaps, and "wild orgies during *hanami*." We were the youngest people there, moving about behind a scandalised group from the South who were *never coming back to the Met,* and audio-guided men too ancient to know about the expediencies of Internet porn.

Shunga translates as "spring pictures." They were mostly created during Japan's elective seclusion from the rest of the world, when no one but the Dutch were allowed in, and then only to a manmade island for trading, often bringing news of Western developments in technology and medicine. Japanese weren't really allowed out, either. That was, at the time, how I understood the pictures. Fantasies of penetration, of breaking through. Overlapping bodies. Mizuko would not have agreed. Later, around her, I had to keep any Orientalist projections to myself. Sometimes she would tell me playfully that I had a Japan fetish, in a voice that sounded pink and soft, and sometimes she would say it like I was truly, *truly* sick. I can't look back at the shunga exhibition or write about it now without thinking of Mizuko. Even though she wasn't there with us, even though I did not yet know of her existence, it feels to me like she was: a spectral presence, watching us from the dimness between the spotlights over each glass case.

In Japan, the erotic is not blue but *pinkku*—pink. I suppose that is why they are called spring pictures, because of the blossom. Pink is also the merging of red and white, the two colours which in Shinto represent female and male. In the West, pink is pretty much for little girls and lesbians. To me, it is Mizuko and the colour of New York.

As we went round the exhibition, Dwight informed me that I was a heavy breather and he had been wondering when to tell me. "It's okay," he said when I looked embarrassed. "It's not a deal-breaker. We all have our *things.*"

"Thangs?" I said, but he had already turned to examine a drawing of an enormous erect penis.

I backed away, holding my breath.

Mizuko was one of the thousands of early adopters who had signed up for Dwight's app before it had been released. She is, or was, who knows now, what Dwight would call "free." The kind of woman Dwight admired, and yet infinitely more refined in her liberation than he could have appreciated. She had, for example, a crying fetish. It has a name—dacryphilia. Mizuko liked to see people crying, and to comfort them. It wasn't a sadistic thing, not really; she didn't exact any form of physical punishment. It was just "cute." She would get someone talking about sad things that had happened. She didn't like it to seem inauthentic, the crying. She didn't want the person to be playing the victim—that didn't work for her. To be genuinely turned on, she had to know they were in an emotional state of some kind. She often took Polaroids of the crier. She had a pink Fujifilm Instax Mini 8. A crying Polaroid of me got added to her collection once. It records a moment when I was happiest, because I knew I was giving her pleasure.

Mizuko rarely cried, except about Rupert Hunter, who made her cry all the time. With anything else, sadness usually made her hard. As in impenetrable. God, when I write about her, every word does that. Turns to innuendo. I mean, she'd threaten to disappear to a mountain monastery rather than cry. She'd say ominous things, for example that she felt stagnant, or she wanted to leave New York. She once claimed the city was selfish and writing was selfish. Sometimes, if she was really sad, she would stamp her feet and recite a poem by Kenji Miyazawa, rousing herself with the closing lines:

> *when there's drought, shedding tears of sympathy*
> *when the summer's cold, wandering upset*
> *called a nobody by everyone*
> *without being praised*
> *without being blamed*
> *such a person*
> *I want to become*

This mainly happened after she had been drinking. She would begin saying her life was meaningless and that she was a terrible writer, and by dawn she would have talked herself round, back into thinking she was a genius.

Mizuko knew writing was her calling, and this certainty fascinated me, as I had spent a lot of time talking about callings with Dwight and he seemed genuinely angry that I didn't know what mine was. "It's not just going to come to you if you don't *try,*" he said as we were walking back to Silvia's from the shunga exhibition. "You have to actively go to it—it won't come to you." This to me seemed contrary to his philosophy about how everything in life should be *user-centric.* If life was user-centric, your future should just head straight for you, or behave like a self-driving car.

I was about to say so, but at that exact moment a woman crossed the street towards me. She removed the earpiece that was attached to her cell and reinserted her straw into her Frappuccino with a noise that made Dwight wince.

"Hey, can I just stop you a sec?" she said to me.

"Okay," I said uncertainly, looking at Dwight.

"So I'm picking up really strong *vibrations* off you." She said this like I might want to know if I had magical powers. Dwight moved between us, as if to block them with his body, but she stepped around him. "I had to cross the street to let you know. Here, take my card."

I snatched it before Dwight could take it. He seemed to feel all strangers belonged to him.

When I got home, I didn't show Silvia the card either. Silvia believed absolutely in her power to see the future, but not in anybody else's. She was able to predict what movie would be on TCM every evening without fail. When I got home that evening she said, "It's going to be *My Fair Lady* tonight, because it was *Gone With the Wind* this afternoon. Cecil Beaton," she added sagely, "made the Ascot costumes black and white because the English king had died and the court was in mourning for six months. Who else would tell you that kind of thing, eh?"

She continued talking as I took off my shoes and sat down on the carpet beside her sofa.

"I went to an exhibition," I said, knowing this was the kind of thing she liked me to be getting up to.

"Where?"

"New York Historical Society."

"Did you take my membership card?"

"Yes," I said, "but it had expired. Don't worry—I had the money."

"What did you see?"

"Quilts."

"With the bee man?"

"Dwight."

"Dwight?"

I nodded.

She tapped her glass for a refill. "Throat's dry."

When I came back in with her vodka, she was watching repeat footage of the Tony Awards. Once I had given her the drink, she spoke in a burst as if she had been waiting to get her words out.

"There are so many conditions these days." She jabbed a finger at the television. "Lesbian gay bisexual . . . And there are so many initials—too many, frankly."

"LGBT?"

"Q," she added, still scowling at the television. "That's the name of the activist group."

"Okay. I'll watch out for them."

Silvia had an appointment at six that evening. It was at the surgery that overlooked the East River where they did medical imaging and there was a constant whir of MRI scans. This time we were in the waiting room until nine. Whenever we were in a waiting room and her appointment was running late and I had got to the end of whatever article I was reading to her, Silvia would tip back her pea-size head and say, "I should have brought *War and Peace*." But this time she didn't say it. She didn't seem to be getting frustrated with the wait at all. Instead she seemed withdrawn, shrinking in her chair, wrapping her lamb's wool around her. She closed her eyes as if trying to retrieve something buried in the past or apprehend something rocketing towards us from the future.

When the nurses finally called her name, I offered to go in with her.

"No." She said it more firmly than I had ever heard her speak.

As I waited in the Siberian air conditioning, the hum of invisible machinery became louder and louder. Maybe simply because the waiting room had emptied out and it was now only me sitting there and one woman behind the desk to absorb it. I had been given forms to fill out on Silvia's behalf. I was used to these and now knew her personal and medical information by heart

—no prosthetics, no magnetic dental work, not diabetic. The ominous rumbling of the machines became impossible to ignore. I suddenly had the sense that by signing her name on them, impersonating her, I was about to push her out of this world and into some other place where I wouldn't be able to get to her.

Back at home, she did not want to watch *My Fair Lady* and asked if I could shut the door to her den.

I woke up at dawn because I heard a noise. I went to investigate and found Silvia standing in the dark corridor, her back to me, creeping painfully slowly towards the kitchen. I had one of those flashes—the sea-glass feel of a well-worn phrase. The name of the game which I had always played with my mother, though she was mostly unaware of it, and yet which I had never considered the actual sound of:

Grandmother's
Footsteps.

11

I went back to bed but then heard her speaking on the telephone.

"I'm sorry to be so insistent—"

I sat bolt upright again.

"—but I'm so helpless here, and you sound very reluctant to send anybody."

I'm here, I thought. *I'm* coming.

I opened the door without knocking. Her eyes did not meet mine, but she gave no sign that my presence was unwelcome, so I sat on the floor next to her in Dwight's WHEN LIFE GIVES YOU LEMONS T-shirt and underwear. The carpet was itchy against my legs, tucked under me. They had grown scaly, I now noticed, probably from Silvia's relentless central heating despite the temperature outside.

She went quiet and let the phone slide down beside her.

"Everything okay?"

"He's not too slick, that one."

"Why?"

"He's not too slick, that one," she repeated.

"How come?"

"I had to hold while he cleaned up the coffee he spilled all over himself. And no one's coming."

"What do you mean?"

Silvia handed me an orange phial—pills I hadn't seen before—and gave instructions: "Not crushed, not dissolved. Finely chopped."

I chopped them on a block in the kitchen as if they were carrots. It occurred to me that if something were to happen to her, I had no idea what to do. There were no instructions for that.

There was a radio in the kitchen. It seemed like the controls had once made sense to someone and then that person had disappeared or died and then someone else had messed it up so that now it made no sense to anyone. Apparently it was never really turned off, only tuned so that most of the time it brooded, suspicious and silent. None of the buttons seemed to make any long-term difference, but occasionally it would burst into life of its own accord. As I was chopping the pills, it came on. Screeching and then burbling, distorted sounds like something gone backwards, and then ghostly voices talking right to me, the opening of a portal to yet another world, it felt, then disappearing again into hazy sound. I was sure I made out my name. I pressed the off button down hard and kept pressing until the noise stopped. I shook the feeling out, jerking my neck violently. I took the chopped pills to Silvia, who had fallen asleep. I left them on a piece of notepaper, drew a circle around them and wrote the time as 03.40, then went back to bed.

I woke up again an hour later knowing something was wrong. I knew that first, before I knew where I was. My laptop was charging in the dark like a lighthouse. I had been having a bad dream where the carpet of my bedroom in England was strewn with tiny shards of glass. To walk across the room, which in the dream I had to do, over and over, I had to tilt my head from side to side to try to see the light shining on them so they would reveal themselves to me in the pale thread. As I adjusted my course to avoid the ones that flashed warnings, I would inadvertently step on others. In the dream I sat on my old bed, upturned the sole of each foot in turn, and saw that the skin was ridged and lumpy, inverting the normal folds of flesh. The skin appeared to have resealed. I had to squeeze each ridge and let the glass prise its way out until both my bed and the carpet were covered in blood.

Out of the dream, I moved very cautiously across the room and listened for sounds from Silvia's den. I thought I could hear moaning. I knocked on the door and there was no answer. Sometimes this simply meant she had too parched a throat to answer, but when I opened it she wasn't on the sofa. Then I heard a groan from Rex's bathroom.

Silvia was on the floor.

"What's going on?"

"Been trying to give myself an enema," she mumbled. "Arm won't work."

I didn't know what an enema was, but it looked like a highly personal experience. From the floor Silvia directed me to the last Fleet Enema twin-pack she had left after her numerous failed attempts and a pair of latex-free gloves. She looked at me with an expression both fearful and sheepish, but her face then wrenched free of those secondary concerns and returned to overriding agony.

"I feel like I'm going to explode," she said. "Do something."

Her voice was faint and gargly, and I was alarmed to see a kind of white crust in the corners of her lips. Her forehead had a film of sweat and her damp hair was flattened to it. Her skin was an alarming yellow, the bones of her temples stretching it like a hide.

"I'm *sorry* to ask you," she kept saying, "so sorry," but there was a pleading look in her eyes. "I'm so sorry. Sorry, sorry, sorry."

"What did the doctor say?"

She could only grunt.

"Are you sure we shouldn't go to hospital?"

"I don't want to," she moaned. "Can't. Have to wait for a lifetime. I don't—"

"It's not that I don't want to do this," I said. "I'm just worried that we maybe need to get proper help. Professional help."

Another spasm of pain screwed her eyes shut and she cried out, so I fell silent.

I gave her two enemas in the end, neither of which alleviated anything at all. She was on her side, gurgling, pale and naked except for her slippers, me crouching beside her, trying to be as gentle as possible. Midway through the second, I thought she was pointing at the message on Dwight's dumb T-shirt, but she was looking at my foot, a mark once a blister, now a scar. I had dozens of them from walking so much.

"Oh no, Alice, have you done something to your foot?"

"I'm fine," I assured her, almost smiling at the question, given the circumstances. "It's fine."

I had never felt responsible for the life of another human being before. I felt young: powerful and without a clue. I wondered if now might be the right time to tell her I loved her. There was a sickly smell of dying flowers and stagnant water. I decided against it. She gasped as I squeezed harder. The bathmat beneath her faintly yellowed. Morning began filtering in through the Venetian blinds, striping us.

I laid her back on the sofa in her den. She insisted on a second round of sleeping pills, which finally knocked her out for an hour while I sat next to her, monitoring her breathing and gripping the cordless telephone. When she came round, the pain had gotten worse.

"I think we should call one of your doctors. Or 911."

She nodded when I said *doctors,* shook her head quickly when I said *911.*

I got her black leather book and found the names of the doctors we saw most: Griffin, who was her GP, and McKurtle, who seemed to focus on the cancer, whose opinions Griffin often dismissed but who was the more sympathetic of the two. I decided to call McKurtle first. I thought his voice would soothe, whereas Griffin might shout at me, but the hard-nosed receptionist said he was with a patient, so then I called Griffin, who said to come in a taxi, he would see her right away.

She could barely stand, and once she was standing, each movement took forever, as if there were something sticky in the air. The viscous feeling—as if we were wading through spit —was relieved only by the swooping speed of the elevator. Silvia kept chanting the word *sorry, sorry,* the whole way to Dr. Griffin's surgery, until she couldn't make sounds anymore, after which she just mouthed it, over and over.

I waited outside while Griffin examined her. His waiting room was covered in framed photographs that he had taken of his trips to Vietnam and Cambodia. They were close-ups of exotic flowers and grasses, temples and fields. I remembered what the official in customs had said to me about the diets of Cambodians. That time seemed unreal to me now, but sitting in the surgery, acting as Silvia's sole guardian, felt no more real in its place. I promised myself that I would tell her I loved her when she came out.

I waited. Thoughts occasionally landed on me like bird feet, the grip of a claw sharp and sudden, and then disappeared. It breached the rules of the surgery, which were printed on little grey cards, to take out my phone, so I scanned both editions of Dr. Griffin's best-selling book on kidney stones. I felt like I might still be asleep. The stickiness in the air was still there. Everyone moved so slowly. The way in which the receptionist, the nurse, and Griffin had all reacted so nonchalantly to the crisis made me feel as if either I was the only one awake or I was the only one who wasn't.

Griffin wanted us to go to hospital: he suspected that Silvia had appendicitis. He said there was no point in calling an ambulance because a taxi would be quicker.

"But she can't *walk*," I said. "How am I supposed to get her into a taxi?" I thought of potholes. I thought of traffic. Silvia's face was ashen. Sweat poured down her neck and darkened her pink collar. "And what do I tell them when we get there?"

This is the note Griffin gave me, on expensive notepaper with his name at the top:

SILVIA WEISS
POSSIBLE APPENDICITIS
COMPLICATED

Then a squiggle I could not make out.

PLEASE CALL — NEEDS CT SCAN ASAP

On my third attempt, I managed to convince a taxi driver to wait for me long enough to explain that we were talking life or death — but nothing infectious — and I needed him to turn into the street I was on the corner of to collect an old lady. Silvia lowered herself in as I stood awkwardly by, not sure how to help and scared to touch her. Griffin's nurse tutted at my ineptitude. Silvia, maybe doubting me too, or wanting to show me she was doing okay, gave the driver an address.

"Isn't that the address we went to last night?" I asked as I registered it.

"That's where I'm supposed to go, isn't it?" She was sweating, eyes bulging. I felt sweat trickling from behind my knees now too. I didn't think it was. I thought Griffin wanted us to go to a different place—a hospital—but I didn't know where it was, so I hoped I'd misremembered the address of the surgery the previous night and we were going to the hospital, because after a while the numbers and avenues all blurred into one. I hoped that Silvia was right, because otherwise it would be my fault for not intervening. I hadn't because I didn't want to be wrong. If I was wrong, I didn't want to be culpable for what might happen to her as a result of wasting time.

The taxi turned into the dead-end street that reached the edge of the river with the surgery from the night before with the loud machinery. I told myself I must have got it wrong about the hospital.

"If it's appendicitis," Silvia said feverishly as the driver counted out the money and I tried to unstick my legs from the leather seat to slide out, "it might go at any moment, yes?"

"Yes. Well, no. I don't know," I said. I knew I could check if I turned roaming on, but it didn't feel like a good idea to know. I edged her into the surgery, moving with her old body as if it were a numb part of mine, and showed the note Griffin had given me to the receptionist on duty.

"I don't think we can help with this," she said. "Does she have an appointment today?"

"Call Griffin," Silvia said through spit that was gathering in her mouth, the plea disappearing like foam in the distance it had to go between her and the receptionist.

We watched her speaking into the receiver.

"Yes," she said, her nod and smile so American and so misleading. "You are *not* supposed to be here—you're supposed to be there."

"Where?" I asked, holding Silvia up by her armpit.

"New York Presbyterian Hospital."

We went through the incremental process of exiting the surgery again, using the side door rather than the rotating one, which Silvia could not keep up with. In the next taxi, the suspension was worse and the driver was angry. I tried to hold her down in the seat as we jerked around.

"I made a mistake." She said it as if she wanted to confess. We were stationary. Her eyes began roving around the interior. "Now I'm going to die waiting."

"No, you didn't," I said. "It wasn't *your* fault, it was Griffin's. He wasn't clear."

When she didn't reply, I wondered whether this was even the mistake she meant.

In the emergency room I imagined someone would address our emergency, but we were confronted instead with armed guards and a woman with a clipboard, who surveyed me as if I might be about to do something criminal unless she could prevent it.

"What is your relation?"

"Her granddaughter." These words no longer thrilled me—they now implied a kind of bondage.

She began talking over me as I tried to explain, flicking my hand away as I tried to deliver Griffin's note about the appendicitis, the complications, and the urgency. I wanted the woman with the clipboard to be terrified for me, to sweep Silvia away behind some curtain and fix everything. Instead she was laboriously slow with the form, looking at me with either boredom or disdain, as if she did not believe a word I said.

"I'm adopted," I explained, as if I were explaining to a police officer that this was in fact my own house that I was breaking into.

After that, the hours passed in sudden jumps. Something was moving very fast (in proportion to the eighty-one years preceding it), which was time running out for Silvia, and something else seemed not to be going at all—the hospital, into whose care this last, fast portion of her life had to be entrusted. It was like staring at an hourglass timer—sand falling, powdery and thin, between two solid bulges that seemed to be growing or shrinking much more slowly than the sand falling between them. I tried to give my note to every nurse and doctor we encountered, but no one seemed interested in it and no one took it, which is why I still have it. Silvia was laid on a cart and wheeled through the maze of hallways, sometimes part of a larger design, a horseshoe or a hexagon, and sometimes just on and on like a warren with no clear structure. Along it were some shut doors and some that opened onto other scenes of suffering, sometimes lone figures and sometimes whole families separated by curtains, and then back to a long, doorless hallway again, in which we were alone.

It seemed we were being shown a longer, scenic route so that we might fully appreciate just how many lives were ahead of Silvia's in the queue for salvation. The fact that we had "walked" in, as the nurse so breezily put it, rather than arrived by ambulance, seemed to count against us. They were resolutely, aggressively, *demonically* composed and even smiled and joked with colleagues they passed. Finally, after some prodding of Silvia's abdomen, we were given the verdict: "We need to do more tests."

The doctor we were with at that moment, the only one whose name I managed to hold on to like a splinter of driftwood in the sea of green and blue uniforms, was Ryan. A colleague of Ryan's had already taken a blood sample, but the blood had hemolyzed, Ryan explained, so he was going to do it himself.

Ryan looked over Silvia's arm and frowned. "Can't find a vein right now," he said. "Flushing needs to be very gentle — they blew up the vein. See that purple lump?"

Another patient was wheeled next to us in the hallway, where he began to sing, flat on his back like an upturned turtle, flapping his arms, simultaneously crooning and conducting an invisible choir from the trolley, his head slightly inclined towards me and Silvia. Without warning, as if suddenly spotting a fish to spear, Ryan plunged the needle into Silvia's arm, clasped in his own. Her face froze in an expression of agony.

"Nope," Ryan said, inspecting the syringe. "Have to try again."

Silvia drew her knees up towards her chest and closed her eyes tight. He speared twice more.

"Got it," he said with evident satisfaction.

"What's your name?" Silvia said, tears sliding out from under her eyelids.

"Ryan," Ryan said happily.

"I'll remember that. It was my first husband's name."

"We need you to have a CT scan," someone said, addressing me more than Silvia, who seemed to have passed out, though on hearing this she woke up.

"Haven't I already had one?"

The person shook her head.

"But I feel like I have. How long have I been here? I don't like going in those tunnels."

"No, sweetheart, it's not the MRI, it's not as claustrophobic. Not really."

"Can't you just open me up now? I'm getting claustrophobic just being in this hallway."

Before the scan she had to drink a liquid—a contrast fluid —that would make her insides into a picture. I tried to explain to the guy who told us this that because of her throat, Silvia had trouble swallowing much except neat vodka. He nodded and walked away. The contrast arrived in an enormous pink beaker full of ice like a Slush Puppie. It took Silvia about an hour to drink it. I sat next to her, helping her sip. Finally she was wheeled away for the scan, and I waited outside, beneath a TV monitor mounted to the wall. It was showing *Who Wants to Be a Millionaire?* The contestant was on his $100,000 question:

Which of the following is now depicted by LEGO figures at LEGOLAND, Florida's Miniland USA exhibit?

A: Crazy cat lady
B: Grain site explosion
C: Crab attacking man's face
D: Public hanging

I had just settled on C when Silvia was wheeled out again.

"I want to die," she said. "I really do."

As they were going to operate, she wasn't supposed to have anything further to eat or drink, but they didn't tell me, so I kept giving her water each time she asked.

"Just wet my lips," Silvia begged. "My mouth is so damn dry."

I complied, using my pinkie to administer tiny droplets. I reminded myself of Dwight. He kept his bees on the roof of his building in Dumbo and carried a pipette with sugar solution on him at all times to save dying bees he found in the street. He used to take it out of his pocket when he was anxious or bored and play with it as if it were a nipple. I tried to send him a message to let him know what was happening; I wanted somebody to comfort me. I didn't know what to say in the message. I tried a few different things. Nothing would come out right. My fingers were all shaky so typing was hard, and yet some of the more absurd autocorrects seemed better suited to the situation than what I could think of to say. Then my phone died just after I sent the message, so no comfort could come from it anyway.

A man in a blue blazer with a badge saying VOLUNTEER came towards us. I followed him around a corner.

"Excuse me, what time is it?"

"Ten-thirty," the man said, smiling as broadly as a barbershop singer.

"At night?" I asked. There was no natural light.

"Yup," he said, still smiling. "What time you think it was?"

"Like lunchtime, maybe."

I had been awake pretty much solidly for two days.

"You want me to get you something to eat?"

"Yes, please."

He disappeared and returned with a sandwich, cling-filmed onto a black plastic plate and labeled HAM & CHEESE. White bread, slit into two triangles. I peeled the top, fibrous layer back, revealing marbled pink ham, shining under the hospital lights like an oil slick, and the narrow yellow of the cheese that had fused underneath it. They looked like they had been treated with something that meant they would never go bad, even if I had to wait there forever.

It tasted only like texture, like frozen moss beginning to thaw. Once I'd eaten, I found I was exhausted. The adrenaline that had been keeping me awake for so long was absorbed entirely by the bread like a mattress. I was so tired that I picked up the pink beaker full of melting ice that had contained Silvia's contrast and began to drink. "Fuck," I said aloud, remembering, and I replaced it on the yellow chest of drawers on wheels that had been left next to us in the corridor.

The chest had a top drawer with a label reading, ISOLATION STICKERS.

The next drawer down said, SHIELD MASKS, SHOE COVERS, CAPS.

The next drawer down said, WHITE GOWNS.

The next drawer down said, YELLOW GOWNS.

By the time I had lowered my gaze to the bottom drawer, I was asleep.

I jolted awake. Tried to stay upright and alert by reading the notice on the wall opposite.

IT'S THE LAW
IF YOU HAVE A MEDICAL EMERGENCY OR ARE IN
LABOR, YOU HAVE THE RIGHT TO RECEIVE (within the capabilities of this hospital's staff and facilities):

- *an appropriate medical screening examination*
- *necessary stabilizing treatment (including treatment for the unborn child)*
- *and, if necessary, an appropriate transfer to another facility*

YOU HAVE THIS RIGHT EVEN IF YOU CANNOT PAY, DO
NOT HAVE MEDICAL INSURANCE, OR YOU ARE NOT
ENTITLED TO MEDICARE OR MEDICAID.

I sat up, fully awake now. I watched my mother—my *real* mother—running past where I sat and around a corner, gown billowing, not stopping but veering away from me.

"Higgins! Why don't you listen to me?" A nurse was wrenching my mother's arm. "Do you want something to drink? Nonalcoholic. Do you want water?"

Higgins, not my mother but a kind of ogress who looked like she might once have played basketball very successfully, rampaged along the corridor towards us. I stood up protectively, in case she was about to ram the cart or knock over Silvia's IV drip.

"You want a muffin?" the nurse asked coaxingly. "How about a meal?"

Other nurses appeared at intersections in the corridor, trying to lay hands on her, but Higgins was unstoppable.

"What are you gonna eat? You don't have any food at home."

Higgins passed us again, smiling a kind of bovine smile, flaring her nostrils at me.

"Obviously a regular," Silvia managed to say through spit. She nodded at a young man who lay facing us with a pink sick bucket between his big sneakers at the end of the gurney, which nearly touched the end of Silvia's. His head lolled to one side; his blue hospital gown stretched open across one shoulder.

Patients and their next of kin swapped powdery gum. An elderly couple were stationed next to us: the man on a cart, the woman behind his head, rigid like a tombstone. They both used the word *charming* to describe things, so I could tell they were married.

"How do folks stay married so long?" the nurse was asking them as she put on the brakes of the cart.

"I don't recommend it," the wife replied.

"But the alternative is being alone, right?"

"That's the alternative."

"So do you recommend *that*?"

"Well, I don't know. I'm not alone, but I don't recommend being a caregiver." She seemed genuinely exhausted. "But that's marriage for sixty-two years."

The nurse whistled her admiration.

"He has a good heart, I know. But high blood pressure." The woman began addressing herself to me as well as the nurse. "We lived in New Jersey when our sons were growing up. Then moved back."

"Because you're in love with the city?" the nurse prompted.

"Yes," she said, sighing. "I'm in love with the city."

The nurse left, and I turned my face to give them privacy.

"Don't be too long," the husband called to the nurse's retreating back. "She's a wild woman."

I went to the bathroom and began to attack my skin in the mirror, squeezing every pore into an angry red mound. I reentered the corridor and tried to bow my head to make it less obvious in the harsh lighting, but when I returned to our spot, Silvia looked guilty too.

"It's humiliating," she said. "I'm embarrassed."

"What is?"

She paused, feeling for a euphemism. "I've messed myself."

I couldn't find anyone who would help get her cleaned up, so she lay there, getting colder. I was angry at myself for finally leaving her side to go to the bathroom at the one moment that I could have been useful, when she needed to go herself. She pointed at the Kimberly-Clark logo on a box of gloves that had been left on the yellow chest.

"I have shares in those guys," she pronounced solemnly. The morphine must have kicked in. "I spend so much time in places like this that I see how much goes to waste, because you have to buy in bulk and it never all gets used."

"That's smart."

By the time we were told that Silvia was finally being taken into the operating theatre, she was delirious, memories coming to her out of nowhere but voiced as if she and I were in the middle of a conversation.

It was time to go.

"I'll be right here," I told her, "when you come out."

"No, don't wait. Go home, Rabbit. Go home."

I remember gasping. *Rabbit.* A sliver of remembered sound hovered above me. I moved towards her to try to clasp it in my hands. I felt myself shrinking. Heard her calling me Rabbit in smaller ears, saw her face from a lower vantage point, felt the voice to be more powerful than mine. Arms. A smell. "Skin a rabbit!" as she undressed me and put me to bed. I felt myself begin to cry, wanting to be so small.

"I can see his handwriting," she mumbled as the brakes of her gurney were taken off and two nurses began to angle her out of her slot.

"What? What's she saying? She's saying something, wait." Now that she was finally moving I didn't want to leave her. I leant right by Silvia's mouth. "Say again?"

"Three," she said, a sudden force in her voice. "Three quarks for Muster Mark!"

12

I retraced my steps out of the hospital, getting lost a few times, back through the sliding doors at last. I wanted to wait for her, but I also wanted to sleep. I wanted her to wake up in the morning, but I didn't want her to wake up without me. Out from cool brightness to muggy darkness. The landscape felt changed, but I couldn't say how.

Sometimes you can tell a homeless person only by the way they don't move, or how long they don't move for. There was one woman to whom I sometimes gave gifts of food I'd bought and couldn't face eating. She always sat on the same metal bench by Silvia's building, occasionally shifting ends with the shade. Only her lack of visible purpose gave her away. With others, it is the sense that they can never stop moving. They push past you with their wagons full of belongings towards some unknowable north. This time my homeless friend was not there, which disoriented me, so that I walked too far. Somehow this upset me so much that I began to cry. Both her not being there and the fact that in my exhausted, blistered, hollowed state, I had walked two blocks further than I needed to and would have to turn back.

When I got home I plugged my phone into the wall and waited for its comforting ping of awakening. The life-starting-over sound. I posted and then deleted a picture of an IV drip I had taken in the hospital. Two people — Dwight's friends — had liked it immediately, but something told me it was a monstrous thing to have done. There were messages on Silvia's answering machine. I didn't know how to work it and was slightly afraid of it, so I unplugged it to stop the beeping, which I could not distinguish from the incessant beeping noises in the hospital I continued to hear in my head.

It was the first time I had been alone in Silvia's apartment. The door to the bathroom was open, still with the yellow stain and the smell of dying flowers. I fell asleep thinking of things that, if I held them in my mind hard enough, might keep Silvia alive through the operation. As I began to slip out of consciousness I got that falling sensation. I realised I had not bought her the flowers I'd told myself I would buy to give to her after the operation. I remember thinking I wanted to get out of bed and buy some in the middle of the night. I remember thinking that if I managed to keep the flowers alive in the deathly heat of her apartment, this would somehow keep her alive in the operating theatre too.

In the morning, Dr. Griffin called and gave me his summary of the night's events. He got me to imagine the head of an asparagus spear so that he could describe to me what had happened in the operation, but the idea made me feel sick. What I understood was that she had survived. I didn't know what the ICU was either, but that was where she was, and he gave me the visiting hours. I walked back to the hospital the following afternoon, when Griffin said she would be awake. I could hear only the creepy, stalker sound of it: *I see you. I see you. I see you.*

I couldn't stop myself. I continued to murmur it under my breath as I bought pink roses on the last block before the hospital.

I see you I see you I see you.

As I walked through the hospital hallway, trying to remember the directions I had been given, I observed myself from above.

I see you I see you I see you.

When I reached the ICU, I was told I was not allowed to take flowers inside. The nurse on duty agreed to keep them in water under her desk but made it clear that this was as big a favour as favours could be; she was supposed to throw flowers in the trash. Silvia had her own room, and her bed looked out over Roosevelt Island. When I went in, I felt immediately shy. More shy than I had felt entering her apartment for the first time, creeping into the hallway as things took shape in the darkness. As she had been then, she seemed to be asleep, but after I sat beside her for a few moments I sensed that she was not.

"I'm waiting," she said.

Slowly she opened her eyes. I felt a pain in my throat like a stuck bone.

"My nurse for now"—Silvia indicated the whiteboard where a name had been written—"is called *Santa*. I make them write names up there because there are so many of them to keep track of. They don't talk or act like real people, most of them."

Her voice was flat. I wondered if I detected reproach in it. I wondered if she somehow knew that I had posted a picture and deleted it.

"Does it suit me?" she asked, following my gaze to the wires snaking between her body and the unmusical machines that attended her. "I always say computers are the scourge of our age."

She tried to swallow the saliva collecting in her throat; the fish-bone in mine would still not go down. "Computers and cancer. It's an excuse for nobody to come check on me in person."

I unpacked my bag onto her legs. "I brought you these," I said, "but you seem pretty well provided for. I don't think you'll be needing much of . . ." I gestured to the neck pillow and an-imal socks with grippy toes I had laid on top of her sheet. "I brought flowers too, but I'm not allowed to give them to you, they said."

Silvia closed her eyes again, as if she hadn't heard. "I had a nightmare. Morphine nightmare, I guess." She kept her eyes closed as she spoke. "Nat, you, that boy you're seeing, Ingrid and the son-in-law, their children and some others—a man and a woman—and a dog."

"And what were we doing?" I asked after a pause.

"You were all there having a party."

"All where?"

"Right there." She indicated with her eyes. "At the foot of my bed. Your boyfriend was in the corner on his machine."

"How did you know it was him? You've never met him."

"From your description, of course. Or I made him up. I don't know. And one of them, the husband, Nat's son-in-law, he came up to me in the bed and pressed his hands down on me, as if he were trying to push them right through me."

"And what happened?"

"I was saying, *Get out, get out.*"

I looked into her face to see that she was frowning with con-centration.

"Then I got out myself and ran across the road and down an alley. I fell into a puddle and then they found me and brought me back to the hospital. I had mud on my face and feet." Her voice had the kind of extreme flatness that is unnatural, like Astroturf compared to natural grass, the flatness that conceals something, like rage or grief. "Then I went back into it."

I flinched. The bone was piercing. I couldn't breathe.

"Outside on some steps a very strange man came across the lawn with a big black beard and little round glasses and gave me a very hard handshake. I knew I must be in the Hamptons. There were young people with tennis rackets, and Ingrid said, *Oh, you missed my mother! Unfortunately, she's not dying, but you are.* She wanted me to swap bodies, and I said, *Who cares?* or something—" Her saliva was running out. "I have more to tell you, but my mouth—"

She flopped her head to one side as emphatically as she could to tell me that she wanted something in that direction. An orange stick was poking out of a white paper cup. It had a kind of swab on the end, submerged in water.

As I was administering the swab to her mouth, the door slid open behind me and the visitor pumped twice on the hand sanitizer. I turned around. A nurse moved past me towards Silvia as if I weren't there.

"Are you able to lift up your tush?"

"*Tush?* I'm not Jewish."

The nurse's eyes narrowed and her expression became cold as she went about bathing Silvia, unmoved by her whimpers.

I left the room, filled a conical paper cup with icy water. I swallowed hard. The bone was still stuck. I moved aimlessly around the ward, reading the noticeboards and the thank-you cards sent to the hospital. There was a very cold room for families to wait in, with a vending machine, a television, and dark leather chairs. I was sick with exhaustion. I sat down but couldn't sleep. When I went back in the nurse was resettling Silvia in the bed and asking her how much pain she had on a scale of one to ten as she touched various parts of her body.

"I need to pee," Silvia said when the nurse touched her abdomen.

"You need to void your bladder?" the nurse corrected.

"Sincerely. I'm going to wet myself."

"You're catheterized."

When she had left, Silvia said, "She hovers, that one—and pats me, which I don't need."

I made a sympathetic face and said, "Is that one Santa?"

"No. I don't know."

The nurse came back in. I moved to leave the room again, but Silvia stopped me. "Don't bother with the bedpan," Silvia said, apparently ignoring the information the nurse had just given her. "I can't go now after all."

"I meant to ask you," the nurse said after a calculated pause, moving her tongue to one side and then the other, chewing it, "you're DNR, right?"

Silvia looked blank. Out of habit, I replied for her.

"What's DNR?"

"It's a form she signed. Means if she loses consciousness, she does not want to be resuscitated."

With a rush of warm saliva, the bone dislodged itself. I swallowed, free at last.

"What does that mean, though, your question?"

"If she wants to—"

"If it's a form she's already signed," I said, cutting in so the nurse could not repeat herself, my voice trembling between extreme politeness and extreme aggression, "then surely you don't need to check, and if you do, you should check her records outside, in private. You should not be asking an elderly woman who has just come out of surgery whether or not she still wants to *die,* as if that is likely to happen. Which"—I shot a look at Silvia—"it's *not.*"

"Okay, lady." The nurse shifted her weight to her other hip and chewed her tongue some more. "I'm just doing my job."

"No, you are *not,*" I heard myself roar at the stocky stranger. "Who even *are* you? Are you a doctor? Maybe you should check privately with one of the *doctors*. Now is not the *best* time"—I took a few paces towards her, and she backed a little towards the wall—"and what difference does it make what she says *now* if she's already written on the form that she wants to die?" I did not wait for an answer. "If she said, *No, actually, I do want to be resuscitated,* it wouldn't make a difference, right? *Not if it is written*"—I began to cry but maintained my shouting through it, like a wind through sheets of rain—"fucking"—I slammed the wall—"written *down.* Then it doesn't make any difference if you try to change it after."

And now I know this to be true for everything.

The nurse left and I crouched down to try and settle my breathing. For the first time in Silvia's presence, I felt completely unselfconscious.

"I belong and donate to a compassion group," Silvia said calmly after a few moments. "And I want to uphold those wishes. No chest compressions or anything."

Tears came again, but silently this time.

"And it's my choice. No one else's."

A loud sob broke.

"It's no life," she said, more gently. "If the heart stops—"

I gasped for air as if I'd been winded.

"It's in my will."

"But that was beyond . . ." I said, staring helplessly at the door for a second, then wiping my face and covering it in my hands.

"My life is nothing. Nothing. These tubes . . . it's an invasion. I don't see anybody. Except Nat. I don't want to. I don't go out. I don't want them to see me. It's over. This is not life as I know it —I want someone to let me die."

"But what about *me*?" I blinked. I realised it felt good to cry now. "I see you. I'm here. I'll always be here if you want. I'll do anything you need me to."

Silvia looked at me intently, and my tears subsided as I took in what she was asking. I held my face for balance and sat back against the wall. A long silence passed in which I fought my instinct to run by stretching my legs out in front of me and grinding my heels into the linoleum. She let the silence grow. Her stare told me that she knew what I was capable of.

"G'day, folks!" Her nutritionist arrived. She did not bother with the sanitizer or seem to notice that I was sitting on the floor, my face wet with tears. "How are you feeling today?"

"I don't feel too hot," Silvia answered meekly.

"I bet you're missing your vodka, aren't you?" This was said without reproach. "Dip your swab in." The nutritionist proffered a flask.

"What a jolly lady she is!" Silvia cried.

"Our secret."

"I like your hair. Are you the one who grew up in Queens? Hasn't she got lovely skin too?" I nodded. The woman had a kind of punk hairdo with piercings all up her ears.

"I like your ear studs. Do you take those out every night?"

The flask came out again.

"I read through the notes and then get a picture and compare what I see when I meet the patient," the nutritionist said, turning to me, suddenly serious, "and I think it will do her more harm than good right now to go cold turkey."

"Sure," I said.

"I don't care for turkey," Silvia added.

I went to the window and looked out at Roosevelt Island. Runners and cyclists went up and down the shore like ants.

"The river is moving really fast right now," I said, my breath misting up the window in the fierce air conditioning.

"It's no river," Silvia said with sudden passion. "It's an estuary." She sucked on the swab. "Not many people know that."

It never ceased to amaze me how she just had the facts always, in her head. It occurred to me that if, or when, she died, a whole load of facts, a body of knowledge, might disappear without a trace.

When I left I was glad. The light outside was strangely yellow, the shadows purple. I could smell something faintly like burning. Coming towards me was a man dressed for rough terrain, clattering a stick along the concrete. When he passed he looked into my face, paused as if he meant to say something, and then continued as if he had thought better of it. I had the feeling that at any moment everyone around me was going to start fleeing from something. Out of the corner of my eye I thought some people might be inching backwards, pretending not to have started making their escape.

I went into a store to buy bottled water. This was an indulgence, but despite Silvia's glowing references, I did not like the water that came out of the taps, which seemed to wall up my mouth as if I had eaten a dry biscuit. I bought a bottle that had a chatty label on the back:

> The Butterfly Effect.
> According to chaos theory, the tiny flutter of a butterfly's wing can cause a cyclone on the other side of the world.

The company had applied the theory to projects they undertook in harsh regions of the world. I considered the supply chain: the bottler, buyer, shifter, drinker, the owner of the store, the harsh region of the world, the label, and the bottle-picker who would extract it from the trash and redeem it for nickels. Exactly as I had this thought, I put my hand into my pocket and felt a hard-edged thing: my psychic's business card. I read the address and realised I was one block from Psychic Boutique.

I rang the bell and a girl answered who was not the girl who had given me the card—the one who had picked up the strong vibrations from me. This new one was called Samantha, though on the card I have it says READINGS BY ANNA. I felt that this was somehow wrong and that Anna, if she was truly psychic, should have come to the door as if she had been expecting me. Nevertheless, I liked Samantha, even though she did try to fleece me out of five hundred dollars. She informed me that if I came to her again, she could get a load of crystals in. She could tell instantly, without me saying one word, which I hadn't, that amber would work nicely. Then throughout our session she kept alluding darkly to her "supplies." I nodded or shook my head like a mute. I didn't want to give her anything easily—I wanted to let the vibrations speak for me—but I couldn't have said much if I'd tried. The choice of letters in the alphabet felt suddenly constricting. It was as though anything I said would immediately trigger concrete to begin pouring around my chair. I couldn't think of any words I wanted to commit to saying if they were going to fix my fate for me like that. After she did the reading, she told me that I would need to come back every day for a week and that the first twenty-four hours after a reading were the most effective if I wanted to use crystals.

"What's your hesitation?" she asked when I became shy about handing over Silvia's emergency credit card. I still couldn't formulate words, and we kept being interrupted by her young sons, who were taking it in turns to come in to tell her that the other one was annoying him. I could hear the soundtrack of a kids' movie in a back room. She gave them her device, which had been facedown on the table next to her like a Tarot card the whole time, to play with.

"I'm sorry," she said. "That one is scared of being alone."

On hearing himself discussed, the boy returned to defend himself. When he was again dismissed, his brother came in wearing a plastic bag over his head.

"Take that off. Cut it out."

Psychic Samantha ripped the bag off him, tugged back a curtain under the table where random household objects were stored, and stuffed it inside.

"I have a headache," he said miserably.

"So put half a potato on it."

"Okay," I finally blurted. "Thanks so much, but I'd better go now, thanks very much for your help."

She told me it was unlucky to share a reading with others, but the main point, the one that I don't mind mentioning because it seems relevant to the story, is that she said I had a kind of evil spirit following me. "Obviously," she added, "that sucks. But if we get you some amber—"

It was a negative energy, jealous and possessive, that wanted me to be alone. Someone maybe with robotic tendencies whom I would have to look after, who would take all my energies and not give anything back, taking even my body from me, and with whom I would be trapped in this cycle of giving and depleting and needing forever. I promised to come back once I had had a think about the crystals.

Walking home, I considered who it might be, this shitty spirit. It could, I reasoned, be pretty much anyone I knew. Susy, most likely. At the last block before Silvia's, I told Dwight to come over, because I did not want to be alone in the apartment again and because I wanted to test him for robotic tendencies. There was something about the way he talked about manipulating *the user,* giving someone using one of his apps an illusory sense of mastery and of choice—like a magician with a pack of cards —that suggested he knew how to exploit the psychological vulnerabilities of humans but that he was not quite human himself.

He had not been inside Silvia's apartment before, and when he arrived he walked around it silently as if he were in church, admiring things solemnly and looking at me with an irritating, earnest expression. I showed him Silvia's three crates. He looked through a first edition of the *Whole Earth Catalog* from 1968, which had been Mark's. He didn't tell me it was very valuable, and when he asked if he could have it, I said yes.

I was hallucinating from exhaustion, but I showed him Silvia's framed photographs and I told him the stories that went with them that she had told me. The jacaranda flame tree from the holiday house, the rockery, the blue-tongued lizards that came out when the family ate shrimp in the garden. Then we ordered takeout, and as he ate, he seemed to forget his solemnity.

"Can I fuck you in the shower?"

I had noticed as I gave him the tour that he seemed particularly excited by Rex's bathroom.

"No," I said. "That's where—" I cut myself off.

"Can I fuck you on the floor?" he continued, undeterred.

"Is this a poem?"

"Can I fuck you in the doorway?" Dwight stood up and put his hands on the frame where the saloon doors were, testing it.

"No."

"Can I fuck you in the chair?" And then, before I could decline, "Can I fuck you on the couch?"

"Not much rhymes with couch," I said angrily.

"Pouch?" he said, stroking his chin thoughtfully. "Cock pouch?"

"I think you mean *codpiece*. Such a jerk."

Dwight had said that one of the things he thought was *special about me* was my knowledge of history—specifically, armour. For some reason it had been an interest of mine when I was about nine or ten: what soldiers had worn to battle throughout history. And, equally inexplicably, it appeared to have come up more than once in conversation with him. This was when he taught me how to make the butterflies, the tool I used with Mizuko when she decided I had the zeitgeist. He'd learnt about it from someone he'd worked with, essentially a Venn diagram on its side, angled to evoke wings. "We can apply this tool to you," he said, "to help you work out what you want to do with your life. In one circle you put all the problems going on in the world, in the other what's unique about you. In the middle you work out what your purpose here is."

Sound knowledge of antique armour had gone into the circle of things that were special about me when I couldn't think of any and was maybe being a bit difficult, given that Dwight was trying to help. We had not yet managed to write anything in the middle circle, the body where the two wings overlapped, but he said that it might take a few days or even months to hit on.

Ignoring my refusals, Dwight now took my hand and dragged me towards Rex's bathroom. I put my free arm out and grabbed hold of the doorway. I didn't want to set foot in it.

"Fuck off," I said. "Seriously. Fuck. Off."

I dropped to the ground and stayed there after he disappeared into another room, reliving the moment of finding Silvia all crumpled and moaning. The stain on the bathmat was becoming a more saturated yellow. The smell of dying flowers seemed to be getting stronger. I looked at the bath and the white plastic handles, imagining how it might feel to be old. Then I remembered that I had left the roses I'd bought for Silvia at the feet of the nurse in the ICU.

That night I dreamt about the roses laid at the wrong feet— the feet of the nurse. Each bit of the dream was like a hyperlink. I pressed on one, wanting answers, and it took me to another. I could never get to the meaning at the bottom of any of the bits. When I reached for the petals of the roses, I was touching a metal seatbelt buckle in a coach, driving by night through a remote place, with a band of mist running parallel to the glass I leant against. Luminous service stations appeared, slowly and then abruptly through the gauze of mist, and slid away again. When I put my hand on the glass of the window it landed on the stone exterior of a university and we went to the top of it, where there was a small garden on the roof. Much later, when I recounted the dream to Mizuko, reading her the notes I had written in my journal, she said it had features of Tokyo University, that my tree sounded like the special gingko there, that one building I described sounded like the kendo building by the football pitch, and that the tunnels under the rooms were like the subway under the engineering department.

"Yes," I said, "I was probably dreaming about that."

Back in the dream, on the roof, we had to choose from a selection of flowers again. I took the roses again, intending to give these to Silvia to make up for the mislaid ones, and when I cut the stems, suddenly I was in a corporate breakout area with Dwight and Walter. "The kind of love we're dealing with," Walter said, as if playing back something that had already been discussed before I arrived, "is beyond words." "That is correct," someone I instinctively knew from his tone to be the CEO said.

"That is why you cannot like us on Facebook. We will not be joining Facebook until you can *love* us on Facebook."

People around me who had been on the coach and the roof but were now with me in the breakout area got up one by one and stuck pink and yellow Post-it notes like petals to a flip chart where notes were being gathered. Dwight read them out. They were written in Silvia's shaky red ink, which she used for warnings:

> *Roses are like kamikaze love pilots.*
> *Roses are like suicide love bombers.*

The CEO decided that he did not like so many mixed metaphors, and so the meeting broke down. As we left the room I ran over to tell him what my Post-it had said, feeling sure it would change his mind: "Love is like those hot towels you're given at some restaurants and then give back when they are cold." He looked at me with disdain. "How would you know?"

I woke up to a noise that I slowly realised was Dwight laughing beside me.

"What are you laughing at?" I said angrily. He laughed so easily he could have done it while unconscious, but I could tell he was awake, looking at something on his phone, from the ghoulish glow, the halo of hair lit up on his shoulders. It was four in the morning. He turned to face me.

"I'm watching this diver high-five a shark. Look."

I sent Dwight away early, about eight, after he attempted to eat some ancient cereal Silvia kept that he found two weevils in. Then I returned to the hospital, to be told that Silvia was in "a state of moderate distress." When she had heard them discuss putting her into a facility, she had assumed they were talking about somewhere like Castle Senior Living and had said absolutely not. I looked up where they meant on Amsterdam Avenue and showed her the pictures on my device. She began pleading with the hospital chaplain, who was making his round.

"You're sending me up *there*?"

"Just for a short while, as I understand it—a matter of months. Then you can go home if we get you some appropriate live-in help."

"But I've got *her*"—she cocked her head in my direction. "She's my Girl Friday. Besides, I've spent my life avoiding anything above . . ." She faltered. "I've avoided going up there for twenty years." She looked to me for help. "Too many ghosts."

13

I still have the list I made as I was packing up her things.

2 dresses (yellow and blue)
1 white jacket
6 underpants
3 vests
4 pairs pyjamas
Valise
Eye drops
Water
Pillow
Pills
Applesauce
Books
Cane
Vodka
T brush/T paste
Trays and liquid soak
Gloves

Wipes
Q-tips
Vitamins

I knew she wouldn't wear anything but pink pyjamas; still, I wanted her to feel she had options. They confiscated pretty much everything but the clothes, saying that such things brought in from outside were not allowed for legal reasons. The first time I visited her in her new home, I took gerberas. Her mouth was so dry she couldn't speak at all, so I only learnt her verdict on them once I had helped her ease the dryness with some contraband vodka, utilised a new tongue scraper she had been given, and turned up the humidifier in her room.

"They're roadside flowers," she said, spit quivering on her lip, "for roadkill."

The second time I took a mixed bouquet that reminded her of crematoriums. During every visit, the conversation again came close to asking me to help end her life.

"They keep trying to make me wear a thing"—she rattled her bony wrist, then let it fall back onto her stomach—"so they can track me. They want to chip me like a dog between my shoulders. They want to know how long it takes me to crap and how often I go so they can tell whether I'm crapping or snuffing it." A shadow passed over her face. "I just want to be invisible."

Dwight had gone to California for work. My new routine, now that he was gone and Silvia had moved to the home on Amsterdam Avenue, was crossing the park to visit her. I would exit where the carriages lined up at the West 77th Street Arch, the rickshaw riders climbing down and unfurling prayer rugs as I passed, the asphalt roar of skateboarders in my ears. There was something surreal, acutely fairy-tale about it—a replica wilderness in the middle of the neat chessboard, me crossing to reach the sick grandmother who was now on the other side of it. There were also costumed children at picnic parties romping under trees and canopies decked with tissue pompoms and candy-coloured bunting, which added to the effect. I lingered like a balloon from parties past, low on the ground, observing the kids filling up water bombs under the park taps. I would time my visits so that after I left I could walk further up to hear the Riverside Church bells chiming seven in the warm, wide evenings, right by where Mark, Susy, and I had lived. The sky was always full of birdsong and evening smells, piano music from a window, the stone buildings glowing against the blue, like cream poured over something tart and hot.

It was nearing the end of June. My three-month visa was drying up fast, which I kept pushing to the back of my mind, and I found myself looking at everything with a new kind of longing. I thought that if I was ever able to live in New York, Morningside Heights was the neighbourhood I'd want to be in.

During this period, which was about two weeks, *what comes up must come down* came to mean that if I went to visit Silvia, which was up, I at some point had to leave and come back down. It was a long, long way, and I refused to take the subway. I insisted on walking as a kind of pilgrimage. Dwight lent me his bicycle, which he was always falling off, but I didn't dare use — it was expensive, too big for me, and had no gears. I was too afraid to ride it and too attached to my walking, but pretended in my messages to him that I did ride it and was grateful for the loan.

On one of my visits I arrived to see two microscooters outside Silvia's room, parked in the hallway alongside various mobility aids. For a moment I wondered if something had happened to Silvia and whether there was a new occupant in her room. I knocked on the door rather than going straight in.

"Enter!" Not Silvia's voice.

Nat was there, with Ingrid and two small children, who were sitting in the corner sharing one device.

"Alice!" Nat said. "Just talking about you."

The children were Ingrid's, Thom and Rosa. Twins. I didn't realise *Thom* was spelt that way until later, because his father insisted upon the *h* so distinctly that he almost pronounced it when saying his son's name, so that I too started breathing the *h* heavily when I said it in his father's presence, as if I had to clear my throat. Out of the two, only Thom seemed interested in meeting me. He stood up to shake my hand and then returned to the corner and his sister and their game.

"Since you're here, let me fill you in on the plan."

Nat had become hysterical about how far the home was from Silvia's apartment on the Upper East Side and said it was "nonsensical" for me to be going back and forth all the time. She kept mentioning a gang of young boys who had been convicted of raping a woman in the park, and Ingrid had to keep reminding her that that had been two decades earlier and in any case they had been acquitted.

"She'll get raped," Nat promised. "I'd have you at mine, but Ingrid's so much closer."

Ingrid, standing right next to her mother at this point, exhaled audibly and nodded with her eyebrows raised very high.

"What's *raped*?" Rosa looked up from the corner as if something were being given out that she might want.

"It's what happens to girls who walk through Central Park on their own at night," Nat explained, as if this were just the system the park authorities had. Same as trash collection.

Rosa returned to the game.

Nat determined that the sensible thing was for me to move in with Ingrid while Silvia was in the home. Ingrid and Silvia did not appear to feel the plan had been finalised. I messaged Dwight from the corner of the room as the women argued about it.

She seems to think I'm some kind of delinquent, I typed.

Did you push back? This was a phrase I heard Dwight use constantly and understood to mean *resist*, but which still snagged somewhere in my brain. I had spent my whole life being malleable and solicitous to people. Pushing, pulling, or any type of force, did not come naturally.

Not really.

"We live right over there, Alice," Ingrid said at last with resignation. "It would be good if you were close to Silvia, we think."

She's hot, Dwight messaged back. *Walter definitely wants to bang her.* He meant Ingrid.

It happened that Ingrid's nanny had been fired the previous day for cursing at Rosa. It was an inconvenient time, as the summer vacation had begun. Ingrid often worked from home, but the kids were driving her crazy. She would love to have me stay if I wanted, just to watch them occasionally. The offer, put like that rather than as Nat had phrased it, made me feel mature. It also suggested that I might still have moments when I could be solitary without getting raped. I had seen adults walking alone while their charges scattered birds, miles ahead on their scooters. Their faces seemed full of wisdom. But it is difficult to tell whether something is an opportunity or a trap when you are put on the spot. I felt the six eyes of Silvia, Ingrid, and Nat boring into me as I accepted. Nat looked at me with an indecipherable expression, somewhere between fascination and annoyance but fixed, as if watching a fly that had lost its way out of the room.

Nat turned to Silvia, lying in state.

"In other news, I've found you a doula, sweetie," Nat said.

"You want to do what?"

"It's a bit like a midwife, but for someone who is dying."

"Mom. Please."

"I want you to meet her. Frank recommended her to me after Lisa died. Most people don't know how to deal with dying people. They just go on about everything else except the main thing."

"Mom. Not the time."

"Exactly. *Exactly* my point. There you go."

"Can you maybe come outside for just a minute, please."

Ingrid and Nat disappeared.

"It'll be good for you," Silvia said when the door was shut, "if you're sure you don't want to go home to Susy. Don't be polite —just say no if you'd rather not, or if you want to go back home to England. I'll be fine."

She seemed to have forgotten that time was almost up on my visa. I said I was sure.

"I know it's a pain to relocate. But it'll be much better for you to stay with other people, I suppose. They'll be a good surrogate family. Much better than being alone without the choice of company, anyway. Hopefully it won't be for long. I'm sorry I've been such a disastrous host."

It shouldn't have felt that way, but I could only think of it as yet another rejection.

When Ingrid told me their address, I thought I'd misheard. They had recently moved to Claremont Avenue, where Mark and Susy had lived, right next to the music school, at the top of a building that overlooked Sakura Park, which is where Mark had made friends with the statue. I was expected the following afternoon. Dwight, who'd got back from California a few hours before, went with me. I'd bought gifts for my hosts this time. Wine that Dwight had chosen with an app that did something if you took a picture of the label. I realised I no longer knew what children played with, or maybe I had never known. In the end I bought two turtle erasers, one pink and one green, from a gift shop on Lexington. The shop assistant insisted on taping them inside plastic for me before she could hand them over. She said they were a choking hazard, even though they were sold loose so could be choked on before they reached the checkout, or the minute they were taken out of the store. I assured her I had no plans to put the turtles in my mouth. Her insistence made me angry, and I told her the rule was illogical. Since losing my temper with the nurse, I had found that I was getting angry more and more of the time.

"You're angry at the system. It's just to do with being in the city," Dwight assured me. "It means you're going native."

"What does that mean?"

"Developing a healthy distaste for authority."

I rolled my eyes at him, but a part of me was thrilled to hear it.

By the time we reached the northern end of Morningside Heights and found the right door, I was sweating. I had only a very small bag of clothes and my journal. (Everything in my small bag must still be there, or I suppose Ingrid will have chucked it. She kept their home spotless. She said she was so anal about it because Robin was OCD about germs, but really she was by nature a total control freak.)

"It's the penthouse," Dwight said, squinting into the midday sun.

The street had that sad summertime feeling that you want to push on to see why it hurts. Behind us, men were sitting on top of the buttressed wall. There were radios playing, soft Spanish lilts and the slush sounds of melting cool boxes. In front of us, the Rooiakkers' building was pale and slim-bricked. Six floors, with a fire escape snaking across the façade. The glass doorway was surrounded by dark green marble, with dark roses on the right side. I peered into a ground-floor window with drawn, discoloured blinds. I checked the building number, in stick-on gold squares with slanting black numbers. I hesitated on the step.

"Trust me," Dwight said, "this is it."

The hallway was walled with last names. I found Rooiakker.

There was no doorman, but the elevator went right up into their apartment if you punched in a code that Ingrid gave us over the intercom. Dwight and I stood in silence inside the elevator, which was slow and rumbly. Gradually we heard the sound of shrieking from above.

"Those are the twins," Dwight said. It annoyed me that he was acting like a tour guide, as if this were his *thang* and not mine.

"I know, I met them before."

The doors opened onto a jumble of shoes and coats, a fleet of scooters, swimming goggles on pegs, and miniature backpacks. Ingrid later asked me not to post any pictures of the children or the inside of their home on the Internet and to delete the ones I had already posted, but you can see all their interiors in magazine articles that have been published online anyway.

Their dog was a miniature thing, a black shih-tzu with hair hanging like a banana peel over its face. It jumped with all its paws at once, lifting itself off the ground and sliding backwards on its needle claws as it tried to get at us.

"JJ, no!" Thom came skidding around the corner. "This is JJ," he said, picking it up and holding the scrabbling paws to his bare chest, then holding it out towards us. "He's very friendly if you like dogs."

"She doesn't," Dwight said before I could lie.

"I like JJ," I protested.

"His real name isn't actually JJ," Thom said.

"No?" Dwight was doing that annoying voice adults use to play along with kids.

"Nope."

"What's his real name? How come you changed it?" I asked.

"It was a mouthful."

I jumped. The voice was not Thom's and came from behind me.

"Robin!" Dwight said, slapping him on the shoulder.

Robin did not slap back, but stood with his hands deep in his pockets. He wore unseasonal heavy denim, boots, and a black cotton T-shirt, tucked in and belted. His shape had a kind of boyishness made bulky, thickening towards the ground, like Play-Doh slowly drooping, giving some features a pinched, pointy look and others a more settled thickness. His hair, Dwight had told me, was dyed. You could tell because it was jet-black, whereas he had little tufts of silver hair which fought their way out of his nostrils and earlobes and laced the eyebrows above his ratlike eyes.

"JJ used to be Janus," he continued. Something about him was familiar. As he spoke, the feeling was intensified by an elaborately English accent. I couldn't tell whether it was an affectation. "I thought Janus was appropriate." I realised he was pronouncing it the Latin way, with a soft *J*. I understood now, from his voice, why Nat thought he was condescending, but it reminded me of certain professors at university, and it instantly made me want to impress him. "Since one can't always distinguish his face from his anus. So you don't know whether he's coming or going."

Dwight laughed way too much, given that I knew he didn't know who Janus was. I wanted to show somehow that I did. That I got the real joke—I wasn't simply laughing at the word *anus,* I knew the names of Roman gods.

"No, the real answer," Robin said when Dwight had calmed

down, "is that we saw a picture of JJ advertised on a noticeboard round here—a classics professor was leaving the city for some reason and couldn't take the dog with him. He wanted to give him to a good home. But the kids wanted to give him a new name, so we called him JJ as a compromise, so he'd still know who he was and answer to it."

Dwight bent down to *interact* with JJ. "Hey, poochy," he said, once, then forty or fifty times more. "Hey, poochy, hey, poochy, I know who you are—yes I do, yes I do, yes I do. I know you gotta poop and pee every three hours." He switched back and forth between dog register and human register. "I love him!" he said to Robin, then back to JJ: "You wanna play?" Again he repeated the words forty or fifty times very fast. "You wanna play you wanna play you wanna play?" Then he started to get mixed up between human and dog voice. "They're manageable?" he asked, but Robin had moved off towards the kitchen. "Hey hey hey hey," Dwight said to JJ, "oh, he's smooth, he's smooth."

I followed Robin into a large space lit by four windows overlooking Sakura Park, the tall trees beyond that, which, now in full leaf, concealed the river, and an enormous skylight.

"Wow," I said.

"Told you," Dwight said, bounding up behind us. He'd come, he kept reminding Robin, to the Rooiakkers' for a drinks party with Walter when RQ + Partners first won the contract to design the incubator.

I noticed Rosa sitting across the room. She was barely credible as Thom's twin; she looked a lot older. She was sitting on the sofa holding an iPad with an expression of intense concentration and did not look up as we entered. She was wearing a T-shirt that bore a rhinestone skull.

"Ro-sa!" Thom called to her as if she were in another room, though all three of us stood before her. "They're here."

Rosa put on a pair of red headphones without looking at us, folded the iPad support so that it sat upright, and sank behind it.

"Poured concrete," Dwight said, circling the toe of his boot appreciatively on the floor.

"Say what you see," Rosa muttered.

Evidently she could hear us and the headphones were a prop.

On one side of the space were four large plan chests, black ones with very shallow drawers, which were stacked and doubled as a long desk as a long wooden board had been placed over them. This, like an altar, had two Mac desktops placed back to back in mirror image of each other. On the other side, with the same clean lines, was a kitchen with a marble island that mirrored the desk. In between, where we stood, was a long, narrow table made of one piece of wood. There was sheepskin, I suddenly noticed, everywhere. It was thrown over chairs, nestling in their laps like pubic hair, or flat on the smooth floor like patches of mould. Framed black-and-white photographs of Ingrid with a bulging alien pregnancy bump seemed to be everywhere I looked.

"Robin took those," Dwight whispered.

Rosa emerged above her device. "You're *adopted*, right?"

"Yes."

"Is that why you're so tan?"

"I guess."

"Hi, Dwight. Alice. Welcome."

Ingrid, as I'd noted on the tour of Roosevelt Island, had the proprietorial gait of a hotel manager. Now barefoot, with enameled toes, she moved over to Rosa and yanked the headphones from the tiny blond head. Rosa looked exactly like her but in every way more terrifying, because Ingrid's expressions did not look right on a child. She was bone-thin, her skin even paler than her mother's, and commanding despite her diminutive size.

"Como estas hola," she said without inflection.

"Hola, cómo estás?" Robin said.

In the time I stayed there, I came to notice that Robin had things he had to do, as I once had, which no one else seemed to understand. For example, he removed all labels from food items, and he tore down cardboard packaging to the level to which its contents had been consumed. "It's his system," Ingrid explained wearily. He fanned magazines on coffee tables at exact intervals. He respected rules, it seemed, as much as I once had, before I went *native*. When Ingrid misused a word in a sentence he would call her out on it, no matter who was there to hear, and ask her to define it, which reminded me of how I'd behaved with Dwight.

Robin showed me around the only private bits of the open-plan apartment, which Dwight continued to call *the penthouse*. I had never been anywhere like it before. Every towel I have ever felt since feels rough compared to the Rooiakker towels. The silky softness of everything left me feeling light-headed, as if I had stood up too quickly. I asked to use the bathroom and sat, recovering, on the edge of a marble bath on a dais—the kind Greek husbands are slain in. There was only one thing I stole. From the bathroom. A decadent scented candle, white-wicked, from the back of one of the mirrored cabinets. It was in a heavy gold container bearing the word ORIENTALIST. I gave it to Mizuko.

When I admired a series of photographs leaning against a wall, Robin halted the tour. "Why do we have those pictures still, Ingrid?" he called. "I thought we agreed."

No reply.

"They're completely impersonal. I've never been to that bar —is it in Havana?" He waited. Ingrid sounded as if she were on the phone. "It makes our home look like a hotel chain."

My room was next to the twins', a kind of playroom equipped with a softball, a keyboard, paintings, potato prints, and an empty guinea pig cage. The poster above my bed said, "From Constructivism to Kinetic Art," an exhibition from two decades ago.

I pointed to a green plastic bowl full of water. "What's that?"

"We're growing a starfish," Thom said.

"You'll probably have lots of company in here, I'm afraid," Robin said.

The twins were supposed to have their own rooms. Ingrid had read a lot of books about raising twins. This was originally Thom's, but Thom insisted on sleeping with Rosa, so now his room was just for play. It had two single beds end-to-end along one wall, so that whenever I lay on one I felt shrunken inside a normal-length bed. Each had an extra bed that pulled out from inside the base for when the twins had school friends to stay. There were little chairs they had outgrown, which now had animal toys sitting in them.

"I don't *want* her sleeping in here!"

Robin held his hand up to say, *Enough*.

Rosa glared at me.

"This isn't even your room, Rosa," Thom pointed out.

Rosa sat on the bed and folded her arms.

A photo of their class was taped to the wall. I pointed to it and said in a friendly way, "Is that your class, Rosa?"

"Yes," she said, her voice sly. "There are only two black children out of fourteen." She indicated the two children. "One is from Africa and the other was adopted, like you."

Robin exited the room.

The adopted kid with the Afro was doing double thumbs up with an exaggerated smile. Two girl children stood back to back, posing with their hands like guns in the centre. Only when I saw Thom's face in the photo could I detect that he and Rosa were related. In person, he was so much gentler that he looked completely different.

Dinner to welcome "the guest," as Robin referred to me, was Japanese takeaway. I was nervous, almost as much as I later was the first time I met Mizuko, self-conscious about how the fleshy salmon kept slipping from my sticks. I took too much horse-radish and it stung my nostrils. Dwight stayed, and Nat came over too. Dwight was insufferably entertaining. He pulled out his own bottle of wine from somewhere, and so the bottle of wine I had arrived with was put in a white, handleless cupboard in the kitchen and to my knowledge never drunk.

When we came to discussing Silvia, I realised I had perhaps had too much to drink.

"I'm surprised she still has the will to live," Ingrid said, and I became teary, and Robin made a strange laugh—not at me, I realised, but at his wife. I felt guilty for allowing myself to sit at their long table while Silvia was in the Amsterdam home all alone.

Robin turned to me. "I was sorry to hear about your grand-mother. It's very, very lucky you were there. I'm sure she wouldn't be alive without you. I bet she's glad you came."

"I'm still digging for a Dutch ancestor," Nat said, to no one in particular.

Ingrid rolled her eyes at the other end of the table. They seemed to despise each other, with a kind of loyalty.

"I've been helping the twins with a school project—"

Ingrid cut in. "That was last fall. The project ended a while ago."

"Okay, so now I have started my own project."

"How are you looking?" Dwight asked, dabbing at his mouth with a napkin.

"Oh, you know, I have some scraps, some things my parents left me. Not much." She shot a look at her daughter, who made a face as if to say this was quite the understatement. "And Alice

helped me set up an account on one of those genealogy websites."

I nodded, sensing that this was the wrong thing to have done
in Ingrid's eyes.

"But nothing turned up. Did it, Alice?"

"Nope."

"Oh. Okay," Dwight said. He was getting that look he got
when he spotted an opportunity. "Family-tree stuff is low tech,
but it's the original tool of connection, a very human tool. Two
parents merge in the creation of a child, and on and on in an
endless chain, and we can map it with—"

"Obviously," I interrupted. "*Obviously* a family tree does
that. You're using all these *words* and you're not saying *anything.*"

Dwight's face suggested that I had gone too native. He continued, undeterred by my outburst, telling us about various companies he had met with in California the previous week. One was
some kind of ancestry project, a "stable storage medium" which
ran like a social network, could run itself for ten thousand years
and record an entire family lineage. Nat craned across Rosa to
hear everything he was saying, which took ages because she kept
interrupting him to ask what certain terms meant. He also described a company that took DNA samples. It was mainly, he
said, to do with health and finding out about any latent genetic
diseases you had, but a popular product they offered was finding
out which other users of the service you might be related to. He
was trying to convince them to market it that way, anyway.

"The tubes," he explained, "are sent to users in their homes,
then sent back to Silicon Valley containing each user's spit. Their
secret history encoded in twenty-three pairs of chromosomes—
hair, eyes, skin, tastes they like and dislike, and then—"

"Could we get one of them? The spitting things?" Nat asked.

Dwight made the same face he made when he came particularly hard: an expression like the stoned *Scream* mask. "Of course. I'll hook you up, no problem."

I shot him a look: *Back off.*

"Or Alice can. I'll send Alice a link to order them."

He took out his phone to send it to me. The table went quiet. Ingrid looked dubious. She was massaging her hair. She examined her nails.

"They're raw diamond and gold—stacking rings," she said when she spotted me admiring them. They made her wedding band invisible. I turned to Robin, who looked at his mother-in-law. Nat was gazing raptly at Dwight. Between them, Rosa sat stroking her loom-banded arm, a spoon protruding from her mouth. She was eating a chia-seed dessert, very slowly. She made a sucking noise on the spoon, then removed it.

"Can I spit too?"

"Of course, honey," Nat said.

"I don't think so," Robin interrupted. "Don't these things cost five hundred dollars and you find out all sorts about how you're going to get diabetes and when you're going to die?"

"I'll pay for it," Nat said, dismissing him with a wave of her hand. "I'll pay for the whole family to do it."

Ingrid looked unconvinced. Sensing this, Dwight added, "Walter's worked with them on something before—he says they're a really interesting company. All former Google. It's just a different kind of search."

"A body search," Robin said, folding his arms.

Ingrid shrugged politely. "I guess there's no harm."

Nat beamed.

Though I was now living only a stone's throw away from Silvia, my visits to her dwindled. My routines were replaced with the

Rooiakkers' routines, primarily the twins': their snacks and their small friends. Thom's toothless friend Anatole, his only friend that wasn't his sister, and Rosa's sardonic first best friend, Brontë, who always had her fingers in a paper fortune-teller. Brontë made one for me: four dots coloured blue, red, purple, green; numbers 1 through 8; then eight locations (subway, log cabin, fairground, coffee shop, art gallery, Japanese restaurant, Barneys, a truck). When they played the game on me, I got Japanese restaurant.

"What does that mean?" I asked, worried. I'd never played this as a child.

"That you'll meet your boyfriend in a Japanese restaurant!" Rosa cried, shrieking with laughter.

"I've already got a boyfriend," I said defensively. It felt like I was being bullied.

The girls became hysterical.

When Ingrid wasn't on site, at Walter's office, or at various council meetings around the city, she worked from home. Her routine involved yoga in the apartment—a special kind influenced by Tantra that involved chanting—which Rosa and I were allowed to join in with, strange food rituals, and brushing with a natural-bristle body brush at certain times. I went shopping for her with lists she gave me. These read like spells. She made her own almond milk, soaking the almonds overnight, then, together with the twins, pinching the skins off one by one, grinding, liquidating, then straining using organic, unbleached cheesecloth. Her bathroom had an array of brown pill bottles, which would sometimes fill me with guilt about Silvia. But whenever I felt guilt about abandoning her and my old routine, I would tell myself that it was really Silvia's fault for not owning a cell phone. That would be a normal way to keep in touch and, as Ingrid put it, *diarise*. In the first two weeks that I stayed at the Rooiakers', I visited her only a handful of times.

Ingrid had chosen the twins' school—a Steiner school across the park—because it tried to limit pupils' usage of technology and balance it out with plenty of pinecones, shells, rocks, and woodworking. I inwardly noted the contradiction between Ingrid's obsession with organic things and natural childhood and how much time she spent on her device. She was a very active Pinterest and Instagram user and had a huge following on both. She had two phones, one iPad, and two laptops. All these little machines, I later thought, when Mizuko read to me from the dreaded book, melting the icecaps. I remembered reading about the butterfly effect, the flap of the wing that travelled through the earth, then the water, then the air. Ingrid could have diarised and architected an earthquake-tsunami-nuclear disaster, no problem. She could have done it with the touch of a button. Robin, on the other hand, seemed disengaged whenever I asked him about the project for Cornell Tech.

"Ingrid's the one spearheading that," he said. "I'm a bit of a Luddite really. I just need a phone to work. She and Walter know way more about that stuff than I do. She hasn't forgotten that I once called that thing she does, with the pins, Pinteresque."

"Like the playwright," I said quickly.

I decided that I liked the way he spoke. The professorial cadences. He asked me lots of questions about studying philosophy and physics, and I was flattered by his interest. I regretted not bringing my difficult books with me from Silvia's (books I still had not touched), as I wanted to impress him by leaving them around the house. When he gave someone his attention, I could see how Ingrid would have fallen for him.

Other than his rivalry with Walter, his borderline OCD hygiene tendencies, and a vague sense of entitlement, he was the enigmatic figure within my new family. At least at first, I could not guess much about his feelings towards me or my presence

in his house. When I Googled him the first time, the search un-
earthed surprisingly little compared to when I did the same for
Ingrid. She was everywhere. Answering questions about work-
life balance and how she raised her children as much as architec-
tural projects. Then it occurred to me that Rooiakker was not his
name. I couldn't remember his real last name, and didn't want to
ask. But then it came to me when I was in the middle of doing
something else. In fact, as I was lying in my long bed making a
collage of what Dwight and I had been up to recently. I typed in
Robin Quinn. When I did so, I felt certain that Nat had not done
her due diligence, or was secretly as digitally illiterate as Silvia.

Robin Quinn had studied at an architecture school in London and, after a few years in a large practice, returned to be a
professor there. But he left England for New York in 2004, after
a third-year student alleged that, following months of inappropriate comments, he'd tried to force himself on her in a car park
after a university function. He was seen leading her semicon-
scious body away from the coat check and outside—he claimed
to call her a cab. The police had found a number of online dating
profiles and a lot of photographs on his computer of women,
mainly bound and gagged, but the harassment case had been
dropped. In its wake, however, a number of other misconduct
allegations were made against him by other women at the university, Robin had been advised to leave rather than dismissed,
and Cooper had welcomed him to New York a year later.

After this, I viewed Ingrid and Robin's marriage with greater
interest. It was impossible she did not know. Whether or not
she believed in his innocence, she had both exonerated him and
proven him guilty by allowing herself, his student, to become
his wife. And yet it did not seem that that transition had fully
occurred. Ingrid appeared to seek out her husband's attention
very little, or, as I watched them more closely, in strange ways. I

got the impression that she was trying to rouse jealousy in him by the way she acted with Walter, and that it wasn't really Walter that she liked best at all. Evidently whatever student-teacher dynamic they'd had was deeply ingrained, as they continued to behave as if their relationship were clandestine.

Walter spent a lot of time dropping by their apartment, which was also an office. When he was there, Robin usually found excuses to go out, like walking JJ. The first time he invited me was the first time I knew for sure that he was not averse to my presence.

"Why don't you come, Alice? We deserve respite from the Yanks."

We would talk about the British school system, science, or Spinoza whilst dangling little bags of JJ's warm shit.

On one occasion, having asked me many questions about my time at university, my thesis, and my desire to please a female professor who had taken a particular interest in me (the same who had advised me to go wild after my exams and unintentionally reduced me to tears), Robin decided to raise the subject. He'd stopped walking and rested his hand on his forehead for a moment, his expression pained.

"It's so hard," he said, "to tread that line between interest and intimacy with a student."

I didn't say anything and he didn't look at me.

"It cost me my job—did you know that?"

I shook my head. How did adults of a certain age not understand how the Internet worked? How foolishly they assumed anonymity. JJ sat patiently on the sidewalk, looking philosophically into the distance.

"You have all these beautiful women coming and going from your office, and some of them are so unbelievably smart and passionate, and you spend a lot of time investing in them. All you want is for them to do well, to help them make contacts after their studies are over, get them into the good firms."

He paused. He seemed to be gauging my reaction so far. I remained silent, and he started walking again.

"A female student made a complaint against me. Two women, actually. They said I made offensive comments and touched them inappropriately. I think that means the shoulder or something. I'm a tactile person. Or I used to be. I used to talk about my feelings openly with my students, and ask them about theirs. Now I have to be so, so careful. It's even worse in America."

My face must have given me away.

"Yes, Ingrid was my student, but we became a couple only after she left Cooper. I always honoured the student-professor boundary with her. But we talked about setting up a practice. Or I talked about doing it and her joining me. When you spend all day with someone, and in the faculty it's often all night too, you forget age differences and those kind of boundaries. You're just two people with a shared interest and a connection."

I shook my head sympathetically; I'd felt the same about my tutor.

We returned with a bag of shit because JJ waited until he was right outside his own front door.

As soon as Ingrid heard the elevator doors open, she called out, "Oh, you're back? I was about to send out the search party." She stared hard at me. "Walter and I have decided we are going on vacation."

I scuttled guiltily past her with the plastic bag to the bin.

"Walter has a house in the Hamptons," she informed Robin as Walter stood by her, nodding that it was all true. "It would be good for the kids to get out of the city and for us to put our feet in the ocean, right?"

"That's all very well, but we can't leave Alice," Robin said.

There was a tense silence.

"Well, she can come," Walter said at last, "and Dwight too, of course." Ingrid walked away and into her bedroom without a word. "Everyone's welcome," Walter insisted. "You guys are family."

"Oh you little devil," Thom murmured from the floor. "That's how they teach us to spell *would* and *could* at school."

"What are you writing, Thom?"

"A story."

"What about?"

"About you coming to stay."

14

Dwight and I sent the Rooiakkers' spit tubes on June 23. For most people, it takes a couple of months after sending away their spit tubes before they get back a list of likely relatives and/or genetic diseases. For Nat, it was only one. Likely this was due to Dwight's suggestion of dropping his name into the part of the form which asked "How did you hear about us?" Because I'd been the one to oblige her by setting up the account, using my email, I got the alert in the car with Dwight on the way to the Hamptons.

They hadn't yet got the results for potential diseases, but they had found a DNA match. I decided not to tell Dwight yet; I hated the way he competed with me to ingratiate himself with the Rooiakkers, and read the contents of the email in silence. The match was for Robin and the twins but not Nat or Ingrid. Just as I was reading, I got a text from Ingrid asking how we were doing and saying that Nat had been reading the company's website and now also really wanted to know if she had the empathy gene—was it too late to ask the spit people? I didn't reply. The email alert had an option to "notify matches," which I decided not to press.

Instead I looked up the match myself. She had written quite

a detailed biography. Then, not satisfied, I looked her up on Google.

MIZUKO HIMURA

Whereas at first it seemed like Robin and Ingrid's home had opened up to me randomly, like a pop bumper or paddle in a pinball machine, after I discovered the match with Mizuko, this chain of events began to feel fated. I leant back in the passenger seat as the car sped along, ignoring the view. It seemed that I was meant to find her. A mysterious power had drawn her towards me, coincidence by seeming coincidence. That feeling deepened as I did more research over the course of the holiday, until it felt like I had found myself, or the self that I would like to be, as Silvia had assured me I would. Though I did not know her exact address, that she appeared to live almost within breathing distance of Robin, and that I lived with him, and that her pictures showed that she was now dating the mysterious Rupert Hunter, our despotic mothers, our absent fathers, the borders we had both crossed, all our many parallels and connections at every point, could not be chance. I saw it as evidence of the hidden connections between things, an all-powerful algorithm that sifted through chaos, singling out soulmates.

"What are you doing?"

Dwight leaned towards me and I turned my phone over.

"Looking at Columbia masters?"

"Yeah."

"For you, or . . . ?"

"Yeah, maybe."

Once he'd turned his eyes back to the road, I deleted my search history.

• • •

Silvia claimed that Long Island was actually a peninsula, not an island. Dwight drove me out of the city along the Long Island Expressway, the LIE. In Queens the traffic was solid. From where we were, we could see the Queens Giant, a tulip tree that was supposed to be the oldest living thing in New York.

"Look it up," Dwight said, pointing.

"'Its estimated age,'" I read aloud from my phone, "'is four hundred years or more. It was most likely an established young tree when the Dutch East India Company sent a group of Walloon families to Manhattan in 1624. This tree is perhaps the last witness to the entire span of the city's history from a tiny Dutch settlement to—'"

Dwight interrupted. "How tall is it?"

"'—one of the greatest metropolises of the world. It grows on fertile, well-watered land,'" I continued, "'part of a glacier-formed moraine created by the Minnesota Ice Sheet when it reached its southern terminus some fifteen thousand years ago.'" I made my voice stern. "'Treat this oldest sylvan citizen of our city with the respect that it deserves. It has survived miraculously from a time when native Matinecock people trod softly beneath it to an age when automobiles roar by, oblivious to its presence. If we leave it undisturbed, it may live for another hundred years or so.'"

"Cool," Dwight said. "I'm going to put the top down."

I had never driven in a roofless car before. The sun was hot while we were stationary, but when we started moving at speed again, the wind became angry in my hair, buffeting me so that I had to close my eyes and smile, even though I did not feel like smiling. I let it batter me, pummel my ears. The wind roared so loudly we couldn't talk above it, and we couldn't hear Dwight's *road-trip playlist.* After ten minutes he put the top up again. There was a strange, civilising quiet as the car sealed shut.

I was in charge of keeping an eye on the GPS. I was finding it impossible to concentrate on giving directions, so I turned the voice on and magnified where we were headed. I liked the names of the roads. Egypt Lane. Further Lane. Abrahams Path. Promised Land Road. Red Dirt Road. Crooked Hill Road. We stopped for lunch at an Applebee's. When we got back into the car, I began again:

MIZUK

MIZUKO

MIZUKO KUYO

MIZUKO ITO

MIZUKO MEANING

MIZUKO HIMURA

I guess I'd been hoping to establish that there had been some kind of error, some spilt spit or tangle of bodily secretions, twenty-three chromosomes that had been improperly filed, that I would put right through this research, but the more I read, the worse I felt.

"What's wrong?" Dwight asked, turning to me again. "Have I done something wrong?"

"I don't know." I wanted him to feel anxious too, but not to tell him what I'd found. Besides, I did feel like this was his fault. I looked up news articles which mentioned the company. This sort of surprise connection had been uncovered before and ended in divorce.

Walter messaged Dwight, which I read aloud for him, noting before I did so the number of messages he had from Hatta and Hae, the identical twins he was in a prodigious WhatsApp group with. Walter's message told us to look out for the *swingers' mail-*

box. Number 69. With a crazy-paving drive. His implicitly more
tasteful house was two further along from that. The crunch of
the gravel drive churned my stomach. I had not decided what
to do with the unwanted information. I did not want to take it
over the threshold and into the house with me. We climbed out
and stretched. I lifted up my arms and flexed them, right into the
fingers, until the part between my shoulder blades made a noise
like a fire spitting. I stayed for a few moments in the glare of the
sun. The house was low and surrounded by dense hedge. Cicadas
stopped as we passed through a wooden gate, then restarted. The
grass on the lawn glowed white in the sunlight like the fine hair
on a child's arm.

Thom came running out to meet us, slowing as he transitioned from soft lawn to gravel. Though he had bare feet, he had
men's sneakers on his hands like big white oven mitts. I realised
that Robin might have a holiday wardrobe that did not include
black, but the sneakers turned out to be Walter's.

"We've stolen them!" Rosa shrieked. "Now he won't have
any *shoes!*"

The twins were wearing matching basketball outfits Walter
had bought them as a recent birthday gift. Orange-and-blue New
York Knicks vests and shorts. Thom looked ridiculous, Rosa less
so—in fact the clothes made her look older, but you could see
her tiny buds through the armholes. Thom wanted to show me
and Dwight the house they had made for a tree frog and a snake
that lived together at the base of an enormous tree in the garden.
They had arranged a ring of gravel stones around it.

"And then this is the human garden," Thom said.

It was large and landscaped, and there was a long dining table, much like Ingrid and Robin's, with two white canvas um-
brellas over it, and woodland beyond. Suddenly there was a

deafening blast of classical music, which stopped as abruptly as it had started. Walter had installed a sound system off in the woods so you couldn't hear the cicadas at mealtimes.

"Whaddya think?" The music stopped and Walter appeared from inside.

"Awesome," Dwight called back.

The twins dragged me inside. Above ground, the house was all glass with sliding walls. Below, Walter had a basement that was the exact blueprint of the floor above, a carpeted cellar with no windows or natural light, where his housekeeper lived and where Walter sometimes tinkered with the pool system. The twins raced around in it with JJ and their scooters, Rosa tailing Thom like the boy in *The Shining*.

Though it was the height of summer and all the sliding glass doors were left half open, a wood fire was burning inside, and three ceiling fans were whirring. Ingrid and Robin were standing at a kitchen island, which made it look identical to their own home. Robin, slicing basil with a demilune, was still wearing black, but Ingrid was wearing white holiday jeans.

"Hi." Ingrid greeted us without taking her eyes off the tomatoes she was chopping. Robin didn't look up or say anything. I sensed they had been having an argument. "Did you just arrive?"

"Yup," I said. "Did you get here okay?"

"Sure did," Ingrid said, still not making eye contact. "Sure did."

"C'mon, guys," Walter said, entering, "arguments in the car don't count."

In the kitchen there was a black lacquered table with an ornamental black bowl like a warped record, with only a very slight depression, perhaps more of a dish. Above it a low-hanging white lamp came down, head height. The dish had something in it that I had never seen before. It seemed to be organic, perhaps a vegetable, but in case it was some kind of art object I didn't want to ask. I later found out it was "white eggplant." Everything in the Hamptons, I came to see, had to be white. There were even, Walter pointed out, white canvas coverings for the fire hydrants.

Walter insisted on a barbecue every day. He liked to stand before its smoking altar, waving wings and legs and breasts, and look at his own chest, hairless beneath his beard. The grill was the kind I imagined people could be cremated in. It was set up at one end of the garden, where a steady throb of dark bees were humping the lavender. By day the house smelt of burning flesh, and by night it smelt of burning insects as moths incinerated themselves on the spotlights on the wooden decking and the darkness rained insects onto the citronella candles.

For that first lunch, we sat down to barbecue number one, and as Walter said, "Welcome Rooiakkers! And Quinns, and Nutts, and—" He looked at me, and I felt yet another twinge of guilt for being there while Silvia was stuck in Amsterdam.

"Hare."

"And Hares!"

"And thanks to you, Mr. Rusc!" Nat held her glass of lime cordial in the air.

"Mom!" Rosa came running up to the table. "Mom, Thom's putting Dad's electrical tape on everything."

"Okay. Thom! Lunch is ready!"

Dwight, now discernibly "out of office," as he kept saying to anyone who'd listen, put on a neon-orange cap which said SAN JOSE SHARKS.

Nat, who hated being excluded from anything, had of course come too, but it was still a surprise to see her. Ingrid looked at the tops of the trees and inhaled deeply, as if she were about to sink to the bottom of the pool and stay there for the whole of lunch. A train horn—*I can't stop I can't stop. Stop! Stop!*

Rosa and Thom began shoveling sweet potato into their mouths, licking meat juice off their fingers, and yelling out QuizUp answers.

"Quiet!" Ingrid warned.

"But this guy's tenth in the UAE for science!"

"How was the drive?" Walter asked his protégé.

I felt my chest seize up. Before Dwight could answer, I cut in. "Fine," I said quickly. "Very straight. The road. Normally I get sick, but I didn't. And Dwight was very safe."

Dwight gave me a strange look. "Beautiful drive," he said. "We saw that super-tall *tree,* we went to a super-nice *Applebee's,* we passed that super-famous *mental asylum.*"

En route, Dwight had told me that the low bridges we were passing under were originally intended to prevent buses from using the road, *so buses with black people in them couldn't get to the beaches.* Did I see?

I watched him take an enormous bite of corn.

Robin looked at the swimming pool, stood, walked to its edge, and scooped out an orange cricket with his hand. "Got to look out for our insect friends," he said to me as he settled back down. "I don't swim either."

"'Don't' means 'can't,' in Robin's language," Nat said loudly.

Ingrid looked at her with a strained expression.

It surprised me that there might be something so simple that Robin had not mastered.

"He doesn't like getting his head underwater," Ingrid added. "Not even in the bath. I think he must have had a bad experience when he was younger, but he says he doesn't remember."

"Water's not my element," he said. "I like solids and I like voids, not something that runs through your fingers."

After lunch we went to the beach on bikes, except Nat, who went with Dwight in his car. Walter led the way. The tarmac was so smooth it was almost creamy, so different from the disfigured New York roads. My eyes narrowed against the sun, sweat creeping into them, making my vision blurry. I hated riding bikes. Susy had neglected to provide instruction, so I had had to teach myself so as not to be teased by other kids, but I'd never been confident doing it. The power lines became white flashes overhead, thick and noodly, then fuzzing back again to golden thinness. With the afternoon sun on my back, I could see my distorted shadow following Walter, Ingrid, and the twins in formation ahead of me. Robin brought up the rear.

We arrived at the kind of wide-open beach that has a big sky above it and a certain kind of feeling that you only get before an ocean. Very flat, with mirror-wet sand right up against the lip of the water, like a polished floor that gleamed for miles. There were dunes behind, figures standing, fishing, but mainly flatness. We had reached the edge of a place, the vastness of water with no world visible beyond it. I walked arm in arm with Dwight. I had momentarily, thanks to cycling, which had occupied both hands and brain, forgotten what I'd found and started to relax. Dwight was listening to Walter talk about the medical waste—hypodermic needles supposedly infected with AIDS—that had washed up all along the Atlantic coast in the summer of 1988, known as "the syringe tide." For a moment, as I held on to Dwight's strong arm, it was bliss.

"You can imagine our ancestors landing on this sort of beach, can't you, Thom?" Nat was staring out toward the horizon, ignoring talk of AIDS.

My heart sank, remembering, and I released my arm from Dwight's.

Ingrid took Nat into the ocean to wet her feet. Thom stood observing and kicking the water. Rosa headed to the vacant lifeguard lookout, climbed up, and jumped off over and over till she collapsed. The rest of us set up on the sand. Robin stayed safely back from the water, a little way from me. Dwight sat between us in a wetsuit he'd produced from his car, on a body board covered in sand that was attached at the ankle. I eyed the white-blond fur matted on his legs, dusky with sand, as he sucked all the red out of a watermelon slab he'd bought from a fruit seller in the car park. Walter snored gently behind me.

Dwight took a picture of us in those positions. His record is public, so I can still see it. This was the exact moment that I found Mizuko's Instagram. I spent almost the whole holiday in this frozen position, my head bent low over her life in miniature. You can see me holding my device like this in Dwight's picture, holding it in one hand, index finger poised on the other, as if poking pins in a voodoo doll. I can see in my downcast eyes that I am starting to fade. Or that the solid world around me, the reality of it, is starting to slide away, like wet sand sinking beneath the water. I have no idea what's about to happen, but I'm walking into it anyway. Writing this, reliving it through the pictures I still have, I feel like I am walking into that ocean and it gets slowly deeper and then suddenly there's a drop and the temperature of the water changes before I'm ready; my footing slips, and before I have a chance to take a breath I'm under.

15

It would be another fortnight before I would meet her for real. Walk home with her, feeling as if I were still in the shallows, not knowing how deep in I already was. After the tension in the café and the sobering talk by the Sugihara survivor, alcohol was welcome and accentuated that feeling of marvellous chance. Mizuko and I drank far more than I was used to over the course of our first evening together, so that I remember it now as a series of lights and darks, as if I were being driven through an underpass that took us from outside the café on Broadway right to her bedroom. 1020 is an unlikely, dark, dive-y pub. Columbia students play pool and darts, and you can sit either in dimly lit little booths or at a long bar. We sat in a booth. For a date, the vibe is a bit off, but I reminded myself that we weren't on a date. If anything, it felt more like an interview—a mock one in which she didn't really have a job to give me and I was pretending that she was someone I'd never met before.

First we discussed my being new to the city, the lecture and bits that had particularly moved us; then we talked about how she got inspiration for her characters and her writing, about both her novel in progress and her short stories, for which she was prepared to sacrifice friends and family, which is how we got onto her childhood, her mother, and why *she* was in New York. At some point the mock interview got tangled into a strange loop or Mobius band, so that I was still the one role-playing being the candidate pretending to want the job but now also asking her questions with answers that I already knew. Everything she told me about herself I knew in outline already. Because of that, and maybe because of the alcohol, I heard it all as if she were speaking in a foreign language. It was exciting to hear her real voice rather than simply reading her captions, but it was less like normal listening than like sonar, charting our strategic positions, my nearness to whatever the next thing was. I knew that if she stopped talking, it might prove to be the end of the evening, but she seemed happy to talk and talk and talk and for me to be silent. By the end, my vision was blurry and my hearing had narrowed around a single, slightly painful note. All I could make out was the sound of her voice hovering above the words, high and searching like a mosquito's, threatening silence wherever it landed.

The silence finally came when I asked about exactly how she used her own life in her writing, intending to impress her with my reading of I-novels, the popular Japanese confessional genre, after which she said nothing for a long time.

At last she said, "For me it's different. It's how I get back at my mom. As far as she's concerned, I've spent the last year not teaching or writing but playing a game on my phone in which I am the manager of an ice cream parlour and then collecting my Himura pocket money every month. I refuse to discuss my writing with her after the reaction she had to 'Kizuna.'"

She said the word like I knew what it meant—like I knew it was a title, and the title of one of her stories. I felt my face burn with embarrassment at just how well I knew "Kizuna"—I could have recited parts of it to her. A small part of me did register that it was an arrogant assumption. Still, I decided I needed to appear innocent.

"What's 'Kizuna'?"

"It's a short story I wrote that went viral." She sniffed. It continues to impress me how fluently Americans, even immigrants like her, speak of their achievements. "It means something like 'Human Ties,' or 'The Ties That Bind.'"

"Okay. Wasn't that the word of the year or something after the tsunami?"

"Exactly. Good knowledge. It can mean anything from the bond between parents and their children to the love you feel for an ex or the duty you feel to your country. Not just positive ties, either. I'm bound to my mother, for example. After it came out, she would have disowned me, except that it would have meant more bad press for our family. She's usually numb to anything but what outsiders think. She wouldn't care if I was upset, but she cares when other people who don't know us get upset. Anyway, if it *did* hurt her, then it was justified revenge."

I knew what this meant. At the root of Mizuko's revenge, and at the heart of the "Kizuna" story, like every other she wrote, was her nameless, faceless father. Hiromi Himura had kept the paternity secret from everyone. It wasn't obvious to me from looking at Mizuko that she wasn't all the way Japanese, but Mizuko had always been sure she wasn't.

"I've signed up to some DNA-matching websites. I'm sure I have relations all over the place in Europe. I *know* he was a *gaijin*."

This was a word that I knew meant "outside person," a foreigner.

"Why won't she tell you who he was?"

"Or is."

"Yes, is. Maybe."

Mizuko snorted and closed her eyes as if this were both too simple and too complex a question to answer. "I've given up trying to work that out." She shrugged, shook her head, then bit her lip. "I don't know whether it's out of loyalty, an insistence on her privacy, or whether it used to be about that and now it's something else. Like pride or stubbornness. Or after 'Kizuna,' when there was so much public scrutiny of her firm."

"You don't think maybe she's just gone so long not speaking about it that now she can't speak about it, even if she wants to?"

Mizuko's eyes darted from the floor to meet mine. I could see she was irritated by what I had said.

"I don't know that you need to be so compassionate. It was probably an affair, and she still has some misplaced loyalty to him or is afraid of the fallout. He's probably a well-known, well-respected person with his own family. Either way, she has put his needs—whoever he is, for whatever reason—first, above mine. That's not what parents do. Parents should make everything as good as they possibly can for their offspring. The next generation, right?"

I thought I should make a concerned face. I felt I should, as a sympathetic stranger, tell her that it was surely untrue, Hiromi's prioritisation of Mizuko's father, but I didn't. Instead I said, "Yes. It sounds like she has really fucked you over."

She looked surprised. "You think so?"

I nodded.

"No one else ever says that. Ever. They always try to reassure me that she loves me more than anything or crap like that. They don't know her like I do. They just think of their own mothers, who are all soft and cuddly, and they can't imagine it. It's a weird thing to do, right? It's not like she still sees him or anything. It's not like it's still going on, the affair or whatever. I used to spy on her all the time, and she was never in touch with any men, *ever*. She never had another boyfriend, so maybe she still loves him, but she just seemed to want to be on her own always."

I nodded again.

"And it made me so *angry*, you know? So fucking en*raged* that even though I was right there in front of her, pleading, she wouldn't just snap out of it. Her flesh and blood. But . . . I mean . . . it doesn't matter. I've given up wishing it could be any different. I keep my expectations low."

I closed my eyes. I didn't know how to show her how I understood. Saying "I know" seemed too small, but neither was it the right time to tell her my version of her story.

I wondered if it would be too strange to recite a passage of "Kizuna" to show her what a good student I was:

> You come into your family, into a moment in history, and
> there has been a conversation going on in the room for so
> many generations before you entered. For a while, when
> you are still unable to lift your head, the conversation
> carries on over it. This is when you must listen and store
> it for when you can finally understand it as language,
> because very soon, when you are on your legs and learn-
> ing shapes and patterns, to turn noise into meaning, the
> conversation will stop and you won't know why.

"If she's looking after his needs and her needs, then I have to look after mine." She ground the cap from her beer bottle into the soft wood of the table. "And if she puts their needs first, over me, then I can put mine over hers." The bottle cap skidded along the table and onto the floor. "She thinks it belongs to her before it belongs to me, but I remember the first thing they taught us on the summer course here, and it's the first thing I tell the students that I teach now: you own *everything* that happens to you."

I nodded. I wanted to stand and swear allegiance.

"I don't believe in family secrets—*any* secrets, actually."

"Me neither."

After that first night, I always maintained a vocal critique of Hiromi, but secretly I felt that it was better than Mizuko realised. Hiromi's straight refusal meant Mizuko had a clear target for her rebellion. Hiromi was silent on one subject, with a definite outline. Better that than to have so many stories and so many contradictions that the outline kept changing and swallowing everything like a swarm of locusts. With Susy there was never a clear line to rebel against, and so I could never get angry.

Though the circumstances were so strikingly similar, sometimes almost overlapping, like Mark claiming to work for a bank owned by Himura Securities, our childhoods had produced very different results. She had always been defiant and angry, a rebel, whereas I had always been quiet and shy, a peacemaker. I picture Mizuko as a child, in a garden, surrounded by overturned plastic chairs, toys scattered everywhere, a fabric Wendy house pushed over, a ransacked paddling pool upturned, and a decapitated head flung far from its hobbyhorse stick. If I'd met Mizuko then, I would have wandered around after her with a toy dustpan and brush, cleaning up. Putting everything back in its correct box. To entertain myself as a kid I would make up rules for games to be played with a theoretical group of children. I never intended to play them, and the children weren't even imaginary in a companionable way; it was just an exercise in constructing miniature worlds that I had sole dominion over. I once pinned the rules of a theoretical water fight to the fridge. I made them up and stuck them there one summer when I had no one to play with and Susy was occupied with drawing in another part of the house. When

I told Mizuko about this, she gave one of her rare real laughs and made me promise to show her the list one day, which I'm including here in case it's still funny:

WATER FIGHT RULES

1. No water inside house
2. Only ½ of a team allowed inside at any one time
3. Time outs are allowed only every ¼ hour
4. The following weapons may be used:

   Water pistols
   Plastic bottles/cups
   Hose
   Water bombs

5. If someone is hurt, the game STOPS
6. No wetting of people on the same team as you
7. No wetting of non-water-fight participants
8. No wetting of clothing/electrical items etc.

"Who were the non-water-fight participants if there weren't even any real participants?" Mizuko asked.

I shrugged, and she laughed even more.

"I like you."

I felt high, or in a state of shock, as if a lorry had braked just in front of me and I'd narrowly avoided death, had felt the air pressure change as it bore down on me within a centimetre of my face and the hairs on the back of my neck stand up. For a second I could not tell whether my blood had run cold or I had become extremely hot.

I couldn't say it back, so instead asked, "Well, is it my turn now?" I meant, of course, to tell her my story, a version I'd streamlined to be the mirror image of hers, but she assumed I meant more drinks.

We were on our third round at 1020.

As I went to the bar to order our fourth, I wondered how best to demonstrate that we were kindred spirits.

When I got back to our booth, I praised her question about the diplomat and his rebellion.

"You say it like it's not for you."

"What isn't for me?"

"Rebellion. Disobedience."

"I know everyone is supposed to go through that phase, but I think I've only just reached mine and am starting to test my boundaries."

I hoped this wasn't too suspect, too like a come-on. I wanted to become intimate, but I wanted to advance by degrees, like the darkness that was descending outside. I wanted her not to know what time it was and not to know that I had anything in mind until it was in hers too.

"The thing about Sugihara's rebellion," she said, "is that he had to disobey orders coming from far away because he met those people face to *face*. It would have been pretty easy for him to turn them down if their appeals had been electronic. If they'd had the kind of border control we have now, it would have been impossible. Imagine throwing a stamp out of a train window. But you'd hope anyone would feel sympathy if they actually saw someone face to face, pleading for a chance."

"You'd *hope* so." I left a pregnant pause, flared my nostrils just a little too much, maybe. The pause became another silence.

"Do you ever miss Japan?"

She shrugged. "Not really. Sometimes it helps to be an outsider. I can't write in Tokyo like I can living here, because there feels too familiar. I know it too well. I don't see it with a stranger's eyes." She looked at my face intently then, like she wanted something. "Tell me about England."

I didn't want to talk about being adopted, as this part didn't quite fit with Mizuko's experience, so I left it out for the moment and went big on Susy's rejection of me and the hurt and paralysis it had caused.

"The last thing she said to me before I came here was to pack less. That was her advice—to live lightly."

I'd thrown the comment out, expecting Mizuko to sympathise. But she said my mother was right in advising me to live lightly in New York. I worried that I detected judgment in her tone, in her expression, which had been encouraging until now.

"I left Tokyo to go to Yale at eighteen, and some people" —implicitly not her—"found it hard."

"The international students?"

"Yes. And students who'd so far lived quiet lives in the Midwest."

"Okay." I wanted to get her approval back in a quantifiable way and groped for information I had stored about her that might win her over again, but my mind was blank. Her interpretation of Susy's comment had thrown me.

"There is definitely this pressure to be everywhere, know everyone, to do and see everything all at once," she confirmed, "and I guess in this city, more than anywhere else in the world, that's almost possible."

"Yeah," I said, as if this tangle of social lives and spaces were something that oppressed me too.

"It's relentless and exhausting," she said, suddenly severe. "I get basically no writing done at all. I'm always slipping out to go do something else. I really need to get away. Go on a retreat of some kind."

"Yeah!" I said again, widening my eyes and nodding slowly but emphatically to show that she had seen into my own symmetrical soul.

"And it can be oddly lonely here for some people."

I turned my expression into ambivalence, a facial shrug, to show that I imagined it could be so for some. I didn't want to say *yeah* again, both because it seemed unimaginative and because then she might think I was a loser with no friends who had no business being in New York, let alone sitting with her in a bar, which I thought she probably already did think, because otherwise why was I taking tickets to talks I thought were about beef, not genocide, and then lingering on afterwards with someone I'd only just met, nine years older than me? I can't have looked that busy. I wondered how to give her the impression I had somewhere else to be without going there. I took out my device and then quickly pocketed it again, realising that this would permit her to take out hers.

"People are constantly moving in and out of New York. Dinner parties at home are *very* rare. No one has the space, and if they do, it's seen as a very intimate thing to do, so it's only done with close friends. I almost always meet my friends in public places."

She said this as though all her friends were potential murderers she'd met online, and I immediately applied it to us. She was telling me that we weren't intimate, but I also heard that maybe I was being bracketed in with "most" people, and that therefore I might count as a nonintimate friend. Which, after only a few hours, was not bad.

Mizuko grew up in Bunkyō, the area of Tokyo where Natsume Sōseki, the famous writer, once lived. The University of Tokyo, where Hiromi had worked for a while before setting up her own assistive technologies company, SEMPO, is there. So is the

Big Egg, Tokyo's dome-shaped baseball stadium. I had looked it all up on Google Earth.

So far I'd managed to keep her away from her many instruments of tortuous communication with Rupert Hunter for about ten minutes. I knew she was running out of power and I denied having a charger in my bag. When she finally retrieved her phone, I heard the words I had been longing for: "Fuck. It's dead."

I bit my lip to catch the smile.

"Dead," she said again, making sure.

She began looking around. I was worried that Rupert Hunter would tell Mizuko embarrassing things about me when they saw each other after this, if he hadn't already done so in a message sent beneath the table. There were things I had said to him I wanted to forget. Once, soon after we had seen each other again in my first year and argued over the tsunami in the media room, I had slipped a note under his bedroom door that read: *Come to my room for bento if you like.* Though I had listed my staircase and door number, Rupert had not come.

But Mizuko did not seem desperate to leave or to go to him —it was possible she wanted to make him jealous—and now that her device had run out of power, there was no reason that I couldn't have her to myself all evening if I managed to keep the conversation going.

I was hungry for the first time in months. I was drunk-hungry. We decided to find food and ended up going to a restaurant Mizuko knew. I can't remember getting there, but I remember sobering up a little inside because it was quiet and we had to talk in something like lovers' tones. It was a miniature restaurant that could seat only seven people at a time on high stools at a long bar. The bar was also where the food was prepared, so we often had to make eye contact with the chef. I remember the feeling of discomfort, hers and mine, with the way I ate the food and the way my lumpy fingers got in the way of the chopsticks. I remember trying to reach one of my legs, hanging from the high stool, towards the floor to stop the room from spinning. The chef gave us hot rice, using a flannel to scoop it out of a wooden bowl, but except for the rice, I wasn't really able to eat much of what he passed to us. I had not told Mizuko, who ordered for us both, about my shellfish allergy. It's not serious, or it has never been serious enough to warrant medical attention, but I do puff up around my eyes and then, depending on how badly I react, down my face and neck. I guess it could, if it was really bad, cause me to asphyxiate.

But I felt I could not tell her this. "It does not *behoove*," as Dwight once put it, "a Japanophile to have a shellfish allergy." I was craving cheese and tomato pizza and remember only two or three of the dozen or so finger-length courses that, in my inebriated, slightly nauseated state, were the hardest to consume. Aoyagi, something which curled up as if still alive and was slapped down on the chef's hand like one of those snap bracelets, and awabi, the abalone or Venus ear. That one was miserable—impossible to eat, and the rubbery flesh had no taste. The dish is supposedly an aphrodisiac and, as it turned out when I insisted on paying for everything with Silvia's credit card, very expensive. I ended up having to hold it in my mouth until I got to the bathroom, where I gagged and disposed of it in the toilet bowl.

When I got back, Mizuko was whimpering.

"What's wrong?" I asked, holding my stomach.

She gestured to the remains of my abalone. "Reminds me of her. She was so good at finding them."

Her was Mizuko's grandmother, Ume, who was an *ama*. Mizuko began to explain that this was not an acronym for "ask me anything," but I had decided I needed to start showing off more. Impress upon her my knowledge so that she would feel it like I felt it.

"Are you serious? Your grandmother was an *ama*? Don't they go to insane depths without oxygen?" She looked impressed. "I read that some carry on diving—without a tank—well into their seventies."

She nodded, a small smile flickered, her eyes met mine; I knew I had her back.

Ama are Japan's famous women divers. They look for things like abalone, the gummy delicacy I had just spat out. They prise them off rocks with a little spatula. *Ama* also hold something of a mythological status in misogynistic Hollywood films, which is how I claimed to have heard about them, rather than from Mizuko's own story. She told me that her grandmother had once auditioned (unsuccessfully) to be in a big Hollywood action movie, but that she had been cast in a few low-budget productions which featured *ama* divers. This had raised her up from lowly origins into the sophisticated world of Tokyo, where she married into the Himura family.

I knew it all already. "Kizuna" moved back and forth between this period of Ume's youth and the 2011 tsunami, ending with her grandmother's foiled attempt at suicide. I'd decided that Silvia was to me what Ume was to Mizuko, just like I had decided that her mother, Hiromi, was my Susy; her absent father, whom I now knew to be Robin, was my Mark; and her relationship with Rupert was as devoid of real intimacy as mine with Dwight. To me, it was clear proof of the existence of supersymmetry, the idea that every particle has a partner. She was mine.

"Were your family badly affected by the tsunami?" I guessed this was how police got suspects to talk, by feigning ignorance or beginning aslant, with polite, general questions.

"I flew into Tokyo a few months after the disaster hit. I went for Ume but was also concerned for the domesticated animals left behind when their owners had been forced to evacuate."

The words were rehearsed, and we had both memorised many of them from the story itself.

"Some were left leashed and starved to death. Since my grandfather died, Ume had been living back in Minamisōma, the place where she had grown up diving. But after the quake, tsunami, and nuclear meltdown, she got evacuated to a school building, where she slept on the floor wrapped in blankets like tinfoil. When communication lines and power were finally restored, she was sent back to Tokyo to live with my mother in the tiny apartment she moved into after I left for Yale. It was really only big enough for one."

I took a sip of the green tea that had materialised on the wooden bar. I noted with growing anxiety that we were the only ones left in the restaurant and the owner was waiting to close.

"When I got there, without my mom's permission, I drove Ume back to Minamisōma. I'd seen on the news that it had become a ghost town within the nuclear exclusion zone. Ume insisted on it, despite the danger and police checkpoints, because her beloved dog, Kathleen, had been left behind. A black toy poodle, named after Kathleen Drew, the biologist who saved Japan by mistake through her research on edible seaweed when its people were starving."

The owner of the restaurant caught her eye, but I nodded vigorously to show that she had my undivided attention.

"'Kizuna' begins with my account of driving Ume back."

So that she could write it up later, Mizuko had filmed the whole expedition with a GoPro camera mounted on her head, the one she used for cycling through Manhattan. Today, I rewatched the footage. Both women are swaddled in vast amounts of clothing to protect themselves from radiation, but over the course of the long journey, Ume gradually, sneakily, and despite Mizuko's entreaties, peels it off, except for a bandanna with a five-point star on it around her head. ("*Ama* culture has loads of superstition," Mizuko explained when I asked about the star. I looked them up: "The *seiman* is a kind of talisman design on their tools and things. It is written in a single stroke, starting and ending at the same point, to symbolise safe return to the surface.")

"She hasn't said anything for a while—is she still here?" In the film, Ume is speaking, and the sound of an embodied voice seems to startle them both. After a pause, Mizuko realises that Ume is referring to their GPS, whose absence suggests she has abandoned the pair to their death wish.

It is silent again. Given recent events, they cannot discuss the weather. There is no available small talk except for the immediate, physical discomforts of the journey. Ume, ninety-two, her knees just visible before a snub of car bonnet, is irritable and hot. Mizuko, rigid in the driving seat, with the air conditioner blowing directly onto her feet, is, despite her layers, numb with cold. I read the story as I watch the footage, because the pair speak in Japanese. The air con does nothing to settle Ume, who can be seen kicking off her shoes and socks and trying to strip down to her vest. Minutes later she bats away Mizuko's hand as it darts toward the dial between them.

Mizuko wonders if the GPS is still monitoring their progress. She has the distinct feeling of being watched by something in the darkness. This makes watching the footage and reading the story at the same time a strange experience, as if she can sense me, a menace from the future, following them along the dark road.

For most of the journey there is no power to light the

streetlamps or the traffic lights, and there are no other headlights on the road. Mizuko passes her grandmother a jar of iodine pills, which are meant to stop the thyroid gland from absorbing radiation. They leave the Jōban Expressway. They are approaching Odaka, Ume's home town, where life has been halted. It is the only place to be hit by all three in the chain of disasters—earthquake, tsunami, nuclear meltdown. Dawn breaks and you can see from the car windows where the wave hit—destruction visible below a tide line of debris, the radiation invisible above.

When the restaurant owner politely forced us out, Mizuko was still in the midst of telling me the story, and so, since I neglected to tell her I had already read it multiple times, I ended up going back to her apartment so she could finish. She didn't actually ask me back, she just kept talking as we got our bags and walked out onto the street, and I kept following her as she talked. When we got to her building, she said that if I liked "Kizuna," which was a ghost story of sorts, then I should come to her annual event on Halloween, where people told ghost stories in her apartment because her apartment was *haunted*. Once her front door had jammed shut so she had had to climb down her fire escape. Another time a perfect circle of water that wouldn't correspond to anything—not pitchers, not glasses, not anything in the whole apartment that might have left the mark—had formed on her dining table. Sometimes there was a sudden temperature drop when she was alone there. She said it wasn't really a salon—that was what Rupert called it; it was more like a *Kaidankai* party. Attendees from their circle of friends at Columbia and assorted strays Rupert picked up at poetry readings brought a ghost story each, or an object—something uncanny and strange. Intellectual circle jerks, really.

"You want to come up and see now?"

I felt a sudden drop in my stomach. "Sure."

I followed her up the red steps and in through the glass doors, noting the carpet, the smells, the ordinariness of the interior. I'd expected something more grand.

In the elevator she told me about the pilgrimage they made every Halloween before the party. "We walk to Harry Houdini's former house in Harlem. It's on this street. Before he died, he and his wife, Bess—they believed in spirits and stuff—decided on a code word they'd use when one of them died to see if they could communicate from beyond the grave. 'Rosabelle, believe.'"

"What?"

"*Believe*. She used to have a seance for him every year on the day he died, which was Halloween. And after she died all these necromancers and people carried on doing it. They go to his house—it's one of the beautiful old brownstones on the other side of Morningside Park."

"They think there's a ghost?"

"Well, not one that haunts all the time, maybe, but that he comes back to communicate on that night. Rupert says that if anyone could break free from death, it would be him."

I must have looked blank.

"You know who Harry Houdini is, right?"

"Sure."

She looked at me suspiciously. This appeared to be a tradition I had missed in her pictures. I dimly recalled a photograph of the brownstone and upbraided myself for not having researched it properly.

"I mean, I do"—I had thought until this conversation that he was a footballer—"but remind me."

"Illusionist. Escapologist. Harry 'Handcuff' Houdini."

"Right, right. I remember now."

"He could escape from straitjackets underwater, or from inside sealed milk cans filled to the brim. Could hold his breath for insane lengths. My grandmother loved him. She could hold her breath pretty well too, obviously."

"How did he die?"

"Peritonitis, appendicitis, something like that. He got punched in the stomach when he was just lying on a sofa. Burst his colon. Bad way to go for someone who could survive being nailed into a crate wearing leg irons and thrown into the East River. He was locked in with lead weights and he found his way to the surface somehow."

"How?"

"People thought he dematerialised. But often he did it in full view—getting out of all these chains and ropes and stuff."

"And what's the house like? Spooky?"

"You can't go in. It's just got a red plaque outside and a reddish brown exterior. We can go look if you want."

"Not now maybe, but yes, I'd like to."

When we got upstairs she got two beers out of the fridge and beckoned me towards her laptop. She wanted to show me the GoPro footage and other stuff—"found materials" that she promised me were not contaminated with radiation. Shoes and bottles, fragments of pottery. Children's toys. Like me, Mizuko had become addicted to amateur footage of the wave. The clips that went viral while the survivors in Japan were cut off and knew far less than the rest of the world, watching their computer screens, about what had actually happened to them. The sheer scale of the devastation. She says in her story that even though much of the landscape is altered beyond recognition, being in the car, driving along the dark road, feels like entering something she knows by heart. Not because it is a place she remembers from actually having been there—she'd never actually been to Ume's modest home in Minamisōma before—but from looking at it on TV from the safety of New York.

All that is missing from the set as they drive is the black wave surging inland. We watched it together that night on repeat. I'd watched it on repeat in my college room. It rears up. The back catches up with the front. Sucking in water ahead of it so that the shoreline is revealed. When it hits, it stops looking like water. It becomes a solid mass, a crazy patchwork of people's lives; household objects, cars, trees. The people capturing the footage zoom in on all the absurd juxtapositions. Fridges rehomed in trees.

Mizuko spots a man's body, or the hump of his bloated back. Ume tells her to slow down, but she doesn't. His coat is beige or the mud and silt has turned it beige, and the creases are hardened. He lies facedown, spat out on the rim of the road. The headlights give the figure a hint of animation. Ume tells her to look straight ahead, but Mizuko's camera is angled right at him.

Further along she surveys the concrete embankments and oyster beds, the market where her grandmother used to buy sea urchins and seaweed. Then all at once the chaos stops. Everything looks normal again. The wave did not reach Ume's house.

The car stops too finally, and Mizuko emerges. She wears so many layers and such enormous ski gloves, just visible moving underneath the camera perched on her head, that she seems to walk in slow motion, like an astronaut. Ume refuses to be padded up again. "I'll die soon anyway!" she says. Beside her granddaughter she is all bobbing, knotty bulges. The abandoned house is more eerie than Mizuko had imagined. They hurry, taking the *ihai*—memorials for dead ancestors displayed on the *butsudan* —and wrapping them in newspaper. There are dead flowers and the remnants of offerings and putrefied remains. Mizuko has to assure her grandmother that the remains are not Kathleen, who then, not in the footage but as a fictional twist in the story, bounds up to them, feral but happy they have tracked her down.

When Mizuko returned Ume to Tokyo, clutching the remains of her old life, her mother was furious. Ume was also upset, because Hiromi was so furious that she felt guilty. After Mizuko returned to New York, Ume wrote a suicide note, apologising to her living family and deceased ancestors for being a burden and having to live with her daughter in her tiny apartment built for one. In the real suicide note, this lament was only the preface, however, to three long pages expressing her grief over the suspected fate of Kathleen. Sometimes I wonder whether Mizuko contracted the parasite then, and had lived with it all that time until it finally reached her brain.

Ume was found hanging from a tree in the park Mizuko used to play in near the house. She was cut down just in time, but not before someone took a picture from an overlooking apartment block and put it online. It looks weird. Like a surrealist tableau created by the wave. Hiromi sent a picture of Ume's suicide note to Mizuko, telling her it was all her fault for unsettling her grandmother with the trip to get Kathleen. Enraged, partly worried that it was true, Mizuko then used the episode, and much of the suicide note, in her short story. When it was published, given the themes, critical attention turned from the writing to Hiromi's company, which designed aids for Japan's elderly population living alone.

Mizuko argued that there was a point to the exercise beyond the creation of a story. She said that Ume was unhappy living with Hiromi and wanted to save Kathleen. Hiromi countered that had they waited, those who had lived in the evacuation zones were gradually being allowed to return to their homes for two supervised hours to retrieve personal items. Mizuko stubbornly pointed out that the personal items they had retrieved, such as Ume's photo albums and *ihai*, would have had to fit into a 45-litre, 70-centimetre square plastic bag, and indeed, there is a line in "Kizuna": "Kathleen was too big for a plastic bag."

When the GoPro film finished, she looked at me, raised her eyebrows, and said, "I know right." She would send me the file if I liked.

The next thing I remember is lying next to her in bed. I snapped awake at the noise of a water bottle changing shape in the dark. It must have been on her bedside. Her elbow was poking into my back. The skin on her legs touched my legs and was alien smooth, not as if she had removed any hair but as if none had ever grown there. The smoothness told me that I had neglected to shave mine. I felt a loop of her long hair touching the back of my neck like the tufted end of a brush. I felt her heat behind me, through my shirt.

Her breath, its milky smell, and her other smell, which I wasn't sure of the origin of yet, like burning wood. I lay there for a few seconds in a trance, taking in my physical proximity to her body. As I tried to imagine what it looked like at that moment, too scared to wake her up by turning over, I remembered the nightmare I had been having. A body: back of a man, facedown in thick mud starting to crack and fissure. A ghost had entered the room with the plastic snap of the bottle and had gone again in the infinitesimal space between the snap and my starting awake.

Something light but sharp pounced on me, and I screamed.

"Cat," Mizuko murmured from her sleep.

We had not drawn the drapes across the two windows in the room, which allowed me to take in my surroundings in the dim light from the streetlamps below. I lay there staring at the teeth marks from the catch on the chain around her neck, Ume's ring on the chain, which had slid around to the back, onto the sheet between us, trying to piece together the sequence of the evening from the details I still had. As I lay, a pink, dreamlike glow seeped into the room, gradually turning a bright, chemical red. The light inched towards the bed, slowly picking out our two bodies—*developing* us, I thought, the way photographs used to be made —until it was daylight and everything had its normal definition. It became hotter and hotter as I stared at the two pinpricks in her neck where her necklace had imprinted itself.

This is just happening so naturally, I told myself. I just have to keep pressing on each link to get to the next; I don't have to know where it's going.

16

I suppose this is the halfway line. The line at which I should have stopped. If I scroll back in time to the Hamptons, I can return to that exact moment of dissolution—when the obsession began. When I looked up from my phone, my mind only partially returned to my body beside the Atlantic, a moment after Dwight's picture had been taken.

Thom, Nat, and Ingrid were exiting the water and coming back up the beach.

"What's the point of having a stinger if you die right after using it?" Thom asked, shouting as he ran towards us ahead of his mother.

"You die nobly—on your sword," Robin answered.

"Rubbish," Nat said angrily, stomping on the hot sand. "You can help another bee that's in distress. Instead of ignoring them and leaving them to die, you can sting on their behalf."

I didn't see what looks passed between them, but Nat did not sit down with the rest of us. She carried on marching back up the beach towards the car.

According to Ingrid, the ocean was dangerous and not for

swimming in. Splashing only. And even at Walter's house we kept a sharp knife by the pool so that we could cut Rosa or Ingrid out by the hair if necessary. It was only for them, since the rest of us didn't swim or didn't have the kind of luxurious hair that would get sucked into a filter.

"No," Ingrid had assured me, inspecting mine with a frown, "*you'll* be fine."

"But Mommy and me might *drown*," Rosa gloated, stroking her ponytail.

Every day of the holiday, the knife glinted in the sun. Rosa flipped up and over like a dolphin or pointed her bottom in the air and flailed her legs for us, and we all waited for her hair to get stuck and for her to drown. She was, I noticed, consistently splashing Dwight, teasing him, or trying to get his attention in some way. Thom preferred to lie on the sun-bleached wood, resting his face on the water, alleviating the itch of a bad insect bite, enjoying the rim of water around his cheeks and the band of dryness around that. He got me to try it with him. He said it was hard to tell after a while what felt dry and what felt wet because what felt normal changed around.

He did this experiment for as long a stretch as he could without running out of breath or scalding his belly on the hot wood. It was true; the wet and dry worlds inverted so that your body felt like it was floating in water and your head felt as if it had poked through into another atmosphere identical to ours.

The argument about bees/stings/swords seemed to have concluded with some kind of commitment to more family bonding time. Ingrid announced over breakfast that the children were banned from playing games on all devices for the rest of the holiday. Rosa narrowed her eyes.

"Dog Genius?"

"Not allowed."

"Animal Planet?"

"Verboten."

"What's the Word?"

"Nope."

"Uno and Friends?"

"No way. We're going to play real games."

Rosa was skeptical. "Like what?"

"Hide-and-seek. I spy. Chess and backgammon, Scrabble . . ." She looked to Robin for help.

"Cards," he added without interest.

"But we don't know how to play chess and backgammon," Rosa cried, wringing her hands as if this were the worst idea she'd ever heard.

"We're going to teach you," Nat warned. "And Dwight and Alice can teach you some real games, I'm sure."

Unimpressed, Rosa walked straight past her grandmother and, keeping her eyes level, dropped like a stone into the swimming pool. She held, Robin realised too late, his phone in her hand.

"If we can't use them, neither can you!" she shrieked as she resurfaced, throwing the waterlogged device onto the side.

Robin didn't say anything for a moment. Even Rosa went suddenly quiet, realising she might have gone too far. Slowly he stood, drawing himself to his full height. His plasticine chest hardened.

"I'm going to count to three," Robin hissed. "By three I want you out of that pool and standing. Right. Here."

Rosa's eyes widened in fear. She looked to her mother for help.

"One."

Rosa splashed around in a frenzied way, unsure whether to get out and run for it or to stay in the relative safety of the pool, where her father did not go.

"Two." Robin began to advance toward her.

Rosa took a deep breath. She plunged under the surface and towards the deep end.

"Careful of the filter!" Ingrid screamed. "Her hair!"

"*Three.*"

Rosa did not surface. Robin stood at the edge of the pool, a black shadow on the water, waiting.

We all held our breath. I wondered if Rosa had actually finally got stuck. Ingrid ran towards the knife and hovered anxiously. Robin removed his watch, flung it toward the grass.

Suddenly there was a loud splash, then a whoosh as displaced water cascaded onto the deck.

"What are you *doing?*" Ingrid screamed. "You can't *swim!*"

At the midpoint of the pool, his feet found the bottom and his head emerged. He pushed sopping black hair back from his eyes. Rosa clung to the lip of the pool at the far end, but Robin ploughed through the water towards her, not swimming but battling against the water as if he were running. He grabbed Rosa by the back of her T-shirt and then held her under one arm, shrieking and wriggling like a fish, as he climbed up the ladder, shirt heavy with water, his jaw tight. We were all standing up, Nat in open-mouthed amazement, Dwight and Walter at the edge of the pool. The only sound was Rosa's shrieking. Robin carried her around the decking, water slopping onto sun-soaked wood, and out of sight. Very suddenly the shrieking stopped.

"We used to play parlor games," Nat offered, though no one was listening, "like murder. Jane Stanton used to play the camouflage game. You hide things in a room by disguising them as other things. So, for example—"

There was a loud thud, a second in which nobody moved, and then an earsplitting cry.

Ingrid dropped the knife and ran.

The rest of us—me, Dwight, Walter, Nat, and Thom—continued eating in silence.

Unlike in New York, where life is extruded from the confines of cramped apartments and out onto the street, things can be hidden in the Hamptons. Each hedge venerated privacy. Where life *was* visible, it was meticulously groomed and well supervised. Compared to the city, I had few observations to put in my journal except ones concerning Walter's home and the people I observed on Main Street. That afternoon there was a queue five blocks long, which snaked around a corner into a car park, for Hillary Clinton's book signing. Nat had bought three copies of the memoir, *Hard Choices,* and insisted we join the line. The others had gone to play tennis at the Maidstone Club and left Nat, Rosa, and me in line for Hillary signing copies of her memoir in the bookstore. Rosa had a sprained arm. She had, Robin said, slipped from his grasp and fallen straight onto concrete.

We stood and shuffled, stood and shuffled, in silence, with Nat spotting people she knew, or knew the names of, in the line.

"You don't want to go there anyway," Nat informed me without explanation.

"Where?"

"The Maidstone."

"I don't?"

"You wouldn't fit in so well there. It's an unspoken thing, but it's a thing." She looked as if she wanted me to press her on it, so I refrained.

I thought this might instead be the time to tell her what *I* knew. How often do you discover something these days—in *the age of information* blah blah—which only you know about? And how often, in this same age, when you find out something that no one else knows about, is it possible to keep that thing a secret?

When I finished telling her, I looked up, my cheeks burning, and she studied me for a moment.

"And she's a writer, this Mizoozoo girl?"

The line moved forward and we moved with it.

"*Mizuko*. Yes."

She licked her lips slowly, rocking. I could see she'd remembered the correct name perfectly. "All the writers I ever met working for your grandmother were absolutely terrible people."

"Oh?"

"They didn't care about anyone but themselves."

I felt my pulse quicken.

"In fact, I'm suspicious of anyone who wants to be a writer," Nat continued.

"Oh?"

We took another step forward in line.

"Silvia and I knew so many." She took a deep breath. "Most had houses right around here. Capote, Steinbeck, Matthiessen . . ."

"That's cool," I said slowly, unsure if it was true or how the dates squared.

"It wasn't like it is now," she said, noting my hesitation. "Now it's all hedge-fund types, but back then your grandmother and I used to get invited out here to stay with all these well-known writers. It was all artists, writers, low rent, quiet. Not anymore. Now you see those little wooden signs everywhere, stuck in the grass around the mansions."

These signs shamelessly listed exactly how many millions per acre were for sale behind impenetrable foliage. I had noticed them too, but Nat loved reading them aloud whenever we passed them. She was again scanning the line for people she knew or knew of. I felt like she was studiously avoiding my eyes, and I sensed the conversation was closed.

We walked home, which tired Nat out, and had leftovers for lunch, just the three of us.

"What should I do about the match, then? What should we do, I mean?"

"We? *We* don't need to do anything," Nat said stoutly. "You, on the other hand, need to get rid of it. Delete it. Shut it down. Pretend you never saw it. You *didn't* see it. It's not your business to know. It was probably a mix-up anyway." She was smiling a fixed smile. "I don't think this is something we should trouble Ingrid with. Or Robin. Not right now."

"But what do you think it means? Is he . . . did—"

"The sun is so benevolent," Nat announced, tucking into leftovers from the barbecue.

I nodded slowly. Evidently the Rooiakker name was more important to her than who Robin might have been in a past life.

"When did you last visit Silvia, by the way?" Her voice was edged with something cruel.

"The day before we left, I think."

Nat did not look convinced. "Have you forgotten you're a Hare, not a Rooiakker?"

When the others got back from playing tennis, Rosa, who'd perked up at the prospect of meeting Hillary Clinton and been ecstatic when she'd got to shake her hand as Nat handed her the two books and I stood awkwardly by resisting the urge to take a picture, now grew pale and silent. Ingrid had the same fixed smile as her mother. Walter, Dwight, and Thom charged about with a ball, oblivious to the tension. Robin, who'd taken his book to the club and abstained from sport in general, and I were the only ones who did not join in the "real games," which Ingrid was determined would go ahead despite Rosa's sprained arm. I sat on a lounger, furtively reading everything about or by Mizuko I could find, and Robin talked on a Bluetooth headset using Ingrid's phone, or did crosswords on his iPad on a sun lounger he had dragged to the end of the deck. The sensation that had plagued me after graduating, of being on the outside of some mystery, peeking in, returned. Each day I moved deeper and deeper into the white glow of Mizuko's world, gripped it harder and tighter in my hand. Each link in the chain led me to greater certainty. I looked up the mother, Hiromi Himura. Her company, the site explained, enabled elderly people to continue living alone in their own homes. It offered services for Japan's senior citizens that included

- Intelligent reminding
- Telepresence
- Data collection
- Surveillance
- Mobile manipulation
- Social interaction

Occasionally Robin would get up from his lounger and stand, legs planted far apart, pointing a silver digital camera at things. He wasn't, I soon realised, taking normal holiday snaps, not of the kids or Ingrid. He was pointing it at odd stuff. The materials of Walter's house. Paving stones. Interesting cracks. A coiled fern. I saw him standing very close to the big tree where the twins had made the garden for the frog and the snake, and I asked him what he was taking a picture of.

"Bark," he had answered. "Beautiful. Come look."

I stepped gingerly, my feet bare in the grass, beside him.

"And look how it speaks to these," he said, indicating a series of Donald Judd totems that made up Walter's art collection. "No embarrassment about taking up physical space. Perfect and complete. Timeless."

I nodded, unsure what to say. He wasn't taking pictures of me or anything, yet somehow it made me feel uncomfortable. He brought a very specific attention to things that made it possible to show something in a substantially different way. He insisted on taking me through his album of shadows, leaves, bricks, pipes, all taken during the vacation so far, his head right next to mine as he hit left, left, left. Up close, he explained, the bleached wood beside the pool could look like a desert landscape, the folds of a towel became a mountain. His photographs reminded me of nothing so much as Mizuko's. They focused in on things or found odd juxtapositions—an inhuman way of seeing, or a way of seeing that meant some things that should have seemed human looked wan and bloodless, and others, which weren't human, were suddenly animated, as if Robin had entered them.

I gave up my journal. I had a secret, which meant that noting qualities of light felt futile. I had been planning on recording the trip for Silvia, but I no longer thought it seemed like a good idea. Even a censored version would only make her feel left out. Besides, I told myself, I was far more interested in what Mizuko was up to than in recording what I was doing. Her world looked neater, so much less threatening than the realities of mine.

I suppose Nat thought our discussion would be the end of it. That generation tends to think in terms of beginnings and endings. They don't understand what you can do with the Internet, or how there's no end to things, no way out. They don't understand that nothing stays private and nothing goes away. It's like the wave—the back catching up with the front.

Walter began teaching Thom to play chess, and Dwight, to

the delight of both twins, introduced the ice-bucket challenge. Though technically, as Dwight pointed out, the ice-bucket challenge was a viral phenomenon and required the use of a device to capture it, it corresponded to a real cause and so was permitted by Ingrid. Dwight's videos of Ingrid bucketing Walter, the twins together getting soaked by Nat, and Ingrid being soaked by Thom (though he staggers under the weight, misses, and the icy water mostly falls on him) are all still online.

"Aren't you going to join in?" Dwight emerged beside me, panting. It would have been the ideal time to instigate my water-fight rules, had I had the heart just then. I looked over at Robin stroking his digital camera. As long as he stayed out of the group activities, I could stay out too. I shook my head. Dwight shrugged and walked away. I sank back, deeper into the parallel universe I had found. I'd scrolled back in time three years to Mizuko's very first picture and was now working my way forwards again so I could follow her footsteps in a more logical sequence rather than randomly clicking on pictures of her.

A recent haircut taken at the hairdresser's.

A black-and-white picture of a woman (Sada Abe).

A Dorothy Parker quote: "Lips that taste of tears, they say, are the best for kissing."

The picture of the picture of her birthday—that was a TBT to her twenty-first; her thirty-second had been in February.

An image she had found of a tattoo she wanted—a three hares tattoo. This was destiny.

Then I saw Rupert's face. He was sitting drinking coffee and holding a *Wall Street Journal*. I gasped.

There were more. A trip to Europe to meet Rupert's parents, who were pictured shelling peas in a country garden with red brick walls and climbing roses.

Fuck fuck fuck.

"Excuse me?"

"What?" I must have said it aloud.

"What are you doing?" Robin said. I'd forgotten where I was.

"Nothing." I looked up.

A pause.

"I've been stuck on a crossword clue for days," he said. "I thought perhaps you might be able to help. You're always so quick. Nine letters, and the clue"—he looked back at his iPad screen—"is a quotation from the Book of Numbers, I know that much. Chapter twenty-three, verse twenty-three, 'What hath God wrought,' and the other bit of the clue is 'Morse.'"

"Sure." I turned away. "Let me think." I covertly typed the clues into my device. "Telegraph?" I said, too quickly. "That was the first message ever sent, wasn't it?"

"*Very* good."

I went back to Mizuko, moving through her pictures with Rupert like a termite. I scrutinised captions, following her grand tour. When the next picture failed to load immediately, I watched the grey wheel with growing impatience. The Wi-Fi seemed to have stopped working.

"Creator and destroyer," Robin called out to me. Luckily, I did know that one.

"That's easy. Shiva."

"You're good."

It could not be coincidence. It seemed to me then more likely that I was a pawn in a vast conspiracy that stretched all the way back to Silvia's first letter and linked everyone who had come into my life since the discovery of the Higgs boson. First Rupert, in Tokyo, then again at university when we were watching the tsunami unfold, then Silvia's invitation to New York, Nat's invitation to Roosevelt Island, Dwight's invitation to Central Park, Ingrid's invitation to Claremont Avenue, and then Dwight's unorthodox invitation to my new family to all please spit. If that could be put down to *chance*, then chance might just as well be called fate. In either case, it seemed obvious to me that my special purpose in life was to unravel Mizuko's mystery for her.

The July sun was hot, and I must eventually have fallen asleep. I woke up as it was getting dark; everyone else had gone, and my nostrils were full of the smell of citronella and immolation. I was on the same lounger, and Robin had his hand on the outside of the crotch of my swimsuit. It was light and trembling, the hand of an old man. I could feel a sliver of the skin of his thumb against the skin on my thigh.

"Alice," he whispered. He pressed his fingers down a little harder.

I shut my eyes; my body began to shake. I tried to control it but could not. Playing dead seemed to be the only option. I tried to feign sleep, sleep without complicity, counting in my head, barely breathing, locking my jaw, trying to freeze my body, but it shook harder the more I tried to control it, to shut it down. Shaking, waking, shockwaves radiating out from the epicenter where his hand lay.

"Food!" Dwight called out from the kitchen.

I kept my eyes shut. It wouldn't be real unless I saw it.

I felt the hand lift. Where it had lain felt suddenly cold. A raw, tender feel like the skin had been peeled back. Footsteps on wood. Silence. He must have crossed the grass. Footsteps on gravel. A screen door whined.

I kept counting. I stayed there until Dwight called out again. "Alice! C'mon. It's ready!"

I pretended I had sunstroke and went to bed. I still had that prickly, shaky feeling up my legs, as if I'd just been in a car crash.

When Dwight came to our bedroom after supper, he was distracted. He had become even more obsessed with the missing plane after the second one, another Malaysia Airlines flight, was shot down over eastern Ukraine.

"The numbers are spooking me," he said as he got into bed.

I tried to sound normal. "Because it's the second time, you mean?"

"No—well, yes, that too. Listen, though: Flight 17, Boeing 777, first flew July 17, 1997, exactly, like, *exactly* seventeen years to the *day* before it crashed, July 17."

"It's weird," I said evenly, not turning to look at him.

I felt hot and was still shaky so got up to wet my face. I ran the tap. It was a stupid modern tap. A jet of individual strands, high-speed, spurted forth. They hit the ceramic of the basin with such force that most of the water was lost before I could catch it. I tried to cup some of it to splash on my face. The water stung my hands. It was impossible. I began to cry.

Dwight came and stood behind me. "What's wrong?"

I gulped. Pressed my hands into my eyes. "All the water is coming out as individual strands," I said, choking.

He looked blank.

"So I can't get it in my hands—it just goes everywhere. I want it to be in one smooth column."

"But it's water. What am I supposed to do about that?"

I began to cry harder.

With no immediate solution, Dwight got into bed, annoyed. When I returned he was facing away from me, towards the wall, reading the back of Walter's *Wine for Dummies* book. I turned onto my side, away from him, and closed my eyes.

I was still awake by the time the sun rose behind the muslin drapes and birds began singing, lying with the sheet pulled up to my chin, listening for footsteps. To escape thoughts of Robin, I went to my shrine. There were three new pictures since I'd last looked. I no longer felt like I was doing anything wrong

—secretly looking at her like this, touching her pictures as I slid down, down, down while she slept. It was public, after all; anybody could have come across it by chance. Nor did I feel guilty on behalf of the Rooiakkers any longer. In the end, I kept it secret from Robin and Ingrid because I wanted it to stay mine. A space that belonged to me. I reached her first picture again. I had that thing in the moment before you fall asleep when everything connects. Mad, allusive; when you lie back, so tired your eyes are smarting, and then suddenly your eyes roll open again so wide, because you have understood something, something big.

At breakfast the next morning Robin acted like nothing had happened, which, after a while, made me feel like I had imagined it, and which then made me feel bad, like maybe I should apologise.

"I found your pawn!" Thom cried triumphantly from under the breakfast table.

Ingrid flinched.

"I'm teaching them to play chess," Walter said quickly as Thom flicked the pawn across the table towards him.

The morning was overcast. Rosa emerged with a red scarf around her neck, a SpongeBob SquarePants T-shirt, and a pink woolly hat with a white hygiene mask pulled up from her mouth onto her forehead. She looked like she had just been spelunking with a head torch.

"Rosa, take that off," Ingrid snapped. "Those aren't toys. They belong to your father." She shot Robin a look. "The air is too clean for him here," she said mockingly. "He misses the city."

"He doesn't like breathing germs," Thom said defensively.

Robin remained silent. Rosa sat opposite him, glaring under the mask. She was daring him again. I shuddered and went back to my story. I was in the middle of my third reading of "Kizuna." That became how I got to sleep most nights after that, letting sleep overpower me despite my fear of it, gradually losing myself in Mizuko's descriptions of the black wave until unconsciousness descended, muzzling me like a white surgical mask. And then in my dreams it seemed that everything I read was materialising around me.

Nat demanded, as it was our last day (the first of August), that we go into town for lunch. She'd barely seen *anyone* here. We drove in a convoy of three cars. I went with Dwight, sitting in the back with Thom while Ingrid sat in the front. As she undid the elastic that held her wet blond hair, I caught a blast of shampoo on the wind. I imagined running my fingers through it the way Robin might. Did he still? Or was that why he had put his hand on me?

Everything in the town was dedicated to someone. There was even a plaque on a rock.

"They're running out of things to dedicate," Ingrid observed.

Everywhere we went there was someone Walter or Nat knew. Nat even took a tour of the neatly rowed tombstones in the graveyard, pointing out dead people she'd been acquainted with in life.

"What kind of chairs are those?" Thom asked, indicating the white ones that were everywhere, milky smooth, with narrow slats and broad backs.

"Adirondack," Nat replied.

"They're all over," he said. "It's like the whole of the outside here is actually somebody's home."

It was true, I thought. It didn't really feel like we were actually outside.

"Also," Nat added, "I don't want to alarm anyone, but everywhere we go I see Alec Baldwin. It's like he's following us."

It wasn't that Robin was feeling awkward or guilty, I decided; he was ignoring me. He was supposed to be contrite, and then it would have been up to me what to do about it. Instead I felt embarrassed and could choose nothing.

At lunch, Dwight explained TriMe, now fully rolled out and making headlines.

"I don't understand your job," Nat said finally.

"*Brand*," Ingrid said, rolling her eyes at her mother.

"Is that a real word?"

Unusually, Robin came to Dwight's aid. "It's a Norse word that meant to leave a mark on something, to burn a mark into it. Like livestock . . ."

There was a loud thud and Nat screamed. An enormous stag beetle had dropped onto the table. It brooded, as if planning its next move, before flying straight into the wall and dropping down dead. I felt intensely claustrophobic, trapped, and I wanted nothing more than to go back to the city.

When we got home from lunch it was late afternoon. Dwight put music on, his road-trip playlist, blasting it out of the speakers in the woods. "Sympathy for the Devil" reverberated between floodlit trees, and he came careering outside, howling the *woowoos* at us. I didn't help Ingrid and Nat prepare the salad for dinner, which was my usual task. I no longer felt I could try to belong with these people. I turned instead to Mizuko, who was spending the evening having a bath. The series showed her reading material (Joan Didion) and her scented candle (Diptyque) and her shell-pink toenails perched on the gold taps at the end of the tub. The last was a selfie with two pink flower emojis placed strategically over her chest where the soap bubbles were not dense enough to cover her.

Meanwhile, it was to be our last barbecue, and I never wanted to see another blackened chicken wing as long as I lived. Dwight began droning on about his work trip to San Francisco again. Nat asked him about earthquakes, and then there was a discussion about other unstable regions of the world and a long, inaccurate explanation of tectonic plates by Nat, using the dinner plates, for the benefit of the twins. Walter was quoting from one of his own articles about how we lived in *uncertain and liminal times*. Then he and Dwight started talking about artificial intelligence—robots that could detect earthquakes. This turned into Walter's claim that soon robots would be doing everything for us, from detecting brain tumours to defending criminals, and eventually no one would have any need for human intelligence.

Robin snapped. "Would you *fuck* a robot?" he snarled. "Would you want to wake up next to one in your bed?"

There was a long silence. Nat had shut her eyes very tightly.

"Yes, I would," Walter said calmly. "I would."

"Me too!" Dwight agreed, with feeling.

Ingrid got up from the table and told Rosa and Thom to clear.

Maybe it was Ingrid who suggested using TriMe or downloaded it herself. Or maybe it was both of them together, by mutual consent—some perverse revenge on his wife for sleeping with Walter, or Ingrid trying to twist a knife harder into his front than into his back, where it seemed to be having little effect. But I suspect it was him, without her knowledge, using some pictures he had of her in her bathing suit to set up shop as a couple. One of the things I knew about TriMe was that an account could be accessed on only one person's device at a time, even if the profile was set to "couple." I had protested that surely this meant that people—lone men—could pretend to be part of a couple, to have a nice liberal wife, in order to seduce women. Dwight hadn't denied it. "We're working on it" was all he'd said.

Later that evening I lay still and silent whilst he fucked me. He seemed more into it than he had in weeks, as if the conversation about fucking robots had flipped a switch. We didn't use a condom; I still thought I was sterile and he said he'd pull out in time. He didn't.

The Long Island CVS pharmacy is a tasteful olive green, unlike any of the ones I had seen in the city. Dwight drove me there first thing while everyone else was packing. I had never taken the emergency contraceptive before and read the instructions and side effects carefully before I did.

"Don't bother," Dwight said, uneasy in the driver's seat, holding out a bottle of water to me.

"Don't bother taking it or don't bother reading about it before I take it?"

"They always say risk of death, dizziness, nausea, flulike symptoms. It's psychosomatic."

When we returned from the pharmacy, everyone was busy loading up the cars. I walked through the gate in the hedge, then stopped dead. There was a body hanging from the big tree where the frog and the snake lived. I walked slowly towards it, wondering how to make a sound above a whisper and as loud as a scream for help. When I went nearer, I saw that it was only the black plastic sheath with the red Saks logo on that Nat had for transporting her smart outfits. It had a handwritten label that said BLACK CARDIGAN (*cardigan* crossed out and replaced with *suit*) and then the word *evening* crossed out and replaced with the word *funerals!* So the label now read BLACK SUIT, FUNERALS! I exhaled deeply and went inside to get my own bag. I had seen Ume hanging from the tree.

17

Why are you all *black*?" Silvia said before hello. "Did someone die on your nice vacation?"

I had purchased my black sack, the priestess uniform I had adopted to mimic Mizuko's. We had returned from Walter's a few days previously. I had mainly slept over at Dwight's, having everything I needed with me, and had gone shopping in Brooklyn that morning on my way back to Morningside Heights. I was uncomfortable. I hated the warm, sickly air inside the home, and on this occasion particularly I was filled with sweetish nausea. For those patients who were not Silvia I felt almost no pity, only disgust.

Monitoring Mizuko meant that I had begun to find any other distractions or demands on me irritating. The home and its inhabitants were especially incompatible with the beauty and dark humour of Mizuko's worldview. I scrolled. There was the original photograph of Mizuko at her twenty-first birthday, in her costume based on the *tokusatsu* film *Warning from Space*. I had watched the film online at the Rooiakkers' house before the trip and convinced Dwight to watch it with me by promising him it would have lots of special effects (special for 1956). In the film, an alien race descends to Earth to warn everyone about an impending disaster. They are trying to warn one man who might have the power to stop it, a professor of astronomy, but they can't make contact with him and instead scare ordinary people in the streets of Tokyo shitless, just because of how they look — these big black starfish with an eye in the middle of their gut — until one of them comes up with a plan. They get hold of a photograph of a famous female celebrity, and one of the aliens volunteers to undergo "transmutation" so that it looks exactly like the woman, whom everyone in Tokyo loves. The doppelganger manages to infiltrate the right circle and explains that a rogue planet (Planet R) is on a collision course with Earth. Mizuko's costume is so cute. She has little pastel stars on her shoulders, a white jacket like a spacesuit, a white helmet, and a little antenna with a pink heart on the top. While Dwight and I were watching the film, Ingrid came in and asked us to turn it down. She was trying to do her kundalini yoga and harness the truth.

"What is it?" she said, after we had adjusted the volume.

"Some fucked-up Japanese movie," Dwight answered, staring in horror at the giant starfish-shaped alien about to undergo transmutation. Ingrid came behind us. Her perfume smelt good, and I felt Dwight stiffen as she leant over him on the back of the sofa, her hair brushing my arm.

"I know this one. I've seen it. Robin made me watch it once."

"Really?"

"Yeah. That *thing* is about to turn into a woman."

"Spoiler alert," Dwight said.

"Robin loves this type of stuff. When I first met him he had a kind of Japan fetish. Hence all the pseudo-Japanese features in here, with the sliding screen doors. Let me tell him you're watching it."

"Hey!"

I snapped back into the room. Silvia rattled the adjustable table that was fixed to her bed. She told me that *they* were taking it out on her. When I asked who, and what they were taking out, she said *years of oppression*. I realised she was referring to the mainly black nursing staff and felt a part of me ball up inside. The Wi-Fi was slow. I switched to roaming. I was rewarded with Mizuko's face—a toothbrush protruding from her rosebud mouth—in a bathroom mirror. She was wearing a grey slip. She must have woken up late. It was already three in the afternoon. The caption read CARPE DIEM.

I felt I had developed a deep affinity with her, as if she were a child star I had grown up with, against whose milestones I remembered my own experiences happening in parallel, as well as various theories, based on her stories and what I could find out about her life online, and what only I—and now Nat—knew. I couldn't piece together precisely how Robin and Hiromi had met. I'd found, after much trawling, a search result for a Hiromi Himura on a webpage that did not seem to have been properly indexed, which in some way connected her with Imperial College. The year listed was the year before Mizuko's birth, but many other years were also listed, and I couldn't be sure whether my search terms made it clear what I was looking to find. Her name might have been appearing in connection with this page simply because she had been affiliated with the University of Tokyo, which in turn might have had connections with or held an academic conference of some kind—I didn't know what—with Imperial College. My search terms, highlighted yellow to show why the engine had picked this out for me, were woven into JavaScript, and others were written in Japanese, so that I didn't know exactly what I was looking at or whether parts of the page were just not working.

I had spent so much time looking at things through Mizuko's eyes, from her exact height or posture, that I felt I could almost predict what she was about to do next. I had decided that I wanted to see her in person somehow, to see if she was even real, not some glitch in which I could see myself in another universe. Initially I had been thinking of trying to stage a collision when she was alone in a public place like the park, but she usually cycled everywhere, even the smallest distances, so my opportunities seemed slim.

Silvia poked her feet out of the end of the bed and asked me to fit her little velvet slippers on them because she was cold.

"Any more ideas about what you want to do yet? Maybe Ingrid could give you an internship?"

"Mmm. Maybe."

"No?"

"I think . . ." I wasn't giving her my full attention. "I think I would have to know how to use CAD and stuff."

Suddenly I felt a rushing in my ears and the prickly car-crash feeling behind my knees. Mizuko had followed her toothbrush selfie from fifteen minutes ago with an aerial shot of a table and a male hand in view, wearing a watch I knew from her other pictures as Rupert's. They were inside the Hungarian Pastry Shop, which Robin, and therefore the twins, called the Hungarian Café, metres away from where I was now. I had been there with Robin and the twins once and I recognised it from the red paint on the wall beneath the rail and the crispy strata of the cake. In any case, she had just tagged the location, so there could be no mistake. If I stuck my head out and to the right, its red-and-white-striped awning could nearly be seen from Silvia's window.

"Hey." Silvia poked me with her bony foot. "Tell me things."

She wanted to know about Walter's glass house, exactly how modern it was, and then to dictate a letter to be mailed to an old friend who lived in France. I forgot to mail it because I was so desperate to make it to the café before Mizuko and Rupert left. I still had the letter in my pocket at the Holocaust talk. I still have it. It's part of the collection under my desk, dated August 10.

From the corner of red I could tell their table was situated at the back and on the right, if you were looking from the entrance. The choice of beverage there is not like what coffee shops in most cities offer now. The choice is beautifully simple. The only cold drinks on the menu are milk, Coke, orange juice (which can be either small or large), seltzer, and cold cider. Hot options include only American tea or coffee, café au lait (which is American coffee with hot milk), hot chocolate, and other teas, which are just called "special teas" and served in a pot. I accidentally ordered milk at first because I was so nervous, then switched to coffee and added a gelatinous cake so I could spend longer there if I needed to. EXPECT A MIRACLE TODAY, advised a rainbow sign by the cash register.

The last time I had been there I'd observed a steady stream of Columbia students, who were territorial about their work spots and writing nooks. I have still got my guest check, which says your name and how much you owe. I kept my eyes on the girl serving me. It was possible that Rupert would recognise me first, but I worried that he would then try to avoid me by leaving. I took a spot near the entrance but facing the back of the room so that I could intercept them if he tried to escape. The waitress called out my name when my coffee was ready and I scowled at her. That was when I first looked directly towards where they were. I could see the back of the empty chair on Mizuko's right and then her back next to it. The solid black curtain of hair. I wanted to go to it, pull it back to reveal her so I could be sure she was not some shadow trick of cyberspace.

Luckily Rupert sat opposite her, so that I would be able to

catch his eye when I went to the bathroom, which was just behind the end of the counter on the left, about three quarters of
the way towards the back. That was my plan: enter the bathroom, rehearse my surprised face in the mirror, exit, catch Rupert's eye, go over, ask intelligent questions re: Columbia, say,
"Actually, yes, by crazy coincidence I am thinking of studying for
an MFA just like yours! I guess you might even be my teacher
then." Begin at the beginning. Know nothing. Tabula rasa. At
the same time, part of me wanted to distinguish myself. To let
her sense the bond we shared straightaway. Maybe subtly hint
at some of my secret intelligence. A special handshake. A nod. I
now completely understood how criminal masterminds could so
easily get caught before the big reveal—the temptation to boast
about the execution was huge.

I pulled the bathroom door shut behind me. The trap was set,
a loop on the ground for the little white foot, a net that would
appear from nowhere. Someone had written out the molecular
structure of LSD across the ceiling. I didn't need to pee, but I sat
down on the seat and stared up at its constellation above me in
order to measure a natural length of time before reappearing.
I was aware that as a guest of Silvia's, and now of Robin and
Ingrid's, I was about to transgress a code. An ancient host-guest
code. But then, hadn't all of them already done that? Did all
New York belong to people and families in their homes already,
or might a part of it, maybe not a physical part but the part
that buzzed and throbbed and shone most brightly by night, be
mine? Sitting on the toilet seat, I felt anxious for a new reason.
Up until now, it had all belonged to me. The information was
contained. I held it—literally—in the palm of my hand. I had
been perving on what Mizuko chose to make public without her
even knowing I existed. She knew nothing about me. By meeting

her in person, face to face, I was sacrificing some of this power, tipping the scales between us.

I unlocked the door, advanced two steps, and produced my grotesque mask of surprise, which Rupert stubbornly didn't see. I took two more steps—grandmother steps—so that I was right next to their table. They still did not look at me. I felt I couldn't do it twice, the surprised face, in case someone else had noticed it. I could tell from his animated expression that he was in the exact middle of telling Mizuko a story.

"But then I literally bumped into Uri, you know, that guy at Oberlin?" He clapped his hands together to demonstrate the climax of his story.

"Rupert!"

They both turned at once.

18

As you know, it worked like a charm. I hovered for a while, asking polite questions, dropping in interests I had siphoned from hers. Then I retrieved my belongings from my table and tangled up the chair legs as I tried to sit down at theirs. The handle of my white enamel cup was too small for me not to burn my knuckles as I drank, but even when it had cooled I left it on the table half drunk to prevent them from leaving. I discovered then, as Rupert declined the ticket for the Holocaust talk, that it is relatively easy to get instant gratification if you are not too worried about what comes after.

"After" began at dawn.

Exactly when the plastic bottle snapped me out of my nightmare with the dead body in the mud, the cat pounced, and Mizuko said *cat* and turned over a few times until we were back to back. When I finally managed to regulate my breathing to match hers, after the shock of the snap and then the sound of her voice, I watched the whole room turn pink, then red, then white. We're back in that room again. Mizuko's bed. The bed in the centre of the bedroom, the centre of the universe, books stacked above the matte-black radiator and against every wall.

When I was finally able to move, I staggered, head pounding, to the bathroom. In the mirror I saw that my face had bloated because of the shellfish she'd ordered. There was a brute ridge where my eyebrows should have been, deforming the shape of my eyes and the bridge of my nose. I looked not unlike Quark from *Star Trek*. Though it had been worth it, a million times, to spend the evening with her and to sleep in the same bed, I did not particularly want her to see me like this. *You could just leave now,* the authoritative drone voice said sensibly, *and then request to follow her. That is the etiquette here really. You've outstayed your welcome already. She barely knows you, and you're in her bathroom talking to yourself. Sure, it's a little tacky to run out on her this early, but she said her apartment is for intimate friends only, remember?* She also said it was haunted, I reasoned back. *Well, you're here, aren't you?*

But if you leave, I cautioned Quark in the mirror, *that's it. You might not get a second chance. Or I guess you might, but you know it won't be at this intensity. It'll be formal and involve saying you'll meet up for coffee and then it probably won't happen. Rupert will be there if it does, or he'll probably tell her that you are seriously lame and not worth following up with. Right now she doesn't know that. Don't go.*

A hasty retreat then, without goodbye, would not, I decided, sit well after the night that preceded it. We had, I felt, bared small pieces of our symmetrical souls to each other, fast, as if playing one of those breathless card games, and I had pretended to be as moved as I had been the first time I uncovered it all myself, back in East Hampton.

I went back to the bedroom, where Mizuko was still unconscious. I had a message waiting for me from Dwight. I'd assured him that today would be the day my period was due, my first since our trip to CVS, and so he wanted to know if it had arrived on schedule. He'd saved the date in his phone. August 11. His presence, intruding into her bedroom with such a crass question, changed the atmosphere immediately.

I replied, *No but packet said it might alter cycle and also mine are often irregular because poly.* I had explained to him that I believed my ovaries were speckled with cysts.

Where are you now?

At Silvia's, on Amsterdam.

How's she doing?

Fine, I typed, feeling sweat pricking my skin under my shirt. *No change here.*

"Can you get me a glass of water?"

My heart plummeted into my stomach, and then my stomach dropped, with the new weight it was carrying, into my pants. I held myself like I had to pee.

"Good morning." It came out with unexpected force; I'd been preparing for so long to say it but still wasn't ready.

"Not tap, the electrolyte water in the fridge." She groaned without lifting her head from the pillow. "I can't even —"

I backed out of the room, into her kitchen. Every surface gleamed as if it had never been used. The fridge was full of neat white boxes.

"Take whatever you want," she called hoarsely on hearing the clink of glass inside the fridge door as I opened it, handling everything softly, like an intruder wearing gloves. "I think there's a Paleo muffin. Whatever you want."

She was desperately hung over, minus the adrenaline that enabled me to ignore it. She raised her head on the pillow, turned down her phone's brightness, and began jabbing at it.

"No reply from Rupert," she said grimly as I handed her a glass of water. "He does this. It's a control thing." I nodded. Of course he did, the bastard. "Why don't you message him and suggest that the three of us hang out today? He'll reply to you. Especially if you haven't seen each other for ages. Say you want a proper reunion."

"Sure. If you want."

I pretended I had Rupert's number, and pretended to be typing the message as she composed the exact wording for me so that she didn't sound desperate or like she was coercing me. It had to sound, she explained, like it was *my* idea. I pretended to hit *Send*. I felt like a child playing with a toy phone modelled on the grown-up object. I didn't mind exaggerating my friendship with Rupert, since she seemed to think she might get to him by me. I could always claim later that the message hadn't sent—say something about its being a British phone.

"I'll let you know what he says."

She spent the morning waiting for the reply in bed, glued to CNN images of the Ferguson shooting, looking like a bird that had flown into a window.

"No?" she kept asking, and I would shake my head.

"No."

I never wanted there to be a too-big silence between us. It made me nervous. Silence was only okay if one of us was looking at a device. There had to be near-constant communication or I felt we would come unstuck from the fast new intimacy between us. I feared that in silence, things I'd meant to keep hidden would rise up by themselves, like steam from an open manhole.

Rupert called time on their relationship approximately three hours and twenty minutes after I didn't send the message inviting him to hang out, so instead of me leaving or him coming, we spent the whole day together, she and I. She lay in bed like a sick child, limply scrolling through pictures, occasionally crying out in pain or making disgusted noises at what she saw. Though Rupert shunned social media (making him godlike to Mizuko), they had all the same friends, so it was only a matter of time, she promised me, before she saw something she didn't want to see. Something that was painful.

"I'm going to have to get an entirely new social scene if I want to avoid him," she said, hunting for evidence of him amongst her friends' feeds. I made a sympathetic face, but my heart leapt up onto her, beat its fists on her heart, yelled, *Me Me Me!*

"I just feel"—she put her hand on her stomach and repeated herself for what felt like the tenth time—"like I've had everything inside me *ripped* out." She made a ripping motion. "But then I talk to you and I forget for a bit and then I remember and I feel it all over again."

When she was not pacified by her device, she spoke continuously about him. If I had known then what I do now, I would have realised that what I wanted was impossible. The more she said about her love for him, the less I should have hoped. Instead, being naive, I saw only how she might be *persuaded* if I provided her with whatever she needed. If I was there to lean on, and if my chest retained the exact imprint of her exquisite head, then she would need only that spot on which to rest. Of course what I should have done was copy Rupert's lead and try to carry on where he left off, treating her like shit. Or maybe it was already too late; you only get one first love. She was mine, but I had not been hers. She was only going to look for some echo of it, and if I had made the right noises, that echo might have been me for a while.

"Sometimes he makes me feel like I am wrong to give up on him because he could be *everything* I want him to be, and other times he makes me feel like I am such a fucking *moron* and that

I should have given up on him the second I *met* him because he is never going to be able to be what I want him to be. It's like the longer I've been with him, the less I've known him—he's only ever been getting fuzzier the whole time. Sometimes I worry that he will just vanish forever, and sometimes I think I'd prefer that so I don't have to deal with the fact of him not wanting me, or wanting someone else. We had basically stopped having sex, you know?"

I did know. She had said this many times the previous evening.

"Well, not stopped, but for *us,* you know, I told you what it *used* to be like, we had definitely been doing it *much* less. Like once a day, and really fast. None of that amazing morning sex where you forget who is who."

I swallowed hard.

"We used to do it *constantly,* but in Paris the most romantic thing he did was roll cold Perrier cans from the minibar on my feet because I had blisters."

This sounded good to me.

"My feet were so sore I had to crawl around our bedroom, even on the carpet. I know I shouldn't give him, like, a second chance, or a tenth, whatever it is now, but—"

I let her talk, imagining her crawling on her hands and knees around the Parisian hotel room, since she did not seem to want anything more from me than occasional solidarity, and as she talked I wandered around the bedroom, touching things I recognised. It was the same feeling of recognition, but much sharper, that I had had when I had arrived in New York and Tokyo. I guess that's the same for most new places now: the new feeling is the sense of actually *being* there, standing in the place you have already seen remotely, not what is actually there.

Her apartment was on the top floor of a building with an

elevator and a concierge and a bike room. She's since moved, so at one time there was a listing for it that had photographs of the inside, taken with a fisheye lens, which had the disorienting effect of making it look much bigger, with all new stuff in it. I screenshot the pictures and zoomed in as far as I could go before it pixelated.

The next day I said she should eat something: What would she like? But she said she was still feeling sick, that thoughts of Rupert had pushed all hunger away, and she wouldn't know what she could stomach, or if she could eat at all, until she saw food. We went to a deli one block away. I tried to get her to pick something, but she was distracted, selecting only a garlic bulb in a white mesh sock and swinging it around in a threatening way.

"Look at this," she commanded, indicating a display of postcards. She was holding up one with an ox.

"What?"

"Rupert is an ox." She alternated between shaking and nodding her head as she verified this on her device. "Yup, he's a fucking ox, I should have known. I should have *fucking known*."

"What are you?"

She spun the display. "A dog."

I spun the wheel looking for me.

The Ram
1919, 1931, 1943, 1955, 1967, 1979, 1991, 2003, 2015

People born under the sign of the Ram are artistic, cre-
ative, elegant, honest, warm-hearted, timid, and charming.
They are also pessimistic, vulnerable, and disorganized.
They depend on material comforts and are very quick to
complain. They do not handle pressure well but can find
their own solution to a problem when given time. The

*best professions for Rams are gardeners and actors. They
are compatible with Pigs and Rabbits but should avoid
Oxen.*

I found her a Greek salad—something told me this might be
what she needed; I suppose I was thinking, Fresh, Greek island,
Mediterranean holiday—but when I caught up with her again in
the next aisle, she was in tears.

"What's wrong?"

She pointed at a packet of extra-long grissini sticks. "His favourite. I buy them specially for, for . . . because he loves them
so much and I—I—"

The bread aisle was too much for her. I tossed the salad box
back onto one of the shelves, the wrong one (something I would
never do in normal circumstances, but we were in the midst of a
crisis, or a miracle, depending on whose point of view you took;
either way, the rules of normal life had gone out the window)
and suggested we go to the cinema instead.

"To see what?"

I listed the first option that came up.

"Is it to do with love?"

"No. I don't know."

She said nothing. We were standing outside.

"Summer is always such a depressing season," she said. I nodded and began to list times and locations. She chose the Magic
Johnson movie theatre for a three-thirty showing. Because it was
such a beautiful day outside, there was no one else in there except for one or two irate people with hay fever. But the movie
was to do with love, and so we left halfway through, but not
before Mizuko had rested her head on my shoulder. When she
leant on me, it gave me shape. It rooted me to the spot. Coming
out into the hot sunlight after the cool darkness of the cinema

was like a rebirth. I came out knowing for certain what I wanted to do with my life, what to put in the body of my butterfly. My calling. My quest. My meaning. My path. My purpose.

She was worried that she was going to be sick. Her eyes were glassy and she did, out in the light, look pale.

"You're just hung over," I reassured her. "You need a Coke. Can I get you a Coke at least?"

She nodded weakly. A single tear slid down her face. I wondered, weird to lick it? Yes. Don't lick. I went to the kiosk in the cinema, bought a ridiculously expensive cola, and pushed a straw in it for her in the way that made a vein pop in Dwight's neck. I went out to where she was sitting on the sidewalk.

"Here."

She looked up as if she didn't recognise me and took the drink.

The look unnerved me. She was clearly experiencing some kind of post-traumatic shock, and I realised I couldn't trust her to remember me if I left her side for a minute.

I took her home, exuding the altruism of a kind stranger who did not want to leave her alone for her own good. She did not seem to see this as a sacrifice on my part. It did not occur to her that I might have other people to see, other casualties and broken hearts to attend to. She said she had always felt more soothed by strangers than by people who were supposed to be close to her. "People like—" She faltered. She couldn't say his name without crying.

I suggested she try the butterfly game. She said I had the zeitgeist. I was doing everything I could think of to keep her away from her phone, trying to entertain her. She mainly stared blankly down at the lock screen of her device, unresponsive sometimes even to direct questions. These were silences, I suppose, in which such a person, a real stranger or new acquaintance, would have excused herself and gone back to her own home, but it didn't feel like I had one to go to even if I wanted to leave her, which I didn't.

"Fuck!"

She held up her device to show me, but I already knew from the look of sheer panic mixed with crazed joy that had come over her face. As she held it out to me, the screen went dark and the vibration stopped. I made my face broad and innocent but was fairly sure I had achieved it with my mind.

"Don't call back," I said. "Here, give it to me. I'll keep hold of it so you won't be tempted."

Her jaw clenched and her eyes widened like I was about to hurt her, like I was about to take away her child. She pulled it to her body, away from me.

"Give it here," I insisted, placing my hand on her wrist and prising it free with my fingers like an *ama* diver, freeing the delicacy from a rock with a little spatula. "Trust me."

19

At home, I settled her on the sofa and brought her cat. While living with the Rooiakkers I had overcome my fear of small dogs (really it was all pets, even my mother's; I didn't trust them) and knew from Thom how soothing holding one could be.

"Take it," I insisted, holding the cat aloft.

"Her name's Michi."

"Take Michi."

Every time I did something like this—pretended to be ignorant of something I knew as well as I knew my own name—I congratulated myself. Michi was all over Mizuko's Instagram. She was obese and ostentatiously fluffy. She let herself be placed in Mizuko's lap.

"She isn't very well, poor thing. See, she's got pinkeye."

Michi had curled herself to face me and I saw that her eyes were a hideous blood red.

"I have drops for her, but I keep forgetting to do it. Do you want to do it, maybe? She scratches a bit when you do."

"Okay, I can do that. Anything else?"

"She's not allowed outside. She's a house cat. That's why

there's net over the windows. Just be careful when you open and shut the door, because sometimes she makes a break for the hall."

"Okay."

"And can you go buy me some tobacco?"

"Sure."

When she was feeling stronger, I suggested we go to the Morgan Library. She said she was sorry she was being a bad host, given that I was a newcomer to the city. I knew the library was one of her favourite places—it said so on her Google Pin. It would get her inspired to start writing something again, or carry on with the novel she'd abandoned, I said. Also I had never been. First she showed me the room where the signs of the zodiac were depicted in the ceiling. Kids from some kind of summer camp, maybe ten or eleven years old, were lying under the rotunda looking up and a guide was telling them a story, so we sat on the floor too.

"The ceiling paintings depict the three major literary epochs represented in the collection. We have Emerson, Hawthorne, Thoreau. You name it, we got it."

"I love *Walden*," I whispered in her ear. "And *The Scarlet Letter*." They were listed on one of her posts from a few years before, when people had nominated their social-media friends to list their ten favourite books, with reasons why.

"Likewise."

We followed the tour into the original library, to the tapestry depicting avarice personified by King Midas.

"Who knows what happened to King Midas?" the guide asked.

No hands went up.

"No one?" She paused. "Okay. Everything King Midas touched turned to gold." The children seemed impressed. "Now, you might think that sounds kinda cool, but you think about it a little longer. Do you really want everything you touch—your food, your pets, your best friend, your mom—to turn to gold?"

"Noooooo," they chorused.

"Imagine it, though," Mizuko said to me suddenly, "if everything you touched . . ."

A feeling crept over me, and I had the distinct impression she was looking at my mouth as she spoke. I felt my lip itch as though a wasp had landed on it.

"You wouldn't ever be able to have physical contact with anyone without killing them," I replied stiffly, trying not to move my lip too much.

"Do you ever wonder . . . like why, or like how, people started kissing?"

I had to fight the urge to put my tongue out onto my bottom lip and feel for the wasp. If it was there it would sting me; the only thing to do was remain still. I must have frowned.

"I'm serious. How did the first kiss happen? Did two people just randomly decide to put their faces together exactly, like nose to nose, so that their lips lined up and then kind of mush them together?"

"I guess." I said it through a clenched jaw, trying to keep my mouth as still as possible.

There had been lots of signs. Explicit signs. We were now so close that we had nowhere to go but back. Unless it was possible —I wondered—to go through? It felt like staring into a mirror, never actually touching the other body even though you pressed yourself against it.

Rupert sent a message to her phone, which I still held captive, every couple of hours, and I did not report them. Even without this information, Mizuko was on a continuous cycle of breaking up. As soon as I began to think she was improving I would have to begin all over again. I came to know the stages in great detail. From tears to rage to glassy-eyed exhaustion to shock and back again. I wanted to find a way to disrupt the cycle somehow and suggested she try something *trademarked,* a method I found online for her called the thirty-day no-contact rule. She was very interested in this, and even paid for a PDF manual you could buy once you had read the free introductory section on how the method worked. It was "guaranteed" to bring back any ex, no matter how bad the breakup had been, but you had to cut them completely out of your life as if they were a cancer. It was not just a case of ignoring them and refusing to spy on them; you had to take proactive measures to guard against their presence in your life. They needed to be locked out completely.

As she read it, I administered Michi's eyedrops, ordered takeout with her credit card, and borrowed some beautiful silky black clothes she pointed to on her rail instead of going home to change. The manual said to immerse yourself in distractions like salsa, swimming, or learning a language.

"What do you think?" I asked when I could see she had stopped reading for a moment, opened another tab on her laptop, and was scrolling through pictures of a girl she thought Rupert liked. "Do you want to try it?" If she refused, I would have to confiscate that device somehow too, I thought. It wouldn't be long before he tried violating her boundaries by email. Now that I've had firsthand experience of Mizuko's silence, I can imagine the chokehold under which Rupert must have been suffering. Tighter and tighter the more messages he sent without replies. I guess I'm lucky he didn't do something crazy.

I had never been tempted to take drugs of any kind and especially not mind-altering ones, but when Mizuko introduced me to Provigil, which she described as mind-*enhancing,* I took two. I was feeling a little wound up already, a little edgy, a little over my head too quickly, but she made it sound like you felt more in control, not less. She said she used it to write, or to level herself out sometimes. I did not want to be excluded from whatever it was that she was going to be doing that day, even though I had once observed someone get stuck after taking Provigil the day before he had to submit a fifty-thousand-word dissertation, insisting on conducting his word count by hand and restarting every time he lost his place. You had to be strategic about when you took it if you didn't want to get stuck. Mizuko acknowledged that this was true. She had once gotten stuck in front of her bedroom mirror, unable to stop applying a shaft of dark red lipstick until she had eroded it to the hilt. When there was no more red in the tube, she began tracing the same circuit with her finger.

I got the same selfish tunnel vision Mizuko promised she got. It was exhilarating to imagine I was sharing a similar tunnel, if not the same one. And obviously I got stuck on her too. Everything else went blurry while she became more arresting, with something like an angora texture at her edges. When I had to go to the bathroom, I sprayed her perfume in the air and walked through it.

"You smell nice," she said as I returned.

"What of?"

"Me."

I noted how much more strongly my nervous system reacted to her praise compared to when Dwight had told me I was quirky and the air had felt stagnant and mildly oppressive. This time the combination of the compliment, the mid-August heat, the perfume, and the smell of her cigarettes, which she smoked inside, made me feel like I was going to faint. At this stage, I thought that my increasingly debilitating waves of nausea might be a side effect of Provigil.

From then on we spent days on it at a time, going on quests

without leaving the apartment—searching for things, counting things, breaking things down. I sometimes take it now. It gives me an attention span that, if I am careful, if I choose the right Wikipedia trail, can keep her at bay for hours. Occasionally it backfires and reminds me of her more than any artefact or sound or picture I have. A line stretches out, wire-tight, under the ocean, a pipeline I can walk back along.

I think it was the fourth or fifth day I had spent at her place and I hadn't been back to the Rooiakkers' once. I suppose they assumed I was with Silvia by day and Dwight by night. Thom sent one message saying, "Are you in tonight for pizza?" and I replied, "No thanks." But I hadn't visited Silvia since I'd left to catch Mizuko in the Hungarian café, and had mostly been ignoring the messages I'd got from Dwight until one arrived that afternoon telling me that there was a crisis and I needed to come right away. I called him and got no answer. Paranoid that it had something to do with Mizuko and my discovery, now the only category of crisis I could imagine, I left the apartment, telling myself I could risk leaving her for an hour. On my way I saw one of the ads for TriMe that Dwight had promised I would.

When I got back to hers, Mizuko didn't even ask me what had happened. She was looking at pictures of her and Rupert together and crying. Worried that Dwight would discover it on my person, I'd left her phone in the bread bin, where she'd evidently found it.

"I saw the picture you posted. A swarm of *bees*? That was the emergency?"

I bristled. I wanted her to think, despite my pledge to stay at her side, that I had a life outside her walls. "My boyfriend keeps them on his roof. They got out. Tried to make a new nest behind a neon sign in a beauty salon opposite his building."

"I know." She sounded slightly hurt.

She had just taken one more from the Provigil blister packet because she said she had something to finish for her first seminar when teaching started again in a fortnight. I tried to make my voice sound innocent and cheerful.

"He needed help getting them back in. You have to wear these funny boots and masks and catch them using a—" I could see she was not listening. I left the sentence in midair, pretending I was finished.

I began laying out food on the coffee table next to her feet. I had bought snacks from the deli on my way back. She slipped down onto the floor and began rolling a quail egg across the tabletop, crunching its speckled shell, laboriously picking, then pulling as a whole section attached to the silky membrane came away. She appeared mollified by the gifts.

"What have you decided to do about—" She made a graceful curving motion to imply a pregnant belly.

I froze. I had forgotten about that. At that moment I couldn't get my brain to contemplate the question, mainly because she had asked me a question at all. About me, not Rupert or, at the most, Rupert and me and how we knew each other. There had been an exquisite moment when I had seen that she suspected, from the slightly exaggerated version of my conversation with Rupert about the view in Tokyo, that we might have been lovers, or at least that a one-night stand had taken place, and I could see both that she'd been jealous and that I had risen in her esteem. I couldn't even imagine an answer that a pregnant person might say. I blinked furiously, made a show of having something in my eyes.

She looked away and studied a piece of shell on her nail very intently. "I had an abortion once," she said. "I didn't want to end up like my mother."

She hadn't talked about anything like this—of her life before Rupert—since the breakup. Nor, which I found even stranger, had she ever written about it.

"I'm going to have a shower." Her first since Rupert had ended things. "See you in a bit."

I sat on the sofa compulsively eating purple radishes. Michi sat at my feet. I gazed into her malevolent, squashed face, her pearly eyes, no longer red, and pink nose. According to a schedule pinned to the wall, Mizuko's first class, on September 3, would be called "What Language to Write In? 3 p.m. Dodge 413."

I listened intently to the sounds of ritual cleaning. I took another pill. She was in there for what felt like ages. How good it must feel, I thought, looking at my own quail egg, to have your tight little shell just peeled clean off like that. Like Mizuko had managed to do practically in one motion. One second of ecstasy before you are eaten. I accidentally dug my thumbnail into the white. When she returned, I was completely wired, staring at the door waiting for her to emerge.

"I feel better," she said with a sigh of relief.

"We should go out somewhere tonight," I said, recalling the part of the manual which said this should be attempted on the fifth day. For me, the promise of the thirty-day no-contact rule lay in the bullet point that said at the end of the thirty days you wouldn't even want your ex back anymore, so it didn't matter if the method hadn't worked.

She sat down next to me in her towel, letting the top part of it drop around her waist as she wrung her hair out. I looked straight ahead.

"Can't," she said. Her long wet hair had left a trail of water droplets from the bathroom to the sofa. "If I go out, I'm guaranteed to bump into him. Especially if I'm trying not to or trying not to think about him. It's the law of opposites, and certainly the law of breakups in New York."

"Unique New York," I said.

"What?"

"Unique New York, unique New York." I smiled. "Try it. Unique New York. Unique New York."

"Unique New York," she said doubtfully. "Unique New York."

"That's it. Unique New York. Carry on. Faster."

"Unique New York, unique New York."

"Faster."

"Unique New York unique New York unique . . ." A smile began to spread over her face too. "Oh god, yes. Unique New York. That feels *good.*"

I'd brought her into my tunnel.

If you were wondering whether I had looked at everything on her phone while I had it, then: of course. I thought that would be obvious, but maybe you're not like me. Maybe you don't snoop. Good for you. It was the most surreal experience at first—to be holding the device, the source of her power, the source of contamination. It felt kind of like holding her brain, and I held it like that, my palm flat, my right index finger light and quick, as if the phone were jellied or slimy. Whilst it was in my possession I covered as much ground as I could. I put in keywords to hook the kind of thing I most wanted. Sensible words like *Rupert, Hunter, Mother, Father,* and, because I could, a few like *sex, sexy, fuck,* and *fucking.* I just wanted to see what would come up. Sometimes messages she had not yet seen, so I had to *Mark Unread.* I went back and forth to the bathroom so many times to look at it that she had actually noticed and asked me if anything was wrong.

The first thing I infiltrated, after I'd read her most recent messages from Rupert and ascertained that no, they had not been discussing me at any point the previous evening, was a folder marked SOCIAL. Inside this I found Dwight's 3 logo for TriMe. My finger froze when I saw it.

After all the sex research I had done while isolated in my room after graduation, admiring Maria Ozawa, I suppose I should have been prepared for the kind of images Mizuko had been swapping with random strangers. It wasn't even what they depicted that was so shocking, but that I knew this person was a real person. I had to sit down mainly because I was shocked, but also because I was turned on. I suppose it was a fight-or-flight response to seeing the pictures. I froze and then fought. Fought in the sense that I masturbated frantically on her bathroom floor looking at pictures she and Rupert had taken of themselves in a mirror. It was a bizarre, not necessarily pleasurable feeling. My blood had run cold, but slowly, as if all the hot had run out; something in my heart felt like it might be breaking, and yet I could not stop. By the time I was done, I had pins and needles and my ass was numb from the ceramic tiles.

"You've been in there for ages," she called. "Are you okay?"

I deleted any incriminating search history and tried to stand up, but my legs were so dead I nearly fell over and had to cling on to the towel rail, which was scorching hot. "*YES!*" I said, everything throbbing.

She was crouching on the sofa, and when I came out she beckoned. "I want to show you something." She had her laptop. Probably more pictures of Rupert. I didn't know how to act after what I'd just done. Her device was in my back pocket and was burning a hole. A hole through which all Rupert's dick pics were protruding and giving me little electric shocks.

"I've been researching writing retreats in Wyoming. I'm look-ing for ones with no Wi-Fi," she explained.

I waited till later that evening, when she had reached the an-gry phase of her breakup cycle, after we had finished a second bottle of wine, and played the road-trip playlist Dwight had put on in the car and later boomed from Walter's outdoor speakers. Mizuko did wild dancing in the living room, moving like she was possessed, mumbling the verses and wailing the chorus.

"We should go somewhere," I panted, jiggling my limbs be-side her. "On a road trip, you know? We could go on the retreat together."

"You need to submit writing in order to be considered."

"I could submit some of yours."

Mizuko smiled and shrugged, ignoring the suggestion. She was still not wearing a bra after her shower. She let her vest's left strap slip over her narrow shoulder. I watched her stamping her feet and pounding her thighs and tossing her head, waiting for her to agitate the remaining strap. She circled near me. I went to refill my mug of wine.

I have reproduced this memory almost every day since it hap-pened. So many times I no longer know that it *did* happen, this one moment, hyperreal, which rends everything in two. When I come back she bends over me, closing her eyes and extending her neck, exposing her throat, her head thrown back so that her nose nearly touches the tip of mine. I look at the thin skin of her eye-lids and see her eyes moving beneath them, and wonder if she is imagining other people in other places instead of me and where she is right now. When she opens them again, looking confused that I have not kissed her, I ask her if she wants more wine, and she slowly pulls a single strand of her hair out of my mouth as I try to speak, tender but strange—the ticklish sensation inside my mouth as her hair is drawn out. This is it, I think, this is the tipping point. The manual foretold it. And from now on I am falling. She kisses *me*. A single thread of spit draws out between us as she pulls away; she breaks it with her nail.

When we go to bed, nothing is mentioned, but she wraps her arms around me and holds on through the night.

20

In the morning, the only sign that anything had changed was that Mizuko announced she was finally feeling mentally strong enough to go outside unaided. She asked for her phone back, and boosted by the kiss, though still neither of us spoke of it, I consented.

Outside meant for a walk, she said, and she wanted to go alone, and then later, to a restaurant with her friends that evening, to which I could come if I didn't have plans. After she got back, I lingered around her all afternoon, waiting for the kiss to be repeated. I had spent the night dreamily replaying it, seeing it from the outside rather than from within the kiss, as if I were watching us on film. But it did not happen again, and when she did not return my loving gazes, I began to wonder if we'd moved too fast. She was still grieving over Rupert, after all. I told myself to be patient.

She spent ages getting ready for dinner, at last emerging from her closet wearing an elegant black dress, full skirt and narrow bodice, with the marshmallow-white sneakers she often wore. I watched as she selected a wide-brimmed black hat, earrings, and an ornate handbag. All her things looked expensive. She had her baby-blue perfume bottle in her hand. This had been the revelation, now I was with her in a real, physical sense—her smell. Now I knew what the milk-and-wood scent was; I could pick it out everywhere, throughout the apartment, where it mingled with sandalwood incense. It's one of my many smaller regrets that I can barely smell her scent when I spray it on myself now. I've become immune.

"You look great," I said.

"Thanks."

I tried to slow her movements with my eyes, to catch her attention in the mirror by staring directly at her. When she continued, oblivious, I wondered whether I should go up behind her, hold her waist like I had done the previous night.

I took two steps towards her, lifted my hands—suddenly made of lead—towards the small of her back, leaning towards her neck uncertainly. I opened my mouth to speak. I don't know what I was going to say—I think her name.

Muh—

She felt my breath on her neck, or heard it, and spun around to face me in alarm.

"You look," I stammered, "amazing."

"You just said that, silly." She giggled and turned back to the mirror.

I wanted to ask why she was making the effort. I had liked her recent disintegration. The greasy hair and smudged eyeliner had been reassuring. She seemed to read my thoughts, however.

"We might bump into Rupert." She said it without taking her eyes off her face in the mirror.

The restaurant was Italian. Three of her friends came. They were from Yale, not Columbia. It was tough. Mizuko kept telling them how *great* I was and how *smart* and how *funny.* She introduced me like a new pet, and of course the attention thrilled me, but it also meant I couldn't speak. I barely said a word, and the friends kept looking at me expectantly. I went to the bathroom to get my shit together and scrolled through some pictures of my trip before I met her, some anecdotes to recall, but still no words would come, certainly not great or smart or funny words. Not the kind they were waiting for. I wanted Mizuko to tell my stories for me, which would also tell me which ones had made an impression on her. She seemed to find everything to do with my relationship with Dwight hilarious, but I didn't feel like talking about that in front of her friends, not now that she and I had kissed. I wanted to phase him out of the equation in case she thought he was an obstacle. When I finally thought of something that didn't involve enemas or old people, the words would pile up in my mouth, reluctant to expose themselves to their audience, and I'd have to swallow them down again.

The situation got worse when they came back to her apartment after and someone put on music. An advert interrupted during a moment when I was the person nearest the laptop, and so somebody said to me—quite threateningly, I felt—*Put something else on.* Obviously I forgot every song I have ever heard in my entire life. In one swift tug, like the tablecloth trick where everything is supposed to remain on the table gone wrong, every name of every artist disappeared too. The only keywords I could think of were the ones on a toy keyboard-and-tape-recorder combo I'd been given as a child, and I hadn't known their meaning even then. *Bossa nova,* for example.

I said I couldn't think of anything, *any music,* except silence, and retreated to the corner of the room, pretending to busy myself by scouring the bookcase there, which held little gatherings of figurines as well as Mizuko's many books. *Heirlooms,* she

31 Jul 2020 2 12 PM

Item(s) checked out to

D4000000562256

The switch / Beth O'Leary
Date Due 21 Aug 2020

Pretending / Holly Bodine
Date Due 21 Aug 2020

Kindred / Octavia E. Butler
Date Due 21 Aug 2020

Sympathy / Olivia Sudjic
Date Due 21 Aug 2020

To renew your items

Paperless overdues coming soon!

had informed me. It was one of the few times she had mispro-
nounced an English word. She said it like *hair loom*. Karakuri
are mechanised puppets, or automata, from the eighteenth and
nineteenth centuries. The word means *device* according to Wikipedia, both mechanical devices and deceptive ones. Mainly they
were made simply for entertainment, but some of them could
also serve tea or shoot an arrow. These had belonged to Ume's
father, Mizuko's great-grandfather, who had given them to Ume
when he died, and they had, Mizuko said, inspired her mother's
obsession with robotics when she was growing up. Ume had giv-
en some to Mizuko. I loved looking at them, but I didn't touch.
I was too afraid I'd break one. In our attic at home there were
two. One was already broken, but the other I had loved to play
with. It was made up of a miniature black mountain with an old
granny on the top sitting in an armchair, and a little rabbit that
ran around and around her at the base of the mountain when
you turned a handle.

"Tell us about Rupert," one of the friends demanded. I spun
around. They were sitting in a ring on the ground. Mizuko was
in the kitchen. The girl beckoned. "We never met this asshole.
Are you friends with him?"

"No way," I assured them.

"But that's how you met Mizuko, right? Through Rupert."

"Well, yes," I said, moving my tongue around my teeth as if
looking for something stuck there. I didn't know what else to
say.

Mizuko reappeared from the kitchen, carrying beers, a cigarette in her mouth. "Take," she said through her partly closed
lips, gesturing to the bottles in her hand.

"Alice was just telling us how she knows Rupert," the friend
said.

Mizuko sat down in the ring, ashing her cigarette into a beer cap. She waited for me to begin, as if she hadn't made me go over everything I knew about him a hundred times already.

"We did a guided tour of Japan together," I explained. "And then went to college together."

"But he's older," Mizuko interjected. "He's twenty-eight, and you're, what, twenty-six?"

"Twenty-three."

"Such a baby!" Mizuko crowed. Everyone agreed, and one of the more patronising friends stuck out her bottom lip.

"And what was he like at college?"

"Weird," I confirmed.

"How?"

"He once pretended to be in Africa when really he was still hiding in his room on campus. Or not even in his room, actually —in a Winnebago."

I felt that the story had been so much better, had made him sound so much stranger than this, when I'd told it before, but I couldn't tell it as I had to Mizuko. When I'd first told her, the night we met, she was entranced. She hadn't even known that the whole coma episode, with Rupert being knocked off his bike, was connected to the Winnebago and the West African harp. She had made me feel *fascinating*. A font of wisdom. ("Why did he never tell me that? I'm beginning to feel like I barely knew him. Go on.")

Now the conversation drifted, and one of the friends started talking about how one of her other friends' younger siblings, also at Yale, was about to launch a company that made beautiful Scandinavian-inspired wooden cabins that people could rent for off-grid retreats. "It's all part of that tiny-house movement."

"Microhouses," I interrupted. "They're Japanese."

"Same thing," the friend said. "The idea is you get away from everything. It's aimed at writers, I guess"—she nodded at Mizuko—"and *millennials*. Like you," she said to me with a grin. "But it's ridiculous. It costs, like, three hundred bucks and you're paying to be marooned in an empty little cabin in the middle of nowhere. Well, Boston. It's a smart business plan, I guess. Making people pay for nothing. Or what used to be free."

"I'd do it," Mizuko said.

"Definitely," I said. I kept my eyes on her, trying to fuse us together again with a private, knowing look. I found it harder to push her buttons—to elicit the same reactions of surprise and thrill—in the company of people who actually knew her.

That night she got straight into bed while I cleaned up and put the bottles down the chute. She was too drunk and tired to even brush her teeth. "Do it for me," she murmured.

"Sure," I said, padding into the bathroom, wetting her toothbrush, and extruding a tiny ball of toothpaste onto the bristles. When I came back she was snoring with her mouth wide open.

In the morning Mizuko shook me roughly awake. She was holding her device by my face where it was half hidden in the pillow. I hate other people being awake before me, and I woke with a horrible lurching feeling.

"He says I'm being *demanding* of him. What should I say back?"

I sat up, blinking sleep out of my eyes, and reached for the phone, which this time she did not give to me but held so I could see it from a distance.

"I can't see the screen," I complained. She brought her hand closer for my consultation but still did not give it to me.

I read.

"Say he can't just turn you off and on again every time there's a problem. You can't just reset." It killed me that Rupert knew he could just evaporate and reappear again whenever he wanted.

Rupert had suggested meeting up with her, and twenty minutes later, after lengthy negotiation with me, Mizuko replied, saying that she would meet him only if it was to get back together.

"But I want to see him *period*," she complained. "Now he's just going to say he doesn't want to see me."

"Trust me, he won't." But this was exactly what I hoped.

Ping!

"See?" Mizuko flung the phone at me and, pointing her chin towards the ceiling so that her hair fell away from her face and the ends skimmed her thighs, screamed.

"What?"

"He did."

"This is because we're not following the thirty-day rule."

She threw herself on the bed and began making a noise like a wild animal.

"We need to go somewhere. Like one of those isolation cabins your friend was talking about."

"But what if he changes his mind and then I'm in Boston?"

I shrugged.

"I *know* I only want him," she said between sobs, the syllables all wrong, "because he doesn't want *me*. How is that even *possible?*"

"It's normal to want what we can't have," I said soothingly.

"No, I mean how can he not want *me?*"

"Look at the manual. See what it says? Every time you contact him or reply to one of his messages, you have to start the thirty days over from the very beginning. He needs to miss you. To know what it feels like not to have you. Trust me, that is literally the *only way* he is going to understand what a terrible mistake he's making."

Mizuko sniffed.

"Okay?"

"Okay."

I consulted the manual. "Anyway, it says that you'll meet someone new on or around day twenty-five, when you'll be radiating breezy confidence."

Once she had seen the high-spec little film that the cabin company had made, in which all the cabins had names and one was marketed as being especially good for writers who needed to disconnect, she was feeling more optimistic about the plan again.

"I'm down on men," she announced, "but pro holidays."

I looked up the details, but they weren't launching until the following month.

"It's hopeless," Mizuko said. "I can't do it anymore."

But she agreed that the best way to stop herself from thinking about him would be to get writing again. She had an idea about a girl called Grainne who refused to eat anything in case her boyfriend had concealed an engagement ring inside it. Grainne was so afraid she'd swallow her engagement ring and choke that eventually she couldn't swallow at all and died.

"But I'm not sure about it . . . I think maybe I need . . . stuff that doesn't have him in it."

A change of scene, I suggested, might help her get stranger's eyes.

"Okay. Why don't you plan it, then? Make it a surprise for me. I love surprises."

The morning of our departure, Mizuko went downstairs to give Michi in her crate to the doorman. He loved looking after her, she said. She made him do it all the time. I went to get provisions from the deli. I bought, amongst other items, two Scotch eggs, since this is what my mother always bought for long car journeys. Mizuko had apparently never seen one before.

"What the fuck is that?" she said as she rifled through the bag.

I explained the concept.

"Thank god. I thought it was a mouldy lemon."

We were going to Texas for a "long weekend," as I kept calling it, even though neither of us had any kind of work to do on either side of it. I'd thought of going to Texas first simply because Mizuko had a friend whom she'd spoken highly of and said she wanted to visit in Austin—a poet and professor. After I looked up his name on Facebook and saw how single and attractive he was, I decided that was out. But Texas had given me another idea.

"So I have an idea for you—for a story," I said slowly as the cab pulled away from the kerb, when it was too late for her to get out. I didn't know how much of Mark and Susy she'd retained since our first meeting, when it had come out all haphazard as a result of nerves and drinking and my sense that this was the one time I would get to impress on her our cosmic symmetry.

At first I think she misunderstood what I was offering her.

"But he's not there, your dad, right? Your adopted dad, I mean. We wouldn't be going to visit him."

I took a deep breath. Clearly I had not impressed it on her hard enough.

"Right. No, he's not there. He's almost definitely dead. But we could go there and just, you know, have a look. You could write about me going to find him or something, like the descendent of the man saved by Sugihara or whatever. You know, a tracking-him-down kind of story."

She didn't seem to get the reference. I maybe knew the details of her life and memories better than she did.

"What was it called?"

"W-a-x-a-h-a-c-h-i-e. Look up Superconducting Super Collider."

When she'd finished reading about it, her face looked animated in a way I hadn't seen since she talked about the Japanese diplomat. Then she made me repeat the details of the story. When I finished, I must have made that blank, bland look. My nose twitched as if I were about to cry. I wasn't, but I did want her approval. I wanted her to write a story about it.

"You look like a little rabbit," she said, putting her arms around me and giving me a brief, hard hug before looking into my face again and biting her lip in a way that suggested she wanted to smile. I closed my eyes and waited for her soft mouth to land on mine.

"For the cover I want the period stain on a white chair." I opened my eyes in surprise. "Why the face? Thrillers always have blood. What's the difference?"

"True."

I saw the taxi driver glance at us in the rearview mirror.

"You're sure you don't mind me writing about it?"

I shook my head vehemently. "No. It's yours."

For the first time I felt like someone had really *seen* me. But I didn't know what it was exactly she'd seen, so I didn't want to speak of it or gesture to it in case that betrayed the fact that I didn't really own the thing.

"Silvia used to call me that," I said abruptly.

"Call you what?"

"Rabbit."

When I had looked up domestic flights, they had all, at this short notice, been absurdly expensive, and I felt I could not abuse Silvia's trust by using her credit card for them. Mizuko shook her head and said she would have paid, since the train was going to be hell.

"Well, I guess I thought it needed to be more of an *experi-*

ence. A train sounds more romantic, doesn't it? And what about hitchhiking? I thought that's how we could get from the station."

I had thought that as a spoiled rich girl she might have seen the charm in this shoestring itinerary, but it seemed she did not.

We took three trains, which were miserable, and slept in our seats, then hitchhiked only the very last bit.

The first time we waited by the side of the road, I began (belatedly) to wonder if anybody actually still did this or whether it had stopped in the sixties. Most of the people who picked us up clearly did so because of Mizuko. If I had tried to do this alone, no cars would have stopped. I looked out my windows for the places where the debris had landed, imagining human body parts, a heart and a torso and feet from the space shuttle that fell to earth when Mizuko turned twenty-one.

Dallas was forty minutes to the south of the site, and as we got closer, the landscape became lunar and the people who gave us rides became ranchers and farmers. We got dropped at the Ellis County Courthouse, which we looked into briefly. Then we went into the Ellis County Museum, which had lots of dusty velvet hats, parasols and quilts, mannequins on top of the cabinets, and, once I had asked where to find them, maps and memorabilia from the SSC. We found a B&B close to the town square, where each room was named and styled after an author. Mizuko chose the Will Shakespeare room on the second floor, which promised a private balcony for morning coffee, afternoon refreshments, "or *soliloquies*."

"For a long time," I read to her from my device, "no one knew what to do about an aborted supercollider. The federal government liked the idea of converting it into an antiterrorism training facility. Someone made a movie there, about a supercomputer that controls a little army of robots. Ellis County sometimes used it as a warehouse to store Styrofoam cups. Then there was a plan to turn it into a mushroom farm and then a secure data storage centre, but the investor slipped on ice and died."

"*Perfect,*" Mizuko said, noting it down.

"And what exactly does the new owner of the site do?" she asked our host that evening.

"Lots of stuff. Guar gum slurries, fluid loss additives, buffers, breakers, friction reducers, spacers, specialty cement additives, root stimulators, micronutrients, nitrogen stabilisers, animal nutrients, coil cleaners, degreasers, and carwash products. The company is called Magnablend."

"And could you maybe take us there tomorrow?"

"Course I can—if you really *want*. You won't be able to see much. I can't get you inside or anything."

"That's fine."

There was a pause in which it appeared he was reluctant to leave our table.

"Do you like living here?" Mizuko asked politely.

"I do indeed—lived here pretty much my whole life."

Mizuko beamed at him, and he finally left us to eat.

Back in our Shakespeare-style room, I began to look at her phone while she showered, but she came bursting out of the bathroom door and I had to throw it beside me.

"Just checking the time," I said quickly.

She was dripping wet, but she'd had an idea for the story and wanted to write it down right away before she forgot. She preferred me not to speak during these moments. I studied her as she typed.

I did not think I was gay. I compared the feeling roused by the sight of Mizuko without a towel to my memory of Ingrid in her swimsuit in the Hamptons, her marmoreal skin and compact, androgynous figure. Maybe I was. Sometimes it felt more like I was looking at women with the eyes of a man, the man directing

Maria Ozawa with a POV camera. Now that I had seen them together, I often looked at Mizuko with Rupert's eyes. With the eyes of all the men who looked at her that way. In some fantasies I would take on the personas of people in her phone, imagining I was them. I was plagued by dreams/nightmares in which I was watching her get pounded, her expression usually one of fury. This was a totally different thing from how I'd felt when we'd kissed and she had held me through the night. But it wasn't completely different from how I replayed it in my head now, again as the voyeur. It was almost more exciting that way, to watch us kiss, than the kiss itself had been. Still, I'd had a hopeful feeling that the moment might be repeated on our long weekend, but the room had twin beds, and it appeared that that phase of the experiment was over for Mizuko.

My eyes strained across the gap. She was holding her phone close to her face, turned away from me, and it emitted a halo of light around her head. Finally she put it on the bedside table between us and fell asleep. I kept my attention on it. I waited. I nearly fell asleep. All at once it lit up and began rutting on the table: *zzz zzzz zzzzzz*. I reached out and grabbed it before the noise could wake her. Reading Rupert's message, I realised I was weirdly warm all over.

By morning my fingers felt like my feet once had from continuous walking in Manhattan—blistered and bleeding, having been unable to stop. I went over it all again, again and again, not caring that I was running her battery low and she might suspect. In some there were props—marbles in her mouth, a set of plastic vampire teeth, white socks. In one she was cutting up a fruit with pink-handled scissors. Little erotic dioramas. Rupert had contorted her into these poses and taken the pictures. I fell asleep fantasising about her and him and sometimes me. Her gold chain tinkling, her dark hair against his chest and then tipped down her back as she sat upright, pale and shuddering. When I wasn't watching from the side, I was between them. A gold hairline crack.

And then I felt a rush of cold air. I saw her face narrowing suddenly as the other side of the picture came towards me; I had been caught watching them through a window. And then I was awake, and shocked to see her standing.

"What are you doing?"

She didn't reply.

"Where are you going?"

"Just shutting the window. Go back to sleep."

At breakfast the host showed us where to find which cereal and which kind of milk. They didn't have almond or coconut options, so Mizuko ate hers dry.

Mizuko asked him about the space shuttle that had crashed to earth on her birthday. He said they had seen a piece of debris on the very same laminated tablecloth I had my elbows on at that precise moment. One of their guests had ignored the police warnings, removed something from a debris field, and attempted to sell it on eBay. People in those days, she agreed, assumed their actions online couldn't be traced.

We got into his truck. As he drove, Mizuko explained what our mission was about. Not the part about Rupert, just how she was going to write a story about my dad and the abandoned SSC and it was going to be called "The Nomad." I sat bolt upright in the back when she said this (she was sitting next to him in the passenger seat). I didn't know it already had a title.

The host pointed across a prairie towards an industrial train trundling past with tankers on it. "I think there's going to be a storm. I'd better get back soon."

We got out of the truck and found a spot where we could see into the compound with a pair of binoculars he kept in the glove compartment. It looked, he said, essentially the same from the outside, at least from this distance, as it had before. To keep the existing acronym, SSC, Magnablend even named their new facility the Specialty Services Complex. Only slight depressions in the landscape suggested the shafts that had been sunk underneath.

"Come on," Mizuko said. "Let's get closer."

It was hard to imagine a landscape less like New York. While the bedrock in Manhattan, except in the middle under Central Park, is said to be perfect for the construction of tall buildings, the geology here, lying over the Austin Chalk, was perfect for building underground. The Austin Chalk is "a geological formation that arcs from Mississippi to Mexico"; I had read about it extensively before I got to Silvia's. The land had to be suitable for tunneling, since the SSC was to be "one of the world's largest tunneling projects," so for that alone the site was perfect. Another advantage listed in the shortlist of sites Silvia had in her crates was "connectivity to the world." Meaning, I suppose, that it was central. Where we were currently standing would have been the centre of a ring 4 metres in diameter and 84 kilometres in circumference. There would have been 4,728 magnets 17 metres long, 2 million litres of liquid helium, and around 2,000 people, mainly physicists, living there full-time. The abandoned tunnels had now been filled with water. We dropped stones into them to hear the splash.

"So you could actually get into it before?"

"Yup," our escort said. "Some physicists even broke in once and took a lot of photos."

"Of what?"

"Rust and decay."

"Why?" I asked.

"Masochists," Mizuko said. Her face darkened. I felt sure she was thinking of her own self-destructive habit of looking for evidence of Rupert with other girls.

"So it was just empty for twenty years?"

"Yup. They made a big deal outta the wrong sort coming here —thieves and dropouts and stuff. There was graffiti, but there weren't—it wasn't as bad as Magnablend made out. They said there were—"

"Multiple alcohol and drug parties." I'd read every article.

"What's a drug party?" Mizuko asked, grinning.

I shrugged, embarrassed.

"So in theory, the Higgs boson could have been found right here, yes?" She dug her toe into the earth. "Like, two decades ago."

"Yes," I said. "And instead they found it in Geneva, the year before last."

"On Independence Day?"

"July Fourth was when they announced it, yes. It could have been found anywhere. At any time. There's not just one."

"Right. But remind me exactly what it is again. I'm made of them, correct?"

Over the course of our journey I had nearly exhausted all the real world metaphors I could think of to answer this question, none of which had satisfied her except the most anthropomorphic, which required adjusting the science.

"They're particles. The basic building blocks of the universe. They are particles which can't be divided up or made into anything smaller."

"Okay. And what do they *do*?"

"They give things their mass. When a particle travels through the Higgs field, which is all around us"—I waved an arm around the emptiness—"it *interacts* and gets mass. The more it interacts, the more mass it has. Think of it like . . ."—I felt for something she would get—"Instagram likes mounting up on a picture."

"Kim Kardashian's boson." She seemed pleased with her joke.

"I guess. So before, we could detect different particles and know them by their mass, but we didn't know why they had that mass until someone came up with the idea of the Higgs field."

"And that guy was your dad?"

"No. Not really—well, no. He was just someone who wanted to help find it. And the Higgs boson is an excitation of the field. That's what quantum—"

"Stop. You lost me. Give me another analogy. I understand the field of snow or the fish realising it's in water, but what was going to happen here? Stick with snow."

"Okay, imagine the Higgs bosons are snowflakes. The collider that was being built underneath here was going to send huge snowballs along a track, nearly at the speed of light, then smash them together. A machine with hundreds of sensors would have caught and sifted the debris."

"And then they would have tracked it?"

"Not yet. The moment they find it can't be sensed directly. The Higgs is unstable. It splits up into particles. It's only after millions and millions of collisions that these fragments accumulate and become a swelling on a graph. The more data there are, the bigger it swells, until it's undeniable."

"So then they say they've made the discovery?"

"Then they know they've found a trace of the Higgs, yes."

"Because I'm thinking in terms of a narrative arc. When would the big celebratory reveal happen?"

"At the very end, I guess. But remember, that's not my dad. He didn't find it. That didn't happen here. This place got cancelled and we left. That's the story, the end of it."

"Well, not the end. Then he left you and your mom, right?"
I faltered. "Right."

I felt as if she had slapped me hard across the face, and my eyes swam, hot and salty. The rejection was bigger than the present moment itself. I understood now why Susy was still engaged in a lifetime of denial that the same man who had fixed her, made her part of his furniture, would turn into the one who left her behind.

Mizuko walked me to the truck with her arm gently through mine. She seemed delighted by the tears, saying "There, there" in a comforting voice but adding that what she was *really* looking for anyway was emotional residue, so tears were good. I could cry all I wanted. She didn't care so much about facts, she explained. But I had felt increasingly that this was what was reassuring about the flatness, the physical emptiness. It was an objective, indifferent landscape—desert and space. Things could be broken down into exactly what they were: earth, sky, storm, train, road, house. I imagined the enormous ring that would have curved under our feet. The particles firing round it again and again until they collided at such force that they released their secret.

The truth was, I had little emotional residue that didn't, in my mind, have Mizuko as its author. The reflection of her face shone in every tear. I could no longer separate out what I felt was my story and what I felt was hers. Susy had occupied every space of that kind in relation to my own history. The only relation to Mark left to take had been an intellectual one. I was the archivist. The critic. The would-be physicist. When I was growing up, anything closer, anything more like identification, always made him evaporate under the weight of my girl-child body. After I'd impersonated him to write the fake suicide note and then pretended to find it in the attic, my brain had cordoned off an area of itself like a derelict house. He became even less real than he had been before. The substance of him was gone, as if my letter exposed him as nothing more than a teenage girl with a box of matches. I had realised, as I composed his words, that I didn't really have any unanswered questions for him except ones about physics, the rules which had governed people for so long and now seemed to be disappearing or irrelevant. The emotional question became why Susy had rejected me. I was interested in that shift, from actively wanting to actively not wanting. Why could we not have found a way to share the grief and make our own little corners of it, the way I had shared Silvia's space?

Susy wouldn't settle on one version for this reason, and her words slid around whenever I tried to pin one down. As a result, her grief had become ugly to me, because the story made no sense. It was like one of those Escher drawings which my favourite tutor had framed above her desk and which I hated: hands drawing hands.

The host and I waited by the truck while Mizuko walked around taking final pictures. She wanted me to take one of her, but just as she passed her device to me, it ran out of power.

"Can you take it on your cell and send it to me?"

"Sure, or I can just post it."

"No," she said, "send it to me. I want to post it."

"Can we both post it?"

"No."

I kept getting the same error notice. There was no signal there.

"I'm having a problem connecting."

"Send it to me when we get back, then."

This picture was part of a carefully crafted post-breakup narrative. She wanted to create the impression that she might have a new boyfriend or some kind of male acquaintance in Rupert's absence. She was relying on his friends seeing it and telling him. I never featured in these pictures. My shadow was the closest I got. I had shelved expectations of another kiss; the intensity of not kissing now worked almost as well—the proximity and denial. But even though she explained why I could not publicly feature in her long weekend, since it wouldn't be sufficiently ambiguous or suggestive of a new boyfriend if I did, I was hurt that I was consistently written out of our life together, and I often looked back over all the pictures she had taken of or with Rupert and wondered when my turn would come.

It came, in a way, that afternoon. But in Polaroid form, and it was not made public. We were sitting in a café in the main square, waiting to leave. She asked me why I'd once wanted to become a physicist and why I hadn't done it. I tried to sound even in my responses. Talking about it made something in my voice tremble. I missed studying physics then so much it stung, tried to deny the possibility that it was the only path that would have been the right one, the only discipline that could have contained and defined me, and that now it was too late, I was a blur, a finger smear of data; all I was left with was the zeitgeist.

Give me time, give me space, give me waves. Rules for how bodies behave.

A part of me had also begun to suspect she was deceiving me somehow, because she seemed so interested in my life all of a sudden. I was half waiting for her to turn around and say, *Only joking.* She didn't. Instead she wanted me to explain, again, the main theories that would be either proved or disproved as a result of the Higgs.

"Which do you believe in?"

"Supersymmetry," I said without hesitation.

"And that's what your dad believed in too, right?"

I nodded.

"What is it?"

"It predicts a partner particle for each particle that we know exists."

"So cute. But what if it's something else? Like, what was it called, the multiverse?"

I was pleased she had remembered at least something from my repeated explanations. "Certain physicists like the idea that someone, something bigger and outside of us, cares. But if we are random, a freak accident"—I shrugged my shoulders and tightened my grip around the coffee cup—"then there is no care. Nothing has been painstakingly revised and fine-tuned. No one's made everything exactly the way it is on purpose to bring us into being exactly who we are. It would be the end of physics, I guess. No order, no pattern, just chaos. Lots of little universes separated by invisible screens and—"

"My therapist would say you're projecting the loss of your father onto the Higgs boson."

I raised my eyebrows and made a face to indicate that I was uncomfortable with her psychoanalysing me. Really, it felt good.

"How do you feel now we're here? Does it bring back any memories?"

I realised then that Mizuko was trying to make me cry. I knew about her crying thing from the TriMe messages. I knew that she liked it when the bottom lip stuck out and the chin puckered. Pretending to cry is like pretending to laugh; after a while you really are. Before I knew it I had hot tears streaming down my cheeks and Mizuko had dipped into her bag under the table and pulled out her mini pink Instax camera and taken a Polaroid of me. She shook it and I continued to cry, harder. Then she laid it on the table and let it develop without saying another word.

• • •

We got a train—a sleeper car—the whole way back. It took nearly two days, and the view was dull. For her, at least. I looked out the window and saw similarities between the landscape and that of the exclusion zone she'd driven through on her way to Minamisōma with Ume.

"Where do you think you could publish it?" I asked after a long silence. My mind had been leaping ahead as I gazed out the train window, and I had got to a vision of a dedication: *For Alice*. Or maybe even in code: *For Rabbit*. She smoothed her hair and said that though she had started off excited by the idea I'd offered her for the story, she'd decided it didn't have enough *mileage*. If anything, it had taken her back to the idea of mining her own family history. She wanted to return to the unfinished novel. By taking my story, I now saw, Mizuko had been testing the boundary between us, waiting to see whether I would hold up a hand and say *Stop*. When I hadn't, she'd decided she didn't actually want it. Like many rich people, she seemed to think things weren't worth having if they came at so little cost.

"I get it—I do get it that it didn't work out for you," she said slowly, half looking at her phone, "but don't *you* get it that it would be so easy for my father to get in touch if he wanted to now? It's not like it used to be."

I began to feel tearful.

Like it used to be meant, presumably, more moral and less networked times, Victorian times, when if people lost touch they lost touch for good. Not for good as in for better, but forever. Or possibly she meant that in more moral, less networked times, like the Victorian times, illegitimate children were more problematic than they are today. I asked which it was.

"Look, either he doesn't know I exist or he isn't curious to find me. Where I am isn't even relevant. I could be anywhere in the world and it would be just as easy for him to find me if he wanted."

I was glad we were going back to the city, and I was glad, above all, that we were not hitchhiking back. I had been carrying around a very definite and growing sensation of nausea, my stomach clenching like a fist without warning, meaning that on the way to Waxahachie we'd had to ask one driver to let us out only five minutes after she'd taken pity on us and stopped to pick us up. Ever since I'd met Mizuko, I'd put it down to Provigil and falling in love. Then, because of my secret voyeurism situation with her and Rupert, I'd decided that the nausea was most likely a moral punishment, compounded by paranoia, sexual fantasies, and semipermanent arousal, but by now, because I was more nauseated and yet hungrier, I had begun wondering whether it wasn't something else, like a tapeworm. Even on the train back, though it was better than being in a car, I was taking Kwells for travel sickness, to keep the nausea at bay. By the time we arrived in Penn Station—after a long time spent staring miserably out the window—I'd figured it out.

I read the instructions three times. As I bore down on the test strip with the stream of my urine, the tip turned pink. I laid it on the floor and watched it from the corner. I was in the Rooiakkers' bathroom again. I'd gone back intending just to get my stuff and say, *Hey, thanks for everything and bye,* but they weren't in, and then I hadn't been able to resist doing the pregnancy test in my pocket right there and then in their beautiful bathroom, even though I knew it was inappropriate. I thought back over each and every one of Dwight's hushed ejaculations: outside, over, onto, never *into* me except then. Walter's house had to be the culprit. Although I had reached this conclusion, when the test did too, I was appalled. Something moved inside my stomach.

The flick of a fish tail. I lay back against the wall with a feeling like resignation.

I now understood a new way in which sex with Mizuko, if it ever did happen, would be completely different from sex with Dwight, in that no part of it would suggest reproduction. It would not imply the fusion of two separate things into a new thing. Orgasms would be waves, bringing in nothing and taking out nothing, emptying us and then letting us swim again. With Dwight, there was no danger of intimacy but there would always be the threat of sperm and egg uniting. That's what I'd been thinking of, I guess—my journey to the CVS pharmacy for the morning-after pill—when I'd told Mizuko I was already pregnant. I'd since implied that I'd already had a termination. Now I needed to do it for real. I was pretty sure it was the kind of thing she'd be very up for doing. There was a high likelihood of some criers in the waiting room. It was the kind of outwardly sisterly act she'd do simply so that she could use it for herself. Very occasionally she had contradicted her hostile stance on having kids by saying things like "I do actually want them, I think, and I want them to be so cute it makes me sick. And I want them to have paws," and then immediately she'd say she didn't really need a child because she had Michi's little paws.

I started composing her a message from my long bed at the Rooiakkers'. Despite my urge to get out of there before Ingrid and Robin came home, I was too physically exhausted to go any further and had collapsed in my old bedroom. I fell asleep in the middle of writing the message, my phone on my chest.

In the morning, one arrived from her.

At first I thought I was in big trouble. She'd sent a screenshot of her TriMe account. I swore under my breath. Did she know? But when I looked closer, I realised what it was.

A message from Dwight on TriMe, screenshot on Mizuko's phone, now saved on my phone. A hierarchy I couldn't immediately make sense of.

Then she sent a follow-up message with the words *Isn't this your boyfriend?*

He was using an alias. A combination of numbers and letters. Mizuko's, as I already knew, was Pearl. Every night I'd lain awake or on the bathroom floor replaying her and Rupert, or her and any of the strangers in her phone. I tried to imagine her being called Pearl for real. The pedant in me wanted to tell her that pearls are basically little shiny prisons that contain dead worms, intruders, skeletons, bacteria. The exhibition at the Museum of Natural History I had seen with Dwight at the start of the summer had a series of x-rays showing how the worm is trapped in the layer of mantle inside the shell.

Yes, that's him, I replied.

Now that I was really pregnant rather than simulating pregnancy, I decided that the psychic who had crossed the street to tell me she could feel my vibrations had been quite correct after all. It seemed I could bring things into being just by holding them in my mind. A lemon, an avocado, a turnip, soon fully formed with nostrils and ribs, each body part downloading faster than you expected.

> *Don't think of it that way or you're going to lose your shit completely. I know it's bad timing. Does he know?*

No, I typed back.

I watched a reply being composed. The instant I replied my power was gone and I felt the foreboding again, my breathing became heavy, the three grey dots quivering as I exhaled.

> *I know how you're feeling—a bit nuts—but trust me. If*
> *you have to think of it, think of it as a parasite. In fact, it's*
> *not even that, it's feeding on another parasite, no offense*
> *—you're hardly independent.*

The crying laughing face three times.

> *A protozoan living in the digestive tract of a flea living*
> *on a dog. That's all you've got, I promise. It really isn't*
> *lovable.*

I nodded dumbly to myself, alone in the long bed in the twins' playroom. I missed sharing with her.

> *Can I come over or are you busy?*
>> *Busy*
>> *Later?*
>> *Could meet at 11?*
>> *OK. Will book appointment for this afternoon at*
> *Planned Parenthood. Will you come?*
>> *Sure. And message him to say it's over.*
>> *But maybe it is what I'm born to do. Like a salmon.*
>> *How like a salmon?*
>> *The way they swim back from the ocean to their natal*
> *river and spawn, you know? They go right to the mouth*
> *of the river they were born in to have their babies.*

After that I didn't get a reply.

I was too tired to walk to meet her, even though it was so near. I could, I thought, perhaps borrow one of the twins' scooters, scoot one block behind Riverside Church and cross to the side with the Olive Tree Deli. That was the midway point between us. There was an uphill section between 120th and 119th, however, so there I'd have to dismount and sling it over my shoulder. I felt impatient that I couldn't just teleport there, be inside her bedroom with one click. I stayed in bed and continued reading about salmon spawning on my device. I learnt, to my dismay, that as they swam into fresh water the female fish "lost their stomachs," which disintegrated inside them to make more room for eggs, and once they had laid the eggs they became listless, died, and were washed downstream and onto riverbanks where they were eaten by bears.

I sent Dwight a message that I copied exactly from the template Mizuko had suggested, without adding any personalisation. *It's over.* With the screenshot for why.

Once I saw the confirmation he'd seen it, I began to get up, dress—putting my hand on my stomach every so often—and pack my things. I could hear Ingrid in the kitchen.

Done, I typed to Mizuko.

I waited for some sign of approval. I could see she'd read the message.

For a while, neither she nor Dwight replied. I sat down again on the bed. Until one of them did, I didn't feel like I could leave the room. I waited for fifteen minutes.

Three pineapples from Mizuko.

I wasn't sure what I was supposed to glean from that.

I sent back two girls holding hands. *Thank you.*

I tried to tiptoe past the kitchen to the elevator.

"Sorry to hear about your boyfriend," Ingrid called out.

"Ex," I said.

She must have heard from Walter, who must have already heard from Dwight. Or maybe she was in touch with Dwight directly now. I walked reluctantly back towards her. At least Robin did not appear to be here.

"I'm off," Robin said, suddenly emerging from their bedroom. 'I've got that lunch at one and then I'm out this evening too."

"Thank you for your input into the circle of trust," Ingrid muttered.

He stopped just before the elevator and said in a tight, sarcastic voice, "Hello, Alice. Nice to see you again." Then he left.

"We've got the tickets to that play on Friday that Walter asked us to get. Robin and I need to go because of the way he behaved on holiday, and I've just been told Dwight isn't coming now you two have had a bust-up, so would you still come? You can bring someone else—a friend? I don't want it to be just Walter, Robin, and me."

I swayed on the spot: a rising wave of nausea. "Sure."

"Okay, great. I'll forward you the details. When was the last time you visited Silvia, by the way?"

I backed away from her question so fast that I left one bag on a chair. The last time I had *tried* to visit Silvia had been right before I'd bought the pregnancy test and was the reason for my being in the neighbourhood in the first place. I'd gone straight from the train station, determined to make it before closing time. They had told me to come back later because she was asleep, and obviously I hadn't. I'd gone to the pharmacy and then decided that since I was so close, it made sense to get my belongings from the Rooiakkers'.

After I left the Rooiakkers', leaving my bag on the chair, I went to meet Mizuko at a bar near her place, and she ran through the gist of what Dwight was going to say and what I was going to say back. When we actually finally spoke, on the phone while Mizuko went outside for a cigarette, he kept saying, "All I'm going to say is . . . ," but that was never all he said, and so that was all I kept thinking about, this disconnect between what he was saying he was doing and what he was really doing, and not the important thing we were supposed to be talking about.

"What did he say?" Mizuko said as she returned to the table.

"Lots. Mainly he said he hadn't actually been using it to physically meet up with people. He said he didn't really see what the problem was with just messaging. He assumed that I knew he was on it. He said everyone was."

Mizuko handed me a cocktail in a marmalade jar. "He's *just* like Rupert—I don't think he really gets it that you're even breaking up with him." I may have given her the impression, at least initially, that things between Dwight and me were more serious, more like an actual relationship, than they really were. She reached out her hand, and I grasped it. "No." She indicated my phone on the table. "Show me."

I passed her my phone.

"Yup. Definitely him."

She compared a picture of him to the screenshot she had. In this, he was still "Active 2 minutes ago," as if time had stopped. "I recognized him from your Instagram."

In the midst of all the other news—and it did really feel like it was all starting to kick off—this piece of information thrilled me: that she had actually studied certain scenes from my life too.

"'Renaissance man and Rainmaker,'" she read aloud. "What a *dick*. And why are random words in caps? *Mendokusai.*"

She pushed her hair back from her face, put her finger to her lips, and repeatedly stroked her nail down the centre of the groove above it. *Mendokusai* translates loosely as "too troublesome" or "I can't be bothered."

I sucked hard on my straw and removed a soggy leaf that was

blocking it. "What is this?" The drink was leaving an odd taste in my mouth and I was starting to feel nauseous again.

"Mint julep."

"Oh."

It was eleven-thirty.

Maybe because I was pregnant, or because I now knew I was pregnant, it had an unpleasant metallic taste.

"You need to get rid of him. You need to never talk to him again. Block him right now, actually. Remove him as a friend. Unfollow. Delete, whatever. Here, I'll do it."

I snatched the phone back.

She studied me, determining whether the action came from disobedience or sadness. I made the face.

"Oh, poor Rabbit, at least we're both single at the same time."

A bus with a large TriMe 3 on the side rumbled past, and we both looked at it, back to each other, and then away again. I tried to make myself cry about Dwight for her, but tears wouldn't come. I played back some things—driving on the Long Island Expressway, walking by the ocean, lying in the park, drawing the butterfly—but then my thoughts returned to the fact of Dwight trying to lure Mizuko into a hookup of some kind, and I had to fight against the urge to jiggle up and down in my seat.

My expression must have looked pained.

"Let's be real for a sec. He was probably just bored at home, getting off. Doesn't necessarily mean he likes me more than you, or even reflect that badly on you, just makes him look like a fool."

"Why a fool?"

"I mean I would never . . ." She waved her hand in the air. "He must be mad if he thinks I would actually go there."

I thought for a moment that she meant she would never get with a boyfriend of mine.

"He's like a four, and he's definitely not my type."

I was silent for a moment.

"Don't get me wrong—I can totally see what you saw in him, that's not what I mean. I'm too old for him, that's all."

She closed her eyes, restarted with a deep breath. I could tell she was about to launch into one of her Internet speeches. I knew the gist by now. My generation, her generation, blah blah blah, *Armageddon.*

This time I decided to interrupt. "So why are *you* on TriMe?"

She looked shocked for a moment, and then as if she pitied me. "*Rabbit,* don't get angry, not with *me.*"

"Sorry. I didn't mean to sound angry."

"I know. It's fine."

What was fine? I wondered. Nothing was fine. I thought back to all the hours spent, mainly while on Provigil, deciphering Rupert's gnomic responses. The most common and infuriating was *It's fine.*

She said she was going to use the bathroom before we left, and I read the most recent messages on her phone without moving it from its position next to her light-blue Columbia card. The last one was from three hours ago.

> *I've seen so many cute videos you'd like but have to stop myself from sending them to you. Have you seen the monkey being pampered?*

I recoiled from the device as if it had bitten me.

I scrolled back up through the chain between her and Rupert. They were still sending each other nude pictures, saying they missed the way certain things felt. After I put the phone down my hands were shaking.

I miss the way you feel.
I miss the way you feel.
I miss the way you feel.

The physicality made me feel sick. The message had his muscles and shoulders and sinewy arms. It moved. I could not stop staring at it, and it reminded me that while I had direct access right now to Mizuko's mind through her device, only Rupert had access to the rest, even though I was the one there, right next to her. When she came back I had a kind of furious rushing in my ears and I couldn't look directly at her.

Then, when we got up from the table to leave, I assumed I'd be going with her, but she said she was meeting "some friends." She repeated this reason for not spending the evening with me three more times that week. I couldn't come because the three different hosts each had a very small table. Everyone she knew in the city had a very small table. Or an average-size table in a very small room. Rooms too compact for me. Yet much bigger than her phone, on which a whole universe could be simulated. I imagined if every single thing in her device—every dick and columbia.edu address, every person or thing she had ever corresponded with who was now trapped inside it in limbo—was given back its real, physical mass. I pictured the chaos. The dicks would push through the windows in the Dutch paintings and into her first-year students. Michi would moult all over, or maybe eat her owner's spit the way pets eat such things. I would be there too, breaking all the dicks.

But even though she had so many social engagements, and work to do before term started, Mizuko accompanied me to Planned Parenthood. She led the way through the metal detector and into the waiting room, where there were leaflets on every surface that read PLANNING IS POWER, with the same in Spanish. I filled out the forms and I felt her watching my pen. I saw her note the way I hovered over the various ethnicities on the form. First the "white" box, then to airspace over the "black" box, a kind of momentary hesitation, a protest of stillness, a staring into the abyss of everything I did not know about myself. She, like me, was made of halves.

I thought I was there to have the noninvasive medical abortion (a pill), but when the doctor examined me he decided I had to wait to have a surgical one, because the fetus was by now more like twelve or thirteen weeks. The size of an egg. When I heard this, tears pricked, which, as I was lying on my back at the time, began to scald my eyes. "I don't know why I'm crying," I said. I also felt sure it could not be so far along, that it must simply be because of my last, irregular period that they had made this calculation. I was sure conception had to be the last night in the Hamptons, which would make it more like five or six weeks. How had it happened before that? In my sleep?

In my folder, which I had to give back to reception, I found a scan of my womb, captioned with the time and date, September 2, on smooth photo paper. I couldn't see anything, though I searched and searched, just as I hadn't been able to see the rabbit in the moon. I was due to return on the first available appointment, the day after the play Walter had tickets for, at the same place, the Margaret Sanger Centre on Bleecker.

Outside, there was nothing moving. The street was cordoned off, with thick black smoke rising from a manhole. Yellow Cabs were crawling past the diversion like the slow wasps that signify summer's end. We decided to walk, or rather, I started walking, and without looking up from her device, Mizuko followed me.

"You're so strong," she told me. "You're so *brave*."

21

It's hard to explain how an infatuation actually starts. It's a state so all-encompassing that it's almost impossible to remember how it felt to live inside your own head before it began. Everything that precedes it becomes a pathway that was always leading there. Time before is valuable only as a resource with which to create a persona, to bind the object of the infatuation closer. I had given my (partially fabricated) past life to Mizuko to make a story that in the end never got told. Or not by her. It is also hard to explain the intensity of the infatuation itself. There is rarely an explanation that seems reasonable to anyone but you. Unless you're part of a cult or viral phenomenon, so that when you weep outside the object of your infatuation's hotel room, you do so in the company of millions. There was no such mass hysteria surrounding Mizuko when I knew her, though from the articles and blog posts I read about her now, I fear it's growing. It was easier in my solitude then to assume I was special. The only person who appeared to harbour feelings to rival mine was Rupert, and maybe, from the way she talked about them, one or two of her students. The day after she accompanied me to the Planned Parenthood appointment, Mizuko's classes began again, and I decided I should follow her. Between classes, she usually worked in the Papyrology and Epigraphy Reading Room on the sixth floor of the Butler Library. I told her I thought it was a good idea to be at her side, or just behind her, as much as possible, on and off campus, to keep Rupert at a distance. The first time I saw him, he was leaning against the fluted columns outside Dodge Hall. When I walked towards him he pretended not to see me, stubbing his cigarette out and walking away. He had the kind of outrageous arrogance that was sometimes mis-interpreted as diffidence, and if not diffidence then Britishness, which allowed him to get away with loitering.

In Dodge Hall I perused the noticeboards, which rustled their many layers every time the doors by her classroom swung open. They were thick with flyers and notices with teeth cut into them. Someone was charging twenty dollars per hour for in-your-home cat companionship; someone else, or the same person, was charging ten times that for chakra balancing. It wouldn't be too difficult, I reassured myself, to find something if I really had to. Silvia's credit card was burning a guilty hole through my wallet.

The door to one professor's room was ajar, revealing a man in a tweed jacket, his face obscured by a bookcase. I snuck a handout from the tray outside the professor's office, then found where Mizuko's locker was, covered in stickers. I wondered if I should slide a love note into the narrow slit of the door. She might find it touching. Someone banged their locker open beside me and I carried on down the corridor and headed out of the building again. I walked along the main walkway that intersect-ed the campus and became 116th Street at each end. Because of the constant surge of people, students and general public, in all directions, this was the hardest topology to monitor. I sat down on a step to read the handout, imagining what it must be like to live Mizuko's cerebral life here. I messaged her but got no reply. I hated it when she did this. Especially if she posted something in the meantime, underscoring her silence. Anytime a silence extended for too long, I assumed she had found out something bad. That I hadn't really messaged Rupert for her. That I had been secretly looking through her phone. Or the other, far worse things I was keeping from her. When I wasn't with her and couldn't follow her, I spent my time watching her go on- and offline.

I was worried that she had tired of me. Like the "Nomad" story, maybe I did not have enough mileage. I did not know how to stay distant from her in order to maintain her interest while getting as close to her as I wanted to be to cultivate attachment. I could see that the charm of what appeared to her to be coincidence was wearing off. My understanding of her had become expected, my familiarity anticipated: the logical, unremarkable outcome of *really* knowing her. No more magical than predicting the days of the week in the correct order. Real intimacy, I worried, pushed people away from you, not closer. Of course I had one surprise for her that, if I engineered it subtly, organically enough, might cement my place in her life for good.

I sat there until the streetlamps came on and the darkness became unequivocal. Still I got no reply, even though I knew her classes were over by now. Finally, though I had wanted to suggest it in person, I sent her another message.

> *Hey, you're probably busy now but I thought we were going to meet up later? I also thought you might like to come with me to this.*

I'd looked up the play online and pasted a link to a positive review into my message: "An immersive, site-specific production, an adaptation of the Greek tragedy *Alcestis*." *Everyone has to wear masks,* I added, to reinforce that this was no basic Broadway invitation. This was cultured, literary, edgy—she could take part.

As usual, sight of the word *seen* nearly triggered an orgasm, or I was going to throw up—I couldn't tell. The play was definitely her kind of thing. Finally she replied with a single word: *Yes.* It wasn't *SO YES,* but it was definitely better than nothing.

I managed to track her down, and that evening things almost went back to how they had been before our trip, which had made things feel strained between us. I felt back where I belonged: in her bed again, eating something dairy-free and frozen, passing the cold metallic spoon between us, the warmth of her mouth still appreciable at the centre, the silver smoothness reminding me of her tongue, soft as velvet.

Now that things seemed better, I wondered if I had been too hasty. The idea of taking her to the play didn't seem as wise now that she was really coming. But now she really, really wanted to go. She said she'd already read all the reviews before I'd sent her the message. It had been completely sold out for months; tickets were being sold on eBay for four hundred bucks, and she'd given up. How had my friend managed to get some? She made me explain about Ingrid, Robin, and Walter. Who they were and what they each did. My chest constricted as I spoke. I asked her more about the play to change the subject. She had read the original; she was *interested to see what they had done,* like it was a house she'd once lived in.

When she went to take a bath, I took her phone instinctively but found that she had changed her password. I tried to work out her new one by tilting the screen under the light so that the heaviest fingerprints might show me. There were, of course, a stampede of fingerprints everywhere. I thought back to how I'd guessed her password so easily in the auditorium before the talk.

Things which had at first felt like signs, if I analysed them for too long, ended up feeling like the movements of my own reflection in dark glass.

"Have you changed your password?" I said when she came back, trying to make the broad, innocent rabbit face.

She frowned. "Yesterday. But I'm going to get an upgrade soon to one of those ones that knows your fingerprint instead."

I felt the nauseous shiver in my stomach—everything from rage to empathy to morning sickness—that I had grown used to and now thought of as being love.

On the evening of the play, we arrived at the entrance to the theatre, which was not a theatre, sometime after the others, as she had insisted on circling around Madison Square Park smoking a joint beforehand because she said it would heighten the *experience*. As we entered, we were each given a white mask with a lip like a manta ray, and a playing card, mine an eight of hearts, that was then hole-punched, which dictated the group of five "guests" you entered the building with. Mizuko went ahead of me and I had to wait. They'd split us up on purpose, and I noted, without enthusiasm, that along the dark corridor leading in from the street there were signs everywhere which encouraged you to forgo friends and enjoy it alone. I waited in line for the next elevator with a group of strangers. I hated it already, and the plastic toggle from the back of my mask was pressing painfully into my skull.

The first room I came to was all marble surfaces and sliding glass doors. After that I remember dark woods, a cemetery, and a cavernous room with strobe lights. From what I could tell, and when I could find them, the protagonist was suffering from a midlife crisis. His wife, Alcestis, spent a lot of time crying on a big white bed or kneeling before a small gold statue of Shiva placed at one end of a deep purple yoga mat that had been exaggerated in length and stretched out like a hall carpet. I saw one bit when the lights changed around the bed so that it became a cage with Alcestis trapped inside. I also managed to see a bit when Alcestis had a lock of her hair cut off with a knife like the one kept by Walter's pool. I had thought there were only three floors, but Mizuko told me after that there were five. In truth, I spent the whole time doing the opposite of what was instructed: forgoing the play and searching for my "friend." Instead of following the characters around the maze, I tried to train my eyes to spot Mizuko, Robin, and Ingrid. With masks it was nearly impossible, and I didn't even know what the Rooiakkers were wearing. With Mizuko, every girl with long dark hair turned out to be someone else.

Certain audience members barged their way around, pushing past me to keep up with the particular characters and plot threads they were intent on following. Sometimes, as a stationary scene was unfolding, grown men would worm their way to the front of the assembled crowd so they would have a chance of being chosen for a special interaction with one of the characters. One reviewer had been taken to a secret room made to look like a cabin in the woods by a woman in a black dress. This was something Mizuko had wished aloud would happen to her. I wandered, looking for my companions but increasingly hopeless, preferring to always be moving rather than to stand still, sometimes lost on my own for ages, going into empty rooms where people could pull out drawers and rifle through things for clues to the story. Suddenly I felt exhausted and lay down in a corner of a dark room until the lights came up and I knew it was the end.

Walter took us to supper afterwards at the NoMad. The restaurant, which belonged to the hotel, was almost as disconcertingly dark as the theatre space next door, but now everybody looked like their normal selves again rather than serial killers at

Halloween. Without the smooth white plastic, each face, even Mizuko's, looked a little too high-definition: fleshier, shinier, the features more irregular, the pores larger. I felt a throb in my chest at seeing Robin's and Mizuko's faces in such close proximity. The throb descended into my stomach and then slipped further down again, as if someone were very slowly unzipping me.

When we were shown to our table, Robin and Mizuko sat next to each other, with Walter on the other side of her, next to me on the end. I studied their faces again, now they were seated. They seemed to bear no resemblance to each other at first, and then gradually my eyes adjusted to the darkness and I saw it. A flicker fading in one and growing in the other. They looked absolutely nothing alike, but they had the same arrogance. They held space in the same way—like it belonged to them. My eyes moved back and forth between them. Mizuko deathly pale, and thin as a child. Her hair hanging over her pointy shoulders, her skinny arms and elbows. It was a rare occasion to see her not wearing black. Instead she wore a tiny blue kilt and a seventies-looking brown-and-white-striped top, with a narrow black choker around her neck. She kept rearranging her plates and glasses on the table in order to take pictures, apparently unaware of or unperturbed by the way that Walter and Robin were staring at her.

"I found it very meditative," Ingrid said. "All that silence, having your cell locked away. I felt like I went into a kind of trance. I'd say it was quite a spiritual experience for me, actually."

Unable to stop looking at Mizuko, Walter replaced the cap on the sparkling water and made a *ng, ng* sound of agreement.

"I know exactly what you mean," Mizuko said. "That was *so* intense."

It was weird seeing her in the company of people *I* knew rather than the people *she* knew.

"Thank you for inviting us," Robin said, with an elaborately gracious gesture, as though the restaurant, or maybe the whole hotel, belonged to Walter. Ingrid glowered at him.

Hearing them discuss the play, I realised just how much I'd missed while looking for them. And though we were now all around the table together, I still felt left behind. Mizuko, I sensed, now amongst "adults," was at pains to illustrate the gap in our maturity. She was making a very lengthy point about freedom of movement and choice and gamification, and I could see that Walter was lapping it up.

"Exactly," he said, "that's exactly it."

Robin stroked his chin, suggesting his detached amusement at finding himself in the company of so many pseudo-intellectuals.

"I loved the whole *random* nature of it," Ingrid said.

She was talking in a strange way I had never really seen her do before. Mizuko too seemed wired. Something about the way she was leaning forward, her hair trailing in the dish of olive oil, so she could fix her eyes directly on Ingrid as she spoke angered me. I made a face at her to say, *Why are you acting weird?* I couldn't tell whether I was imagining it or she was just stoned.

I found it all totally draining. Before I had lain down, the play had been nearly two hours of walking. I wondered if it would be okay to lay my head on the nice soft tablecloth and close my eyes now. I was too exhausted to even worry about what would happen if I did. My body tried to shut down my brain, to bring it down by force onto the table. My plan had been to dissect Mizuko's career and family history in conversation, so that Mizuko could work it out for herself, but now I felt a poison seeping into my brain every time Robin gave her sidelong glances and every time she ignored or belittled me in his company. The poison was causing a painful swelling near my heart, and near my crotch, and yet at the same time it was turning all my limbs to lead, infecting me with sleep so I was powerless to stop the conversation. Maybe I didn't want to let this happen after all. Maybe she didn't deserve it. I felt increasingly impotent, my eyelids drooping ever lower as I watched the conversation take turn after turn that excluded me, knowing little of the New York theatre scene. The more powerless I felt, the louder their laughter and obvious comradeship became, and the more certain I was that handing Robin to her like this would be a mistake. It would cut me out completely.

When Mizuko got up I gripped the table, pulled myself up, and followed her. "Where are you going?" I demanded, more feebly than I wanted.

"I have to pee," she said, giggling. "Is that okay?"

I went with her. "Are you messaging Rupert?" I asked, trying to control my voice. The thought gave me a sudden surge of electricity. Renewed energy in my limbs.

"Actually, I'm not," she said through the door. It sounded like there was something more. There was a pause. I said nothing. "Can I tell you something?" she asked slowly.

I froze, then slid down onto the floor of the bathroom, staring at the door she sat behind. It was either going to be the thing I most wanted to hear or it would be the thing I least wanted. "You can tell me anything—you know that," I said calmly through the door, like a hostage negotiator. This might be the moment, I thought, to do a trade.

"Oh god. Okay, wait there." There was a flush, during which I began to shake. I felt as if my legs might never walk again. Finally the door opened. I looked up at her, tugging at her skirt and staring over my head at her reflection in the mirror.

"So guess who I just matched with?"

22

The cordless phone never stops ringing. I am in Silvia's apartment. Silvia is not there. I open and shut cutlery drawers and cupboards with fancy glasses from days when Silvia must have hosted parties, not knowing what I am looking for.

My face feels rubbery. I am certain the skin has become thicker, or my fingertips are completely numb. Far below my skin, like an underground stream faintly trickling, I am sure there is blood. But I do not feel one hundred per cent alive. I do not feel like the same person I was when I woke up yesterday, which feels like the same day because I have not been to bed.

Answer the *phone,* that's all you have to do to make it normal. Otherwise you are just standing there with that noise and that's what makes something about this scene feel not quite right.

You need to know that you are overreacting. This does not correspond in any way with the reality of what happened. All that happened is that you went to a strange play and you spent the whole time walking around on your own, and then to a hotel, or to its restaurant, and you could have fallen asleep on the table you were so tired, but then you couldn't have slept because you were full of adrenaline, and then you went to a party and Mizuko left without you and then—and then—you walked home all the way from wherever they took you and then you came here to where Silvia isn't but in every other respect it is still the same as when you were last here. Before.

So there *is* a before and there *is* an after. That isn't made up. But it's just a passage of time, no big change that changes everything.

I let the cordless phone ring. It goes to the machine. The people from Silvia's home leave a message with no information in it, just to call back. I keep checking my phone. Nothing. Her last picture was taken at the party—her in the middle with two friends.

It was my fault. The nearness. I guess it was inevitable.

Everyone, Dwight said, was on it.

Less than one mile away, the screen said.

When she had come out of the toilet stall in the NoMad, she had said she was always getting slightly older white couples like that sending her messages. Or guys who were into lolicon. She couldn't give me a reason why she had the app, except for why not? It existed; she'd seen the ads. Rupert, she said, had always wanted to try it. A threesome. It seemed like the easiest way to keep him interested in her.

She wouldn't show me if any messages had been sent between them. She only flashed me the profile: it was Ingrid's hand in one picture. Her stack of raw diamond rings. The face had been cropped.

I could not hide it, but nor could I get up off the bathroom floor, so I told her, in as calm a voice as I could, that it made me feel "weird."

She made a face and nudged me out of the way to wash her hands. "Knew I shouldn't have told you."

"No, you should. It's fine."

"Why weird? How close are you to them really, anyway? Don't tell them I told you, obviously."

I suggested we make excuses and leave, even though our food had just arrived.

She rolled her eyes. "It's not like I'll necessarily reply . . . Not if it bothers you this much. But you need to remember, Alice, I'm much older than you. It would be different if one of them were coming on to you."

I could only open and shut my mouth.

"They sound pretty open-minded if he changed his name to his wife's."

"What? Who told you that?"

"You told me that. Last night. I'm not talking about it anymore. Not after the way you just reacted. They're not that old, not compared to me, remember. Why do you look so grossed out? Get up."

"How do you know how old they are?" I asked, still from the floor.

"Duh. It *says*. Thirty-six and fifty-six. I don't think you can lie about your age on it because it's lifted from—oh, well, I guess you could."

"Can we just go?"

"I left my purse at the table."

"Go get it—just tell them I'm not feeling well. It's morning sickness, but just say I'm feeling sick. Say I've been sick."

She gave me a hand, and I staggered towards the reception area.

I sat in a high-backed black velvet armchair. She seemed to

be taking a long time. I sent a message telling her to hurry up. I was worried she had sat down with them again, that Walter might have persuaded her to stay. Finally she appeared. "Car's here," she said.

My nausea intensified in the car. I tried to look at the road ahead and pretend I was driving to make it better; it's odd that even imagining being in control of the car can do that. After a few minutes I realised that the driver was not going where I had thought, and where I was mentally steering his car. We were going down, not up.

"Aren't we going back to yours?"

"No."

"What address did you put in?"

"There's a party Rupert might be at, in Brooklyn."

The driver and Mizuko talked to each other while I sat in silence. He complimented her on her shoes and asked if she was a foot model.

"Do they slip off easy? That's what they ask the foot models to do—slip half the foot out so you can see the arch."

I made a face at her like *who the fuck is this guy?*

"How much you pay for them?" he persisted.

"Aren't you supposed to be driving?"

"*Chill,*" Mizuko said firmly. "My rating."

We picked our way to the front door of the building.

"Lots of them will be anarchists."

"Right."

"And the people whose place this is own this amazing bakery called Bird and Daughter."

I kept nodding as we entered the hallway and descended a staircase towards the noise of people.

"And they're pretty much all poly." I glanced at her. "Polyamorous," she added, seeing my confusion. "It's all pretty incestuous, actually."

I felt like I'd missed the bottom step.

We made a circuit and Mizuko decided Rupert wasn't there, so we found a corner and she bowed her head over her device, her hair falling around it so I could not see what she was doing. I *had* to look at her and appear to be engrossed in whatever it was she was doing; otherwise I was standing there staring without anyone to talk to.

"Who are you messaging?" I asked dumbly.

"R—" She broke off, reading a reply that had just come in, overhanging the one she was writing.

"Rupert?" I checked.

"Mm."

When Mizuko did eventually introduce me to people at the party, she said the same things she'd said with conviction in the Italian restaurant—"Meet my new friend Alice," or "I've adopted her," or "It's *love*"—but more absentmindedly, like she was only going through the motions, after which she faded away somewhere, leaving me to fend for myself. The only person I distinctly remember talking to was a guy with plus and minus tattoos on his knees who had a six-month probation job for a tech company and said he knew Dwight. We sat next to each other on a sofa where people were passing around brownies. I assumed they were hash brownies, so I had only a tiny bite of one. "It is moreish," I said politely, "but actually, you don't want too much. Thank you."

Plus and Minus told me that the government was tracking him. "They're probably tracking you too," he said when I laughed nervously. "What do you do?"

"Me? Nothing. I just graduated."

He made a surprised face. "Oh. Well, they probably are anyway, if you're coming to parties like this. Most people here are on a list."

I must have looked blank.

"Agitators," he said. "But even if you just sit tight, be good, and buy shit, your identity is being traded all the time, and with your permission. It's like dust—tiny specks of your skin and hair."

The one bite of brownie was perhaps stronger than I had realised, because my skin had started crawling.

"So what do you actually do? You stop phishing scams and stuff like that?"

He looked offended. "Not exactly. The kinds of company that want to hire me are the security firms and defense contractors that make software for the government."

"What do they do?"

"Track people's movements, predict future behaviour by mining data from social networking websites. You can get a really intimate picture of a person's entire life—their friends, the places they visit."

"I know," I said. "I mean, I imagine that they can."

I don't remember choosing to get so completely high that I burst out of my own skull and became a kind of mist, a fresh dew on every face, but I remember the command *Open your mouth and shut your eyes,* and I remember someone holding my lips back, exposing my gums, and someone else holding my head and stroking me, and then the bitterest thing I have ever tasted, and then someone else asking me how I knew Mizuko and me saying dreamily, again and again, "She's adopted me. It's *love.*" And then I lay back like a sleepy child having its clothes taken off. Arms aloft, my feet liberated from their shoes. "Skin a rabbit!" I said sleepily, like I felt sure Silvia had said to me years ago when she got me ready for bed. Then I let myself be borne along in a primordial blur of limbs, keeping my eyes shut against the light overhead. Two couches had been pushed together to make a padded playpen. Outer layers were draped or thrown over the sides. I was not certain if voices addressed themselves to me, so I mainly did not answer them. I felt my mouth colliding with hard objects and heard myself shout "I'm falling!" which gave rise to a wave of laughter and stroking. "Okay." I giggled sheepishly, stroking my own arm.

I could feel my spine turning to fuzz. I became bodiless. I'll never forget that feeling, but when I try to picture the scene now, I have nothing. No faces, maybe vague shadows, protuberances and depressions like faces in the moon. I end up picturing a simulation we were shown at school the first year our notion of science was separated out into three—biology, chemistry, and physics—of what the universe supposedly looked like moments after the Big Bang.

When the police arrived at the party, I didn't immediately put two and two together. Everyone started yelling, "Feds! Feds!" The word meant nothing to me, but they began corralling us in the basement. I put on clothes—a man's.

Some people climbed out of a small window up onto street level and escaped that way. It didn't occur to me to try to do this myself, but I watched with detached interest as Plus and Minus made use of a leg up. Someone passed around a cupped handful of pills. "Quick, swallow them." Obediently I took what felt like three. There were black spots in front of my eyes. A ringing in my ears: sirens or music, or something else. Maybe because I did not try to leave, or because I did not recognise the officers as representing any danger—or because the large and sweaty denim jacket I had put on had mysterious origami squares of powder in the pockets—I was one of a handful of guests taken away in a van. When we got out we were taken for fingerprinting and photos, and I smiled until my jaw ached the whole way through. When they were done I could not stop staring at my hands, which now looked like cartoon paws. I wanted to show Mizuko and have her hold them, squeeze them: *How cuuuuuuute. How cuuuuuuuuuuuuute.*

The concrete cell was small, and a quarter of it was taken up with a toilet without a partition, but despite this I remember thinking the room had a really nice vibe. Slowly it occurred to me that I was happier there, and more at home, than I had ever felt anywhere in my life. I spoke at length with my cellmates, whose lives I understood instantaneously and as profoundly as if I had lived them—was living them—myself. I lived all of them not one by one but simultaneously. Of course I now understand that I was under the influence of a psychoactive drug consumed primarily for its euphoric and empathogenic effects and was not in fact having a vision of agape. Someone told me I needed to drink water, and so, to reassure them and show my appreciation for their concern, I kept calling out for water, but no one came.

After a while my incessant commentary on the oneness of all beings became a low murmuring and finally silence as I lay back against the cool, miraculous solidity of the cell wall. A voice to my left asked if I was okay and I told it I loved it and was deeply sorry I did not know its name. My cells—the cells in the skin on my back—felt like they were popping one by one wherever I pushed into the wall. I tipped my head back. From somewhere behind me, beyond a bright rim, I heard singing.

I don't remember them asking me any questions. All I remember is giving Mizuko's name as my own. Then, when I was released without charge, I walked west, thinking of Columbia floating westward, stringing telegraph wire behind her—a picture I'd seen pinned to a noticeboard in Dodge Hall. I muttered the words *Go West* until my jaw could not move anymore. I had a dry, bitter feeling in my mouth. I walked under sky spreading pink, through Prospect Heights and then north through Fort Greene, saluting strangers who caught my eye on their way to work. I could have gone to Dwight's, but then I remembered we had broken up, and then I remembered Mizuko. My cell had been returned to me inside my purse, but it had died. I wanted to continue walking, or my legs would not let me stop. I felt as if I were being directed, and so I felt I could let my mind wander and be free, knowing it was all being taken care of. A benign force was propelling me on. I stopped in front of a sign that tumbled a blood-red LED message perfectly in time with my heartbeat, over and over again in a way that hypnotised me for some minutes:

HAVE A GREAT DAY AND
MAKE GOOD CHOICES
HAVE A GREAT DAY AND
MAKE GOOD CHOICES
HAVE A GREAT DAY AND
MAKE GOOD CHOICES

YES, I promised, the words moving through my veins.

I crossed the Brooklyn Bridge and arrived at City Hall. *I am a daughter of this city,* I announced, one arm held aloft, the exact pose I imagined when Susy spoke of Mark as a young man, the divining rod, as a few early workers and street cleaners continued on their way.

The pink sky began to cloud over, and gradually the oneness of the universe began to drain away. The light became white cloud, bleached into ordinary. I noticed I was sore and incredibly thirsty. I sat down on a traffic island that for a moment I thought was the park on Pearl Street, which confused me for some minutes, making me think I had not come up at all but gone down further. The thought exhausted me, so that I could not stand up again. I asked a passerby, who confirmed that I was in midtown, and this exchange gave me a small amount of energy to stand and walk again. Only when I got to Silvia's, smiling feebly at the doorman, who recognised me and gave me a key (something I'd never had when I'd lived there with Silvia), did I remember that she was now in Amsterdam and that I was technically still staying with the Rooiakkers.

I considered heading towards her place, but the thought of going all the way up there now made my legs buckle. The apartment was deadly quiet and I could hear my breath and my heartbeat in my ears as if I were deep underwater. Pressure on my back. Suddenly cold, a shadow over the sun, a biting feeling in my kidneys. I stood by the sink running the tap, passing my hand in and out of the soft flow, in and out, drowning the sound of my breathing with the pummel of water on metal. New York tap water had never done anything to quench my thirst. I went into my old bedroom. I lay down width-ways on the bed, keeping my feet on the floor, but a sharp pain, as if I had leant on a burning hotplate, seared through me, making me leap up again. My phone bleeped from the pillow, where it now had enough power to turn itself on. As I held it, smooth and solid in my hand, I remembered.

The cordless phone began ringing, ringing, stopping, ringing. I went back into the hallway to hear the message. It was Amsterdam. Call back. I went looking for aspirin in the kitchen but forgot what I was looking for. I realised I smelt homeless and became so desperate for a shower that I began undressing right there in the kitchen. Disrobing like a child, dropping the strange things I was wearing onto the floor with disgust, and limping, hard-footed, as though my feet were all bone, towards Rex's bathroom. Skin a rabbit. I wanted to remove every layer, right down to the muscle. There I stopped, shocked by the sight of myself in the mirror. I was covered in bruises: some small and distinct as grapes, some faint and stippled, others cloudy and creeping like rot—finger marks, bites, grazes. I stood on the edge of the bath to see the whole of me at once, pushing my hair from my shoulders to see how they climbed right up around my neck. I was mesmerized. It was like I was looking at somebody else, but when I touched them they hurt just like it had hurt when I lay on the bed. I could, I thought, tell that I was pregnant. My breasts were fuller, and there was a very soft swelling between my hipbones. I felt dizzy standing on the side of the bath, felt something give as if a sinkhole had opened up beneath me. I half fell, half lowered myself onto the bathmat. *Don't hit your head.* Was it the drone or had I told myself? I'd heard it in the voice of Susy, who greatly feared slippery surfaces and had always said this type of thing as if I might be intent upon concussion.

If I had had a friend other than Mizuko to call, this would have been the moment. I would have said, *I think I have just accidentally taken part in a gangbang in a dingy basement that looked like a serial killer lived there before being escorted off the premises in a police van after everyone in the neighbourhood called 911 to report a disturbance.* Then they might have come over and held me for a bit, stroked my hair, got me to an STI clinic. I would have realised that Mizuko was a terrible human being. But I had no one to call except her, and she didn't answer, and so this was not a funny story or even a surprising story I could tell someone and I continued to think of her as a goddess.

When I got into the shower I felt a tiny astringent something as the shampoo foam ran between my legs, something pucker-

ing, like there was a small tear. I heard the sound of the voices
at the party gurgle up at me from the plughole and I began to
shake. Mildly at first, then violently, until I had to steady myself
by holding on to the plastic handrails.

When I finally turned the water off I realised I was bleeding.
I checked my body in the mirror, but I knew already. I became
very stern with myself and sat on the toilet in the brace position.
If I am not stern and businesslike with myself in moments like
these, which are not planned for, then I know I will have an anxiety attack. Out of the shower, where the water had disguised it,
the slow bleeding became fast haemorrhaging. When it was over
I turned to face the toilet bowl and knelt down to look at what
was inside. The blood was clotted and dark at the bottom but
sending up red billows like a flare that was turning all the water
pink and opaque so that it became rapidly more difficult to see
what was in there. A part of me held on to the idea that this was
occasionally a feature of pregnancy in the early stages. I had
read, under the lists of fruits and vegetables, that spotting could
sometimes happen. I reached my hand into the water and tried to
dredge the bottom. I did not want to flush it without being sure.
I searched for images of miscarriage online—kneeling by the
toilet, gripping the ceramic with my free hand in order to try to
stop my shaking—and then used the toothbrush holder to scoop
out the pink water and transfer it carefully into the sink with the
plug down. I worked meticulously and calmly, using my hands
as a sieve, until I found what I was looking for.

*P*lease *pick up.*

Then, to give this message a different weight, more gravity than the near-identical ones hovering above it, I asked if, since she had had her abortion administered by mouth — which means you are fully conscious when it happens, like a heavy period — she had seen the fetus when it came out, and if so, if she wasn't too busy doing whatever it was she was doing, wherever she was doing it, would she perhaps check on the tiny, fleshy part of me I had saved from the water?

No reply.

Not even *seen.*

Or, I added in a second message, I could send her a picture and she could evaluate remotely.

Sent stayed grey and flat. I waited for the blue — the bright, beautiful blue that would create a neural pathway between us.

To make it absolutely impossible for her to ignore me unless something was very, very, imminent-apocalypse kind of wrong, I sent one more:

I really need you right now.

I turned back to the sink, considered the rich red sashimi I had salvaged. In texture similar to what I had spat into the toilet bowl of the Japanese restaurant with Mizuko. I laid it in the palm of my hand to examine. I looked for bones. I couldn't see anything remotely human, and yet I felt a kind of kinship I had never felt before. As I held it, it appeared to move, then to shrink and curl up at the edges like one of those fortune fish.

It occurred to me that my follow-up appointment at Planned Parenthood had been booked for today. I wondered whether I should call them and cancel. Was it like that? Like a dentist? Even if this wasn't *it* and I was still pregnant, I did not feel like today was the right day to be sedated.

"Strange, strange thing," I said to the fish. Its edges were crisping in the central heating. "It's like you knew the date."

As I went on cradling it and it became increasingly leathery and indestructible-looking, I considered the prophecy I'd ful-filled. I had claimed to be pregnant—this had come true. I had decided to get rid of it, and that too had come to pass, a matter of hours before I was due to be sedated and have it suctioned out. A tingly feeling arrived in my fingertips. A powerful feeling, ten times the intensity of taking photographs. At the same time a part of me, however, felt bereft of exactly that feeling. Though I had chosen already, I had been cheated of the feeling of having chosen, good choice or bad, and had it replaced with a kind of inevitability. A box somewhere on a form, the black box, had been ticked once, and that was that. What had happened, the way the world had become receptive to me, its native daughter, now felt like no choice at all.

Mizuko still did not reply.

I laid my fish on a piece of kitchen towel. I took one of the last four Provigil pills I had in the beaded purse Mizuko had lent me, which I had managed to hang on to from both the party and the police station. I positioned myself in front of Silvia's library, got down four books from a shelf at random, and waited for the tunnel to open.

The first was about classical civilisations. I focused on creating exact mental pictures of the artefacts described. The materials: wood, stone, clay, glass. The small objects: phials, coins, beads, rattles. The simple tools. I thought of the textures—linen, wool, metal, earth. Soon the sound of the city below faded out. I wanted to fill my mind with as much of this other, older world as possible so that there would be no room in it for her. So that she would not even have been born yet. In this world, she had not abandoned me at a party, because she had never existed. Her sudden, anachronistic appearance in this world of amphorae and togas would be greeted with shocked silence, and she would have to retreat again, embarrassed, as if she had stumbled into the wrong room.

I got to a subheading, "Vestal Virgins." They got to live together in Rome's only college of full-time priests—daughters of the city—and they lived free from the usual obligations, like marriage and children. That could be me, I thought. I'd definitely have been a vestal if I had lived then. The cordless phone rang out somewhere in the dark, shimmery heat, but I ignored it. The vestals took a vow of chastity and spent all their time observing rituals, the main one being to tend a fire that was never allowed to go out. And that's Silvia's central heating, I thought, vowing to live with the discomfort more gracefully. On the ides of March the virgins processed around various shrines, picking up little human figures made of rush, reed, and straw, and then went to the Tiber, where they threw them into the water. The book suggested that these figures were substitutes for human sacrifice and absorbed all the pollution and evil within the city, so sacrificing them brought about purification.

My eyes were dry, and I forced myself to blink. I felt my brain accelerating. I lay on my back on the living room floor.

Silvia's phone rang again, mocking my silent one. I ripped the cord out of the wall, and the abrupt peace gave me not just relief but the feeling of mastery. This was, I supposed, what Dwight meant by *pushing back*. Resisting forces that were unpleasant or disagreed with you. Noises that threatened to oppress you. I returned to my spot on the carpet, where I lay on my back with my knees up to help my cramps.

I stared intently at my phone. It lay next to my head on the carpet. The longer I stared at it, the less I recognised what it was. It had turned into a stranger. A deaf-mute. Dark and resolute. Nothing about it suggested that it might be an object one could communicate with. Stroking it with my fingers or holding it to my head and trying to talk felt as useless as talking into a stone. I flipped over and shot my arm out to surprise it. *Snap out of it!* It felt horribly light in my hand. So insubstantial compared to the impression it gave of solidity. I found a picture of one of her favourite scenes from *The Parent Trap*, with subtitles along the bottom. I offered it up. Bait. I waited. No one liked it. She did not like it. By dusk, an angler quitting empty-handed, I deleted.

I decided to leave the apartment and take my little red fortune fish across to Roosevelt Island, where I had met Dwight, Walter, and Ingrid for the first time. I sealed the fish in one of Silvia's heavy cream envelopes, deciding that like a vestal, I would proceed to the triangular park at the end of the island and throw it in the water.

Outside, everything seemed to be thrumming, making the same noise as the noise inside my brain, but much louder. It seemed to be that way round, rather than that the noise in my brain came from outside it, but it became hard to tell. It had a kind of rhythm—*dugadug dugadug dugadug*—like a chain in the teeth of something, drawing up an anchor from somewhere far below. The sky vibrated with the sound, shifting thick, then thin, rippling, some great murmuration behind it.

I made it to the park before closing and climbed the steps that led up to the triangle of grass very slowly, unsteady on my feet, holding the envelope in both hands and close to my chest. At the top I walked straight through the middle of the triangle towards the vanishing point, to the open granite enclosure at the southern tip of the island. Once there, I sat down on the stone blocks, cold despite the sun, and stared vacantly into the grey wake— the current made it look like the island was moving—until I felt a light touch on my arm and heard someone telling me it was time to go home. And where was that?

I got up to go. The warm bath of serotonin and dopamine had now fully evaporated. I began to despair. I didn't cast the envelope into the water. I found I couldn't part with it yet. When the park closed, I sat down on a bench by the funicular and made long, air-tearing noises, my lungs heaving and grating. And then I fell asleep.

When I woke up I was disoriented. It was dark and my bones ached. The metal grille of the bench had burnt itself into my bruises. With panic, I saw that my device was nearly out of power. I could not let it die even for a moment in case it would be the one moment she tried to call.

I went back to Silvia's, noticing the emptiness more acutely this time, now that it was dark and there was no familiar sound of TCM movies or light flickering from her den. I sat on the floor just inside her front door, charging the phone at the first plug socket. But here the Wi-Fi symbol was showing only the very epicenter, no radiating waves, so I shunted further and further until the cord wouldn't stretch anymore.

How could we have got this far, got this close, for her to disappear? I haunted her, vehemently refreshing every few seconds, watching the wheel spin like an instrument of torture. Cranking the walls and floors and ceiling so that they moved closer and closer in. The picture from the party was still her most recent. I stared and stared and stared at it.

WHERE ARE YOU

When the Provigil finally wore off, I realised I was desperate for the bathroom. But after I'd been, I had not taken two steps before I needed to pee again. I went back, repeated. I stood up again. I needed to go again. I sat down again; this time there was only one drop. I got up and left the bathroom again, and then again the burning sensation of having to pee. I spent most of the night in the bathroom, in this cycle, on repeat. Every time I tried to leave I felt as if I needed to pee again and my bladder would drag me back in. If I managed to pee, even one drop, I would be rewarded with a sharp, burning pain that subsided for only a second before it was replaced with the desire to do it all over again. My device was still taunting me with its black mirror. I jabbed at it and it told me only the time, or it told me numbers. I felt sure that on the twin times or the mirrored times she would call, and when they came I would tense up, and then she wouldn't.

I threw the phone across the room. She made me terrified and sick and I depended entirely on her for sustenance, even though what she gave me was as good as air. I wanted out. I started to look at flights home from the floor of the bathroom, Skyscanner open on one tab, a cystitis symptom checker on another, and

Mizuko's arrested online activity on a third, fourth, and fifth. It was unlike her not to have posted anything for over twenty-four hours.

I was out of Provigil. I needed a new visual stimulus. I began searching for images of the bedrooms at the NoMad. For images of Robin and Ingrid. I looked through Dwight's pictures. I looked at the routes between their three apartments on Google Maps. This helped me to create pictures in my mind of what she was up to. I imagined that when she had left the party, she had gone back to the restaurant, up to a hotel room at the NoMad to join Ingrid and Robin. My inflamed urinary tract—the desire always to pee, squeezing every last drop of liquid from my body until there was nothing left—now felt absolutely connected to Mizuko's failure to respond.

WHERE ARE YOU

Somewhere, signals were being scrambled. Neurons were firing out and being deflected. There was a blockade. An invisible dome that bounced my missiles right back. Maybe the Rooiakkers were to blame. Sex game gone wrong. Ties tied too tight. That happened all the time. Bodies in suitcases. Forgotten safe words. Circulation cut off. Something was stuck, that was clear. I wondered if I should go to their apartment. I imagined myself loping towards Claremont Avenue. *Unhand that woman!* I pictured punching Robin in the stomach repeatedly. But I could only do this through pictures. I could not imagine my real, physical body ever entering their perfect, pristine home again. The idea quickly made me feel ashamed. They'd be laughing. Dwight would be too, and Walter. Robin's stomach would take the punches like Plasticine, my hand sticking in and being sucked into it like a trap. I imagined Mizuko's eyes narrowed in catlike pleasure.

WHERE ARE YOU

I had sent the same message so many times the words formed perfect columns underneath their predecessors. That's quite cool, I thought. I sent another.

WHERE ARE YOU

I hoped that if something had happened to her—not a sex game gone wrong, but something that absolved her of guilt for this torture—she would look at this when she finally got to her messages and think it was funny or cute. A performance piece. Endurance art.

I went to the kitchen for more water, not for thirst but so I'd have something to pass through my kidneys, saw the stranger's clothes on the floor, and for a moment thought there was an intruder in the apartment, until I remembered I'd worn them to enter it myself. I tried to imagine what Silvia might advise me to do at this moment, and returned to the stack of books to try and re-create the effects of Provigil without the pill itself. I arranged them in a ring around me and left my device on the other side of the ring, telling myself I could not go to it, nor to the bathroom to gratify my phantom urge to urinate, until I had read *one whole book* cover to cover, after which I was allowed out of the ring to use the bathroom and to check the time—which was no longer time like a time of day or night but digits, a numbered countdown—and then I had to return to the ring to read another and start the process over again. For double immunity, I imagined Silvia overseeing this system in the silence of the apartment, but I could not control my thoughts or keep her out of them. She's going to be dead, I thought. She'll be dead, and then everything will be fine.

I turned the lining of Mizuko's purse inside out. Coins, pellets of gum, fuzz and hair, receipts, and one Provigil fell to the floor.

At last I felt myself glide into the familiar state of deep concentration. My brain oily and smooth again, the fragments put back together with gold, all the tangled paths narrowing to one, whose sides rose up and enclosed me like a tunnel. I felt my powers return. The ability to unlock the meaning of every sign if I just looked at it hard enough.

When I order the drug now in England, it arrives inside a pouch for rose-hip supplements. Did it affect my behaviour towards her at the time? I don't know. It locks you into your own way of seeing things, I suppose.

I came to a chapter about Pandora. At last everything starting to make sense. A chain between me and—*dugadugadugaduga-duga*—her. I came to a word that made me slap my forehead in astonishment. *My phone is the jar.* My phone is the fucking jar. The mistranslation of *pithos,* a large storage jar, as *box,* Silvia's book told me, is usually attributed to Erasmus when he translated Hesiod into Latin. Fucking *hell,* I thought, shaking my head at this flagrant textual corruption, my teeth chattering. That's *big.* I should note that down. I looked for my journal and realised it was at Mizuko's. Was she reading it now? Laughing with Rupert at my juvenilia?

The combination of my urinary tract infection, the oppressive central heating, and my concern for Mizuko's unexplained silence meant that the Provigil did not last as long as usual at its normal intensity. I felt the chain stick, and then the other metaphor I was using to help make everything more bearable, the tunnel, also begin to disintegrate. This happened before I had even finished the book, and so the last few chapters were a struggle. I had to read them with my hands cupped around my eyes like blinkers. When I finally finished it, I allowed myself to go to the bathroom and then, only then, to check my phone.

Nothing.

Twenty-four became thirty-six became forty-eight became blocks that were days, not hours. I guess this would be when she had her seizure and Perry called the ambulance.

It was the medium itself, I now felt, as much as Mizuko, that I was enslaved by. I began to run from room to room. I'll exhaust myself again, I thought, and then I'll fall asleep and I won't know that time is still passing. I had removed her timestamp from WhatsApp for her during the breakup with Rupert, but she had since reinstated it. I checked it right before I started running. She had not been active in days. When I stopped running, it said "active 19 minutes ago." I gave a sharp intake of breath, hit myself in the head with the heel of my hand, and threw the phone to the floor as if it had scalded me.

Maybe she has lost her phone.

Maybe someone else has it.

Maybe she lost it at the party.

Maybe Rupert has it.

Maybe she is now using Facebook from her laptop and so that is why she is active on there—

Maybe Robin has it.

—but cannot read any of her messages and her phone just rings and rings.

It would truly be wonderful, a miracle, I thought, if she had mislaid it, because then she would be unable to contact the Rooiakkers on TriMe. Or see my WHERE ARE YOUs.

I had, while chained to the toilet, downloaded TriMe with the idea of standing outside her building and seeing if the proximity made her appear on my screen. I was already inundated with messages from white men saying that their girlfriends had always wanted to have sex with a black woman. But now every time I got a message alert I thought it might be her, so I decided I had to disable it. Her silence had to *mean* something. I could only bear it if I thought of it as a message I had to decode. Not an absence. In the stillness and silence of Silvia's apartment, I sat down on the floor, prayed that it was still and silent where she was too. Then I lay down and prayed that the prone position I was currently in was her position too. Alone. I had black magic. I closed my eyes, darkness, as if that might let me see what she saw. A neon-pink 3 flickered and instantly disappeared again into the dark. The sight of it on my own device now made me sick. I held my finger down on the menu screen; each little app logo began to vibrate. I deleted the 3. I contemplated deleting everything. Cleaning it all away. The idea had a charm, a self-cancellation, many little suicides, a way to dispatch myself without actually going anywhere.

I did not cancel my many selves completely, because then if she did try to get in touch with me, I would never know. I would do just one more thing. One gesture. I poured myself a glass of Silvia's vodka, circled my phone a few times, then pounced on it. *Unfollow.* It felt good for one second.

I may also have been experiencing a sympathetic form of encephalitis — encephalitis being inflammation of the brain, which she was diagnosed with. The numinous glow was always a false dawn. Each time the screen returned to darkness, I would stare at the faint greasy patina of my fingerprints, tracing the configuration of buttons I'd pressed to induce this fever. *Unfollow.* I began looking for loopholes that might let me undo what I had done. They hadn't even been real buttons. They didn't exist except in the instant I'd brought them into being by touching the now-dark glass. They were, I recited, buttocks clenching with the memory of Dwight, skeuomorphisms. Part of a gratifying simulacrum which overlaid an invisible field whose laws I couldn't hope to understand, much less reverse, designed to make me feel as if I'd depressed something when in fact I hadn't.

I lay on my back willing it all to end. After a time, I found a small section of the carpet that let me feel something else. A cool spot that grew cooler and larger the harder I pressed into it, until it became the exact outline of me. Until, after a brief panic that I might be incontinent as a result of the UTI, doomed to die alone, leaving only a stain on Silvia's carpet, I felt revitalised, and ruthless. I decided to confess everything. I would write the truth of the matter down. I would be brutal and unsparing to us both, and after reading it she would see herself as I saw her and so understand me as I really was. Now I wonder whether everything would have turned out fine if I hadn't. I saw it as a message of love. A ritual cleaning. A stripping back of everything I'd tried to conceal from her. How I loved her, how I hated her, how it wasn't really chance that had brought us together, how in another way it really was. The patterns and paternity I had uncovered.

I wrote quickly, sensing that the appropriate time for confessions was drawing to a close, after which one would be most unwelcome. I suppose I also wrote it anonymously, though that didn't signify anything but my intimacy with her at the time. If someone had sent me something like that, I'd have assumed it was from her.

I felt myself swimming to the surface as I wrote. My legs kicking, my arms outstretched and grasping, as if very soon I might be up in the light. Once I had finished I felt exposed, as if the sea had drawn back from the shoreline like lips revealing gums. It would be impossible, I thought, after reading it over to myself, for a wave not to come rushing back in. It would be impossible for her not to come back to me with all the force of shifting earth, rearing ocean, a wall of water behind her. I admit that some parts of it were fairly provocative—they were intended to be. As I say, any response seemed better than silence.

So that it couldn't be instantly forwarded to the others it implicated, and to endow it with a sense of occasion, I decided to print it rather than emailing. She had said she only read things properly in print, could only really, truly understand something if she could hold it.

Outside, I felt an invisible field all around me that I swam in, every step slower than the last, the air thickening until I felt like I was wading through ketchup. Crowds seemed to form and throng around me wherever I stood. I had grown accustomed to being nameless and faceless in the city. My anonymity—the impersonal nudge and natter of the crowd. But now every face I passed showed some kind of recognition. First, the guys in the lobby seemed much friendlier than usual, then my homeless friend on the bench was back and acknowledged me with a hopeful wave. Then people I didn't know. Random people on the street looking at me as if they knew me, and I thought I heard one or two whispering my name. The city knew me. It could distinguish my cry from a million other cries, the way people say mothers know the cry of their own child.

I went to use a computer in a convenience store that no longer exists but that seemed to be built entirely out of stacked newspapers and six-packs of bottled water. I can see the interior of the store now: narrow and dusty, with baroque flourishes of vacuum-packed fruit. I was now excruciatingly thirsty, despite being enclosed by walls of water, and still desperate to pee, so that I wondered if I was in fact hallucinating. I tried to be quick, but I had to find a system of moving the mouse, directing its capricious rollerball where I didn't want it to go in order to get where I did. The keyboard had an unpredictable delay between my typing and words appearing, so that first I typed wrong and then I deleted wrong and then I got trapped in that circle over and over. After ten minutes I considered aborting the enterprise, but then the screen froze and so I couldn't. Abandoning it then would have meant leaving my confession open for all to see.

I doubt if anyone had used that computer in years. The screen was set into one of those busts, warm beige, like ancient stone at sunset. The warmth increased with its resistance. I was clearly dragging it back into a battle it had been assured was over. When I thought I'd won, the printer closed ranks. It was then that I made the first public sound that I had made in days. "*Fuck,*" I said, like a bark.

I paid for the printing, a correct stamp, and a large brown envelope. Brown hands appeared over the counter with a receipt, which was faintly comical to me but which I kept as proof that I had sent something. I like to collect evidence of my life, and I also like to leave it around for others to puzzle over. I began pulling at the hairs on my clothes and letting them fly around, so that if, for example, I was murdered after this, my DNA would be all over the city and the case would remain a talked-about but unsolved mystery.

I was so jumpy, so unaccustomed, since my correspondence with Silvia, to using real mail, that I very nearly inserted the envelope into a waste-disposal unit. But I did send it. Or rather, I dropped it into the correct metal box to be sent. I wanted it—very literally—out of my hands. For someone else to bear the weight of it. I calculated she would receive it within forty-eight hours.

I went home and waited for each of those hours to elapse. As much as I feared her reaction, I feared her continued silence more.

Yes, some things resisted. Some things felt like countersigns. The keyboard had been chalky, the keys stuck. I didn't have the right change. But I don't think that if I had waited for this episode to pass, I would have been able to avoid writing what I wrote. I don't think it would have passed unless I'd written and sent it. It was about twenty pages long in total, with various subheadings and footnotes. The part I regret is the assumption that she'd actually gone back to the hotel. The perversions I imagined to be taking place. The depraved scenes that had come to me, composites of images I had seen on her phone, with faces and features reallocated. I had wanted to goad her into admitting it, because I didn't know if she had, so I wrote about it as if I knew for sure. The more I wrote, the higher my fever raged, waves of arousal and anguish coming faster until I had to type with one hand and quiet them with the other between my thighs.

When another forty-eight hours had dragged by and I still hadn't heard from her, I asked the guys in the lobby if they would mind calling my phone to check that it was working. It was an English phone, so I figured this was reasonable, and I started to acquire a more stable frame of mind. Maybe there hadn't been enough in my account to pay my phone bill. Maybe I'd reached my roaming limit. The phone proceeded to vibrate in circles on the desk, and everyone at that moment began grinning as if we were all friends.

At first, sending the confession by real mail had felt like a genius device. I would not have to sit by my phone and watch for the signs that indicated it had been sent and seen. Slim but solid paper would, I hoped, convey me better. Now I had to consider the very real frailties of the system. Ludicrous, in fact, to entrust something of such magnitude to a mailman. A perfect stranger. I looked up stories of nefarious New York mailmen. There was one who had willfully upturned the lives of ordinary people like myself by hoarding 40,000 pieces of undelivered mail. The city was crawling with thieves and malcontents. And yet how treacherous, I thought, after such neutrality, bordering on indifference, and occasionally open hostility, when the whole city finally seemed alive and tremulous to my touch, a seething structure reaching out to meet me and accommodate my every move, as if I had been expected and was welcome there, that *she* was the only thing in it that would not respond.

24

This kind of torture has a particular name, of course. As you'll know already, I had been *ghosted*. And at this point you're thinking, She should have walked. Disconnected. Got the fuck out. Let me tell you, there was no out. It was a locked box stronger than any magician ever broke free from. As indestructible as it was invisible, made of nothing but permeating everything.

When I headed up towards her, eight days had passed. Despite my solitary confinement, I felt talked out.

"Can you tell the difference," the sky asked slyly as I walked out again under it, "between a sunrise and a sunset?"

I considered. It was a metallic twilight, the dying sun invisible but for the many lucid reflections bouncing off the buildings.

"No," I said.

"No? In that case, why should this be the end?"

Neon began to sizzle into life as I started walking. I could hear it, a growing intelligence all around me, as if a swarm of bees crawled behind every glinting surface. I remember thinking, I must simply be native now, a fluent speaker. Just by walking, I had learnt the city's language. I understood all the coded messages flying around, each one with its distinct smell and colour becoming integrated in my mind, and I saw who sent them and where they went and who read them. I could suspend each one of them—hold them in the air like flies in a spiderweb—then set them moving again with a motion of my wrist. The chefs in rubber shoes, bent over, smoking, the invisible people hunched inside sleeping bags, the dazed businessmen leaving work, all on their cell phones, became parts, and their parts became cells, and their cells became smaller until they were the same as what throbbed in the sky and all around me. I could now connect the sour smells of rubbish overflowing with the chlorine disinfectant from outside the table-dancing club and the place under the bridge which always smelt of urine, and it was a pattern. Like a musical phrase that repeated. Every neon sign I looked at I could see through and through and through into the wiring and then the particles firing and then the smaller things inside those.

I reached the park at 73rd and headed towards Levin Playground. I stuck my head into the spray hissing from the pale granite drinking fountain. On the other side of the park I moved faster. Along 96th to Columbus. I looked down to see a trail of small footprints like a cat's; "Amazing," I said aloud, shaking my head in wonder. The prints had left their imprint in fresh sidewalk, leading me towards her.

I started to feel scared when I saw Nussbaum & Wu on the corner, the signs for Nails and the Housewares store on the corner opposite, which told me I was there. Her building was still there, and showed no signs that anything had changed. It remained an imposing mushroom grey, with a set of classical columns flanking the doorway. In the centre, above the entrance, an iron fire escape climbed down the façade. Dark window frames bit into the stone. Still the familiar red steps up to the door. White air-conditioning units protruding from the windows. Same decorative moulding and cornices. Hers was on the top floor—the sixth.

The bodiless voice of Perry, Mizuko's doorman, surprised me as I tried to slip past his usual spot in the entrance. His head buoyed up from behind the desk.

"Hey, Alice."

I had often picked up deliveries from him, and he must have grown used to seeing me there. Perry told me the story, the bits he'd seen with his own eyes: the paramedics, the arrival of the mother from Japan; the rumour in the building he'd had to quell that it was Ebola, and the little that Hiromi had told him when she got back from visiting her daughter in the hospital the previous few nights. Mizuko lived a ten-minute walk from St. Luke's, and Hiromi had gone back and forth several times daily. Visiting hours for critical-care patients were limited to fifteen-minute intervals but could be repeated throughout the day. Late last night Hiromi had left for the airport, explaining that Mizuko had now recovered and would be coming home soon, but she had to get back—she had work, and she'd had to leave her elderly mother, who was very frail, alone while she was away. She needed to go back to her.

Every time he said Mizuko's name out loud I felt some of the old nausea creeping back. The faint feeling. I felt my magic power slipping away.

"She got a parasite of some kind. That goddamn cat, I bet. Demon. Disgustin' animal. She's not even supposed to keep a pet in the building. I got me and my whole family checked out by the doctor 'cause we had it stayin' with us when you two went off on your trip to the desert. Did I tell you she had a seizure right here in the middle of the lobby?"

I nodded. "Where's Michi now?"

He pointed a finger heavenwards.

"Dead?"

"No, no—upstairs. I think her mother's been feeding it."

He let me in with the spare key Hiromi had been using. "Did you see?" he called out after me as he headed back down the hall. "That guy at the hospital in Dallas died today."

"Mmm," I said. I didn't know who he meant, and was grateful when the elevator doors closed behind him.

> *Begins with flulike symptoms. Extreme tiredness, fatigue, breathing problems, dead limbs, strange sensation of sore throat . . . Some people make a full recovery from encephalitis. But for many, encephalitis can lead to permanent brain damage and complications, including*
>
> - *memory loss*
> - *epilepsy, a condition that causes repeated seizures*
> - *personality and behavioural changes*
> - *problems with attention, concentration, planning, and problem solving.*

I'd never heard of it, and it was the kind of thing I could imagine Mizuko cooking up. I told myself she wouldn't go that far for a story. I reminded myself of what Perry had said. The paramedics. Unless she had somehow done it to herself? People did, it seemed, do things like that. I searched *self-infected parasite.* People seemed to order them online and swallow them fairly regularly. Weight loss, digestive problems, all kinds of things. I tried not to doubt her. I wanted to believe it, and that some benign force was turning the tables in my favour.

Michi was hiding under the sofa. I bent down and she shrank from me.

"Hi, Michi! So is it you I need to thank?"

We rarely get the chance to see things anew. I remember a Latin translation that caused me to fail an exam at school because one of the words, translated for us at the bottom of the page and intended to help, was *invalid*. I read this to mean false, null, illegal. The opposite of *valid*. But it was meant to be understood as invalid as in a sick person. It torpedoed my entire translation. Instead of tending to the sick, the priests were being accused of fraudulence and neglecting their duties. Even though it didn't match up with the grammar, or the story, I kept on returning to that word to check, and every time I saw it only as I had done already—invalid, null, void.

It took some minutes for the new situation to sink in. Pretty much the only scenario I had not imagined was that I would be able in some way to start over. And yet it seemed a miraculous erasure had occurred—as simple as deleting a search history or restoring factory settings, a memory neatly wiped around just the mark I had made on it. Except for her phone, of course. That would have to go.

I realised I did not know precisely what a seizure was. Stop a moment to think of your life without Wikipedia. Sweet source of eternal comfort. Ministering angel of information. Think of your life without the option to Internet search.

> A **seizure** is a sudden surge of electrical activity in the brain. A **seizure** usually affects how a person appears or acts for a short time. Neurons conduct electrical signals and communicate with each other in the brain using chemical messengers. During a **seizure**, there are abnormal bursts of neurons firing off electrical impulses, which can cause the brain and body to behave strangely. The severity of **seizures** can differ from person to person. Some people simply experience an odd feeling, with no loss of awareness, or may have a trancelike state for a few seconds or minutes, while others lose consciousness and have convulsions (uncontrollable shaking of the body).

I tried to imagine it. The **seizure**. Her brain's electrical impulses travelling towards me across the grid.

The apartment had a new kind of smell, like minty chewing gum and boiled rice. It looked different, but I could not at first say how. There were some new things: a pale pink rice cooker, some tea canisters and packets of the same surgical masks Robin used. I flinched, and then felt something brush my ankle. I looked down to see only the leaves of Mizuko's indoor plant, a kind of palm. Some of the lower leaves had begun to die, but in a way that seemed strange the longer I looked at them. A perfect curve from green to brown, an exact line between life and death. There was an old pizza box in the trash. The crusts rattled like bones inside when I picked it out. I tried a piece of pepperoni against my tooth. It was hard and covered in amber dust. Days old.

Before I touched anything else, I went straight to the cabinet in the bathroom where Mizuko kept her Provigil and, pumping spit into my mouth, swallowed one. Then another. I went to the bedroom. At this point I realised I had not thought through all the possibilities. I saw my confession; it was like seeing a friend from your infancy, whom you are too shy to approach now. It had been opened but replaced inside its brown envelope, my childish handwriting, her address and the word *urgent,* all laid out perfectly on the freshly made bed. Next to it another envelope, this one unopened, a similar creamy thickness to the one I had enclosed my fish in, with neat Biro kanji on the front. *Water, child.* Her name.

I found her phone. It was out of power. Once charged, it was still useless to me—I did not have her thumb. I put it in my pocket. Then I turned to the envelope. Its physical relation to my brown one suggested it was a reply.

25

Y ou got a delivery to make?" Perry indicated the various packages under my arm.

I nodded.

"I didn't think nobody wrote letters nowadays."

I nodded again, then shook my head instead.

"Kids your age are all *e*mails and *Face*book. You want me to send them for you?"

I shook my head, clutching them tighter, and started moving towards the door.

When I took it, I had her justification for "Kizuna" ringing in my ears: "You own everything that happens to you."

Here was an envelope. It was right here in front of me, so it had *happened to me,* even if it wasn't addressed to me. In any case, it appeared that Hiromi had read what was in mine.

In all the assumptions I had made about Mizuko's paternity, I had not thought much of Hiromi's inner life. She was the piece of the puzzle that didn't really fit unless I sanded her edges down. I steeled myself with the notion that if anyone was to blame for the blood knot that now tied Robin and Mizuko together, it was her, not me. But also I had never considered that she could be a victim of any kind, because Mizuko had never presented her that way. Mizuko was the victim. Hiromi was the adult. Adults could not be victims. Her job had made her seem an even less sympathetic character. I mean, she made machines that looked after old and vulnerable people in their homes, removing the need for human contact. In my mind she was close to a villain, and I worried that she might have fitted her invalid daughter's apartment with various sensors—a telephone that could check a person's pulse or glucose levels, or a toilet that scanned waste for signs of disease, the kind of things her company made. Maybe, I wondered as I ripped open the back of the envelope, she had been tracking my movements since I had entered her daughter's apartment.

The first thing to say is that I couldn't even read the letter. Not directly. It was written in Japanese, so once I had opened it, having readied myself on a bench above Morningside Park where I could see for miles, I had to get up and go find someone who could. I guess that when I did, any trace of moral boundary disappeared, but at that point I felt no more responsibility to Hiromi or Mizuko than I did to the tiny basketball players whose shouts and thuds and ringing metal I could hear echoing from the park courts below me. The women were in that moment strangers, playing a different game from mine, and the rules from one did not apply to the other.

I first approached someone on the street who looked convincingly Japanese, but she wasn't. Next I approached a woman in a Japanese supermarket I knew of nearby, but she looked at me with fear in her eyes. Then I saw an Asian-looking kid sitting in the window of a Starbucks, and he confirmed that he could read

Japanese. I offered him some money and he agreed, writing in between the lines the words he could.

As I have mentioned, the practical consequences of something are often indirect and unforeseen. I think of that when I think about what I wrote in my not-entirely-true confession. The World Wide Web was originally invented for physicists at the Large Hadron Collider to share information, to share objective facts, to find one version of the truth that cannot be denied. Its architects can hardly be blamed for the plague they have let loose. Sometimes it's the other way round: you know only the consequence and not the origin. I read today about an earthquake supposed to happen in America any moment now. Scientists worked it all out from a place near the Washington coast called the ghost forest, where all the cedars are dead, killed by saltwater. The ground in which they were rooted dropped down during an earthquake—the growth rings told the researchers this because they all died simultaneously, not slowly but suddenly. The scientists matched what happened in the ghost forest to what happened on the northeast coast of Japan, thousands of miles west.

> On the eighth day of the twelfth month of the twelfth
> year of the Genroku era, a six-hundred-mile-long wave
> struck the coast. Though tsunamis are the result of earth-
> quakes, no one felt the ground shake before the wave
> hit—it had no discernible origin. When scientists began
> studying it, they called it an orphan tsunami, like an
> orphan line on a printed page. Finally they matched that
> orphan to its parent. The pieces fit together perfectly. And
> now they have tubes with samples of the seafloor, history
> written for people who can read it, people who can then

*work out the earthquake's recurrence interval, a two-hun-
dred-and-forty-three-year cycle.*

I walked through the heart of Columbia, 116th Street, part
of the same route Mizuko had walked with me that first time,
when her silky coat had been floating on the summer air and everything had felt so smooth and easy that I'd wanted to laugh. I
laughed now, not with happiness or because anything was funny
but in solidarity with myself. I could choose any reality I wanted,
and Mizuko would have no choice but to live in it with me, at
least for a while. She'd chosen me once already, in a way, it had
been a choice of sorts, and that was enough, it was permission. I
walked all the way to the Hudson River and found a spot where
I could stand looking down over the water. I took my brown envelope, still with her name and address on it, still marked *urgent*.
Then I extracted Mizuko's phone from my back pocket and put
that inside too. Then I put those into a large plastic zip-lock bag
from her kitchen. I put in her other device, her little MacBook,
as well to weigh it down. Then I sealed all of them—my confession, Mizuko's two devices—sliding the zip slowly and with
ceremony, and dropped the bag down into the fast-flowing river.

It was what I had imagined I'd do with my fortune fish on
Roosevelt Island—return it to water—only this time I had actually managed to. When I saw the bag disappear beneath the
surface, I had to clench my teeth and suck my tongue against
the roof of my mouth to stop some primal sound from escaping.
Then I felt a hand on my shoulder and let out a cry of surprise.

"Can you take my photo?" a stranger said.

"Sure."

I walked back past Saint John the Divine. I had never been
inside. Something about the outside of it had always oppressed

me. It was built on the site of an orphan asylum, and the external architecture, as Robin had described it, had the look of a schizophrenic. It was originally supposed to be all in one style, and then the plan was changed, but some of it had already been built, I suppose. And I think that happened more than once. There was a lot of stop-starting and abandoning and subsequent revivals. It is still not finished. So construction and restoration are going on at the same time. And that was fine, I told myself, it would be fine. There was never one truth. Even the Higgs could still be used to prove opposing theories, its mass falling between them on a chart. Besides, I told myself, my breathing heavy, eyes widening till they bulged, I was post-truth.

That night, lying in her bed but without her, I dreamt of Ume's thick feet in beige ribbed socks, secured within double-strap leather, hanging from a tree before she was cut down, the same dream that haunted Mizuko in "Kizuna," and a voice calling me from darkness at the bottom of the ocean.

26

She came back to me at 10.01 the next morning, a mirror time, as I'd expected.

Keys turned.

"Hello?" I called.

No reply.

When I came into the living room, she looked only a little alarmed to see me. "Where's Mom? Perry said she's gone."

I nodded. "How are you feeling?"

She didn't look at me as she spoke. "Drowsy. Sick." The words came out automatically, as if she were used to answering the question. Then she said, "It's weird to be here. I feel like I've been gone for years."

"But you remember me?"

She turned and faced me for a moment. "Yes. You're Rupert's friend."

She circled the apartment slowly, unsteadily, practically oblivious to my presence. I tried to make myself feel the way I imagined she might. I thought about how I'd feel if someone had taken the whole summer away from me. A part of me was relieved at the idea. I wondered whether it was better to lose all your memory and start over completely or to lose only a part of it so that the job was part construction, part restoration, like the cathedral. I thought of returning home to find that something had been taken from you, or destroyed. I thought of the wasp —a mud dauber, as Thom had informed me, assuring me that they were solitary creatures who hardly ever stung—that had plagued my bedroom at Walter's. Every time Dwight or I opened the door it would appear, head straight for the blue book on the second-lowest bookshelf, and disappear behind it, where it would begin making a high-pitched sound like glasses shaking in a cabinet or a screw coming loose. I had peeked behind the blue book and seen that the wasp had made a series of cylinders that looked like miniature urns. There were five of them on the paper edge which faced the wall. I had stared at them for a long time, then taken another book and sliced them away. The nests had left five sandy marks behind, like fingerprints. Instantly I felt that this was a wrong thing to have done. The mud dauber, who'd learnt her flight path by heart, continued to return and to dive hopelessly at the bookshelf, as if she could not believe it—what I'd done. Her long labour of love, the painstaking creation of a home for her young, had disappeared. She came back again and again, in an ever greater frenzy, until I could not watch anymore and decided I had to kill her the next time she flew in.

I brought Mizuko some green tea. "Can I get you anything else?"

"Where's my cell phone?"

I shrugged. "Maybe it's still at the hospital. Did you collect your belongings?"

"They said I didn't come in with anything. They just showed me the cut-up clothes I was wearing, in a plastic bag, and I said no thanks, I didn't want them back."

I shrugged again. "I'll look for it—you sit down. But I did a bit of research while you were in the hospital. They say looking at screens should be avoided for a while at first."

She lay gingerly on the sofa, as if she'd never tried the position before. "But how come you're here?"

I carried on pretending to look under and around things, opening drawers and shifting papers haphazardly.

"I wanted to look after you when you came out, of course. Your mum had to go back to Tokyo. I spoke with Perry, and we think it's best if I stay for a bit. With you."

"When I first woke up I thought . . ." Her voice trembled. "I couldn't really move my mouth or make words, but I felt instinctively that we were so much better with each other. She was being like a proper mom somehow, and I thought . . . I don't know what I thought, but it felt really good to know she was there. I felt bad, almost. That she was being so nice to me."

I saw she had not touched the tea. I removed the stewed tea-bag and ran some hot water into the cup. Michi seemed to sense that she was a prime suspect and didn't come out from wherever she was hiding.

"I really don't want to be alone right now. I shouldn't be alone. I was so depressed thinking I was going to come home to an empty apartment. I couldn't remember Rupert's number." Her voice tightened as if she were going to cry.

I reached an arm around her, told her to lean on me. "Well, it's fine, because I'm here and I'm not going anywhere. I promise."

When she leant stiffly and obediently towards my chest, I saw that she had a bald spot on the top of her head like a Capuchin monk. It thrilled me to see it. I breathed a sigh of relief.

"It's going to be fine."

27

The first immediate difference in her personality I noticed was that she had become religious about personal hygiene. Though she didn't leave the apartment, she used hand sanitizer to go on every journey, between the kitchen and the hall, her bedroom and the bathroom. Though for Perry Michi was in disgrace, Mizuko refused to accuse her of anything, and when I urged her to let me take her to the vet, she shook her head. I asked her to tell me about what the parasite had looked like in the x-rays—*a ribbon* —and how long—*two centimetres*—and what the scans of her brain had looked like—*gyoza*—and how the doctors had first spotted it—*a strange ringlike thing*. I tried to imagine burrowing into her, eating my way all the way up into her brain. To a hippocampus that she said was cute and looked like a seahorse.

We decided that from now on I would deal with Perry, delivery boys, and tasks that required leaving the apartment. I wanted to be her link to the outside world and so happily played the role of tributary, bringing her gifts and tokens. Sometimes, on my way back from an errand for her, I imagined I would open the door and see a trail of clothes leading to her bedroom and find them there together. Sometimes Rupert and Mizuko. Sometimes Robin and Mizuko. Sometimes Ingrid too. Sometimes all four. This got stronger the longer I was away from her, until when I came up in the elevator and walked towards the apartment the feeling would make my heart pound and I'd have to push my key into the lock and run into the bathroom, lean my back against the wall, and reach my hand between my thighs.

The second immediate change was that she got migraines, which meant she often had to lie in bed with her curtains drawn against the daylight. At first she ate most of her meals in there, and every so often I'd find food, like the furry skin of an edamame bean, under the pillow. When she did leave her bed she was listless. As well as banning digital devices, I said she wasn't allowed to read books at first. Not for the first week of convalescence. Sometimes I bought a newspaper, scanned it, and then read to her in bed about beheadings and infectious diseases and chokeholds. I also got her interested in the missing plane, and I seemed able to hold her attention on that for a while.

"The black box that investigators are searching for is about the size of a shoebox, weighs around 10 kilograms, and is actually orange."

"Orange?"

"They changed it so they were easier to find."

"Okay."

"Shall I carry on?"

"Yes."

"'Aviation experts warned back in March that the crucial moments of doomed Malaysia Airlines flight MH370 may never be discovered, as the black box that records details of the flight may have overwritten key data.'" I looked over the top of the newspaper to check she was still listening. Her eyes were wandering around the room.

"'A black box actually consists of two boxes, a cockpit voice recorder and a data recorder. The flight data recorder records a stream of flight information, while the cockpit voice recorder stores conversations and other noises made in the cockpit.'"

"Say that again?"

I repeated myself more slowly.

"Got it."

"'Each of the boxes is about the size of a shoebox and weighs around 10 kilograms. They are made of aluminium and are designed to withstand massive impact, fire, and high pressure. Although the original flight recorders were painted black, the color was changed to orange to make them easier to find by investigators.'"

"Typical."

"'The black box on Malaysia Airlines flight MH370 is made by the U.S. firm Honeywell Aerospace. It is programmed to record cockpit communication on a two-hour loop and delete all but the final two hours.'"

"Why?"

I frowned and continued reading, this time in an exaggerated way. "'*This is because* it is normally the last section of a flight that determines the cause of a crash. In the case of Air France flight 447, for example, the cockpit voice recorder provided a valuable insight for investigators into the confusion that overcame the pilots. In the case of MH370, however, it is thought that the crucial moment for understanding the flight revolves around the period during which its communications systems were disabled and it took a sharp turn westward before flying silently for about seven hours. Although the flight data would have survived had the boxes been found in time, the discussion in the cockpit immediately after the flight lost contact with air traffic control would have been overwritten, unless power to the recorder was lost at the same time. The black box sends out a ping, activated by immersion in water, that can be picked up by a microphone and a signal analyzer from about a mile away. However, the battery of the pinger on MH370 lasts for only thirty days, and so even if the boxes are found, the mystery may never be solved, as six months have passed since the tragedy. The depth of the area of ocean that investigators are searching ranges from 1,150 metres to 7,000 metres. The detector could have picked up the black-box pinger down to a depth of about 6,100 metres, or 20,000 feet.'"

"My head hurts. I'm going to take a nap. Finish reading it to me later."

"Do you want some water?"

"That's your solution to everything drink more water."

She had said she could imagine me as the *otoban san* at school, which means the little person on duty, the one who volunteers to clean out the rabbit hutch. It's true that I was conscientious, full of plans and rules. Since my kidney infection I had been scrupulous about drinking water, and I said we should see her unmooring, her memory loss, the loss of her devices, as a big opportunity. Brisk, businesslike platitudes I had heard from Dwight. She had always talked of going off grid, I reminded her. I would now hold her to it. Maybe a retreat to some tasteful Scandinavian-inspired cabin in the woods where a person could build up her soul and psychic defences again. Columbia could find a substitute teacher. I said we could treat it like an experiment—try to make it to thirty days.

"Like a Zen Buddhist nun?"

"Yes, I guess."

She smiled weakly.

"I'll set you up a little shrine at your desk to write. I could go to some flea market and buy a typewriter."

"I wouldn't know how to use one. I'd just use a pen."

"Yes, sure, a pen is fine."

"A nice silky one."

"Yes, I'll go out and choose you a nice silky pen."

"And what would I write about?"

"Oh, anything. You could write about this — about the hospital and losing your memory, about the parasite, the seizure. You could make up the bits you don't remember . . ."

"My mom going home."

I paused. "That part too."

In solidarity, I said I would give my device to Perry and have him lock it away for me in storage until the thirty days were up. It would soon be, I reminded her, November, National Novel Writing Month, NaNoWriMo, which she'd planned to get her students to do. She could try to finish hers that way, but starting early, in October. She looked uncertain at first but gradually became excited by the idea. I outlined our neo-Luddite manifesto to Perry, and he looked both confused and impressed as he put my device in a little box.

I had thirty days. These, if I was careful, could be made into what felt like thirty weeks, or even — if I was very careful, and very frugal, and broke them down into small enough fragments — into thirty years. Her brain seemed to have rewound to the exact moment she'd collapsed on me outside the Magic Johnson Movie Theatre. She was limp and pathetic and woozy and I loved her, I realised, even more because I knew how completely it was doomed. I wanted to calibrate every moment of it, to curate each day like a picture. While I would probably never have her undivided attention if she was writing, I would at least have control over what came in and out of her life in isolation. She had, after I had stirred her up about the most recent abandonment, vowed never to speak to her mother again. Same for Rupert, she promised. He was the real parasite. He had drained her of all her energies. He didn't really want her to be a successful writer with new friends. He was jealous. He was demented. He could not be allowed to trap her into that cycle again.

I suggested we get rid of whatever traces of Rupert were left around the apartment. I bagged T-shirts, odd socks and cufflinks, a letter he'd written something on the back of.

"Do you need this?" I asked, turning the letter over to its printed side. It was a bank statement.

"No. And chuck the electric toothbrush. He bought it for me," she said glumly. "Whenever I put it in my mouth I think of him."

I went straight to the bathroom and bagged it. "I'll buy you a nice normal one."

She looked at me as if I were the most understanding person in the world.

"I'm normally a fun person. I just can't stop being sad right now."

"You are fun."

She gave a pitiful sigh.

"Anyway, I'm not going anywhere—don't worry."

She did look worried. "Sometimes when he hugged me he would hold on for such a long time, and sometimes he squeezed really hard, like he would never let me go, but then I'd always be waiting for him to go instead of just enjoying him holding me. I'd be waiting for the moment when I would feel his arms loosening around me. I was so fearful of that gradual loss of pressure."

I looked at her hard. "Well, now you can breathe, without him weighing down on you all the time. You can get your own space back. Make new memories."

She nodded feebly.

"We can do it together."

A baby bubble of laughter. My heart soared. It made everything feel okay, this natural, hiccupy sound.

After we rid the apartment of Rupert, I suggested that it was possible that her cowardly mother had installed sensors, which brought on a second denuding of the apartment, with multiple trips to the garbage chute, both of us back and forth like marching ants. You could hear the stuff slide away to the very bottom of the building. The first things we suspected were the kettle and the bathmat, but once we began putting pressure on them, most of the appliances and furnishings in the apartment turned out to be a part of a conspiracy, devices intent on manipulating us in some way, distracting or spying on us. Physical things were dispatched. I had a drawer, and the photograph of Ume remained, but by the time we were done the apartment looked very bare, containing little but the mattress, two lamps, her grandfather's *kintsukori* bowl, a collection of nonfiction books, *The Golden Bowl,* a dictionary, and a thesaurus. Mizuko loved reading the dictionary. She liked it when there were multiple meanings for words and when opposite meanings could be contained. I started reading the Henry James novel. Let her tell me certain anecdotes again.

I knew the loop we were on.

There had been one kiss before—after the movie, before the seizure—and now I was waiting for it to replay itself. I put my faith in it. That's how a loop worked. I could ask her questions that were not really questions. I knew the answers. I could even quote her, pretending I didn't know she had said it already. I could move at inhuman speed, meeting her wherever her mind darted, like a machine that had been built to know her.

Do you think we will still create statues of people in the future?

Answer: *No, because we will know too much about them.*

"Oh my *god*." Mizuko put her hand to her face. "You're telepathic."

I could regurgitate her opinions from old statuses. I had a memory that went forward in time as well as back. Sometimes I knew a thing about her and I had to wait — wait for ages as a weird demented look came over me — until she would finally give me a relevant opportunity to use it. Sometimes there wouldn't be an opportunity exactly, but I'd manhandle it into one. And then she'd look at me oddly and say, "Well, maybe we're twins."

There was that familiar face. The face of someone drinking in kindness from a stranger. It was like time travel. The steps of a dance that only one of us knew. Next, I was sure, would be the kiss.

The following day I set her up with pen and paper. I remember my relief, sliding into blackness, to see her begin. I felt sure my place in the story would now be cemented — she wrote about real life, osmosing whatever was in front of her onto the page. She was writing *Kegare*, the half-finished novel, longhand, starting over because she had thought of a new way to "make it work." I was happy for her writing to take longer, because then I thought our time could go on longer. But she was writing in Japanese. I knew only that *kegare* was a Shinto concept. It was a kind of defilement, "a spontaneous result of amoral forces." Things that produced *kegare* included death, menstruation, disease, and childbirth, but it could also be produced just by mixing up different physical spaces, like the outside and the inside. *Kegare* would be the result if you brought the outside in with you, for example by not taking off your shoes. It could be transmitted from person to person, even indirectly, through touching the same things and breathing the same air. There were rituals you performed both to contain it and to dissolve it.

When I asked her about her idea for the story, she said it was to do with how the tsunami had mixed everything up: objects and spaces and people displaced, the insides of homes sucked outside and the outside pushed in, with sofas in the branches of trees and a muddy car that had ploughed into a bedroom. The mixing up of these realms had created impurity. When I asked her what was different now, in what way precisely she had found a way to make it work, she would say only that it had been inspired by *my generation*. The way we thought we were so tuned in to the rest of the world, gleaning information at the touch of a button. In fact, she said, we were drawing a veil over it, or, the worst of us at least were letting ourselves ooze out over everything else.

"Like what? Bleeding, sweating, crying?"

"Yes. But even just the way you see the world and you project it, project yourself, onto other things."

"Doesn't everyone do that?"

"Yes, and they always have, it's just getting easier and easier. The scale is new."

It was always disorienting when she did this. I had seen her as a vital part of forming the way I saw myself, by seeing, reflected back to me, a body of history and experience that I felt we shared, which was more than family and DNA could do to shape a person. Yet she saw herself nowhere in me. She was fully formed, and nothing about me was special except my phony intuition into the workings of her own mind. To her, I was only a splinter of some much larger entity that she wished to place under a microscope.

Sometimes I would get a small window into what was going on in her writing, when she would look up from her work and ask for a synonym. She was convinced a word existed, a noun, that meant the loss of feelings for someone who was for-

merly loved—a word for the act of falling out of love. I said I
couldn't think of it. It wasn't in the dictionary either, not the one
she wanted. At moments like these I knew she was in danger of
Wikipedia. I would watch as the thought of giving up my experiment and searching online crossed her face and then I would
point resolutely to the hand-drawn calendar we'd taped to the
wall. Not yet. Time was not up.

Left to our own devices, or lack of them, we became a cult,
and yet one in which I was never sure which of us was the char-
ismatic leader and which the gullible follower. I still can't decide whether it was actually me who had a tyrannical hold over
Mizuko or just she who held one, holds one, over me. I sat behind her in the bath and washed her hair for her, around the part
which had been shaved and now had stitches. But as the thirty
days dwindled I began to mistrust these too. I touched them with
searching fingers. They might signify all kinds of things, I reasoned. None of it told me for certain that she had lost her memory. I greatly regretted jettisoning her phone and laptop now. If
I'd been calmer, if I'd had more time to hide things and make
good choices, I would have had them unlocked and ransacked
them for information on her whereabouts while she had been
out of contact. These black boxes were now somewhere in the
river, their pings slowly fading. We didn't wash her hair much,
and it developed a nice tacky texture. I liked to look at the short
patch on her skull, growing quickly, which told me she could not
know. Gradually my bruises from the night of the party turned
bluish grey. Mizuko never asked about them. By the time they
faded I had a fretful feeling. She was in my hand, the size of a
plum, by turns an object and a living thing I was afraid of.

She was supposed to go for checkups, but the hospital had
no means of contacting her and Mizuko said it wouldn't make
a difference anyway. She had found the hospital experience

traumatic, and besides, the way they had dismissed her from Accident and Emergency the first time proved that they were incompetent. They hadn't even been able to keep her electronic devices safe in the patient property lockup. She didn't ever want to go back there.

She would work until six or seven every evening. Then we usually ordered food and drank beer. I would often wake her up by accident in the middle of the night.

Stop jerking.

You keep jerking.

Sometimes I could be happy, imagining a benevolent future, but the luminous, happy mood would always shift overnight and by morning we'd wake up in different positions and strange tangles and things would be wrong without my knowing why.

In the last week I felt her withdrawing. What was once everywhere, an ocean I imagined myself to be drowning in, was now barely deep enough to bathe in. I saw her warmth draining away and couldn't stop it. On night twenty-nine, I couldn't sleep and got up to use the bathroom. When I turned on her bathroom light a fan started whirring, and this woke her up, so I had to turn it off and pee in the dark. When I got back into bed she was evidently awake, furious but silent, with her eyes shut tight. Then she opened them suddenly, reached her hand out, and I thought she was reaching for me so went towards her and accidentally knocked her arm so it pushed the glass she was reaching for over and then it smashed on the floor.

"Leave it. Do it in the morning."

"Day thirty," I said.

"I know."

I woke up to find a bloodstain on the sheets. For a moment, half asleep, I was scared that her head wound had opened. Then I realised I'd got my period. My first since, confirming that I was no longer pregnant. The sight of the round red stain, in the exact middle of the white sheet, was a relief. When I got up to clean the stain I forgot about the broken glass and it sliced into my feet.

She was angry and told me to clean the floor as well. I crouched down and remembered my nightmare the night Silvia became ill. I hadn't thought of Silvia in weeks.

I could see she needed novelty. I didn't need to climb inside her skull to know that. It was visible in every move and word she said. Slowly my presence had become second nature to her again, and it had happened before I'd been ready, without the long-waited-for embrace.

That day, day thirty, was the day snow came. While she worked on finishing the last paragraph of the last chapter, I did not leave the apartment. I watched from her window, as if from a ship that had been becalmed, as all around grew white and still. Then I got up. Moved things around. Usually when I did this, it attracted her attention. Not this time. I couldn't sit down, but I couldn't stand either.

At about six in the evening she got up from her chair, walked towards the wall, and crossed off the final day on the chart. A big red line through the number. "I'm done," she said. "It's finished."

I tried to smile.

"I think maybe we should celebrate," she announced, "to mark this day."

She came behind me, took the glass of water I was holding out of my hands where I sat, put it on the coffee table, then stood before me. I imagined her bending forward, her mouth floating like a blossom towards mine, damp and pink and metallic. I imagined her lifting her dress and sliding my finger inside her, to a hard place that made me hold my breath and press my tongue into my teeth. I imagined she held it there with such force that it was hurting the little triangle of flesh between my fingers. I wanted to release the tension from the moment. To relieve the imagined pressure on my finger. I looked up at her face, wondering what she wanted me to do, but her eyes were closed. It would need to be me who did it this time. I wondered if all this time she had been daring me to take control. My hand hovered. The same trepidation as when I'd unfollowed. It would have to be now.

The intercom sounded so loudly it seemed to shake the apartment. We both jumped.

"Who the fuck is that? You answer it," she hissed.

I cleared my throat.

The buzzer was being held down. Rupert's voice became audible through the door. He was calling her name.

I could see she recognised his voice too, but her expression was otherwise indecipherable. I looked through the peephole and his face bulged towards me, so I stumbled backwards into the apartment.

"What should I do?" I whispered.

I turned round to find that Mizuko had rushed into her bedroom. "I can't let him see me like this," she called. "Tell him I'll be right out. He can wait in there with you."

I looked out at the fire escape. It was dark and the snow hid most of it, the flat planes of white making the ground look much closer than it was. I considered the time it would take to unscrew the lock on the window.

I heard her pulling on clothes. I grabbed my backpack, went to the window, the screw dusty but easy to loosen. In one swift motion, I slid out into the cold.

As I climbed down the face of her building, I could not shake the feeling that this was exactly the kind of thing one of her characters, one called Rabbit, would, in the last scene, end up doing. By the final level I wondered if she was making me do it, telling me to run, so I obeyed. I did not stop until I reached the street.

28

At the bottom, I stooped, panting, looking back up for a white face at the window, which didn't appear. I blinked at the moon. People were dashing through the street, over the grey ramparts. I saw properly for the first time that the city had changed season. Everything looked smooth and strange, some things beyond identification under a shroud of snow. I put my hand against the icy metal of a streetlamp. The world became quiet. I stood still. I couldn't walk away. I continued staring back up at the window, waiting. I waited so long my neck ached, and my back, where my kidneys were, did too, from the cold. It didn't feel like there was any option but to wait. Someone like Susy would have gone back. Denied everything. Wrestled the situation back under control. But something was compelling me to stay where I was. To see if Mizuko would come to me. Or maybe, as the psychic had suggested, the evil spirit was following me and wanted me to be alone.

After half an hour, the mounting sense of rejection was too much to bear, and I began to inch along the street. *I'll never, ever, ever come back,* I told her with my mind. *Who is going to look after you now? I'm going to start walking, and if you don't come and stop me, that's it. It's done. It's over. It's dead.* On reaching the corner with Nussbaum & Wu, I stopped again. Waited for her hand on my back. The nothingness hung in the air. It was worse than rejection. *It stops here. At this corner. When I turn. Now.*

For a moment I felt a kind of relief. A sensation of freefall similar to what I'd felt on my first walk in New York. I could go anywhere, be anyone; no one knew me. I began following banner signs that hung from streetlights, advertising a free exhibition of Romare Bearden's "Black Odyssey" at Columbia. It was open for another fifteen minutes. The rooms in the exhibition were warm, but I could barely make out the scenes in the picture frames. When I reemerged it was very dark, starless, and colder. Too cold to snow.

The glow of the streetlamps sat heavy and thick above me. As I walked aimlessly, in the direction of downtown, I returned to my theories. That Mizuko and I shared the pictorial equivalent of DNA. That a sympathetic magic existed between us, no matter how far apart we were pulled. That we defied physical laws of time and space, waves, gravity, the rules laid down by physicists which governed our physical universe (earthquakes, tsunamis) and physical bodies. And yet somehow our connection had led to the opposite of intimacy. My search had led to its opposite. I had never felt so isolated and disconnected, even from myself.

I wondered if it had been a bad move to leave like that. I wondered if I should go back up. I had been so wound up and tense for the last week, waiting for the end, that I'd just run for my life. Assumed the buzz at the door was the sign to flee. *ZZZ ZZZZZ ZZZZZ ZZZZZZZ. TIME UP! THIRTY DAYS OVER. Intruder detected.* I had taken only my small bag, which had Mizuko's copy of *The Golden Bowl* in it. I had left without any of the stuff in the drawer, and without retrieving my device from Perry's storage room.

I had to go back for that, at least. It would help weigh me down. Stop the floating feeling. And maybe she would be there, in the lobby, or coming out of the elevator. With Rupert?

"You just caught me, I was about to leave. Here you go," Perry said, sliding it across the desk. "And you didn't even miss it, right?" His tone was sarcastic.

"Right," I said, forcing a smile, gripping it in my freezing hand. "Did you let him up?"

"Who?"

I stared hard at him.

He began to look uneasy. "I went down to the storeroom for, like, a minute. Is there a problem?"

"No," I said, but I knew my voice gave me away. "Everything's fine."

"You wanna check it still works?"

I looked down into the dark screen, tap-tapped. My own face reflected back at me. I was waiting for Mizuko to come. To tearfully take me back upstairs.

"I guess it's out of power."

I knew mine had gone too.

I moved along the street, away from her building, as if I were adrift in deep space. Up or down, left or right—these were no longer meaningful choices; whichever way I went, there was nothing behind anything. I walked aimlessly towards Riverside Drive. The verges belonged to a strange new park, packed shiny and tight like cheeks crusted in salt. I walked until the cold got so deep into my bones that I couldn't feel my feet hitting the ground. I went up to Grant's Tomb, then across to Sakura Park, where the pagoda was covered in snow. I cleared snow off the swings. It was the quietest I had heard the city.

I could see the Rooiakker apartment clearly through the slim, leafless trees, and walked across what turned out to be very deep, unmarked snow to get a better look. Each footstep held for a moment and then broke under my weight so that my leg would plunge down to the knee. The snow got into my shoes and melted into icy water. I reached the edge of the park, where it drops away onto Claremont, and saw the lights come on just as I stood there. I crouched down. I stayed there for a long time, wondering if anyone would come out. After twenty minutes, when no one did, I got to my feet, stiff and cold and wet. Then I walked down—down, down, down, until I reached the Apple Store at the bottom of the park, where the crowds began and gave me warmth and someone asked for directions but I couldn't make any sound come out.

When I turned up at Dwight's in Dumbo, I could no longer feel my body.

"I need to borrow money for my flight home."

"Hey," he said.

His upper half was contained in a shirt that was tight and navy, and I noticed a gamy smell coming from him. He said he was pleased to see me, and I said "likewise," in a way that could have been heard as insincere by someone not raised a Mormon. He said it was lucky I caught him as he had been travelling a lot for work and was currently in between Airbnb guests. Instantly I remembered everything I hated about him. But it was, in a way, comforting to know that he had not changed at all.

Dwight's company made me feel even more anomic. I watched us without interest, heard us only faintly, like strangers below my window.

He told me about his latest client. "We want 'Realising the Potential of a Connected World,' but somebody already has that."

He was holding a silver bottle like a bullet that had the name of his gym on it. He waited, but I didn't have any comment to make about the slogan.

"I've also been invited to be on the panel for a conference about smart cities."

I remained silent. I could not even pretend. Then he showed me the hare in his freezer that he was going to make a ragu out of. I asked him to explain smart cities to keep him talking while I used his laptop. His screensaver was still set to the incomprehensible map of the subway system. I began looking for flights.

"Oh, look," he said, smiling. "There's one of my ads."

It had snuck up at the side of the tab I had open. *What is the reason for your travel? Business, leisure, family?*

He cooked for me, even though it was nearly midnight. Hare pappardelle. He said it was supposed to be funny. I must have looked blank, as he said he didn't want me to be upset. I said I wasn't upset, I was tired and upset about something else. He was convinced I was upset about the pasta sauce and said that since hares are also called snowshoe rabbits, because of their big feet, we could call it that instead if I liked. Snowshoe ragu. He said it as if I were a baby. A baby that he needed to feed with a spoon like a train going into a tunnel. Then he laughed and laughed and laughed.

Dwight had gone hunting for the hare himself, upstate. He had his snowshoes in the hall for effect. He pointed out their special bindings. I thought of him tracking the hare and the hare probably thinking that he was just a big joke in expensive snowshoes. It was likely because the hare thought of him as a total joke that he had managed to shoot her, because she had sat down to laugh and hadn't been able to stop. The hare that had died laughing slow-cooked while he told me the story. The whole apartment smelt of it by the time we went to bed. He'd removed the bones and left the meat in chunks, soft enough to extrude through the colander and out into something glossy. After I ate, I found I had forgotten the name for everything and could no longer even remember where I was, or that I was unhappy.

As he carried me from the sofa, he said he was too tired to change the bed linen from his last guest, so would I mind if we just slept in those sheets?

"Oh."

"Yeah?"

"Was it a couple?"

"No, a single woman."

"Bit creepy."

"But not really."

"Here, charge my phone."

I get what I call big-small dreams. They're not exactly dreams; they lie in wait for me on the border between sleep and wakefulness. I have had them ever since I can remember. I have them in addition to the falling sensation that most people get right before they fall asleep. Big-small refers to the sensation of big meeting small. Of strange scales, which seem to contrast so greatly that the moment of their meeting is like an explosion, which then collapses all distinctions between them for one instant. A unity of opposites. First I am nothing but a tiny, tiny person with a tiny, tiny hand, and I am pushing on a door that reaches from the ground up to the sky, in slow, slow motion. My minute hand moves towards the door over what feels like an infinity; the explosion when my hand and the unimaginably giant door meet—*click*—lasts only one second. Less. The instant after the explosion the ratio flips and I am nothing but an enormous finger pad, each line in the skin like a tyre track, magnified a million billion times. There is a tiny pin, the sharp point of it, and my spaceship finger is moving down towards it, slowly through space. When it pricks the skin there is the explosion and it flips again until I fall asleep or I wake up.

On my tour of Japan we were shown rocks that rise out of the sea like vast incisors, with a house built into them and a proper roof on top but only a tiny archway carved into the rock, where the sea seems to have whittled it away. My big-small dreams look a bit like that. Tiny fingertips with mighty power. One thing becoming its incompatible opposite and back again. I know that this sensation signaled that I was beginning to wake up. My finger began to hover before an enormous Mizuko doll. Then at some point during the night, Dwight began to have sex with me. I was full of pasta and had no power in my limbs and no voice to stop him. He had recently, but not recently enough, shaved his scrotum so that it grated against me like sandpaper.

Waking in the morning, I had to remember grief all over again. It was sunny, a white winter sun, and that made me sad. He was pacing the room speaking to someone.

"Apparently she's really good at html, which is all I care about . . . Yeah, yeah." Pause. "Yeah, my favourite part was, *Steve, do you need me to condense that for you?*" He slapped his chest and laughed. "Right, right. I told them it's fallen through the cracks because it's no one's baby."

He saw me staring at him from the covers and grimaced. "Sorry," he mouthed. I shrugged.

If I stayed in any one position for too long, the gnawing pain of having lost Mizuko would overcome me. I climbed out of bed. I thought of her; I pushed back. Would she miss me? I pushed back. Silvia had written, *You have to develop some self-control.* But that idea made me think of the way Mizuko had written *Kegare* in thirty days and of Zen Buddhist nuns, which made me think of Mizuko sitting in a little dojo in a black kimono with long sleeves, tracing her lineage back to Shakyamuni Buddha and no longer caring about me or what secrets I had kept.

His call was finished.

"So you need me to lend you the money for the flight?"

I said he was very generous—he shut his eyes and beamed, an expression of beatific helplessness, as if to say he could not stop the flow of generosity charging towards me, he himself was fully charged—but that I did not want his help any longer.

"Honestly, it's fine. I got an app that finds me ones that are cheap as shit, like five hundred bucks. Let me lend you the money. You can pay me back when you get to your mom's house."

"No. I mean it." I didn't want to owe him anything.

29

I went to Amsterdam. I had taken care to avoid walking past it whenever I had run errands for Mizuko. Now that the dark metal benches, the railings, and the strip of grass that snaked around the exterior were snowed over, I almost didn't recognise it.

Nat was in Silvia's room, wearing black, with black sunglasses pushed up into her hair. She was collecting up Silvia's things, alongside a nurse. Silvia's funeral, she told me without ceremony, had been that morning. The nurse looked like she might have been about to comfort me, but Nat said, "Don't bother. And don't be fooled by her good manners." And, turning to me, "I've told them all. Told them that you're a devil."

I stared at the floor, feeling tears pricking at my eyes, my vision blurring.

"She's the devil disguised as a little lost orphan," she said in a raised voice, addressing Silvia's emptied room. I stood in silence, the nausea from all those weeks ago returning. "Though you did manage to pull the wool over Silvia's eyes with all your pleases and thank-yous."

The nurse, whom I didn't recognise, quickly exited the room carrying a stack of folded sheets. I wanted to appeal to her with my eyes, but Nat had now fixed hers on me, and I could do nothing but stare back at her as tears started to fall. The sharp, superficial pain at being spoken to unkindly had obscured the deeper pain, which had not yet turned into something hard and heavy.

I left the room without saying a word.

I found myself doing big, meandering loops around Morningside Heights, hoping to see Mizuko and Rupert. Not so I could talk to them, just so I could see. I walked up and down the street. I went to the Hungarian, I went to all the usual haunts. At the back of Riverside Church, I saw the posters on the lampposts for the exhibition. I went again—it was still free and warm. There weren't many rooms and there was less of a crowd, and I quickly saw that Mizuko and Rupert weren't among the people there. This time I paid closer attention to the pictures and the black figures populating them. I stared at them for a long time, wondering what I was going to do and how I was going to get home. When I came out it was already dark.

I walked to Silvia's apartment. Two Tonys offered me their condolences, but I still couldn't speak. The weightless feeling started to harden and the heaviness arrived. I sat on the floor.

Silvia's cordless phone rang. It was the funeral directors; they had called by mistake, hoping to get Nat. After they apologised for their mistake, the man wished me a safe trip home. I felt so heavy that I could imagine plummeting through the floor to the very bottom of the building. It's disconcerting to have an undertaker wish you a safe trip. Nor had I yet decided I was definitely leaving, but the casual, decided way in which the undertaker said it made me realise that everything was really over.

I didn't know how I was going to find the money to get home. For the past month I had been spending Mizuko's. Before that

I'd used Silvia's credit card when I needed it, but I decided that it had probably been frozen.

I lay in the apartment, putting off whatever it was I was supposed to do now. I read a book about the healing power of dolphins. Snowflakes slid down against the glass while beyond it they flew upwards on the wind.

The apartment continued to fill with flowers, though I did not know who the senders imagined was there to receive them. I took some of the dollar bills Silvia kept on her tip tray. I took some of the larger notes I knew she had in one of the drawers in the study. I went for a short walk around the block to a shop with a sign saying WE BUY FUR. I took some of Silvia's fur coats I'd seen in her closet, but the man was rude about them, which I did not realise was the prelude to his making me an offer, so I left. I went back to the apartment and waited. I was waiting for someone to arrive and stop me. As I moved around in my personal oblivion, bumping into things below waist height, I understood why Silvia had continued to sleep on the couch after Rex died. If everything stays the same, it seems possible for someone to come back. One part of me didn't want hope—I wanted it to be decided—but then I also didn't want it to be decided at all.

The last night I slept there, there was a big yellow moon. I stared at it with Silvia's binoculars. I remembered the guided tour and Rupert's father. The people in the town were celebrating by making "moon-viewing rice balls" and collecting *aki no nanakusa,* which are grasses that flower in autumn. These, our guide explained as she gave us each a handful, were bush clover, pampas grass, arrowroot, fringed pink, agueweed, and Chinese bellflower. There's an emoji you have probably never sent: the moon-viewing ceremony emoji. It has the moon, a heap of mini-mochi, and the pampas grass. I have a handful still, pressed dry into a paper leaflet which explains the story:

*The Old Man of the Moon one day looked down into a
big forest on earth and saw three friends sitting together
around a fire. These three were a rabbit, a monkey, and
a fox. He decided to find out which of the three was the
kindest, so he went down to earth and changed himself
into a beggar. He asked the three friends to help him,
saying that he was very hungry. The monkey brought back
fruit, and the fox brought back a big fish. However, the
rabbit was unable to find any food, and so he asked the
monkey to gather some firewood and the fox to build a
big fire. Once the fire was burning very brightly, the rabbit
explained to the beggar that he didn't have anything to
give him, so would put himself in the fire to cook so that
the beggar could eat him. Just before the rabbit jumped
into the fire, the beggar turned back into the Old Man of
the Moon and told the rabbit that he was very kind but
that he shouldn't do anything to harm himself. Because
he decided that the rabbit was the kindest of the three, he
took him back to the moon to live with him.*

I realised that I wanted my mother. I wanted the feeling that
Mizuko had described of being reunited with her own in the
hospital. The call was short. I explained where I was and what
I needed her to do for me, and then I had to correct my present
tense, to refer to Silvia in the past. Susy's voice was small but
reassuringly the same. "So come home," she said.

I was delayed in the airport by the man who looked at my
passport. I had arrived with endless hours to spare but had forgotten about my spent visa. I finally managed to board, just as
the gates were closing. The British accents onboard, especially
that of the pilot, piping into the cabin, reminded me less of myself or my mother than of Robin. I cried silently for most of

the flight. When my neighbour asked me to turn out my reading light, I watched the flight path on the screen in front of me. Weird digitised cartography. A red line. Green and blue. Borders. Sea. Glitches. Gone.

On arrival, I went to the electronic passport gate. I wanted no face to check mine, no repeat of my arrival at or departure from JFK. I wanted to slip quietly into the electromagnetic field of home. The kind of impersonal validation of my identity, my sameness, that the smart border control system is perfect for. My machine was taking longer than those of the people on either side of me. I wondered if the change I felt had taken place inside me was really that seismic. I pressed my chip harder into the reader and looked more sternly at the facial recognition monitor. Nothing. I thought of Mizuko's new story, the novel. Man had such impenetrable means to stop the outside world from coming in, and so little to stop our inside world from surging out, wrestling any foreign object into submission. I tried the old trick. *I'm one of you,* I told the machine. *Now let me in.* It refused, and I joined the back of the adjacent queue.

30

I was ready to head for the train, had planned to move quickly through arrivals so as not to feel the sinking feeling of being unmet, but at the gate I saw Susy waiting for me, bearing a sign decorated with scratchy Biro drawings of rabbits and my name. Maybe she had once called me that too; if she had, I had forgotten.

The emptiness inside me, a numbness where hunger should have been, had increased ever since I'd left New York. In a way, it had helped me feel closer to Mizuko. Like the way Silvia had slept on the sofa, it made me feel as if things hadn't landed yet, that the shock was still new. Normality turned out to be far worse.

"Darling."

She took my bags. She looked just the same. I tried to take one back from her.

"No need," she said. "I'm a Libra. Well balanced."

It was a phrase I had heard her say so many times before, and something about hearing it just then, its simple equanimity, made me cry again.

From watching Silvia, I'd learned that one of the worst things about being ill is that most other people find your suffering opaque. With this sadness it was different. I felt that I needed to nurture and protect it from people's understanding. I wanted Susy's sympathy because I wanted comfort and to feel less alone, and yet I also didn't want it—I didn't want my personal grief to be part of something universal right then.

"It's okay," Susy said. "I don't blame you for leaving. I didn't see what I was . . . I didn't realise what I was like before."

I had once located our house on Google Earth and showed it to Mizuko. It is at the end of a long road shaped like a fish-hook. The road turns into gravel for the last stretch and makes a loop around the house, so that you can always hear someone arriving. As usual, the brindle dog came running out to frighten me until it recognised me, when it looked embarrassed. I entered the hallway with the circular walnut table where the post was kept.

"I forgot to tell you the dishwasher's not working, so take your glasses, plates, cutlery, et cetera, into the shower with you —it saves us hot water."

"Okay."

I put my suitcase down and the brindle dog stared at it in an interested manner, and then I followed Susy to the kitchen. I had no sense of what time it was. There was a clock above a shelf of china milk jugs, but it had long been broken. Dried flowers and bugs lay at the bottom of glasses. It was all exactly as I had left it.

She had her back to me at the sink and was listening to *Gardeners' Question Time*. The sound of it, accents and concerns —the normalcy—seemed crazy.

"That's my present from Charles," she said, turning and indicating the kitchen table, where she had apparently given up trying to assemble a Magimix. I remembered how strange her

eyes were, nacreous and lilac-coloured. They were complement-
ed by her oversized baby-blue fleece, magnified by her glasses,
and slightly loose in their sockets. I rubbed mine, which were
raw from recycled air.

"Who's Charles?"

"I can make smoothies with it, he says. I don't know why he
thinks I'll want to do that."

My heart felt heavier even than it had on the floor at Silvia's,
as if it were sinking into my feet and then dropping like a stone
to the bottom of the deepest ocean.

"I don't know who Charles is, Mum."

"He's my new friend." Her eyes darted to the door. "He's responsible for bringing out the new me." She smiled to herself,
then shook her head. "I did actually take my raincoat. I hope I
didn't leave it in the airport."

"Under that chair. What does that mean, your new friend?"
My mother hadn't had a new friend in years, and certainly not
a male one.

"Special friend." She glanced up briefly and gave me another
thin smile. Maybe she had changed. Up close she looked older
than I remembered her. She moved more slowly. Her grey hair
was matted at the back. Most of all, she was being unusually
obliging.

"I'll go put my bags away. I'm exhausted."

I climbed the wooden staircase. The other dog, the decrepit
Labrador that could no longer make it up the stairs, lay at the
bottom watching me go.

Since I had gone to university, my room was usually referred
to as a guest room. Someone had left a heart-shaped cushion on
the bed. I took off my shoes and socks. My feet were swollen
after the long flight and marked by the scars of old blisters.

I got up in the middle of the night and unpacked. I realised I'd left things at the Rooiakkers' and Mizuko's, but I had gained things from Silvia's. In the morning I went up into the attic. Things scattered and ran for cover under my feet. Leaving the boxes largely intact had seemed to comfort Susy. As if things could turn around at any moment and Mark would be back to claim them. Now I understood this strategy very well. It seemed less like madness. In fact it made complete sense. I found the box I knew contained the single copy Susy had had made of "Alice in Dallas."

There was a time when everything had not yet separated . . .

"Hello?"

I spun round to see Susy standing behind me. She was holding a coil of thin, shiny rope and what looked like a sheet folded over one arm.

"Hi?"

"Hi." She stood over the hole where I had perched the ladder.

"What are you doing?"

"I've done a portrait of one of Charles's friends' dogs. I've started doing dog portraits. This one was a Tibetan terrier crossed with a poodle. Do you want to see? He offered to deliver it for me this afternoon, so I've got to wrap it up. That's it over there." She indicated behind me to the painting.

"Very nice. How much is he going to pay you?"

"Well, he's an Arab, so he's promised to pay me in pistachios."

"Pistachios?"

"Yes."

"So he's literally nuts?"

She made a hurt face so I apologised.

"I made a coffee cake to celebrate your return."

"That's nice."

"I should really get rid of this stuff. Charles bought me a book by a Japanese woman where she tells you to—"

"I know," I said, flinching. Mizuko had told me about the phenomenon when we'd cleared out her apartment.

"Her method involves gathering together and communing with everything you own, then—"

"I *know* what it is." My voice broke.

"Okay." She looked alarmed. Hurt. "Shall we go downstairs and talk about what's going on?"

We descended one by one and went to the kitchen. There was an extravagant winter storm outside. The tinfoil sky flashed beyond the window, rattling in the frame, and once or twice a white fork like a vein. Through the opposite window, which looked out onto the other side of the house, the light was pale, picking out where the wall was still broken from the last big storm, with the scorched telegraph pole and the burnt tree. Now she sat opposite me at the table, delicately folding and refolding her napkin. I could tell she wanted me to begin, but I did not.

"Your outfit is rather fun."

I was wearing my black sack. "Thanks."

"Wait!"

She decided she had to give me something, and she went to her bedroom and came back with a little figurine under a glass dome.

"What's this?" It looked like a sheep wearing a dress. I vaguely recognised it as a cheap Christmas ornament we'd once had on the tree. It didn't look new.

"It's a Christmas present."

"Aren't you going to wrap it?"

"I thought you should have it now—in case you leave again. Because I wanted you to know I'm sorry."

I nodded. The word hit something very deep. I had hated her because she suffered, and now, for a reason I couldn't be sure of yet, I didn't feel that way anymore.

"It's okay," I said. "I've worked that out for myself."

"So tell me about it all."

"What all?" I was stubborn. My newfound understanding had immediately grown into surliness. Now that she was being nice to me, it seemed like a good time to be the rebellious teenager I had never been able to be before, when she'd been difficult instead.

"Your trip."

I burst into tears again.

"Oh, Alice, what's wrong?"

"Nothing," I said, sobbing.

"Come on," she said, "it's me."

"I know. That's partly it."

Parents tell their children not to talk to strangers, but as the statistics show, it is rarely strangers you have to worry about. It's exes, family members, neighbours. Besides, hardly anyone gets classified as a stranger anymore. We're talking to strangers *all the time*. I was worried that if I told her the story, she would identify with it too much. That her sympathy, however well-meaning, would make me possessive, angry again. She was always making things personal, seeing only their relationship to her rather than what was complex about them. And yet her request touched me. A skimming stone, bouncing towards me even though I tried to repel it.

"Well, then, what's the plan now? You can't stay here forever."

My plan was indeed to stay there forever.

I got up from the table and went to her study, otherwise dark but for the warm glow of her computer. I was not supposed to use it. No one was allowed to touch it, but her password was always the same.

MARK1968

Then my fingers stumbled over the keyboard as I typed her name.

MISUKOP MIZUKO HIMRIENA HIMUA. HIMURA.

Susy came and stood in the doorway.

"What are you doing on my machine?" The gentleness in her voice was gone.

31

It is 23.32 p.m. I still believe in symmetry, so this will be the last part. You've reached an end if you come back to where you started. I also remain superstitious about certain numbers. I use 23 and 32 for my lottery tickets, for example. It extends to dates. I still see *signs*. Today felt like the right day to make this public, because a piece of the missing plane was found washed up on Réunion, the island in the Indian Ocean. It's human nature to attach our little stories to something bigger, but the memory of some people really does hold so much more than their life ever encompassed. Sugihara, Mizuko's rebel Japanese diplomat, was born on the first day of the new century: 1.1.1900. I like to imagine his parents taking in this date as they looked into his face for signs of themselves, the midwives eating simmered burdock root, sweet black soya beans, stroking him behind the ears, and all of them knowing he would be in some way special, destined for some great role. But the part of the Holocaust talk that resonates most with me now is no longer the part about the heroism of Sugihara and his signing all the fake visas. It is the part about what happened to him after—his living in obscurity, selling light bulbs door to door.

Other than the numbers thing, I thought I'd got my problem under control when I took up gardening. That's why I chose a basement flat with a garden. I wanted to pick up tools. To mow a lawn and listen to the radio with the sun shining off the extension cable like a river in the grass. I wanted to get healthy. Gain weight. I saw a doctor. I went in case there were any remnants of the summer inside me—sticky, slender fish bones that needed to be scraped into the bin. He was dismissive of my concerns and said my body would have let me know by now. Did I have what was known as female intuition? I said I'd had my feminine intuition somewhat scrambled in the past.

I left Susy in spring. I scheduled moving out to take place on the exact day in April I had left for New York the year before. I thought it was a good way to start over. The money Silvia had had—after all her medical, legal, and tax bills had been paid by the executors—she left to me. Otherwise I could never have moved out. Getting my own place was a big part of starting over and beginning to feel better again. I didn't imagine that owning a physical space would make as big a difference as it did. I have my own threshold that I carry myself over, and I am the only one with a key. I enjoy being self-contained and self-sufficient.

I arrived with grow bags and hives and mini-manger-trough planters, riding the second wave of gentrification to break upon Wood Green. I remember that the churches in Harlem had homemade signs on their noticeboards with warnings like MAKE ROOM FOR PARASITE SODOMITE GENTRIFIERS, but in Wood Green, no such resistance. Not much happens here. Which is nice. I'm after that kind of vibe. Nor is it a fashionable place where people come to do nothing. There are no GONE FISHING signs. It's just an okay place where people live. I chose this neighbourhood because it made me feel apathetic when I first looked round, which is how I wanted to feel. Since I've moved here a Chinese takeaway on the main street has ominously renamed itself from whatever it was before to the Golden Bowl, but other than that, the landscape is the last place on earth that might call Mizuko to mind.

I like to spend my hours crouched on the hot, wet soil under the tarps, looking for leaf-miner flies and spider mites, spanking things and letting little clods of black soil fall onto my shirt. I like cutting things down best. Anything I can do with a power tool. I listen to the radio always, so I have the comfort of voices but no pictures.

Moira is after privacy, not incarceration. If you watch this thing grow, it will envelop you . . . Today *Gardeners' Question Time* is being broadcast from Weymouth. I note things down. They are discussing *a wonderful energetic rampant prune*. And they are right, Moira. To be safe from the world, you should not have to lock yourself out of it. But I am more careful to keep the outside outside and the inside inside. I have a soft pair of indoor slippers, a shoe rack for my gardening gear. For a while this seemed to do the trick, and I felt that whatever contamination I had helped to spread, the boundaries I had helped to break, sprinkling flakes of myself all over the surface of New York like so much fish food, had been forgiven.

But then they found a body.

For a few days she was just a female body, found after water turned to ice. Then, through dental records, biometric data, phone calls, she gained a name. The reports said that Hiromi Himura, fifty-six, of the Himura banking family, had been visiting her daughter, a resident of New York. The reports added that

Ume Himura was found, long dead, shortly after Hiromi's body was found. The picture Hiromi had taken of Mizuko, *Kakusei, Waking!* was now circulating online.

I read the same few news articles over and over. Ume had not established that Hiromi was missing, despite having failed to return. It was a relief that she had not been moved into a home. I felt that Ume would not have liked the ground beneath her moving again. I imagined her lonely death, remains decomposing into a human stain on a carpet. As I read, I began making short little huffs from my stomach. The only relief I could find in this ending was in how deeply it pained me.

I suppose you will want to know what the letter said. Not mine, I don't want to share that—some things should stay private—but a translation of Hiromi's. Its intended recipient should at last receive it.

Dear M,

I'm sorry for this. Another failing, I know. You won't believe it, but I came to America to try and be a good mom at last. I fed Michi and bought a rice cooker, for example. I waited for you to wake up so I could tell you in person. I'll be a good mom now. Granny wanted to come too, but she is too old to go long distances, so I left her at home. But she was very worried. I was so happy when you began to wake up that I sent her a picture message, but I don't think she ever turns on the cell phone I got her.

The waiting gave me time to think about some things I regret. I realized for the first time how much I do love you, and I promised myself I would look after you when you woke up. I thought we could start over. And I would tell you the things you always wanted to know.

That was what I planned when you were still unconscious, and then the evening that you first opened your
eyes they sent me home and said to come back in the
morning. I came back full of hope and big plans, but
when I got back to your apartment there was a package
for you. It was marked urgent, so I opened it. I'm sorry
for that, because you know how much I am a private
person. Even writing this is not easy for me, but I know
it is the only way for us both to have what we want. It is
my choice to have a secret in my life, just as it is yours to
make it known, if that is what you want, when I am gone.

Granny says that even if you live through an earthquake, there will be a tsunami, and even if you live
through the tsunami, radiation will get you. We are never
done. I was foolish to think I might be. Knowing you
were okay, I felt such relief, and I thought it had finally
changed—the numb feeling, sometimes even the anger
I felt towards you for so long. But I was wrong. This
is not your fault, and there is so much love that I wish
I could give you now that I can finally allow myself to
feel it. I understand why you wanted to know him, and I
understand why you want to be known yourself, because
I know what it is to be denied. Please know that I was
never hiding you.

You think I don't understand why you write stories
that upset the ones close to you for the benefit of people
far away, people you will never even meet. I once felt
something like it, and I once tried to tell strangers what
happened to me, even though I never told you or Granny.
I will tell you now so that I don't disappear without giving you your answers first. I thought it would be obvious
to you. I just couldn't bring myself to say it.

I was raped. In 1981. Nine months after, I had you. So.

Your father—the word makes me feel so odd—was living in the same university building as me. When I came back I told people I had rejected my place, since in the end I was there for only the first term. Granny was the one who wanted me to go, because she was so determined for me to be a scientist like Kathleen Drew. She fought my father so hard to let me, and finally he gave in. I got there, and at the end of my third week I went to shower and I left my bedroom door on the latch. When I came back a man was there. He said he had come to tell me I shouldn't leave my door on the latch. He seemed a lot older. I thought he was trying to be kind. But the next time I went to use the bathroom in the middle of the night, I left my door on the latch again. When I came back in that time he was standing right behind the door, enraged. He said he had told me not to do it. I must be stupid. He did not desire me, he informed me, he said he simply wanted me to learn to do as I was told.

After he left I was too scared to leave my room. I didn't know which door in the hallway was his, or if he was on a different floor. All night I lay awake. When I had to pee I went in a flask. I jumped out of my skin every time I heard footsteps pass outside. I waited until the morning, when lectures began, and then I went to the representative for international students and he told me to talk to the police.

The first question they had after I told them my story was why had I left my door on the latch? When I saw that they did not believe me, I became upset. I didn't know how to explain myself, even in my own language. I got confused and I started to feel ashamed. My English was not so good then, even when I was calm. When they took me to the station, the second account I had to give of my story, in front of the right officials for them to write down, was slightly different. I mixed up the order of certain things. They seemed to think I was not telling the truth. I told them I hadn't slept all night and I would like an interpreter to help me, but they said they did not have anyone who spoke Chinese.

When something is written down, that's it. I don't even remember what I wrote or whether it made any sense. Their questions made me feel like it was all in my head. They suggested I was homesick in a new place, wanting attention. I was eighteen. I didn't know about sex, nothing about rape. I didn't know that I should make them examine me there and then. Instead I had to leave the station and go back to my bedroom.

I didn't sleep that night or the next. They said they would find a match for my description, and I waited for a call or a visit, but no one came. I went to the international rep and told him I wanted to change rooms, and he said he would try to put me somewhere else.

After a few weeks, an officer came to tell me they had found him. Robin Quinn agreed that he had been in my bedroom but said he had not forced his way in. He told them he had been invited. It was, the officer said, my two slightly different versions against his single consistent one. Robin Quinn said I had consented and must now be regretting my decision.

I was written off as homesick foreign girl who had made a bad choice. Who felt regret at the loss of her innocence. There was nothing else. I called my mother and told her I was coming home. I said I'd made a mistake.

When I got back I didn't talk about it. I could barely talk at all. The longer I didn't, the fewer words I had, and the less I could manage to make myself say.

It has made me a difficult person to love. Even Granny says she didn't like me as much after I came home. She thought I blamed her for sending me away. Tell her that isn't true, by the way. I wish there was one person to blame. I see and read about people like him everywhere.

I got the idea for my company because I hated the thought of a person being scared in a room on her own. I remember lying facedown, my arms pinned against my back, on my own floor, in my own room, surrounded by my own things from home in Tokyo—my single bed and my tennis shoes under it, my desk and my lamp and my pencil case—and thinking, Why don't they help me? Why won't they sound the alarm? And when the police looked around I wanted to shout, Tell them! You saw it, it happened right here. I can't prove it alone. Afterwards I didn't trust them either. I felt like all my everyday belongings and bits of home had betrayed me when I needed them to be on my side. I abandoned most of my belongings when I went back to Tokyo.

If I say I understand why you need to tell your stories, maybe now you can understand why I did not tell mine. The risk of not being believed again was too much. I started to think that maybe I had made it up. Maybe it was in my head. But then I found out I was going to have you. It's all come around. You take real things and turn them into fiction. I wish I could say I wanted you. The truth is I didn't, and I knew I wouldn't and couldn't love you. I went along with the pregnancy at first because I

felt too unsure of my own mind to stop anything that was
happening to me. The idea that I couldn't separate what
was true from what was false was so terrifying. I couldn't
even trust myself to walk out the front door, let alone
make a choice. Not knowing myself like that was more
frightening to me than the stranger in my room. That was
the worst thing—being hollowed out like that. That, in
the end, was why I kept you. I wanted to know it had
been real, to have some permanent mark. You were my
burden of proof.

My mother tried to make me end it. I think she
suspected. My father was, of course, furious, but that
only made me colder inside and more determined to go
through with it. I remember thinking, as you grew inside
me, that I would never let a man make me do anything
ever again. I hoped that by pushing you out with all my
strength rather than lying back unconscious and having
another man put his hands between my legs to remove
you, the last trace of him would be gone.

I hadn't anticipated that when I saw you it would
feel worse. It would be like replaying the whole thing in
slow motion. That's the only reason there are almost no
pictures of you as a baby, except the ones Granny took.
I could not look directly into your face back then. You
had been an abstract something, at worst a foreigner,
inside my body, but outside it, you were like my enemy.
I was afraid of you, because I was sure you and he were
one. When they put you on my chest in the hospital I
felt trapped, held there by a helpless baby, pinned back
against my will.

Granny wanted to look after you, and I let her. She
tried to get me to change the name I gave you. She said I

was depressed and it wasn't fair on you to give you a sad name. I know you will look after her now.

I told myself I was doing the right thing—what child wants to know that story about herself? One parent a criminal, the other a victim, and she is half of each? But I thought silence was better than a lie. So many times after we fought I wanted to lie like a leaf on the ground to be stepped on. Just to disappear. I was afraid you would bring him back into our lives. Since I spoke to the police I have never said his name out loud. Never looked for him. I didn't even know until now that he had changed his last name. When I read the contents of the letter that came for you, I didn't anticipate how it would hurt me, how it would turn me into a mother, someone to feel protective of you and at the same time pain, not just because of him but because in finding him you were rejecting me.

I want to die away from home. Too many people in Japan go to the same old spots. The Sea of Trees is full of morbid tourists now who take photos of the hanging bodies and even steal their belongings. I do not want some creep taking a picture with me in the background.

I will always be there if you need me, because I will always be part of you. The part of you that would not be denied.

H

I think back to when reading this used to make me cry, and I hear myself make short little huffs of breath as if I am choking. But I do not know the people I am crying for anymore. I don't let myself sympathise—I think it would be wrong. I don't compare Robin with my birth father, or myself with Hiromi, or Ume with Susy, or even Mark with Mizuko anymore, though they are both experts at disappearing. I don't know, I can't know, but I almost did. When I read it now it's like I have broken into a reality that is not mine, and when I step out of it, as if I had removed my headphones and heard the city again, it is easy to close the door behind me.

What I can link is the two letters. At first I felt only a very dim connection between my confession and hers. It was a circumstance of Mizuko's life that I had not known, that had not been part of the picture I had of her, and so therefore it could not exist. Nor could I really admit to myself that Hiromi had really gone. Gone to Tokyo, sure. People were mass, and mass was energy, and energy never died, it just went somewhere else. I tried to think about death, to imagine it, but I couldn't. Mizuko would say that if someone from *my generation* dies, they continue to live online. They are stuck all around us, bumping up against our fingers. Sharp objects sensible through cheap fabric, like the lining of a purse. Their world smells of Juicy Fruit gum, and the air tastes of copper coins like blood. We know and they know they're lost forever, but neither of us can quit our search. But slowly it dawned on me—my own role in the story, and what it had cost Mizuko: the loss of one parent after gaining another.

Working out that I am *not Mizuko* has been an important step towards feeling better. If I have hit on a moral, it is this: the body is our natural barrier. There were lines I should not have crossed, and I did so without permission. I was looking always for correspondences, but meaning is found through difference.

But then there is inheritance. I guess the lines blur while we assimilate. I had started to recover. Moving gave me the impression that I'd managed to build a wall between then and now (except that the new life was founded on the money I inherited), but then the physical contents of Silvia's apartment arrived. Including the three crates. I sat in the garden, laying out each item on the ground. First as if there had been a crime scene, then, as the accumulation grew, as if there had been a full-on tsunami. Her blue grid tray for pills—days along the top, then rows for morning, noon, evening, bedtime—reminded me, with a little pulse of electricity, that she was not just somewhere else; she was gone. I read or turned things over, seeing things in them I hadn't seen before. I still have the sealed envelope with the red fish inside, which I've kept, and the last letter Silvia dictated to me, which I did not send. Maybe this won't be an issue in the future, as there will be hardly any physical remains of a human lifetime; we'll just give our grandchildren our devices. Can you imagine trying to divide up all the things in them? *For Carol: this attachment.* Maybe, as Mizuko said, we won't even really die, just carry on in the feedback loop we are stuck in. Instead of connecting with new things, widening our worlds, algorithms have shrunk it to a narrow chamber with mirrored walls.

I made it through a month in my new home with all these old objects—painting walls and sanding wood and feeling generally stable—without trying to contact her. Then one morning I cracked and ate two Provigils for breakfast. I watched the footage she sent me from her trip into the exclusion zone with Ume, listened to the Holocaust talk online, and set up a new Instagram account under the guise of a new business venture: New Leaf Gardening. The card with the ram on it—the one I had read with Mizuko in the deli—suggested that the profession would suit me. I took the name from a van I saw in the Hamptons. It belonged to Mexican gardeners at work with a Strimmer on Walter's fortifications. Because I could not stop myself, I searched for the triangular park of Roosevelt Island on Google Earth, next to the smallpox hospital, covered in a creeping green. I went down and down until I landed on the blades of grass and the goose dung and the dew. I felt all my self-sufficiency, my own Walden Pond, seeping out of me as if I'd sprung a leak. *Self* soaked into everything around me—the floor, the walls, the one window, the grass. The words on the page.

I returned to the chapter in Silvia's book about Vesta. When the virgins entered a collegium, they left behind the authority of their fathers and became daughters of the state. So any sexual relation with a citizen was considered to be *incestium*. Impurity. As a ward of the state until my adoption, I figured I was guilty of this many times over, starting with losing my virginity to Dwight. The punishment for breaking the oath of celibacy, I read, was to be buried alive in the *campus sceleratus,* in an underground chamber. The vestal had to be buried alive, because this was the only way to kill her without spilling her blood, which was forbidden. To kill her they created a kind of legal fiction that they weren't really killing her. They buried the nonvirgin priestess with a nominal amount of provisions, so she would technically be descending not to burial in the city but to a habitable room, resulting in a lingering death by slow suffocation. I stood considering this fate as potentially being mine while I installed the mirrored cabinet doors, pulling them ajar when I had finished to test the hinges, so that I saw myself as an infinite regression getting smaller, smaller, smaller, an endless corridor through which I could retrace my steps.

32

I've been following an American man, an "adventurer," which could be any American man, who has been hunting the missing plane. In Nosy Boraha, a Madagascan island, he recently found a bag—brown leather, pale stitching, green tartan. Crusted in salt and darkened with water damage, the zip detached except at the ends. On the same beach he also found a camera case, the sole of a shoe, and a prayer cap. Another bag turned inside out and ravaged so that every seam hung loose from the body like tentacles. On a sandbank off Mozambique he found a white triangle that appeared to be a piece of plane. The object has the words NO STEP printed on it. The authorities of the countries searching have decided that if nothing is found by the time they have covered the entire 46,000-square-mile search area, a search which is due to be completed this month, the hunt will be left unresolved. The adventurer promises he won't give up.

I don't know if I can either. I am currently using Google's Street View to follow the route Hiromi would have taken from her daughter's apartment to the river.

I walk my eyes along West 113th Street to Riverside Drive.

This part of the route has been photographed by the satellite in bright sunshine at the height of summer. Then, when I urge the arrow on, crossing Riverside Drive towards the water, the satellite images become wintry. As I push through the bank of trees that separates Riverside Drive from Henry Hudson Parkway, the dazzling summer light, white gold radiating upwards from car bonnets and green leaves, turns to a malevolent winter orange, emanating from an unknown source in the overcast sky. The images show another time from the street before, and I suppose the whole map, the whole world, is made of these different bands of light. But I can't help thinking of the shock I felt when I finally realised it was winter, on exiting Mizuko's apartment. The summer was long gone, but I hadn't noticed until then.

When I come out the other side of the dual carriageway, onto the Hudson River Greenway, the trees instantly lose their leaves, as if in fright at the speed I move, the stress of the jump, and they become black and bare. Silhouetted against an even darker sky. The eerie orange light is gone. It is bleak. The city has a hopeless aspect—grey water and dimly distinct sky. It was here that she waded out into the river, clutching her large suitcase to her chest, the handle of which she had security-padlocked to her belt. In addition to what she had brought from Tokyo, she'd packed a lump of loose concrete, an ornamental paperweight of Mizuko's, a doorstop which had also belonged to Mizuko—a clear glass orb with air bubbles suspended inside—and a large leather-bound dictionary for good measure.

When I got back to thinking that way, I felt like I was trapped and that communicating with Mizuko (but really just myself) was the only way I could be led out of the maze I had created for myself. I didn't know whether she had deleted the accounts or blocked me. I held on to the idea that she was angry because I had run out on her, when all anybody ever did was run out on her. She didn't reply to my emails. I only had her Columbia one, and I realised that by now that might be defunct. The messages must be stuck somewhere in the tube of light underneath the ocean that connects London and New York. I wanted to tell her what I knew, but I couldn't.

WHERE ARE YOU, I mouthed at the screen.

I was actively looking for her name at first, but after a while it just started popping up even when I wasn't. I'd searched her name enough times by that point so that anything to do with her would seek me out without my soliciting it. At first this gave me a perverse kind of hope, as if she were trying to be in touch even though she now appeared to have either blocked me on everything or shut down her online self so that she was totally sealed off and private. I set up the alerts for her name. It was through trying to find her that I discovered I was being impersonated. Someone had used my public pictures and set up a fake account. There were pictures of me and Dwight and Mizuko, with our real names and odd, hostile captions I hadn't written. The false sense of mastery I'd once had in creating these little image grids was inverted. Anybody could do the same to me. I became convinced that I was being watched.

Because self was still leaking everywhere, a part of me began to think it was Mizuko rather than a stranger. I hoped that there might still be a reunion. I hoped it in the shy, sly way hope comes out of the jar, the mistranslated box, last—after everything and everyone else has escaped.

I guess I haven't really broken my pattern, because now I am writing this, almost as compulsively as I wrote my first confession. As I wrote, a feeling of peace came over me. Then, as I wrote more, the feeling of peace left me and was replaced by sadness, guilt, then anger all over again until I got back to peace. When I wrote about Mizuko she felt less real, so in a sense I think when I started I was trying to empty her rather than bring her back. Writing in short bursts usually made me feel ordered and together, as if I had just taken a shower. If I did it for too long, it started to feel like I was having a nightmare. I would start to feel like it wasn't even me writing it, like watching someone access your desktop remotely, or the drawing of the hands that are drawing each other.

My reflections amount to a love story that is mostly made up, from memories that are mostly false, between people who were mainly not there. The things for which she was not there have her in them now more deeply because of her absence, and her effect on my way of seeing them. Anytime I note her absence from a thing, she arrives at once, as if summoned, entrenching herself more deeply than she exists in my memories of times when she *was* there, so that time, the sequence of what really happened, seems to curve around her. I found it hard to write the bits where the things that were at first surprising or even shocking became normal incrementally until I couldn't see that they were anything but normal, because everything else had shifted just one centimetre here and one centimetre there, moving at the speed fingernails grow, until finally everything just clicked into exactly the wrong place.

The purpose is no longer just to possess Mizuko but to give back what I took from her. The law of opposites says don't send a message to your intended recipient if you want her to read it. So I am making it public. This rule has also been at work on me while writing. At first I thought I was writing to her, for her, about her. It is still all those things on the surface, but now it is deeper, wider. I scrolled back through the pictures I have saved to the cloud today, and suddenly it went at a crazy speed all the way to the beginning. I feel I am complicit in what happened to Hiromi. Initially my instinct was to hide my role—certainly not to write about it. The earlier confession went so wrong, and I was ashamed. I think I tipped it into the real. I go back to the convenience store, my words frozen on the screen as if inscribed in stone. Words I can't delete or wash away into an ocean. I think of her body sinking with the weight of them. Just when I think they have sunk to the bottom, they float back up. They fill the air. When sunlight catches on webs in the garden I think of them; they break and blow around me. I pull out moulting hairs and let them go but find them later on my clothes. They stick.

I hope when this is done I'll be able to get back into my happy gardening vibe that was so healthy for me. I want to go back to my routine and my morning ritual with the compost, but it will probably be that my life will split in two. New Leaf Gardening in Wood Green will be happening in parallel to a fantasy that runs along the bottom of that screen like a ticker. Alice will be fine. Rabbit will stay up tonight, and every night. Resending and resending, reopening the page to see if she has responded, if anyone has. The spinning wheel will make my eyes hurt and everything else will go dark.

Acknowledgments

Emma Paterson, for everything. Lauren Wein and Elena Lappin, most sympathetic of editors. In their different ways, Pilar Garcia-Brown, Rosie Price, Zoe Nelson, Stephen Edwards, Rachael DeShano, and Liz Duvall. Colin Thomas, both for his generosity and for his wonderful daughters. Quentin Jones, Osamu Watanabe, ONS and Taka Ota, for fated introductions, guided tours of Tokyo, early book buying, and a language lesson. For their inspiration, Jane Partner, Tamara Follini, and Gayle Guest. My grandparents, John and Su, for their coffee machine, kindness, and moral support, and my parents, for their infinite patience.

OLIVIA SUDJIC was born in London in 1988. She studied English Literature at Cambridge University where she was awarded the E.G. Harwood English Prize and made a Bateman Scholar. *Sympathy* is her first novel.